"Peter Telep's research into Marine Corps operations and the people who carry them out is meticulous. A great read for everyone, but especially past, present and future Marines. Well done and *Semper Fi*!"

—Tom Marino, Former Sergeant (0331/0311), USMC

"The story line is exciting and fast moving. I liked the concept that the main good guys were former Marines who were bonded by their service in combat. I thought that it was an interesting and perhaps plausible scenario if such a threat ever developed. I would want to be a part of a reaction group like that even if it was loosely organized."

—Fred Frederiksen, Former Sergeant (0311), USMC

"I was completely engulfed by *The Secret Corps*. Mr. Telep understands that Marines always have a strong bond and will always help each other, as the roots drive deep. He does an excellent job with the meticulous details of the weapons systems and setting the stage for the action. I literally felt like I was there. This is a great adventure from cover to cover."

—Corey Peters, Former Sergeant, USMC

"This story reminds me of what it means to be a Marine. Becoming a Marine is the most proud thing a person can ever do, to serve next to your fellow Marines, that pride never goes away. Just ask a vet from any other branch and they will say they served in the Military.... ask a Marine and he will always say he served in the US Marine Corps. *Semper Fi.*"

—Ray Johnson, Former Corporal, USMC

"Peter Telep understands that there are three things a man must have in his life in order to receive fulfillment: a war to wage, an adventure to lead, and a loved one to rescue. When we read his writing, it is obvious to us all that Mr. Telep 'gets it.'"

—Master Sergeant James "Johnny" Johnson, USMC (Ret)

Praise for *The Secret Corps*

"It's about time a solid thriller writer looked to the ethos and extraordinary combat capabilities of U.S. Marines and gave the genre a welcome boost. With advice and counsel from real Leathernecks who know the breed intimately, Peter Telep has written a roller-coaster story that genuinely evokes the colorful character of the Corps."
>   —Captain Dale Dye, USMC (Ret)
>   Marine, Author, Actor and Filmmaker

"After reading this book, I am awed by Peter Telep's attention to detail and how plausible this story could be. His portrayal of Marines (lingo/mindset, etc.) is spot on, and his character development is impressive—mainly because I identify in so many ways with each character's backstory (some of their stories are the same as mine). Anyway, wonderful job, loved it."
>   —Master Sergeant Clifton Lee, USMC (Ret)

"Exciting and fast moving. Peter Telep covers all potential territory in the current operating environment. Entertaining reading that incorporates real Marines, current technological challenges, and takes place in the Jacksonville, North Carolina area."
>   —Colonel S.W. Davis, USMC (Ret)

"Peter Telep has written an imaginative and enjoyable tale. The read is swift, riveting, and contains a bit of painful realism in this fact-based fiction. The players from Johnny and "the boys" to the Marine Corps Band of Brothers will all seem larger than life to the uninitiated, but let me assure you there is not one in this story that would fail to live up to the challenge."
>   —Lieutenant Colonel R.C. Adams USMC (Ret)

"Reading about actual events in my life, with fictional twists and story lines, was extremely amusing for me. I can personally tell you that Peter Telep did his homework—from our verbiage and personality nuances to the gear and equipment we use. He also extensively researched the agencies, local and federal, as well as the little details, such as road names, to make you feel as if this story were real! I truly enjoyed reading this novel!"

—Joseph "Willie" Parent, Former GySgt USMC

2D Force Recon / 2 Marine Special Operations Battalion

"Simply stated, I liked the book; I liked it a lot. It firmly grips you and genuinely personifies our Corps's character/characteristics (cohesion, loyalty, selfless devotion to duty and each other, to name a few) routinely resident in Marines and their units. And after knowing Johnny for over twenty-eight years, I can state that this story is very believable."

—Major J. W. Dorsey IV, USMC (Ret)

Vice President, Glock, Inc.

"*The Secret Corps* was a bittersweet read. It's a perfect blend 'factual fiction.' The accuracy and detail brought me back to my time in the Marine Corps and sparked memories of so many great people and amazing stories. I truly appreciate and respect Mr. Telep's desire to make his novel as realistic as possible, and it is—often painfully so. The bond between Marines can never be broken. In *The Secret Corps*, you really get to understand that. I am proud that I contributed my expertise to its creation."

—Josh Iversen, Former Staff Sergeant, USMC

"This was an awesome read. The story line pulled me in and kept my attention to the end. Mr. Telep has done a fantastic job of capturing the life long brotherhood that we share as Marines and our drive to accomplish the mission. *Semper Fi!*"

—Gunnery Sergeant Eric N. Gordon, USMC (Ret)

———————————— ❖ ————————————

"A Marine is a Marine. I set that policy two weeks ago—there's no such thing as a former Marine. You're a Marine, just in a different uniform and you're in a different phase of your life. But you'll always be a Marine because you went to Parris Island, San Diego or the hills of Quantico. There's no such thing as a former Marine."

—General James F. Amos, 35th Commandant of the Marine Corps

"...They were from two completely different worlds. Had they not joined the Marines they would never have met each other, or understood that multiple Americas exist simultaneously depending on one's race, education level, economic status, and where you might have been born. But they were Marines, combat Marines, forged in the same crucible of Marine training, and because of this bond they were brothers as close, or closer, than if they were born of the same woman..."

—Lieutenant General John Kelly USMC, in a speech 13 November 2010 at the Hyatt Under the Arch, St. Louis regarding Corporal Jonathan Yale and Lance Corporal Jordan Haerter, KIA 22 April, 2008

"We should bleed America economically by motivating it to continue its huge expenditure on its security as America's weak point is its economy, which already has begun stumbling because of the military and security expenditure. America is not a mythic power and the Americans, after all, are humans who can be defeated, felled, and punished."

—Ayman al-Zawahiri, successor to Osama Bin Laden

———————————— ❖ ————————————

THE SECRET CORPS

PETER TELEP

Ulysses Press

Published in the U.S. by
ULYSSES PRESS
P.O. Box 3440
Berkeley, CA 94703
www.ulyssespress.com

ISBN: 978-1-61243-609-8
Library of Congress Control Number: 2016934500

Printed in the United States by Bang Printing
10 9 8 7 6 5 4 3 2 1

Acquisitions Editor: Casie Vogel
Managing Editor: Claire Chun
Cover design: Peter O'Connor, www.bespokebookcovers.com
Interior design: Jake Flaherty

Distributed by Publishers Group West

This book is dedicated to the United States Marine Corps, and to every Marine who
has ever served... past, present, and future...
We are forever in your debt.

Support our men and women in the military:
operationshoebox.com
semperfifund.org

Preface

The United States Marine Corps is one of the smallest combat forces of America's military, yet Marines have a reputation for leaving the largest footprint on the battlefield. For over two centuries, the Corps has been transforming young men and women into warriors with few peers. Their commitment to each other, to the mission, to the Corps, and to our country is embodied in their motto, *Semper Fidelis*, "always faithful."

Admittedly, it is difficult for civilians to comprehend the bond that Marines share with each other. General William Thorson of the United States Army said, "There are only two kinds of people that understand Marines: Marines and the enemy. Everyone else has a second-hand opinion."

When asked, the Marines themselves talk about going downrange and trusting their teammates with their lives. They describe the mutual respect they have for those who have become one of the few, the proud. They discuss friendships and the common desire to uphold the storied traditions of the Corps and make their forefathers proud.

The bond is about honor, courage, and commitment, yet it is even more... an almost mythic and secretive intangible that has intrigued me for years. With this challenge in mind, I set out to capture lightning in a bottle and turn it into a novel—a lofty ambition to be sure.

The Secret Corps could be more accurately described as a hybrid between fiction and nonfiction. The characters are closely based on four veteran Marines who epitomize that extraordinary brotherhood forged in the Corps. These men took me under their wing; they taught me to fire their weapons and to think like them. They shared their stories of great triumph and heartbreaking loss. They treated me, an outsider, like one of their brothers. They helped me discover that I could use their bond as the very backbone of my plot.

The old saying about Marines is true: they can be your best friend or your worst nightmare. Their generosity and their ferocity are extreme.

—Peter Telep, Winter Springs, FL

Prologue

"We all knew each other before that night in Fallujah, but afterward, something changed. We realized we couldn't say goodbye after leaving the Corps. We had shared a large part of our past together, and you don't walk away from that. Our experiences shaped who we are, and, in turn, we shaped those around us."

—Johnny Johansen (FBI interview, 23 December)

Four riverine patrol boats thundered upriver beneath an overcast night sky. The boats were in column formation and running blacked out. Their five-man crews resembled cyborgs with Night Observation Devices (NODs) jutting from their helmets. These were the hardened Marines of Small Craft Company, 2nd Platoon, 1st section, the innovators who had roared through the deserts of Iraq with their boats in tow, drawing curious stares from officers and enlisted alike. The unit's primary mission was to provide tactical mobility, personnel transport, and a fire support platform in support of Military Operations in a Riverine Environment. When insurgents began exploiting the Euphrates River to smuggle weapons and personnel, the Marines—in typical Marine Corps fashion—stepped up with a large caliber maritime response. They deployed heavily-armed aluminum jet boats with solid cell polyethylene collars making them the most dangerous and maneuverable craft on the water.

On this particular November morning in 2004, three hours before sunrise, the crews of Small Craft Company were transporting a platoon of twenty-eight men divided into "stacks" designated Alpha and Bravo. Each stack had boarded one of the thirty-nine-foot-long boats. The men straddled the pairs of rodeo seats positioned between the coxswain's station and the bow, or they sat on deck along the gunwale. This GCE or Ground Combat Element was primarily from 3rd Platoon, Second Force Reconnaissance Company, a special operations capable unit that belonged exclusively to the Marine Corps. These boys had basic infantry skills as sharp as an officer's Mameluke sword, but they were much more than infantry. Each had earned the coveted Military Occupational Specialist "0321" designator. They were reconnaissance men trained as static line and free-fall jumpers and combat divers. They could scout and patrol like a disembodied squad who had returned from the afterlife. What they knew about assault weaponry, breaching demolitions, close quarters combat, and raid techniques would buckle a bookshelf were it printed in hardcopy. Most importantly, they were the eyes and ears of their commanders.

Out on the riverbank, another pair of eyes was riveted on them, eyes belonging to a fourteen-year-old spotter named Yusef who had buried himself in the mud and was armed with a pair of binoculars looted from an Iraqi soldier's corpse. He had picked up the four boats shimmering in silhouette and tracked them as they swept by. He reached for his cell phone. Not in his pocket. The other? He reached again. Nothing. It was gone! He would have to run to the next spotter's station to alert the compound. He waited until the boats passed, then pushed up on his elbows like a zombie heaving from the mud. Barely two seconds later, the skies opened, and the rain pummeled him with a vengeance. He fell twice before reaching the edge of the field.

A gunnery sergeant on the second boat probed the rutted riverbank with his NODs. About a hundred meters off now, date palms thrashed in the wind like some unearthly cheer squad glowing phosphorescent green. Beneath them lay clusters of one- and two-story homes constructed of cement or cinder blocks, their flat roofs festooned with power cables, their windows darkened, their inhabitants sleeping under extra blankets to combat the cold. Beyond those homes, and past the kebab shops where the old men usually loitered, stood the twisted hulks of cars stripped to their bones. Those chassis formed a winding fence near a field draped in darkness. It was here, along this part of the riverbank, where the danger grew more enigmatic, where the opportunities for cover and concealment were the greatest.

The gunnery sergeant detected movement in the field, a collection of shadows that seemed to wrestle with each other. He looked again and found nothing. He flipped up his NODs and took a deep breath. A mistake. That god-awful stench boiling up from the water was produced by Fallujah's runoff system now swollen from an earlier deluge. Raw sewage was coursing through the garbage-filled streets and forming dozens of poisonous tributaries. The men around him waved off the noxious fumes while the rain drummed louder and the outline of the ancient city appeared and vanished like enemy recognition flash cards in a training class.

As the boats rocked through more wake turbulence, the gunnery sergeant clung to his seat and stared back at the field. There was no fear in his gut, only a premonition that began to gnaw at him. He cursed off the feeling. Nothing to worry about. Easy day. No Drama. And besides, this operation was nothing compared to what his father had been through.

One summer evening, after a pack of cigarettes and a few shots of Jim Beam from a cracked glass, the old man had finally broken down and told him about his time in the U.S. Army and the fighting in Vietnam. He recounted the December 1966 attack on Landing Zone Bird, a fire base located in the Kim Son Valley some fifty kilometers north of Qui Nhon. Over 1,000 North Vietnamese Army regulars overran the fire base's perimeter, which at the time was manned by only 170 American troops. Presidential Unit Citations, Distinguished Service Crosses, and one Medal of Honor were awarded to those who had fought, bled, and held the LZ that night. Consequently, there were few people or situations in the civilian world that ever frightened the old man. He said that men are like steel: they both need a little temper to be worth a damn.

All of his life, Gunnery Sergeant James "Johnny" Johansen had lived by his father's words and refused to let adversity stand in his way. He had joined the Marine Corps and risen to the rank of gunnery sergeant. Now he was 3rd Platoon's senior enlisted man and "platoon sergeant," advising the commanding officer and ensuring optimal standards of proficiency, conduct, and cohesion in the unit. On a daily basis he demonstrated that his men were the smartest, toughest, and most readied force in the world. There were none better.

Johnny leaned toward Staff Sergeant Paul Oliver, the B stack leader who was hunkered down beside him on the boat. He mouthed the words, *"Easy day. No drama."*

Oliver grinned.

Because there were so many hard days in the Corps, and the drama in country was particularly high this past year, Johnny had become fond of those phrases to put his men at ease. He would tell them they were "all that and a bag of chips" and that they were all over this mission "like a fat kid on a cupcake." They knew that if there was one man above them who truly cared about them it was Johnny. They would walk through Hell, and he would walk with them. "Thanks, Gunny," they would say. "You're the man, Gunny."

* * *

Soaked and out of breath, Yusef reached the next spotter's station where he found his counterpart, Malik, fast asleep inside the small earthen bunker. Yusef shook the older boy awake and shared the news. Malik snorted and said there was no way to tell where the boats were headed and that the other spotters upriver were now tracking them. Yusef argued that they should call the compound anyway. Malik widened his eyes and shoved Yusef against the dirt wall. "You woke me up for this! Let someone else do it, and let someone else take the blame for crying wolf."

Yusef spied Malik's cell phone tucked into a mesh pouch attached to a backpack. He reached into the pouch, snatched the phone, and took off running.

* * *

Staff Sergeant Josh Eriksson commanded the second patrol boat, radio call sign Game Warden 2. He spoke over the boat's VIC-3 system, informing Johnny that they were ten minutes out from phase line green and reaching the Objective Rally Point (ORP). After crossing that line marked by a terrain feature, they would make their final radio checks and ensure all weapons systems were operational. The Ground Combat Element would stand and prepare to disembark.

This was the fourth mission Josh had run with Second Force, and he enjoyed the camaraderie and vivid tales of buffoonery that Johnny and the others shared in their down time. Johnny was a popular and charismatic leader with an enormous network of friends throughout the Corps. Josh respected him because he had taught his boys to appreciate Small Craft Company's mission capabilities and did not write them off as taxi drivers. Johnny and his men counted on the boat teams as a Quick Reaction Force (QRF) should the need arise, and they valued Josh's obsessive attention to planning and maintenance. Through reciting the Marine Corp's Rifleman's Creed, Marines learn that the rifle is your life. You must master it as you master your life. For riverine operators, the boat is your life, and Josh was intimately familiar with every square inch of his, from the hydraulic bow door to the aft heavy machine gun mount.

Officially known as Small Unit Riverine Craft (SURC), the patrol boats were, in effect, high-speed death machines on water. A skilled coxswain could pull a hard 180 degree "J-turn" and put the gunners back on target in seconds. Violent emergency stops from forty-plus knots were accomplished within an incredible single boat length. Josh was the captain of his boat and the section leader who commanded all four. He thumbed a dial on the VIC-3 panel to his left, switching to the platoon net so he could check in with the other boat captains, who each responded over their 152 radios.

To his right sat his coxswain, Lance Corporal Wilson, whose attention was split between the boat ahead and the Furuno Navnet radar positioned left of the wheel. The radar's screen glowed dimly, and Wilson was monitoring his speed and searching for obstructions in the water. Each range ring showed him one quarter of a nautical mile.

Up near the bow, Lance Corporal Duffy stood tall at the boat's MK-44 minigun station mounted to the SURC's port side and fitted with a heavy gun shield. Arguably the sexiest weapon on board, the minigun was an electrically driven rotary machine gun whose six barrels spun like a bundle of axles to unleash salvos of tracer-lit fire that lashed out from the boat like a dragon's tongue. The other bow gunner, Lance Corporal Blount, manned the M240G 7.62mm machine gun. Blount and Duffy alternated between the minigun and the 240 "Golf" so they were proficient with either weapon, and Josh was pleased to have his two favorite bulldogs peering out from behind their gun shields, searching for prey.

Standing behind Josh at the aft gunner's station was Corporal Keller, who kept a firm handle on "Ma Deuce," the nickname for the M2 .50 caliber heavy machine gun. Keller had an ammo can attached to the gun with a belt of .50 caliber sitting in the cradle. He caught Josh glancing back at him and lifted his chin, as if to say, "Ready to rock-n-roll, Staff Sergeant."

These were Josh's men. This was his boat. He loved them as much as he loved the Corps, which was why he could converse for hours about his unit and constantly brainstormed better ways to exploit their gear and win more fights. He even sported a tattoo on his left outer forearm that depicted the POW/MIA flag in silhouette, along with the words: I AM MY BROTHER'S KEEPER. He literally wore the bond between Marines on his sleeve.

When asked why he joined the Marines, Josh would narrow his gaze and without hesitation state that the Marine Corps saved his life. To describe his childhood as rough was like describing the sinking of the Titanic as a "little boat accident." Suffice it to say he had come a long way from that mobile home park in Asheville, North Carolina, where his father had nearly died from an overdose and where he had been blackmailed into some criminal activity that had nearly sent him to prison. He had taught himself to look at the world through the eyes of his enemy, realizing that sometimes *you* are your own worst enemy. The mistakes he had made were never far from his thoughts, but they were lessons learned and made him who he was today, leading this section of boats, calling over the 152 and the intercom that they had reached the Objective Rally Point. Now they were approaching the Shark's Fin—a hairpin turn in the river that posed great danger to the boats because the small islands and irregular shoreline were a nesting ground for insurgents.

* * *

When he looked back through the torrential rain, Yusef spotted Malik racing over the asphalt like a coal black skeleton with colossal eyes. Malik narrowed the gap between them as they splashed up the road, pieces of broken asphalt pinching the soles of their bare feet. Yusef needed to slow down so he could dial the compound, but Malik would stop at nothing to reclaim his phone. The man who had hired Yusef had promised a large bonus if he provided information that became valuable to the insurgency, and notice of these boats could be very valuable. Yusef needed to pass it on, despite Malik's cynicism. Gritting his teeth, Yusef ran faster toward the crumbling ruins of four houses that had been demolished by an air strike. Maybe there, among the piles of twisted rebar and slabs of concrete, he could lose his pursuer.

* * *

Staff Sergeant Joseph "Willie" Parente glared at the old iron bridge, its triangular girders gleaming like perforated teeth in the gloom. It was from here, back in March, that the charred and dismembered bodies of two Blackwater contractors had been strung up like cattle in a butcher shop. A convoy of SUVs had been ambushed and those men, along with two others, were brutally murdered in an incident that had sparked the First Battle of Fallujah. All Willie could do now was shake his head in disgust as the rain momentarily stopped and the rusting green underbelly of the bridge passed overhead. A fresh sheet of rain confronted them on the other side, and then they started into the Shark's Fin turn, leaving the bridge and the nearby Fallujah hospital behind.

Willie was Alpha Stack's leader and seated aboard Game Warden 3 with the rest of his men. The boat's captain, Sergeant Corey McKay, was an articulate and generous operator, a warrior prodigy who bought beers and told good stories that made him seem much older than his youthful face suggested. He lifted his voice and announced they were hitting the bottleneck. His gunners remained vigilant, covering their sectors of fire with an efficiency both expected and appreciated by everyone. As the coxswain rolled his wheel left, the boats swept parallel to a liver-shaped collection of small islands divided by a lattice-work of channels. Unsurprisingly, a few rifles cracked in the distance, but none of those reports was followed by an echoing thump along the boat's collar or clang off the armored plates. Two more pops resounded from the islands but apparently the rest of the insurgency was too cold, too wet, or too tired to fight.

"Hey, Willie, phase line green," Corey said over the intercom. "Three minutes out."

"Roger."

He reached for his radio and dialed the platoon's internal net so he could notify Captain Zabrowski, who was seated up near the bow with the platoon's communications chief, Sergeant Edinger, and the corpsman, HM2 Milam. Although the captain did monitor the boat's intercom, oftentimes he was speaking with "higher" on another channel and unable to catch every report on the intercom or internal net.

At the same time, all four coxswains set their engines to 1800 rpms so that the harmonic tone made it difficult to identify their exact number and position. This was an old trick proven effective by running drills with troops on the shoreline. Those men would turn their backs to the water and listen as boats passed. They were asked how many and in which direction those craft had traveled. For the most part, they failed miserably, meaning the insurgents would, too.

With the captain notified, Willie gave the order, and the men stood and began their last minute comm and equipment checks. This was Christmas morning seconds before opening the presents, and nothing could stop that familiar and formidable rush of adrenaline warming Willie's chest like a shot of Jim Beam. The boats would make a final turn and reach the Riverine Landing Site (RLS) just a kilometer ahead.

Willie took a deep breath and steeled himself. He was a card-carrying member of an elite gun club that had once been called *teufelshunde* or "dogs of the devil" by German soldiers in WWI because they fought with such ferocity. The shadow he cast was centuries long, and the sight of him in full combat gear struck the enemy cold. He was a weapon of destruction. A warlock. But it was not always this way.

Staff Sergeant Joseph "Willie" Parente had once been a spindly school kid from Fairhaven, Massachusetts who had worn thick glasses and a patch over one eye to correct a vision problem. His father, a veteran Marine, was a long-haul truck driver gone for weeks at a time, and his mother worked for the Titleist Golf Ball Company, whose corporate headquarters were on Bridge Street in Fairhaven. Every time his father left home, Willie donned his cowboy hat and holstered his six-shooter cap gun. He assumed his post in the front yard. His two older sisters would inform the neighbors that he was protecting the house until their dad returned. Years later, he joined the Corps, did a stint as a 0352 TOW gunner (antitank missile system operator), and was also on the battalion's rifle and pistol team. He had worked harder than ever to become a Recon Marine, and now he was at the top of his game, deployed here to Iraq to participate in the Second Battle of Fallujah and Operation Phantom Fury. Along the way he had earned an additional nickname: "Bare Knuckles Willie," after a run-in with an insufferable staff sergeant who nearly cost him his career.

"Drifter," Corey began, addressing the unit by their call sign. "Thirty seconds to mark. Stand by."

Sergeant Heredia, the platoon's 3rd Team Leader, turned back to Willie and nodded.

Willie clutched the gunwale. It was game on. The riverbank materialized through the rain. Beyond lay the hillsides and swaying palms leading up to the compound.

* * *

Yusef was picking his way over the broken pieces of concrete when the cell phone slipped from his wet hand and tumbled into the mountain of rubble. He had no flashlight, no other way to see where it had fallen, and Malik was coming now, clutching pieces of rebar that jutted from the rocks to form handholds.

"I dropped your phone! I can't find it," Yusef told him.

Malik was nearly on him and shaking a fist. Yusef swallowed and turned to get out of there. He padded across the summit of splintered concrete. One foot gave out. He lost his balance, slipped, and plunged backward.

The sharp piece of rebar penetrated his back and went through his left lung as he hit the slab. These details were lost on him, of course. He knew only the pain and reached up to feel the blood-soaked metal jutting like an arrow from his chest.

Malik leaned down and gaped at him.

Yusef struggled to breathe. "I'm sorry."

Malik shook his head. "You get what you deserve." He retreated down the pile and shoved his head into the larger crevices, still searching for his phone.

The rain kept falling, but Yusef no longer felt it on his cheeks. He lay there, listening, as Malik continued moving across the rubble. "I found it!" he cried. Yusef heard him shoving smaller pieces of concrete aside, and then the older boy groaned as he forced himself down into the rocks. Yusef craned his head and watched Malik disappear up to his waist. A moment later, he wormed himself back up with the phone clutched in his hand.

"Call them," said Yusef. "My family needs the money."

"If this call is worth anything, then *my family* will get the money, not yours. Not the family of a thief." Malik flipped open the phone and began to dial.

* * *

Sergeant Corey McKay stood beside his coxswain, Corporal Ochoa, as the latter expertly piloted their boat behind Game Warden 2. The lead boat, Game Warden 1, was turning just offshore to the right flank, working security for the insertion, while Game Warden 4 banked to the left. The goal was to insert the Ground Combat Element as quickly as possible and with a minimum of maneuvering.

"Thirty seconds to mark," Josh called to the other boat captains. And then it was time: "Mark, mark, mark."

Corey and Josh took their boats head-on toward the riverbank and slammed right up onto the shoreline, the sandy bottom scraping along their aluminum hulls. The hydraulic bow doors were already groaning into position, and the stacks of ground troops were leaping onto the bank, their boots making sucking noises in the mud. They bolted toward the hillside just upriver, where the shoreline gave way to a cluster of towering bulrushes. Corey and Josh took a head count, as did Johnny and Willie.

Sometimes an operation like this would call for a false insertion or extraction, and the boats had already conducted one prior to reaching the rally point. Now, as the last man from each stack exited, the coxswains threw their engines in reverse. The boats exfiltrated to the left in their current order. They coxswains kept their engines turned away from the landing site to avoid exposing them to fire and to reduce their noise signature.

The single wave insertion had gone off without a hitch, the gunners marking their fields of fire, the zone identified onshore by a security team who planted infra-red strobes. Corey's coxswain followed the lead boat to another small island. They brought the boats in tight to the shoreline, near the stands of trees and a tarpaulin of taller bulrushes beneath which they found excellent cover. From there they would wait, monitoring the platoon net for the call to extract.

The men on Corey's boat were consummate professionals, standing tall against the wind-swept rains. Corey shifted out from beneath the control station's awning. He flipped up his NODs and drifted back to his aft gunner, Corporal Quiroz, who banged fists with him then immediately returned to his fifty cal. Corey went up to check on the bow gunners, not that they needed his supervision, but he wanted to show his gratitude for them standing up there in the miserable weather. Their grins said, *"Oorah, bring on the storm."*

Corey glanced across the bow toward Josh's boat, nearly lost beneath the heavy reeds drumming on his hull. That tapping, along with the falling rain, filled his ears with a white noise that further concealed their position. The gunners scanned the opposite riverbank, but this was a more rural area with broad fields and few houses, a well-chosen hide position. Corey's night vision revealed little more than the oily water lapping at the shore. He thought of Johnny and Willie and the rest of the GCE out there and how he had almost become an infantryman himself. He had left the small town of Girard, Pennsylvania with the goal of transforming himself into a 0311 rifleman but had emerged from infantry training school as a 0331 machine gunner, which was just fine with him. As is often the case with many recruits, he had had no long-term intentions of joining the Marine Corps. Yes, he was getting burned out in high school, but he was not failing, just getting worn down by the grind. Coaches told him he was a damned fine baseball player and could take his skills somewhere and maybe earn a college scholarship, so that had been the original plan. As fate would have it, he had linked up with a friend, Dusty, who was a few years his senior. Dusty had joined the Corps and shared stories of his experiences. Corey was intrigued and wondered if he had what it took.

His first deployment was to Colombia and Honduras. He was thrilled to be a part of an eighteen-man team of experienced operators who groomed him into a maritime warrior. The unit acted as a quick reaction force, did humanitarian work, and supported drug interdiction operations for the DEA. During those nine months, Corey was meritoriously promoted, and his commanders told him he was well ahead of his colleagues who had joined the Corps with him. The sandy-haired kid from a sleepy football town in Pennsylvania had made his mark and was continuing to do so half way across the world in a country booby-trapped by a crazed and suicidal insurgency.

Corey returned to the control station and checked his watch. The platoon should be nearing the compound. Any minute now, some Marine in those hills would recall the famous quote from Gunnery Sergeant Dan Daly, who, in 1918 at the battle of Belleau Wood, urged his comrades to attack by shouting, "Come on you, sons of bitches! Do you want to live forever?"

* * *

Asad al-Zahawi shuddered over the beeping noise. For a moment, he was not sure if the sound originated in a dream. He reached over to the night stand and fumbled for his cell phone. The boy on the other end said he was Malik and spoke in a broken lilt, his voice infected by nerves or by the sound of falling rain seeping into his phone. He spoke of boats headed toward the compound, of Americans, and of the bonus he wanted if the information was correct. Just as al-Zahawi sat up in the bed, a knock came at his door. He answered to find his brother-in-law with a rifle slung over his shoulder. "My spotters called. Four boats. A platoon of Marines."

Al-Zahawi shook his head and spoke through his teeth. "They found me."

His brother-in-law raised a palm. "Calm down. We'll move quietly. And remember, we have Allah, along with every neighbor you've helped on our side. You lifted them all out of poverty. They haven't forgotten you, and most already belong to the insurgency."

"Where are the Marines?"

"Just outside. We can't get to the cars. Not yet, anyway. I'll give you some men, but stay here until I call for you."

Al-Zahawi reached under his bed and slid out his AK-47, along with two magazines. "I told you I wanted to leave. You promised I'd be safe." He rose and nervously stroked his graying beard. "I turn fifty this year. I hope I live long enough to celebrate that birthday."

"You will. My men will stop them, and we'll get you out.."

Al-Zahawi snickered. "How many do you have?"

"Over one hundred."

* * *

Johnny held back his assaulters as Willie's security team pushed out to the row of palm trees marking the edge of their last covered and concealed position. Ahead lay twenty meters of pockmarked ground that terminated at a square formation of compound walls rising nearly three meters. Partially eclipsed behind those walls were a pair of two-story block homes with, Johnny estimated, two to three bedrooms each. Their flat roofs and arched windows protected by ornate metal screens were not uncommon in Fallujah; however, surrounding them was an improbable and lavish landscape design featuring fountains, imported shrubbery, and topiaries better suited for a palace. According to aerial photographs, three late model sedans were parked inside. The entire compound was owned by Asad al-Zahawi's brother-in-law, and recent intel gathered by an Army Operational Detachment Alpha team indicated that the insurgency financier himself was staying at the compound. Coalition forces had been trying to capture al-Zahawi for months as he used foreign fighters and couriers to smuggle cash in bulk across Iraq's porous borders while creating a complex array of indigenous money sources. He garnered most of his funding from petroleum-related criminal activity, kidnapping, bribery, and blackmail.

Attached to the platoon and crouched beside Johnny was Sergeant First Class Nunez, an operator from the ODA team who could positively identify al-Zahawi from the dozens of other bearded men wearing ManJams and sandals. Johnny had earlier warned Nunez to shelve any ideas he had of being a rock star; his job was to stay alive so he could ID the target, not get himself killed trying to prove that Army SF guys were superior warriors. Nunez said he had nothing to prove, that SF guys already were masters of the universe. Johnny had chuckled. "You think you're all that and a bag of chips, huh? We'll see." For his part, Nunez remained tight on Johnny's heels, safe and sound.

In addition to Nunez, Sergeant Ashur Bandar was attached as a linguist (MOS 2712). He was born in Kuwait, raised in Syria, and taken to the United States as a boy, where he received his legal citizenship because he had never been a legal citizen of Kuwait or Syria. Like Corey, he grew up in Pennsylvania but had gone on to graduate from Penn State. Instead of joining the Marines as an officer, he enlisted because he wanted to get down and dirty as an infantryman. Indeed, every Marine in 3rd Platoon spoke some Arabic, but Bandar, known as "the terp" (short for interpreter), was the go to guy should they need rapid fire information.

"Hey, Johnny, it's Willie," came a familiar voice over the platoon net.

"What do you got?"

"Looks clear so far. Could be some guys on the roof behind those ledges, but I doubt it with all this rain. We'll keep an eye on them, though."

"Roger."

"We're moving out," Willie added.

The platoon's advance on the compound was so well-choreographed that it seemed twenty-eight men were being guided by a single mind. The security teams split off into static positions from which they would establish a base of fire along the perimeter, while Johnny gave the hand signal, and his twelve men pushed through them and charged across the open field to the main gate, which was secured by a rusting chain and thick key lock. A pair of bolt cutters rendered the lock useless. Team Leader Oliver gently removed the chain from the gate and opened it just wide enough to pass through. Sergeant Brandt, Bravo stack's assistant team leader, hustled off with his six men toward the house on the left, while Johnny took his six, including Oliver and Nunez, to the right. Four Marines from Willie's team trailed the assaulters to provide added support, while another group exploited the assault team's movement to the gate. Once there, they broke off to circle around the back and open the rear gate, should the assaulters need to extract out back. The idea of a precision raid was to advance on the objective as quietly and simultaneously as possible, avoiding anything that might give up the assault team within the compound's walls.

In a perfect world and on a perfect night, their high value target would be lying fast asleep in his bed, and the first thing he would hear was his front door exploding inward. By the time he sat up and rubbed the grit from his eyes, a Marine would have a rifle jammed in his face. "Don't move, motherfucker." Their target would recognize those instructions because he was a fan of American action films and because he assumed the word "motherfucker" was the preferred pronoun of the United States Marine Corps.

Working alone, Sergeant Pat Rugg, the lead breacher from Florida who had the grin of an alligator and the shoulders of a black bear, rushed forward to unfurl the green-colored detcord and place the sticky side along the hinges of the metal door. The rest of the team stacked up and held security behind him near two palm trees and a row of manicured shrubs. In case the charge failed to detonate, the others carried a sledgehammer and a Halligan bar like those wielded by firefighters to pry open residential doors. The assistant breacher, Sergeant Tom Marshall, had a pistol grip pump action twelve-gauge shotgun with breaching rounds, along with an alternate roll of detcord. Johnny hunkered down with the others and turned up the volume on his radio.

"Alpha set," came Willie's voice over the platoon net.

"Bravo One is almost there," answered Johnny. "Brandt, how you doing, son?"

Brandt answered tersely, "Bravo Two is set."

"Roger that."

Trailing the shock tube behind him, Sergeant Rugg returned to the group. Nunez assisted by holding up the breacher's blanket to protect the team from any shrapnel triggered by the blast. Rugg now clutched the Qualtech firing device, a remote-control sized igniter with dual initiated priming system that was attached to the end of the shock tube.

Johnny reported to Captain Zabrowski that Bravo One and Two were ready and that the breaching charges were set.

"I have control," the captain announced over the radio.

Rugg removed the Qualtech's safety pin, then threw a lever, releasing the second safety.

Zabrowski began his countdown: 5, 4, 3, 2...

The last second used to hit Johnny the hardest. *Esprit de corps*, he knew, was rooted in all Marines. Without it there was no way to survive that moment between the verge of battle and the battle itself, a moment once riddled with self-doubt and untested faith in his brothers-in-arms. Now, after all these years in the Corps, after watching bravery come fully alive before his eyes as bleeding Marines carried each other from the battlefield, he knew beyond a shadow of a doubt that he could trust these boys with the mission and with his life.

Rugg pressed the firing button. Pale-orange light flashed from the doorway, followed by the sharp bang and powerful concussion of explosives. From the other side of the compound came the echoing rumble of Brandt's charge.

Johnny was already on his feet, raising his M4A1 rifle. He sent off Willie's four men to the cars, where they would lie in wait for anyone attempting a break.

Staff Sergeant Oliver jogged out front, hollering, "Clear!" He was first to the door, which had blown off its hinges and collapsed in a mangled heap. Tightly behind him were Pat Rugg, Tom Marshall, and Sergeant Carlos Padilla. They flipped up their NODs, activated the SureFire flashlights mounted to their rifles, and entered the home. Johnny, Nunez, and Bandar brought up the rear. They were five assaulters, one intel guy, and one interpreter.

As the stench of the explosives wafted into their faces, they crossed into a large foyer tiled in expensive white marble. The beams of their flashlights cut like lasers through the swirling dust. Now they would employ initiative-based tactics to clear the rooms, remembering to fill all voids in security; flow to meet the danger area; then go assault the next danger area. The phrase was "fill, flow, and go," and the Marines practiced clearing rooms until they could do so almost unconsciously, relying on muscle memory and the rhythm of their breathing and boots.

Beyond the foyer lay a living room with a wall of sagging bookshelves, the kind made of thin particle board and pumped out of Chinese factories. The furniture looked equally inexpensive, as if the owner had built the houses but run out of cash before he could properly furnish them, or perhaps he did not care. The place was a tacky knockoff of a rich man's house. Weird juxtapositions like this were common in Iraq. Staff Sergeant Oliver pushed forward with his guys and cleared the living room and adjoining kitchen, while Johnny, Nunez, and Bandar started down a short hall toward a staircase, from where the putrid scents of body odor and stale tobacco made Johnny want to hold his breath.

Oliver rushed up behind Johnny and muttered, "Clear down here." He started up the stairs with the other Marines—

Just as someone tossed a grenade into the stairwell.

* * *

Willie was staring through his NODs, letting the infrared laser generated by the AN/PEQ4 mounted to his rifle play over the rooftops. A parapet about a half meter high spanned the perimeter of each roof, and he felt certain that at least one or more snipers would take advantage of the cover provided by those low walls.

Without warning, the windows of one house flickered with light a half-second before a muffled explosion shook the ground. As he reached to key his microphone, automatic weapons fire ripped across the compound walls, originating from the north, where the densely packed neighborhood lay hidden behind curtains of rain.

"This is Bravo Two," called Sergeant Brandt. "My house is secure. There's no one home."

"Johnny, sitrep, Johnny?" Willie called.

A reply came, but it was not Johnny; it was Captain Zabrowski, who began to speak but his voice was lost by so much weapons fire on Willie's position that he dropped to his chest as the palms shredded above him, pieces of fronds and bark flying like confetti. The incoming ceased long enough for Willie to raise his head as Sergeant Heredia's voice cracked over the net. He reported contact to the north, contact to the south, contact to the west.

Jesus Christ, they were being surrounded, Willie thought. Had they been setup? An intel leak? What the hell?

Willie noted that Brandt and three of his Marines had reached the roof of their house and quickly hit the deck as the parapet came alive with ricocheting rounds.

"Drifter, this is Bravo Two," called Brandt. "I can see them moving up. Large numbers. Company size force, over."

Willie's men at the back gate said they were pinned down by withering gunfire from at least two machine guns and a dozen or more riflemen.

"Johnny, sitrep?" called Willie. "Come on, Johnny!"

* * *

In the second that Johnny had spotted the grenade, he had spun back to face Bandar and Nunez and had extended his arms. Driving forward like a defensive tackle, Johnny knocked them squarely onto their backs and shielded them with his own body.

Meanwhile, unbeknownst to him, Staff Sergeant Oliver, a young man barely twenty-six, had made a decision—and in that instant he became every Marine. He fought during the founding of our nation and was a devil dog in Europe. He flew with the leathernecks of the South Pacific and battled with the "Frozen Chosin" in Korea. He waded into the blood-stained rice paddies of Vietnam and reconnoitered the enemy across the scorching deserts of Kuwait and Iraq. He was a special operator infiltrating the Taliban in the tribal regions of Pakistan and a bulldog trekking up the perilous mountains of Afghanistan.

And because he was every Marine, he did what every Marine would have done. Without hesitation. Because he was a member of a fraternity of courage and sacrifice.

Staff Sergeant Paul Oliver leaped onto the grenade.

It all happened in one second. Not enough time for Oliver to recall those glorious winter mornings playing football with his father in Youngstown. Not enough time for him to picture the tears falling from his mother's eyes when he had told her he was joining the Corps. Not enough time for him to agonize over leaving behind his wife and newborn son... but just enough time for him to remember his heritage, his duty, and his desire to save his fellow Marines.

Johnny screamed for Bandar and Nunez to wait there. He scrambled to his feet, returning to the shattered staircase, where Oliver was lying on his side, missing an arm, a leg, and most of his face. Johnny checked the man's carotid artery for a pulse. There was none. Rugg, Marshall, and Padilla had fallen back into a small alcove. They were badly shaken, had taken some minor shrapnel wounds, but were otherwise okay. With his stomach twisting in anger, Johnny signaled for them to follow. He took the stairs two at a time, opening fire to force back whoever had tossed that grenade. His breath was labored, his ears ringing from the explosion. He turned into a hallway about five meters long with three doors, two to the right, one to the left. The beam of his flashlight caught something near the left side door, a gleam of metal, and Johnny's rounds chewed into that door jamb.

A figure spun from the farthest door on the right, and Sergeant Rugg was already pushing past Johnny to hammer that bastard onto his back, the insurgent's blood-covered AK-47 tumbling from his grip.

Within the next heartbeat, a second man appeared, lifting his arms into the air, but his attempt to surrender was cut short by a third figure who appeared from behind and gunned him down. This third insurgent, whose face remained hidden in the shadows, was not wearing ManJams but a western-style dress shirt and slacks. He continued firing before ducking away. Johnny and the others shrank to the walls, their rounds striking the man's ghost.

"Bandar, Nunez, get up here!" Johnny shouted.

"Bravo One, this is Drifter," called Captain Zabrowski. "Do you have our package?"

"Sir, I think we got him cornered. I need a minute."

"You got thirty seconds. They're cutting us off from the river."

"Roger that, sir. On our way."

* * *

Josh got on the radio and told the assault force commander that no one was cutting off his men from the river, not if Josh and his four miniguns had anything to say about it. He called up the boat captains on the 152, and they blasted out of the bulrushes like a biker gang roaring away from a dive bar, their sterns sinking, the water churning white behind them as they got up on step. Bad to the bone, Josh thought.

As heart-racing and breathless as the situation was, Josh knew his boys would keep their cool and rely on their training. They needed to get on the landing site as quickly as possible but also be aware that the site might change, given the scope and location of the enemy force. Friendly elements along the riverbank needed to be accounted for at all times, with situational awareness and weapons discipline never higher. Communication was the key to it all, and as they cleared the island, Josh learned that the GCE needed his boats directly behind the compound. He shared that news with his men, along with a report that a platoon-size force of insurgents carrying small arms and rocket-propelled grenades was setting up along the riverbank, preparing for their arrival. "It's coming boys. It's gonna be a shit storm."

* * *

"Tell him to drop his rifle and get out here," Johnny told Sergeant Bandar as they crouched down at the end of the hallway.

The terp lifted his voice and spoke rapidly in Arabic as more salvos of gun and RPG fire boomed from outside.

No answer.

"You tell him he won't be hurt," said Johnny. "But if he doesn't come out, we'll kill him and every one of his friends."

Bandar shouted again. Nothing. The terp shrugged.

Johnny gave a hand signal to Rugg, Marshall, and Padilla. They sprang from their positions, and Johnny led them down the hall. Once they reached the open door, Johnny swung into the room, his flashlight panning across the walls.

* * *

Willie was lying prone and about to tell Johnny that five insurgents had slipped past the main gate and darted into the house. However, before Willie's fingers ever neared his push-to-talk button, two more insurgents rushed from behind, their sandals slapping in the mud. Willie rolled, firing nearly point-blank into the first, who had not seen him, then he squeezed off another round into the second one's chest. Two more rounds into each man finished the job.

However, killing them was like shaking the bee's nest. Another surge of fire drove him back onto his belly, the rounds coming from one, two, even three directions, the fools catching themselves in the crossfire.

Sergeant Brandt and his men were already coming down from the roof with orders to clear a path toward the riverbank, but they, like Johnny's team, were getting pinned down inside the houses. Willie's men near the rear gate had caught a break during reloads and fallen back into the compound All three cars had been struck by RPG fire to explode in succession and drive the men posted there back to the walls on either side of the front gate.

Even with the advantage of the night vision to "own the night" and superior weapons, there were just too many insurgents, and they kept coming as though off an assembly line. Staff Sergeants Daniels and Boatman, who had taken up positions on the northeast side of the compound, reported new contact to the west, a pair of machine guns whose fire was so relentless that they were unable to fall back.

Willie thumbed his mike and ordered Sergeant Heredia to grab a few Marines from the main gate. They needed to locate those insurgents to the west and suppress them long enough for Daniels and Boatman to exfiltrate. Heredia broke free from the tree line, and Willie followed him, running a serpentine path to the gate, whose iron bars rattled and lit up like short-circuiting Christmas trees under a fresh onslaught.

Lowering to his haunches, Willie caught the attention of a Sergeant named Freeman, while Heredia grabbed another. Heredia and his teammate circled around the burning cars while Willie and Freeman headed for Johnny's house. Freeman was a Sasquatch who hailed from Jamaica, Queens and enjoyed sucking on empty brass casings as though they were breath mints. Despite his size, he could run like a marathoner. By the time they reached the flattened metal door, Willie was out of breath but motivated to rush inside because more gunfire popped from the back of the house, sounding like ammo cooking off a burning tank.

Willie tensed and cursed as the metal door creaked under his boots. At the end of the foyer, a pale-faced bearded man squinted in Willie's light and brought his rifle to bear. Willie had three rounds in the man's chest before the man ever squeezed his trigger. As the insurgent fell, Willie and Freeman hit the deck on either side of the wall as another insurgent stole a peak around the corner and fired wildly toward the noise.

* * *

Corey gritted his teeth as muzzle flashes lit up the riverbank. Clusters of bulrushes along with a mound about three meters back from the waterline gave the insurgents both the high ground and well-covered firing positions. The GCE's path back to the boats was now twice as dangerous.

Rounds struck the bow and the armor around the control station. The insurgents always targeted that station, believing if they took out the captain or coxswain, the rest of the crew would abandon the fight. They did not realize that Marines were cross-trained heavily because they were always only one bullet away from someone else's job. The hierarchy went from captain to coxswain, then bow gunners to aft gunner.

Josh was on the radio to check the status of the GCE before the boat gunners opened fire. "They got our boys blocked," he reported. "They'll rally on the other side of the hill till we call clear. Let's go!"

All four boats throttled up and sped downriver, with Corey and Josh turning directly toward the bank. The insurgents assumed they had adjusted course to put the guns in better firing positions. They did not expect Corey and Josh to barrel head-on into the fire.

With the wind whipping over them, and rounds ricocheting everywhere, Corey ordered his bow gunners to open up, even as the captains of Game Warden 1 and Game Warden 4 did likewise. The sight of four miniguns lighting up the bulrushes with tongues of crimson fire was enough to take Corey's breath away. The mechanical buzzing of all those guns, and the thought that death could be only a second away, gave him the most incredible rush, one that was well-nigh impossible to duplicate on any college baseball field.

The riverbank came barreling toward them, with enemy positions scattered like pawns on a chessboard of mud. The water jet engines roared louder. They would hit the bank in just a few seconds. This was the way Marines fought—leaning headfirst into the danger. Corey grabbed his rifle with attached grenade launcher and held his breath.

* * *

Johnny's flashlight shone into the face of a graying Iraqi with a long beard of steel wool. This was the man in business attire, and he shouted something in Arabic as he raised his hands. His AK-47 lay on the nearby bed.

"Don't move!" Johnny ordered. He was a second away from exacting payback—trembling with the desire to do so—but his training took hold.

Bandar came in behind Johnny and fired off a few words in Arabic, his tone hard and uncompromising. Sergeant First Class Nunez appeared a second later.

"Is this our guy?" asked Johnny.

Nunez's gaze widened in recognition. "Yeah, that's him!"

Shots came from down the hallway, probably out near the staircase. Somebody shouted, "Get down!" But it was too late. Marshall, who had gone to the doorway to cover them, jerked as rounds pierced his neck and chest. He convulsed and slumped to the floor.

"Get 'em!" screamed Johnny.

Sergeant Rugg cursed and dragged Marshall back into the room while Nunez and Padilla squeezed past them to return fire.

"He's bleeding out real bad, Johnny," Rugg reported.

"Do what you can!"

Shuddering with the desire to help Rugg but knowing he needed to get their package ready to travel, Johnny sloughed off his pack. He opened the main zipper compartment and tugged out an extra plate carrier vest, one they dubbed a "bullet bouncer" or "bouncer" that was part of their Full Spectrum Battle Equipment (FSBE). He gestured for al-Zahawi to put it on, after which he zipper cuffed the man's wrists behind his back and pulled a balaclava over his head, turning it backwards to blind him.

Rugg lifted his head. "Sergeant Marshall is dead." His report was punctuated by a triplet of gunfire that bit into the doorpost above him.

Letting that fully register in his thoughts was both time consuming and dangerous, Johnny knew. Dwelling on Oliver and Marshall now would dull his senses. There would be plenty of time to grieve later, too much time, in fact.

"Johnny, it's Willie, over."

Willie's voice swept him back to the moment. "Yeah, Willie, I'm up on the second story. We got the guy, but we're cut off."

"We found Sergeant Oliver down here."

"They got Marshall, too. So you're here?"

"Yeah, I'm with Freeman at the bottom of the stairs. There's four of 'em. You force them back into the stairwell, and we'll take it from there."

"Roger." Johnny regarded Sergeant Rugg, who was still on his haunches beside Marshall. "Pat, I need Nunez to carry Marshall. Carlos will stay with the terp. I'll escort Mr. Money Bags here. Right now, you do like Willie said and corral 'em into the stairwell. When Willie's through with them, you get Oliver on the way out."

"You got it, Johnny." Rugg took a deep breath and rose. There was a sheen in the man's eyes born of a weary determination. He turned off his flashlight, flipped down his NODs, then burst into the hallway and sprinted off, releasing a blood-curdling war cry as he opened fire. The insurgents would believe he had a death wish or had gone insane, but big Pat Rugg was just being a Marine.

Taking Rugg's advance as their cue, Johnny gave the signal, and the others followed, with Johnny clutching the back of al-Zahawi's shirt and shoving him forward.

The four insurgents took one look at the enormous Cyclops trouncing toward them, assumedly wet their pants, then scurried away. They were thumping farther down the stairwell when the rat-tat-tating of familiar rifles boomed and lead peppered the ceiling above the stairs.

"Johnny, you hear me?" shouted Willie. "You're clear!"

"Roger, we're coming down!"

Willie and Freeman were dragging the bodies out of the way as they descended. Rugg was already engaged in the grim task of hoisting Staff Sergeant Oliver over his shoulders. Freeman helped by accepting Marshall, since, he too, was a pack mule of the first order. This freed up Nunez to work security as they moved.

Johnny notified the captain that they had confirmed the ID of their package and were exfiltrating down to the boats. They returned to the front entrance and kept low on either side of the doorway. Johnny saw how they could exploit the cover of the burning cars, heading there first instead of making one long hike to the gate. He shared the plan.

Freeman and Rugg were nodding, and Rugg spoke for the both of them, "We're good to go, Johnny. We're just slow carrying these guys."

Bandar gestured to Sergeant Padilla who was watching over him. "Let me and Carlos go to the palm trees and draw some fire while you guys make the break."

Johnny shook his head. "I'll send Nunez."

"Come on, Johnny, let me fight."

Johnny eyed the young man, searching for any signs of weakness. "Sergeant Bandar? Padilla? Get out there and draw some fire." He winked at Bandar.

The interpreter returned the wink. "Glad we speak the same language." He charged off across the metal door, with Padilla in tow.

By the time they reached the palm trees, they had captured the attention of at least six insurgents who had been concealed behind the burning cars. At that instant Johnny realized that if Bandar had not made his offer, the group would have been ambushed. Those insurgents had been perfectly hidden, and Bandar's desire to contribute had just saved them all. There it was, *esprit de corps*, flying high like the stars and stripes, right before Johnny's eyes.

Meanwhile, Willie was already lobbing one fragmentation grenade, then a second, striking a one-two punch, the frags blasting apart at least three insurgents behind the cars while the rest retreated toward the back gate with their tails between their legs. Nunez got a bead on them and took out the last man before he could join the others. Johnny hollered to move, and they double timed across the courtyard and ducked behind the nearest car. Once a beautiful black Mercedes sedan, the vehicle was now lying on its side and spilling gas, oil, and radiator fluid like a dying beast. The rain sizzled as it fell on the super-heated quarter panels and doors, and all that burning rubber and melting plastic released a toxic smoke that had Rugg and Freeman coughing.

Al-Zahawi kept standing tall, and Johnny shoved him down, onto his knees. Rugg and Freeman set down Oliver and Marshall so they could rest before the next trip to the gate. Johnny skulked around to the front of the car and targeted two insurgents up on the rooftop of the adjacent house. He caught the first one in the head, and the man dropped off the ledge and plummeted with an eerie, almost underwater slowness. The second guy reacted and dove to the side, but Johnny anticipated that and caught him in the neck. He fell prone on the ledge, one arm draped over the side and dangling like a pendulum.

"Nice work," Willie said.

Johnny glanced back, nodded, and then he lifted his voice to Bandar and Padilla. "Come on, now. Move!"

Bandar rose and bolted toward them with the agility of an Olympic track star, and there was certainly enough gunfire to send him dashing from the mark. Padilla kept tight on his boots, whirling back once to cover their rear.

AK-47s popped and cracked from somewhere behind Johnny, and Bandar took a round in the leg. He stumbled, turned, then caught another bullet in the side that sent him toppling. Padilla could not stop in time and fell over Bandar, both of them smashing into a puddle. More guns cracked, and the mud around them erupted in a dozen tiny volcanoes.

Johnny craned his neck to the gates, where four insurgents had appeared. Rugg and Nunez were on them, though, emptying their thirty round magazines in a retaliatory strike that had the word *vengeance* engraved on every shell casing. When their rifles fell silent, there was nothing left alive near those gates.

After ordering Willie to keep an eye on al-Zahawi, Johnny sprang from behind the car. He raced toward Bandar, who was being hauled to his feet by Padilla. Johnny took one of Bandar's arms and draped it over his shoulder, then he and Padilla carried the terp back to cover.

"Johnny, I can't feel my legs."

"Don't worry about it, son. You think about what a rock star you are. I didn't see those guys behind here. You drew their fire. You saved us all."

Bandar's eyes creased into slits, and he nodded.

The second he was able, Johnny called for HM2 Milam but learned the corpsman was tied up with four other causalities. He lifted his voice to the others, "We need to patch him up before we move him again." Freeman, Rugg, and Nunez were already digging through their packs, producing morphine and trauma bandages, while Willie reported more movement out near the rear gate.

* * *

Josh clutched the gunwale as the patrol boat crashed into the riverbank and the bow rose and shuddered across the mud.

Four insurgents were literally three meters away, firing at them as Lance Corporal Duffy swung the minigun around and stitched fiery lines across their makeshift bunker. Mounds of earth spewed in all directions.

A wave of gunfire came from the bulrushes, within which several insurgents had concealed themselves. Rounds pinged off Duffy's gun shield before he fell back into the boat, clutching his thigh.

"Get up there! Get on his gun!" Josh barked to Lance Corporal Wilson, then lifted his voice even more. "Duffy, you all right?"

"Aw, yeah, Sergeant," he gasped. "Yeah."

"Be there in a second."

The coxswain left the wheel and slipped out of the control station, rushing up to re-man the minigun and put fire into the reeds.

At the same time, Corey and his men were trying to suppress another wave of insurgents bounding over the hill to reinforce their brothers. His machine gun and tracer-lit minigun fire struck much higher lines than Josh's, casting the entire riverbank in an otherworldly glow. Corey himself was thumping off rounds from his rifle's M203 grenade launcher, the explosions decimating insurgents and terrain.

Josh glanced down at the SeaFLIR, a forward-looking infrared imaging device. On the screen were the heat signatures of the GCE attempting to fall back to the riverbank. Their lack of movement suggested they were cut off well before the last hill. Johnny's group was still inside the compound behind the burning cars. After assessing the SeaFLIR's data, monitoring the platoon's internal net, and receiving intel from higher regarding the GCE's status, Josh knew that if he and his boys failed to clean up this shoreline, no one was going home.

I am my brother's keeper...

He got on the 152 and ordered Game Wardens 1 and 4 to get in tighter and direct their fire across the bulrushes, while Wilson and Corey's minigunners concentrated on the crest of the hill. The boys on the 240 Golfs would continue suppressing additional contacts near the waterline or off to the flanks.

Josh started toward the bow, where Lance Corporal Duffy was still lying on the deck, waiting for him... but then he stopped. From the corner of his eye, he detected movement to his left about twenty meters down the riverbank. He squinted into his

NODs. An insurgent was just coming out of the reeds, standing waist deep in the water. He lifted an RPG onto his shoulder and took aim at Josh's boat.

* * *

On three, Willie led the others back to the gate. He arrived first, and when he turned around, he frowned at the team dragging toward him like a pack of badly wounded wolves. Rugg was carrying Oliver, Freeman clutched Marshall, and Padilla had Bandar on his back. Johnny had let his rifle dangle on the single point sling and had drawn his M45 MEUSOC pistol. He shoved al-Zahawi with one hand and used the .45 to cover their rear, along with Nunez.

"Brandt, it's Willie. I need you and your guys at the front gate."

"Roger, on our way."

"ETA?"

"One mike."

"Right on."

Willie slipped past the gates and outside the compound walls. He was there but a second when salvos of AK fire ripped across the dirt not a meter from his boots, followed by more chiseling into the concrete at his shoulders. He crouched and hustled back through the gate and behind the wall, where he caught his breath and faced Johnny. "Maybe a squad out there under those palms to the left. We need to get past them, over two little hills, then over a big mound just before the water. What I don't like are all those reeds down by the water. Too many covered and concealed positions. It's a gauntlet all the way."

Johnny grimaced. "Where the hell is Brandt?"

"Should be here any second now."

A distant shout seized Willie's attention. From behind both houses came more members of the Fallujah homeowners' association, at least a dozen rifle-toting men, maybe more. They appeared enormously upset over the Marine Corp's violation of their covenants by shooting up two houses in their neighborhood. They split into three groups, taking up firing positions along the walls and behind the cars.

"We need to go now," Johnny ordered. "Go, go, go!"

"I'll hold back and buy you some time," Willie hollered.

"Watch your top knot."

Willie grinned. That was a line from a movie they both loved: *Jeremiah Johnson*, and a reference to being scalped by Indians. No chance of that here. These natives preferred to dismember you, burn you, then drag you through the streets before hanging you from a bridge.

Johnny shoved al-Zahawi past the open gate. Brandt and his men showed up a heartbeat later, and Willie hurried back outside the compound to cut loose an entire thirty-round magazine on the insurgents positioned behind the palm trees, suppressing them and clearing a path for Johnny's group. They splashed off through the puddles, heading toward the river, with Nunez and Brandt's four Marines dishing out heavy fire to the flanks.

Willie returned to the rain-slick wall and chanced a look around the corner, past the gates and into the compound. The insurgents had been reinforced by another six or seven men. There were over twenty now, nearly ten squatting near the cars and the rest lying or crouching in and around the landscape or peering out from the windows. As Willie rolled back from the corner, they began shouting to each other. Echoing footfalls drew near. He took a long breath. Overcome. Adapt. Complete the mission. But how? By remembering who he was.

The Fujita-Pearson scale, which ranked the severity of tornadoes from F1 through F5, still needed revising to account for United States Marines like Staff Sergeant Joseph "Willie" Parente. Standing on the shoulders of every great Marine who had come before him, Willie spun away from the wall like the F6 twister he was. He rushed across the gates to the opening, where he emptied another magazine into the compound, driving the insurgents back toward their covering positions. He ceased fire and pitched one and then a second flash-bang grenade toward the houses, exploiting their detonations to blind the enemy and reload. He noted with dread that he had blown through seven rifle mags, with only three left. As he reached the opposite side of the gates, the clang of a grenade against the metal framework sent him racing along the wall. The grenade exploded, tearing one of the gates into a smoking piece of abstract art and raising a chorus of screaming from the insurgents. They were coming for him.

* * *

Josh brought his own rifle to bear on the insurgent shouldering the RPG. Even though he stitched a line in the water straight up and into the target's chest, killing him instantly, the man's RPG still flashed.

The whoosh and streaking light were the last things Josh heard and saw before he shouted, "Hit the deck!" The rocket exploded, sending shockwaves through the entire boat. The stench of fuel came immediately, and the port side engine coughed and fell silent. With smoke clouds swelling, Josh crawled back to find Corporal Keller. The aft gunner was lying across the starboard deck, bleeding profusely from multiple shrapnel wounds to his legs. "Hang in there, Artie!" he cried, then he faced the riverbank.

Seeing Josh and his men were in trouble, the insurgents directed all of their fire on Josh's boat. Lance Corporal Blount turned toward the hillside and returned fire, and what seemed like a hundred rounds clanged off his gun shield and mount, off the canopy behind him, and off the deck. Blount remained at the gun, emptying his ammo can. As the gun fell silent, he dropped behind the gunwale, groaning that he had been hit.

As Josh tensed over which of his men to treat first, the starboard side engine sputtered and began to lose power, presumably its fuel line also damaged. All three gunners were down. His coxswain was manning the minigun and about to need a reload. The boat was dying on the shoreline. Josh slammed his fist on the deck. He was not out of the fight. Not yet.

* * *

Placing Corporal Ochoa in charge of his boat, Corey leaped off and splashed into the water. He came slogging around the back of Josh's SURC, grabbing the collar and hauling himself onboard. He took one look at Corporal Keller bleeding out across the deck, then swung around at the sound of shouting.

Yet another RPG was being directed at them from beside the bulrushes, and Corey raised his rifle and punched that man onto his back before he could do any more damage. Two more riflemen appeared behind him, and Corey fired a grenade at their boots, then ducked as the explosion sent them hurling in opposite directions. He dropped to his hands and knees and faced Keller. "How you doing, Corporal?"

"I need a beer."

"Roger. We'll get you some help first."

Josh rushed over and crouched down. "Nice shots! I owe you!"

"Forget it," Corey replied. "Time to own this river!"

"Hell, yeah! If it ain't wet, it ain't worth it!"

That was Small Craft Company's motto, and Corey loved hearing it as he hurried to get some bandages on Keller's wounds.

* * *

Johnny and his group neared the last hill overlooking the riverbank. The stench of gunpowder permeated the entire area, and hundreds of shell casings shimmered as gold flecks across the mud. To the rear, Brandt and his men traded fire with a few more insurgents who had ventured out from the palms to try their luck along the pathway's edge. They highly underestimated the precision of Marine Corp riflemen, but what they lacked in forethought and aim they made up for in sheer numbers. A few turned into ten, who turned into fifteen, and it was all Brandt's men could do to keep them at bay.

Johnny crouched behind the hill. "Hey, Josh, it's Johnny, you with me, over?"

"I got you Johnny. You'll have to get the package to Corey's boat, though. Got some catastrophic damage over here."

"Roger that, are we clear?"

"Not yet. Still got a few contacts on the flanks. Standby."

Brandt came running up behind Johnny and hunkered down. "Sergeant, everyone and his mother's coming—like the whole goddamned town."

Johnny smiled darkly. "They can't get away from us now."

The young sergeant almost returned the grin, and he understood Johnny's reference; he understood it big time. Lieutenant General Lewis Burwell "Chesty" Puller was one of the most, if not *the* most highly decorated Marines in the history of the Corps. When commenting on how he was surrounded on all sides by the enemy and was outnumbered 29 to 1, the legendary Chesty issued those same words: *They can't get away from us now.*

Brandt cleared his throat. "We're going red on ammo."

"I know." Johnny crawled to the top of the hill and hazarded a look over the top:

Two of Josh's boats were belching out enough fire to kill a legion of men, let alone a string of loosely organized insurgents. But there was always that one lucky rat who pulled through, that one rat bastard who could sneak up on a boat along the shore and toss in a grenade, and the boys from Small Craft Company were doing their utmost to exterminate him.

RPGs struck thunderclaps near the compound, and they were closely followed by more gunfire. The platoon net came alive with reports of the security team being overrun.

"Josh, we're running out of time here."

Captain Zabrowski got on the net and confirmed that everyone should fall back to the boats. The insurgents were advancing en masse toward the river.

"Okay, Johnny, you're clear," cried Josh over the radio. "Bring 'em down!"

* * *

As the first two insurgents ran past the shattered gate, Willie express shipped them to Allah with a pair of double taps, then he was back on the move. He sprinted toward the end of the landscaping, where a fountain of three lions spitting water lay near the driveway. He reached the fountain's square base and ducked behind it. He turned and came up again, sighting three more insurgents who had clambered past the gate. Two went down, but he missed the third, cursed, and fired again, nabbing him in the leg. Willie scrambled to his feet and was back on the run. Shoot, move, communicate. Never stop.

In hindsight he should have stolen a moment to recheck the roof line, because when he broke away from the fountain, a distinctive booming resounded from high and behind, and the hairs stood on the back of his neck. The neighborhood watch was now armed with Russian Dragunov SVD sniper rifles, and they had found him.

He was half way across the open field, perhaps twenty steps away from a quartet of tightly placed palms, when a single shot echoed off the compound walls. His boot gave way, as though his foot were no longer there. After another step, excruciating hot pain woke from the base of his heel and shot up his leg. The rational side of his brain said stop. The recon side said run. He compromised and limped his ass over to the trees, collapsed behind them, then released his empty magazine and shoved home another. Only two left now. He tilted his rifle down toward his boot, and the attached flashlight told the story. A bullet hole was torn in the sole of the arch, with a blood-ringed exit hole coming straight out the back of his heel. The best he could surmise, a round must have ricocheted off the ground.

With fresh bark exploding into his face as the sniper who had caught him set free another two rounds, Willie raised his rifle toward the muzzle flashes. He found the man's silhouette, range roughly 100 meters. He relied on the laser and on Kentucky windage, making adjustments on the fly to account for the wind and rain. The outline of the sniper shifted out from the parapet. Willie aimed slightly to the left and took in a deep breath. Smooth and steady pressure on the trigger. He took the shot. Low and to the right. Startled, the dark figure began to pull back from the ledge. Willie's next round would be even more interesting. He fired, and the silhouette slumped as the dead do, the shot so accurate that Willie only half believed he had made it. He laughed aloud until more insurgents detached themselves from the walls and came running at him, wailing like banshees as they opened fire.

Caught off guard, Willie emptied his magazine, dropping all four. He ejected the empty mag, and then shoved in his last one, swearing over the waste of ammo. Thirty rounds left for the rifle. He still had his .45, with one mag in the pistol and two extras. The Corps issued them seven-round Wilson combat magazines, but Willie and most of the other guys had purchased aftermarket Chip McCormick ten round magazines for a little extra firepower. That seemed like an awfully wise choice now.

Willie began picking off more men as they attempted to advance. His plan was to drop the nearest guys then make his break for the riverbank. He sent two into the mud, clutching their chests, but then a more ambitious idiot Willie nicknamed "Moe" appeared from behind the walls with an RPG propped on his shoulder. Willie switched to full auto, blowing through nine rounds to level him and the other two stooges who had joined him. By the time he broke off fire, another four insurgents were flitting like little demons to the flanks. Muttering a curse, Willie emptied the magazine, unsure if he had struck them but convinced it was time to fall back.

He grabbed the palm tree and heaved himself to his feet. The fire in his leg was a three-alarm blaze now. He hobbled farther into the shrubs and palms, past some tall, wild grass, and toward a deep scar running across the ground about thirty meters away. His left hand cleared the rifle from his workspace, allowing it to hang at his left side from the sling. At the same time, he drew his .45 with his right hand. He repeatedly craned his head back, hearing them cut through the underbrush behind him. The scar ahead became a V-shaped irrigation ditch leading down to the river. The ditch was about three meters across and roughly two meters deep, although it was half-full with rainwater. There was no other cover, so Willie picked up the pace and headed there, groaning aloud as he did so, his eyes burning with tears.

As he neared the long furrow, the first shots came in, blasting up the mud to his left, then to his right. He spun and splashed onto his gut, raising his elbows and balancing his .45 in both hands.

The ManJam squad had momentarily lost him. Three men drifted off to the right flank, two to the left. The rain and darkness had worked wonders, as did Willie's night vision so he could study them.

But then, from the shadows to his left came a loud and rhythmic squishing sound, and as he turned, he came face-to-face with an insurgent whose eyes bugged out. Reflexes took over, and Willie shot him in the head. The insurgent fell, and Willie cursed because he had just given up his position.

As he dragged himself onto his hands and knees, some clown fired on full auto in Willie's general direction, sewing a line across the back side of the irrigation ditch. Once the man's rifle went silent, Willie repressed a scream and forced himself to his feet, running the last few meters to the ditch, putting his full weight onto his wounded foot. He slowed, tripped, then slammed face-first onto the ground, his elbow hitting a rock, his hand opening reflexively and sending the .45 skittering into the water. He crawled forward and tugged himself into the ditch, rolling sideways across the muck. His momentum carried him like a log down the embankment, and he splashed completely under the water. He came up, chilled and gasping, his hands groping through the mud, searching in vain for the pistol. Damn, his wife was right again. He did have two left feet, and he should have learned to dance.

* * *

Once al-Zahawi and the rest of the group were safely aboard Corey's boat, Johnny hightailed it back over the mound, intent on finding Willie. The staff sergeant was not answering his radio, and no one else had seen him. Knowing Willie, he would chose the most covered line back to the riverbank, so Johnny backtracked along that more wooded path. While he would never admit it, a hollow feeling swelled in his chest, a feeling that Willie might already be dead. And no, the Marine Corps could not afford to lose a man like Staff Sergeant Parente. He was always out front, always there to provide whatever the platoon needed. He did his job without complaint and was competitive to a fault, always ribbing Johnny for not pushing harder, even when both of them had already set the envelope on fire.

Rounds buzzed over Johnny's head, a few splitting open the trunks behind him. He picked up the pace and kept on because he had steel in his back and a brother he needed to find. An AK-47 set to full automatic rattled from the adjacent field. In a matter of seconds, Johnny was at the perimeter, crouched down and counting six men converging on an irrigation ditch on the opposite end of the field. They weren't fleeing... they were *chasing*...

It was not a question of math. If it were, then it would be six against one. No, it was a question of stealth and speed... and, of course, who was the most aggressive Recon Marine on the planet. That would be Johnny Johansen, the guy wearing the man pants, the guy who was all over this moment like a fat kid on a cupcake, the guy who was definitely all that and a bag of chips. Imagine that. Easy day. No drama.

After checking his rifle to ensure he had a full magazine, Johnny grinned crookedly. He pictured himself drinking Jim Beam from a cracked glass and reflecting on this night as though it had already happened, grab-assing with a bunch of young guns who were holding their breaths. They wanted to know what happened next. It was time to show them.

He vaulted from the tree line and opened fire.

* * *

Willie considered crawling out of the ditch to retrieve the insurgent's rifle, but more men were coming, maybe twenty meters off now and closing... Multiple rounds cracked from above and continued, with AK-47 fire popping in between. Next came the sharper crack of a pistol. Without warning, an insurgent leaped into the water directly in front of Willie, not expecting him there and acting as though he was fleeing from someone. Before the man could bring his rifle around, Willie reared back and delivered a "Bare Knuckles Willie" blow to the man's nose, breaking it instantly.

As Willie reached out to seize the man's rifle, another man jumped into the ditch, he too, trying to evade the hellish fire blazing from above. Willie seized the end of this man's rifle, wrenched it out of his hands, then reared back and batted the insurgent's head like a baseball. Meanwhile, the first guy, who had dropped his rifle was reaching for a pistol at his side. Willie batted the man's arm, dropped the rifle, then delivered another bare-knuckled blow to the insurgent's face. He punched the guy again and again until the thug's teeth caved in. With the insurgent stunned, Willie grabbed the man's pistol and shot him. It was only then that he remembered to breathe. His chest rose and fell twice before he spun toward the sound of boots shuffling from above. He tightened his grip on the pistol.

* * *

Johnny had spotted the last two riflemen jumping into the ditch, and he steered himself there to finish them. A single gunshot had him leaning into his trigger, but when he neared the ditch, he found Willie completely covered in mud and aiming an old Makarov at him.

He lowered his rifle and sighed. "You weren't answering your radio."

Willie reached for the radio pack on his vest. "Aw, hell, I knew it was quiet. It got shot up. It's dead."

Johnny frowned. Willie would not have called for help anyway. "You all right?"

"Took one in the foot. Exit wound in the heel."

Johnny's eyes widened. "They got you in the heel just like Achilles. That was the only way they could shut you down."

"What're you talking about? I'm still in the fight."

"Right on." Johnny proffered his hand and hauled Willie out of the ditch. As they turned to go, Johnny looked back and wished he had not. A crowd was gathering outside the compound, rallied by more gunmen. With a chill winding up his spine, Johnny shoved Willie's arm across his shoulders, and they sloshed off toward the river.

* * *

By the time Johnny and Willie reached Corey's boat, the gunners were laying down suppressive fire on more insurgents flooding down from the compound. Meanwhile, Josh's boat was being towed off the bank by another. All four SURCs exfiltrated to the left. Johnny asked Corey if they had taken a head count, and they had, so he slumped down next to Willie, leaning back on the gunwale and breathing the deepest sigh of his life. He glanced over at his friend. Their gazes met for a moment, but they turned away, staring half-dazed at the bodies of Staff Sergeant Paul Oliver and Sergeant Tom Marshall lying on the deck beside them.

Later on they would learn that of the twenty-eight men assigned to the raid, only fifteen had returned. Small Craft Company had nine wounded but all would make it. Al-Zahawi's financing of the insurgency would grind to an immediate halt. CIA paramilitary operations officers in country were transferring him to one of their "black sites" in a process known as "extraordinary rendition." They would reduce al-Zahawi into a babbling idiot who would tell them everything they needed to know. Johnny hoped he knew a lot, because extraordinary men had paid for that intel with their lives.

* * *

By morning, Johnny and the rest of the platoon returned to Camp Baharia, located about two miles southeast of Fallujah. The base was named after the Arabic word for Marine, *mushaat al-baharia*, which roughly translated as "walkers of the Navy." Baharia was once a Ba'ath Party retreat called "Dreamland" and was a favorite haunt of Saddam Hussein's two sons, who watched boat races from the nearby artificial lake ringed by palm trees. Willie received treatment at the hospital tent and learned that the bullet had not struck any bones. Meanwhile, the survivors of 3rd Platoon and Small Craft Company were debriefed, after which Johnny convinced the company commander to allow Josh and Corey to remain at the camp before returning to their unit the following day.

That evening, they all gathered in Johnny's cement bungalow. Alcohol was banned on the base, but Johnny and Willie always kept a little whiskey in their living areas, some Jordanian Industrial or even a little Johnny Walker Blue Label sent from home for a special occasion. The ice came in 3' by 1' rectangular blocks, and they would chisel it apart with their knives for whiskey on the rocks. With a friend standing guard at the door, they raised their glasses, first in a toast to those they had lost, wishing them *fair winds and following seas*, and then to each other: "Never above you, never below you, always beside you."

Chapter One

Present day...

"I didn't believe it at first, but then the pieces came together. It was huge. It was crazy. We weren't sure who we could trust, but that never stopped us."

—Corey McKay (FBI interview, 23 December)

The journalist from *WIRED* magazine sashayed into the warehouse like a Victoria's Secret supermodel trapped in a red business suit and wireframe glasses. Her name was Susannah, and Dresden could not remember or pronounce her multisyllabic surname, not that it mattered. He had assistants to manage those details. The lithe and lovely Susannah thought an expose on one of America's largest private equity firms and its co-founders would earn her literary accolades, and she had spent the better part of a month hounding Dresden's staff for the opportunity. He had read her curriculum vitae touting her degree from Colombia, and he had scanned her freelance articles in *Forbes* detailing human rights violations perpetrated by ISIL. The Islamic State of Iraq and the Levant, more commonly known as ISIS in the media, distracted journalists like her—even as other terrorist organizations lurked in the shadows. While Dresden had agreed to the interview, he had done so only after scrolling through her Facebook account, whose privacy settings still allowed him to admire her profile picture.

He insisted they meet at one of his companies, UXD International, a munitions recycling operation seventy-four miles west of Houston. The 100,000 square foot facility lay on the outskirts of rural Columbus, on a desert plain situated far from any densely populated areas, given the nature of their work.

Since the global war on terror had begun, Nicholas Dresden and his senior managing director/co-founder, Edward Senecal, had transformed their once tiny firm into a powerful conglomerate with high return portfolios. The firm's growth was the result of purchasing specific defense companies including manufacturers of firearms and ammo; service providers of aviation and signals intelligence; and two very large defense contracting companies. UXD in particular designed, constructed, and operated demilitarization facilities for destroying and recycling conventional and chemical weapons around the world. Recycling of old and unwanted munitions resulted in the production of TNT and a variety of other products exported overseas for commercial mining use, including slurry explosives well-suited for underwater blasting applications.

Dresden had brought the journalist here so she could witness for herself UXD's many successes—and because he was well aware of her agenda. She planned to confront him about how, during the past decade, political change in the White House and the drawdown and/or withdrawal of forces overseas created substantial losses in revenue and a steep decline in share value. Many of his companies were hemorrhaging; consequently, her article would depict him as a fifty-nine-year-old dinosaur staring up at an asteroid-filled sky.

Now, as she gaped at the colossal warehouse and the munitions stacked from floor to ceiling, Dresden flashed his perfectly capped teeth, ran fingers through his shock of gray hair, then led her to the edge of the balcony where the hustle and bustle of the shipping dock unfolded like a stage play before their eyes. Forklift operators loaded towering pallets of recycled explosives onto eighteen-wheelers; shipping clerks took inventory of incoming and outgoing merchandise; and another team of clerks manned stations on an assembly line that sealed boxes and marked them for shipment.

"This place is amazing," she began.

"We're very proud of it."

She swiped a finger across her smartphone. "So do you mind if I record?"

"Go ahead."

"How did all of this get started? I mean the firm, everything."

He snickered. "That's already well-documented. You didn't Google me before you came here? Didn't read our Wiki page? I'm shocked."

Her gaze lit on him. "I don't care about what's already been said. I care about what you have to say now... with your inflection, your bias, your insights."

Dresden thought a moment. He found her reply flattering and felt compelled to impress her, which, of course, was all part of her plan. "Here's something I've never told anyone, something you won't find online. It all started with bananas."

"Excuse me?"

"That's right, bananas."

She stared over the rim of her glasses. "Is this some inappropriate joke?"

"Not at all. Hear me out. Eddie and I were in our twenties and aggressive bastards back then. We were at a dinner party and somebody commented on the rising heart attack rate among the African population. A doctor in the group asked about the year's banana crop."

"What do bananas have to do with accelerated death rates?"

"We learned that the failed banana crop reduced the natural source of potassium in the African diet. The results were reflected in increased cardiac events, especially in undiagnosed coronary victims. You combine that loss of potassium with a poor health care system, and the result was a soaring fatal heart attack rate."

"Wow, I wouldn't have made that connection."

"Wait, it gets better. Somebody in the group suggested it'd be a great time to sell the Africans bananas. That's when Eddie began looking into a banana farm in Costa Rica. We formed D&S Equities and sold stock to everyone at the dinner party as a way to raise capital. We put it all together in one night with a handshake—nothing more. Within a week we had it all on paper, and Eddie went down to Costa Rica, bought out the banana farm, and we started shipping bananas to Africa. I was told we saved many lives."

"Sounds pretty crazy. And risky."

Dresden hoisted his brows. "Far better is it to dare mighty things, to win glorious triumphs, even though checkered by failure... than to rank with those poor spirits who neither enjoy nor suffer much, because they live in a gray twilight that knows not victory nor defeat."

"That's very eloquent. Who said that?"

"Theodore Roosevelt, and as you can tell, I love to recite it to all my employees. But the truth is, Eddie and I were just a couple of fast-talking frat boys from Princeton, and we didn't have any of our own money in the pot. Fortunately, the risk paid off. We used our profits to buy a startup pharmaceutical company in Canada that makes statin and warfarin type drugs. Eddie's Canadian, and *Health Canada* is a hell of lot easier to work with than the FDA."

"So you sold bananas to Africa to maintain healthy hearts, and now you sell cardiac drugs in case the bananas aren't enough."

Dresden nodded. "That exact business model is working right here. The DoD pays us to make their munitions and pays us again to destroy or recycle them."

"Sounds like a win-win. So how did you go from bananas to bombs?"

Her turn of phrase amused him, but instead of lifting his grin, he lowered his voice. "If you want to know, you'll have to turn off the recorder, and you won't be able to print any of this. Still interested?"

She consulted her smartphone. "You're off the record."

"Do you know anything about the Iran-Contra Affair back in the eighties?"

She winced and slowly shook her head.

"I keep forgetting you're just a kid."

"Last time I looked, I was a woman—with all the parts."

Now he winced. "I'll have to agree. Anyway, back then, Reagan decided to get involved in the Nicaragua civil war. Something called the Boland Amendment stopped the federal government from providing military support to overthrow the Nicaraguan government. Despite that, Vice Admiral Poindexter, and his deputy, Lt. Colonel Oliver North, diverted millions of dollars to the rebels. That money came from a deal where we sold anti-tank and anti-aircraft missiles to Iran. Around this time, the CIA approached Eddie and I, and using Iran-Contra funds, D&S Equities created Smith Armory. As a private entity we brokered ongoing arms deals to Nicaragua and Iran."

"Why did they pick you guys?"

"There was a splinter group in congress. They were concerned about the erosion of presidential power. They realized that using private companies to wage wars created another barrier to congressional oversight and heightened secrecy for both the planning and the execution of declared or undeclared wars. We were their guinea pigs. They wanted an unknown company to work through, and by taking the risk, they rewarded us with covert preferential business opportunities, like inside intel on mismanaged companies ripe for takeover. Our firm grew rapidly from there."

Her gaze narrowed on him. "Do you ever feel guilty?"

"About what?"

"Your companies profit from war. Without conflict and bloodshed, you're out of business. Does that bother you?"

Dresden stiffened. "No."

Susannah consulted her phone and read from a note: "I was looking at some reports on world international terrorism activities released by the State Department.

It seems the administration's unwillingness to engage in a ground war doesn't bode well for D&S Equities."

Dresden snorted. "It doesn't bode well for America. Islamic Extremists have found safe havens in Syria and Iraq, and we're doing nothing to stop them from training and equipping their fighters. This country is vulnerable, despite all of the vacuous assurances from administrators who spend more time covering their asses than protecting this great nation. The Boston Marathon bombing and the Charlie Hebdo attack in France could happen again... doubtless they *will happen again*... no matter what they tell you, my dear."

Down below, the company's Executive Director of Shipping, Tom Barryman, gave Dresden a thumb's up, the signal that he was ready to give them the tour. Barryman had been with the company from the beginning, a second career after retiring from the Dallas Police Department. He was about Dresden's age but waddled like an aging mallard while Dresden sported a triathlete's physique from his incessant training.

Dresden gestured to the floor below. "Tommy wants you to see our static detonation chamber. It's a machine that helps us destroy the bombs."

Susannah removed her glasses to expose her stunning blue eyes flecked with green. "I have to be honest, Mr. Dresden, my editors want me to ask you some hard-hitting questions about your other companies and the tremendous losses you've incurred—"

"—which you just did. I'm glad we got that out of the way."

She sighed. "I understand why you've brought me here, but before we go any further, I want to be upfront because I respect you. What you're doing here is remarkable, but my editors want a story that focuses on the drawdown and downsizing of the military and its associated contractors and companies."

"Of course. But it doesn't have to be that way, does it? You could focus on how my business and our partners plan to evolve."

She glanced down at her phone. "Dare mighty things, huh?"

"Absolutely. And, of course, you'll find me much more agreeable. Shall we?"

Dresden escorted her down the stairs and across the shipping department, where Barryman handed them hardhats and safety glasses and led them to the far end of the facility, a five minute walk at a brisk pace. They passed through two security checkpoints with X-ray machines and entered another room, where the static detonation chamber rose from the center like an enormous blue refrigerator box surrounded by a spaghetti-work of scaffolding and staircases. Barryman took them behind the chamber to show them an adjoining room where a multi-jointed mechanical arm automatically loaded missiles into crates that were towed along on a conveyor, through a double airlock, and into the chamber itself. At the moment, the system was down for routine maintenance but would be up and running in thirty minutes.

"That's the feed system up there," said Barryman. "Our original feed only had a diameter of 150 millimeters and a length of 400. Weight was limited to three kilograms for each feed, but we just installed this new system, and we can accommodate most anything out there, missiles wider and taller than us."

"So the bombs go inside and what happens?" asked Susannah.

"The chamber is superheated to 1,022 degrees Fahrenheit, so the explosives deflagrate and detonate. The gasses are destroyed by explosive effects and pyrolysis in the main chamber. Anything left is further treated to remove any pollutants. The scrap is retained until we're sure everything's safe and been completely destroyed."

"It's a very complicated and very expensive garbage disposal for things that go bang," Dresden said with a wink.

Susannah gestured that she wanted to take a picture, and Dresden urged her to do so.

"If you want to come back in half an hour, I can show you how it works," said Barryman.

"Thank you, Tommy. We'll let you know," said Dresden.

"Okay. I need to run. Two big shipments heading out tonight. I'll catch up with you later. Great to see you."

"You, too," Dresden replied. He regarded Susannah. "So now that I've convinced you that we're not just profiteers, we can get the hell out of here and have dinner."

She glanced down at the wedding ring on his hand. "Will your wife be joining us?"

"She's back in New York working with one of her charities. If you feel—"

"No, not at all. You're old enough to be my father. I was just curious. I thought it might be interesting to get some of her insights."

"The real dirt on the firm, huh?"

"Exactly."

"Well, if you're nice, I'll tell you a few more stories."

"I did read about your trip to Afghanistan last year. Why did you want to embed with Special Forces troops? Didn't you think it was too dangerous?"

"That's a very long story."

"Was it something on your bucket list?"

"You might say that."

* * *

They had reservations at Del Frisco's in Houston, and the drive over would take about ninety minutes in traffic. As Dresden sat with Susannah in the back of his limousine, he offered her a cocktail, and then they continued their conversation. She pried again about his trip to Afghanistan and why a man pushing sixty would put himself in harm's way. He allowed her to speculate about wanting to see firsthand how the products and services supplied by his various companies aided troops in the field, or how he had gone to the mountains as part of some rich man's macho fantasy weekend. When she was finished with her shots in the dark, he told her about how his father had fought in North Vietnam, Laos, and Cambodia with the Navy SEALs, and how his maternal grandfather was a member of a Naval Combat Demolition Unit during WWII and battled the Germans on Omaha Beach.

Dresden's paternal grandfather, Franz, was an Army doctor in allied-occupied Germany, circa 1945, and he was the reason why Dresden had gone to Afghanistan. He took a deep breath and began the story.

One night Franz was working at an aid station in Berlin when a Muslim named Beb Ahmose rushed frantically inside, carrying a young boy in his arms. He spoke in broken English about how a Jeep filled with drunken GIs had struck his wife and son, that his wife was already dead, and that his son needed immediate medical attention. The boy's leg was broken and he was having trouble breathing. Ahmose said he pleaded with the GIs to take his son to an allied medical facility, but they laughed and drove off. Franz said he would do what he could, but their small aid station was poorly equipped and only meant as a stabilization facility before patients were shipped off for further treatment at area hospitals. Ahmose begged Franz to treat the boy and insisted that they not go to a hospital. While this struck Franz as suspicious, he treated the boy and managed to stabilize him.

Interestingly enough, Franz Dresden was also a member of the OSS, the Office of Strategic Services and the predecessor of today's CIA. Using his OSS connections, Franz gathered intel on Beb Ahmose before the father and son left his aid station. He learned that Ahmose was actually an Egyptian and part of a Muslim delegation caught in Berlin with his family at the close of the war. It was well documented that the Muslim Brotherhood had strong ties to Nazi, Germany, and Beb Ahmose was a confirmed spy and courier for the Muslim Brotherhood in Egypt. Franz received orders from the OSS to capture Ahmose, but he did not. By the time the boy was sutured and stabilized enough to travel, Ahmose learned of Franz's prying and killed him using one of the surgical knives Franz had used to operate on the boy.

"So Ahmose escaped Berlin with his son, leaving my grandfather in a pool of blood. I went to Afghanistan because I was following a lead on Ahmose's whereabouts, but we came up empty on that trip."

"This guy Ahmose killed your grandfather in World War II, and you're still seeking revenge? He's probably dead. Then what? You'll try to kill his descendants?"

"I'm not sure why I'm looking for him, or what I'd do if I found him or his family. Maybe I'd ask for an apology. I need closure, I guess. For many years, my father was obsessed with finding him, and it almost feels like my duty to continue the search. He passed away last month, and you know what he told his only child while he was in the hospital? He only had two regrets: that he never found Ahmose, and that I never joined the military."

"I'm sorry to hear about your father."

"Thanks. When the firm took off, he told me how proud he was, but then right there at the end, he showed his hand. He wasn't proud because I never became a real man. I didn't serve my country."

"Why didn't you?"

"I don't know. Back then, my father was such a hard ass, and I started rebelling, doing drugs. I become ridiculously liberal. Then I got into Princeton and thought anyone in the military was a retard or a criminal. Baby killers, you know. Besides, it all worked out."

She nodded, thought a moment and said, "Honestly, I didn't expect you to be this forthcoming."

"I'm sure you didn't. So now you have a choice. You can ignore my wishes and take everything I've told you and put it in your article. In that way you'll continue to make the assholes who own your magazine rich. Or... you can respect my privacy and accept my offer to come work for me restructuring our public relations department. The position pays double what you're making now, and our offices are on New York's Third Avenue, so you won't have to move."

Her mouth fell open in disbelief. "Are you serious?"

"Yes, I am. This *was* an interview. But it wasn't mine. It was *yours*."

Chapter Two

"I've spent most of my life looking at the world through the eyes of my enemy, and the strange thing is, when it came to this, I agreed with the enemy on a lot of things."

—Josh Eriksson (FBI interview, 23 December)

Edward Senecal, co-founder of D&S Equities, wept over his son's hospital bed. Emile, not yet thirteen, had been rushed from his bus stop and transported to St. Michael's in downtown Toronto with massive blunt force trauma injuries to his head and chest. His nose was broken, along with several ribs. A lung had collapsed, and he was already in a coma as his brain continued to swell. He had been intubated and placed on a ventilator. The doctor had warned them of extensive and possibly permanent brain damage—if he survived.

Emile's injuries had not come from a terrible fall or from a car or from some other ungodly accident. They had come from three classmates wielding baseball bats. Senecal's poor son had been beaten to the ground like a rabid dog in a third world country.

It had all begun several hours earlier, when Senecal had been sitting in his office in the Canada Trust Tower on Bay Street and brainstorming ways to get the U.S. Congress off the fence regarding a $250 million dollar Department of Defense Contract. In addition to co-founding D&S Equities, he was the CEO of Aero-Vista Ltd., a fixed and rotary wing drone manufacturer with avionics and airframe assembly plants in Toronto and the United States. The Air Force was ready to do business, but with continued controversies over drone deployment and with only limited threats on the horizon, Senecal was unsure if Washington would ever commit. He had been at his window, staring at the multi-colored skyscrapers arranged like the components of a motherboard inside some immense computer, when his smartphone rang and broke his train of thought. Mimi, his thirty-four-year-old wife, stammered as she told him what had happened. Three boys had been threatening Emile's younger sister, Celine, during their walk home from school because she was not wearing a burka like a decent Islamic girl. The boys had crossed to a row of shrubs where they had hidden baseball bats. Emile came to his sister's defense, shoving her out of the way and getting beaten before a local school bus driver saw what was happening, pulled over, and chased off the boys. By then, of course, it was too late. Meanwhile, Celine had run straight home to get her mother, and she was all right, but Emile… Senecal burst to his feet and beat a fist into his hand.

How had it come to this, in his city, in his life?

Edward Senecal could proudly trace his French Canadian ancestry in an unbroken line all the way back to the 1600s, arriving in "New France" alongside Samuel de Champlain, the founder of Quebec City and one of the most charismatic figures in Canadian history. Senecal considered himself an honorable man with closely-held core values. Family, religion, and his country were upper most in his thoughts. He was a student of history with an acute and heightened sensitivity to social oppression and injustice. He was, after all, a product of his own history, some ancient and some surprisingly recent. The ancient oppressions by the Catholic Church, the French-English assimilation, and the language issues beginning as far back as 1760 still festered in present day politics.

Now it was the Muslims who were changing his way of life and traditions. He was regaled by constant anecdotes of Islamic dominance and Sharia Law legislation throughout Europe via emails and phone calls from a sister-in-law in Paris and his brother in London. He felt the tightening of yet another constriction on Canada—his Canada—with a burgeoning 3.2 percent Muslim population, which was second only to Christianity. Somewhat claustrophobic, the social situation was still manageable and did not begin to choke until the Muslim population in the Greater Toronto Area, his family's sanctuary, exceeded five percent, making it the highest concentration of Muslims in any city in North America. He wanted to believe he was a tolerant man, that the story of his life proved he was, but when he was made to feel like a foreigner in his own country and when the foreigners themselves began to dictate how he should live his life, well, a line had to be drawn in the sand.

And now this.

Mimi was down the hall in the ICU's narrow waiting room. She had vomited twice from the stress and was now comforting Celine. Senecal took his son's cold hand and pressed it against his own tear-stained cheek. He remained there, trembling with fear and anger and utter frustration before returning to his wife and daughter.

"I just got off the phone with the police. The boys are in custody, and there are news vans outside and at the police station," his wife said.

"What were those boys thinking?" he asked.

"Eddie, please," she said, flicking her glance to Celine, who was staring blankly as she rested her head on Mimi's chest. "We have to pray now. That's all we can do."

"Did you reach your mother?"

"She and Dad are coming. What about Nick?"

"He was in Houston for some bullshit interview, but he's leaving now."

"Why don't you sit down?"

He glowered at her. "You want me to sit? I'm ready to kill somebody. Those hajis beat our boy, and now we might lose him!"

"Lower your voice! You sound like one of those jarhead generals."

"Emile might have brain damage!"

"Eddie, please..." Mimi began crying.

He stood there, panting. "All of this political correctness. This world wants us to believe in everything—so that we stand for *nothing*. Nothing! They beat my boy!"

"And now what? They're going to pay? You're going to go kill them and wind up in jail? We're the victims. Don't change that by doing something stupid."

"I'll be right back."

"I'm warning you, Eddie! Don't do it!"

"I just need... I need to go for a walk."

Senecal bolted from the room. He took the elevator to the lobby. There, he found a rear door leading to the loading dock. He stood there, breathing in the cold evening air cut by the faint odor of diesel fuel and tobacco. Off to his left, two nurses were sneaking cigarettes in the alley. He glanced away, scanning the street as though he might spot one of the boys. His stomach churned with helplessness. He was a fifty-eight-year-old man with a young wife and kids. Every day they made him feel young, but tonight he was painfully aware of his age. He thought of his pistol collection back home, the 1911s, the Glocks, the Berettas, and the Sig Sauer P226 with 124 grain +P ammo in his night stand. He imagined himself bursting into the houses of those boys and murdering their families, shooting each and every one of them pointblank in the forehead. He poured gasoline over their bodies and watched them burn on their front lawns. His imagination ran even more wild with heinous acts he could commit against them. And then he saw himself behind bars, lying on his thin bunk and cursing over the hum of fluorescent lights, a hum that penetrated his skin, a hum that drowned out his perception of time and space, a hum that would carry him to his grave. Mimi, of course, was right. Retaliation against these particular boys would only get him locked up and further ruin his family. Mimi, Celine, and Emile needed him more than ever now, and he would be a man for them. He would provide for them a safer country. He would protect them from any future harm. He dialed the number to a pre-paid cell phone.

"Jesus, I can't believe you're calling now," said the man on the other end. "I heard about your boy. I saw it on CNN."

"I'm sure the pundits are running wild with stories about tolerance and intolerance and the rest of that bullshit."

"Yeah. What can I do for you?"

"I want you to reach out to our friend in Namibia. We're ready to move forward."

"Slow down, Eddie. You need to be sure."

"Did you not hear me?"

"Look, you're under a lot of stress. You need more time."

He snorted. "Are you kidding me? What have you been saying for the last six months?"

"That the time couldn't be better."

"Then what's the issue? Or maybe you've been full of shit from the beginning."

"Calm down. I'm just saying that once I put this ball in play, there's no stopping it. Do you understand? No stopping it. Are you sure?"

"I have never been more sure about anything in my entire life."

"And what about Nick?"

"He's good to go."

"I find that hard to believe."

"I don't care what you believe. You just make it happen."

"All right, then, Eddie. I'll call him tonight. We'll be in touch."

Senecal thumbed off his phone and closed his eyes. It was done.

* * *

Dresden arrived at the hospital by one a.m. and found Senecal fast asleep in the ICU waiting room. His wife was beside him, but their daughter had been taken home by Mimi's parents. Dresden had called Senecal when he had touched down at the airport. The man had sounded exhausted. Dresden could not imagine what he must be going through. He and his wife of thirty years had never had children or adopted, and this was one of those rare moments that made him glad that Victoria was infertile.

"Eddie, I'm here," he said, tugging on Senecal's shirt sleeve.

Dresden's partner was about as tall and athletically built as he was, but he refused to acknowledge or embrace his age and was still dying his hair blond, even though it was obvious in his eyes that he was pushing sixty. He tugged a pair of glasses from his shirt pocket, propped them on his nose, then rose from the chair and gave Dresden a brief hug. "Thank you so much for coming."

"Of course."

"There's an all night place down the block. We could get coffee."

"That's all right. How is he?"

"They're trying to control the swelling on his brain. Not sure how much brain damage yet. Probably a lot. He's on a ventilator. The doctor said we could lose him."

"Eddie, I'm so sorry. I can't believe this happened. They went to a private middle school, didn't they?"

"Yes, it's at the end of our block. They walked home every day, never a problem, until these three little Hajis moved into our neighborhood."

"They'll get theirs. You and our army of lawyers will make sure of that."

Senecal closed his eyes. "You have no idea."

"Are you all right?"

Senecal opened his eyes and regarded his sleeping wife. "No, I'm not. Let's go somewhere."

As they left the waiting room, Dresden noted an intensity in Senecal that brought out the veins in his forehead and tightened his gait. That was to be expected, and this was not the first time Dresden had witnessed his friend grieve; the man's first wife, Elisabeth, had been diagnosed with stage IV cervical cancer only six months after they were married, and Senecal had held her hand for five long years.

"You remember the first day we met?" he blurted out.

Dresden frowned. "Where's this coming from?"

"I'm asking you."

"Yeah, I remember. Super bowl twelve party down in Trenton at that girl's house, what the hell was her name?"

"Doesn't matter. You wouldn't take the bet."

"Because it was ridiculous. I remember now... the Broncos were going to slaughter the Cowboys."

"But they didn't. They got raped. Eight turnovers, I'll never forget it."

"Yeah. I thought I'd be taking your money a little too easily," said Dresden. "I should've known better."

"I heard you didn't bet anyone that night. You weren't in on the pool, nothing."

"Where did you hear that?"

"From that girl. What's her name. Is it true?"

"You're asking me this now after what? Thirty something years?"

"Sure."

"All right, it's true."

"And you've spent your whole life hedging your bets."

"I hate losing."

"You've never taken any risks. Ever."

"Come on, Eddie. You know we've both taken *huge* risks."

"No, you've never just closed your eyes and dove in. You always have to analyze it to death before you make a move. You talk about daring to do mighty things, but every risk you take is calculated."

"Knowledge is power."

"And what do you do with that power once you have it? You put it in a box and store it up on the shelf in your closet? Or are you man enough to use it?"

"Eddie, I'm worried about you. Your son's lying back there in the ICU, and you have way too much on your mind. I don't know where this is going, and I don't want to know. You take some time off. Take as long as you need."

"Time is the one thing we don't have. Not anymore. Yesterday we were selling bananas, remember?"

"Funny, I was just talking about that."

"Yeah, and here we are, a life time later. Blink of an eye, right?"

"I'm going to pray for your boy." Dresden clutched his friend by the shoulders. "And you, and Mimi, and Celine."

"Suddenly you found God."

Dresden pursed his lips. "Whatever you need, I'm here."

"I called our friend in Washington."

"Regarding this?"

"No. I told him we were ready to move forward. The ball's in play."

Dresden began to lose his breath. "You're not serious."

"The time is right."

The hospital walls narrowed, and for a moment, Dresden felt the blood escape from his head. His breath grew shallow, and he reached out to the wall for balance. "Repeat what you just said."

"I told our friend to cut it loose. I told him you were good to go."

"Why did you do that?"

Senecal began to answer. "Because—"

"—because your son got beat up? Jesus Christ, Eddie, do you understand what we're talking about here? Jesus Christ!"

Senecal grabbed Dresden by the shirt collar and spoke through his teeth. "Listen to me. What happened to my boy was just the straw that broke the camel's back. If you want to pretend that we haven't been sitting on this for years, then you go ahead. You make yourself feel better about it. You do whatever you have to do to make peace with your new found God. But the game is on, and you're on the team—because you *know* what happens if you're not. Everything we've built is gone. Our legacy goes up in flames." Senecal shoved Dresden back into the wall, then raised his palms, as though the violence contained within his hands was not his own.

Dresden tried to imagine the chain of events that was about to unfold, but the horrors flashed like pieces of abstract art created by those aforementioned flames. "Why didn't you come to me first? I've been your partner for over thirty years!"

"You're right. And I'm sorry for that. But I know you, Nick. You wouldn't take the bet. You won't ever take the bet. So I took it for you."

Dresden began to choke up. "Dear God, Eddie. Dear God."

Chapter Three

"It all started with Johnny's brother, and it's weird how different they were. Johnny was always closer to us, so you could see why he had his doubts."

—Willie Parente (FBI interview, 23 December)

Johnny drove his pickup along a dirt road that meandered through a wiregrass ridge shaded by longleaf pines. These were the Holly Shelter game lands, with over 48,000 acres of hunting and hiking grounds situated a few miles northwest of Johnny's home on Topsail Beach, North Carolina. In the back of his black Tundra, protected by an insulated cap covering the flatbed, were Bomber, Musket, and Rookie, his three Gordon Setters. The dogs were a large breed and coal-black, with distinctive markings of rich mahogany on their lower legs, paws, and muzzles. They paced and wagged their tails fiercely in anticipation of the hunt.

Quail hunting in the late afternoon, especially in early December, would be a real challenge. Johnny preferred to arrive just before sunrise to catch the birds while they were still on the roost. An even better strategy was to scout them the night prior, homing in on their calls as they linked up with the covey. If he hunted them too late in the day, they would be scattered, decreasing his chances of bringing home a limit bag. Consequently, Johnny had planned to go hunting in the morning, but no plan ever survived the first enemy contact—or obligations at work. He, Corey, and Willie had been wrestling all last week with a new proposal at the Triton 6 office in Sneads Ferry, and the entire project needed its final red team scrub. An independent group known as a "red team" had been hired to find flaws in the proposal, and now Johnny and the others were making their revisions. Red teams were used throughout the military and civilian communities to challenge organizations' effectiveness. Unfortunately, their work often nixed any chances for taking a Monday off. Johnny could not complain, though, because life after Operation Iraqi Freedom and the Corps had become both productive and gratifying in ways he could not have imagined.

Once he retired from the Marine Corps, Johnny had linked up with Willie and Corey to form Triton 6, a company that provided maritime instruction, equipment, and support to the defense and law enforcement industries. For the past eight years, they had been awarded and had completed government and private sector contracts all over the world. It was interesting and exciting work, and Johnny loved it because his twenty-three years in the Corps were a valuable commodity and put to good use. He and the boys could pick up government contracts here and there and procure a few consulting opportunities in order to pay the bills. Collectively they could provide a service unmatched in any industry. Johnny would remind potential clients that they had the experience of traveling to far off lands to infiltrate, close with, and destroy any enemy; if they had accomplished all that armed with creativity and a small force, then why not offer the same knowledge and expertise to private businesses and the government? Smaller, more agile forces, brought less required communication, red tape, and tactards into the equation of making decisions. For larger contracts, they would partner with companies like Warrick Marine (where Josh had become vice-president), Dillon Aero, and DOS, Inc., who had the infrastructure to support them.

A second way they did business was to develop and shape company pursuits by predicting and recognizing global requirements, such as identifying the need for security at large sporting and entertainment venues, along with other gatherings in the U.S. and abroad. They would collect intel from news sources to identify trouble areas and present solutions to international clients. Securing those foreign deals was much more complicated and involved establishing a strong relationship with a local agent who would get them through the door to meet with flag officers and staff. The real trick was to find a reputable agent (whose fees were dictated by his own success rate). However, even after securing this go-between, meeting with the clients, and making the best possible presentation, some large deals fell apart because of deep corruption and nepotism within that foreign government. There was no way of determining why a contract was lost because of those unknowns. If a deal was secured, then the U.S.'s Foreign Military Sales Office served as a facilitator between Triton 6 and the purchaser to ensure that all business was completed legally and that Triton 6 was not willfully or accidentally supplying weapons or training to enemies of the United States. The sales office also made sure that all International Traffic and Arms Regulations (ITAR) were being followed. These regulations involved items found on the United States Munitions List (USML) and dictated that if Triton 6 wanted to share defense-related information or equipment with persons outside the United States, they needed authorization or special exemption from the Department of State, which they had obtained many times in the past.

As Johnny and the others had been putting their final touches on the proposal, Daniel had called with an invitation for a late lunch. Johnny had not spoken to his brother for nearly a month, even though he lived nearby in Holly Ridge and was a professor and program director at the University of North Carolina Wilmington. Daniel headed up the NC State Engineering 2+2 Transfer Program and was "the resident rocket scientist and chief pogue," according to Johnny. Daniel admitted that he felt guilty for not calling in a while. Johnny said he was nearly finished at the office and still itching to get out in the woods, even if they never saw a bird. If Daniel wanted to meet, he ought to join him at Holly Shelter for a few hours. They could grab a burger on the way. Daniel had reluctantly agreed.

This was not the first time Johnny's brother had come hunting, and as usual he had balked about carrying a shotgun and said he would rather observe. With that attitude, he would never get any better and continue to make wild shots like "Granny" on the old *Beverly Hillbillies* television show. Shaking his head over that, Johnny climbed out of the pickup truck and took a deep breath. The air smelled like winter, reminding him of apple cobbler and hot chocolate and bonfires. Being out here in God's country was pure joy, even if only for a few hours. He met Daniel at the tailgate.

"Why don't you put on your man pants and take a shotgun?"

Daniel made a face and adjusted his glasses. "All right, Johnny, if it makes you feel better, I'll put on these man pants you're always talking about. Do you have an extra pair lying around?"

Johnny narrowed his gaze. "Look here, you watch the news? You hear about all those burglaries at the Cottages? They just had another one last week. You got no choice. Every man should own a gun."

Rolling his eyes, Daniel tugged open the tailgate. The dogs leaped out and began sniffing around the truck while Johnny pulled forward the gear and handed Daniel a hunting jacket with bright orange patches on the chest and sleeves. Next came a similarly colored ball cap. Johnny donned his jacket and hat, then handed Daniel a Winchester 20 gauge shotgun and some boxes of #8 birdshot. He reminded his brother to keep the muzzle pointed skyward. Johnny's shotgun of choice was a Ruger Red Label over-and-under 20 that the boys had given him when he retired. He absolutely loved the shotgun's cut-checkered American Walnut stock and opted to run a skeet choke on the first chamber and a full choke on the second. The skeet choke allowed for a close range shot that opened the pattern. The full choke was meant for a tighter long-range second shot.

As they started away from the truck, the dogs fanned out. They were already dressed in their orange vests and wearing their electronic collars. Johnny made sure he was tracking them with the GPS-enabled touchscreen remote. He could monitor the dogs' direction, distance, and speed, and he could even tell when a dog was pointing or had treed some prey; in fact, it was a lot like watching troops on the ground during a search and destroy mission. Between all the maps, saved trails, and other settings, Johnny had yet to exploit all of the system's features. Technology like this made hunting a lot more fun and ensured his dogs would not get lost.

Satisfied that the system was up and running, Johnny regarded his brother. Daniel's graying beard now extended more than two inches from his chin, while Johnny remained clean shaven after all these years. "You know who you look like?"

"No, Johnny, I don't."

"Like Charlton Heston come down from the mountain."

"Give me a break. Professors wear beards."

"Because you think you look smart?"

"Because we hate shaving."

"You look like you've turned on your country to go fight a holy war."

"So which is it? Am I a jihadist or Moses?"

"Shave it off. You'll look younger. I bet Reva would love it." Reva was Daniel's wife of over twenty years. She was born in Delhi to an Indian mother and British father but raised in the United States for most of her life. She had stunning blue eyes, and Johnny often flirted with her to get his brother's goat.

"It's become increasingly difficult to make that woman happy."

Johnny snorted. "Viagra."

"No, that's not it. Ever since the girls went off to college, she's retreated into her insurance business, and I've taken on more responsibility at work. I see her for an hour a night, and then we're in bed, watching TV until we fall asleep."

"What's wrong with that?"

"That's no life."

Johnny stopped and faced his brother. Behind him, the pine trees formed an elaborate maze across the pale yellow grass, and somewhere in the distance, a shotgun boomed. "What's wrong with you?"

"Remember the proposal you guys did for that contract in Brazil?"

"I'm trying to forget it."

"You remember how you asked me to proofread it?"

"Yeah, so?"

"So I never told you, but that meant a lot to me."

Johnny drew back his head. "We just wanted to get an opinion from someone on the college side of the house, somebody outside the military."

"That was the first time you ever came to me for help."

Johnny stood there, wondering where this conversation was heading. He thought back across his life, trying to recall a moment when he had sought Daniel's assistance or advice, but it was true—the only thing he could remember was that damned proposal. Sure, there were times when Daniel had volunteered to help Johnny with his homework, but Johnny always said that if he could not grasp the material, then he deserved to fail and would take his licks like a man. Besides, older brothers were supposed to be the stronger ones. Why couldn't Daniel just accept that? "What the hell's the matter with you? You're bringing up this old shit, getting all sentimental. You sick or something?"

Daniel grinned. "You'll never change. Subtlety's not your thing. Cut to the chase. Get busy. You're on the train or under it."

"I'm serious," Johnny said, sharpening his gaze. "You okay?"

Daniel nodded and started off. "You're right, Johnny. I need to put on my man pants. Let's go hunt some birds."

"Dan, wait. Something you want to tell me? Something you need?"

"I can't spend my whole life coming to you for help. I got everything covered."

"You and Reva okay? I mean, really? Is mama cheating on you or something? You cheating on her?"

"Jesus Christ, Johnny, no. I just... sometimes you think you know somebody, right? But you don't know them at all."

Johnny thought about that. "I've told you before and I'll tell you again... there's only three kinds of people in this world: wolves, sheepdogs, and sheep. I'm a sheepdog. Always have been, always will be."

"And what am I, Johnny?"

"Look, whatever's bothering you—"

"Say it."

Johnny hoisted his brows and spoke more emphatically. "I said whatever's bothering you, I'm sure you'll work it out. The old man didn't raise no dummies."

Daniel made another face.

Johnny frowned. "What?"

* * *

Northern Bobwhite quail were distinguished by the feather coloration on their heads. Males had a white patch under their necks and white lines above their eyes. The body feathers of males and females were a combination of brown and black, and buff and white, affording them perfect camouflage. The name "Bobwhite" originated from the sound produced by the male, who seemed to be whistling the words, "bob-white," but to Johnny, the bird's call sounded like a squeaky wheel.

They hiked for an hour across a ridge line and descended into a field with native grasses whose seeds attracted the birds. The dogs led them away from sections of thicker grass, since the birds were too small to push through those, and they also avoided any open areas that made the quail feel too exposed. If Johnny caught the dogs getting a bit "birdy" after spotting their prey, he would blow into his hawk caller; the shrill cry would trick the quail into believing that danger was wheeling overhead. The bird would freeze in his tracks.

As they neared a woody draw with last night's rainwater streaming down into the depression, Rookie froze and leaned forward, his tail thrust skyward. Bomber and Musket locked up like PFCs at attention on Parris Island. Near the top of the draw stood a thick, weedy area, and Johnny hunkered down and squinted in that direction, his breath coming heavier on the air. It was one of those perfect and rare moments during a hunt when everything lined up according to plan. They had approached the dogs from behind. Rookie, the youngest and least experienced of the three, had located the birds. He had gained that experience and had behaved beautifully, turning off his natural instincts to attack and waiting for his master.

Johnny caught Daniel's attention and motioned his instructions. They would approach the weeds in a straight line, always aware of the dogs. Daniel nodded his understanding. Johnny indicated with his free hand that Daniel's range of fire was from his center line and off to the right, while Johnny's was off to the left. Hunters never crossed mid-point to shoot a bird flying on their partner's side; it was poor sportsmanship and dangerous. Also, they never took a shot lower than the horizontal plane because they could hit one of the dogs. Johnny pointed to the safety on Daniel's shotgun, and Daniel waved him off and mouthed that he was ready. Johnny gave him a curt nod, then slowly rose and stepped toward the dogs, ever wary of the grass crunching beneath his boots. The wind was in their faces now, which had helped Rookie find the birds. Johnny's hackles rose. He paused and glanced at his brother, who skulked forward, his gaze never more intense. Something had come over Daniel. His jaw was set and his eyes had bugged out as though they were patrolling the bombed out streets of Fallujah. The pencil-neck boy was long gone. He appeared angry, even bitter, but over what?

For just a second, Johnny saw himself in his brother's eyes, and he related to that bitterness. After more than two decades in the Marine Corps, Johnny was finally up for promotion to master gunnery sergeant. But when the promotion list for E9 had come out, Johnny learned he had been passed over. In that instant, he decided he was done making the rest of those men look like HE-roes. He was better qualified than those who had leapfrogged over him, but kiss-ass politics, along with his brutal honesty, had screwed him over big time. He would adhere to the words he always shared with his Marines: it's either up or out. You're either climbing the ladder or getting in the next guy's way. With just five months left on his enlistment, it was the perfect time for his EAS, End of Active Service. Most Marines in his position would have waited until the next promotion board and used the year to transition into civilian life—but not Johnny. He would practice what he preached and lead by example. After all, how could a senior Marine Corps NCO spend all of those years teaching his charges how to be Marines and then ignore his own words? That would make him a two-faced politician. Admittedly, shedding the uniform felt like crossing a swamp of unknown size, armed only with his experience in the Corps. Did he have enough planks for what lay ahead? He had no choice but to find out. He was a Marine. A sheepdog. Easy day. No drama.

He resumed his pace, and as they neared Rookie, Johnny gave the command for all three dogs to flush the birds. What might have been a magnificent explosion of feathers and thumping wings became a lone quail bursting from the weeds.

Daniel swung his shotgun in the wrong direction, right past Johnny's face. Johnny ducked a second before the shotgun boomed.

"Die!" his brother shouted. He fired again. "Die!"

"Dan, what the—"

"Holy shit, I got him!"

"You almost got me!" Johnny turned and picked up the Garmin from where he had dropped it while ducking for his life. He rose and glared at his brother. "What were you thinking, cowboy?"

Daniel struggled to catch his breath, his face glowing like a plum. "I was thinking I'm the sheepdog now!"

Johnny wrenched the shotgun out of his brother's hand. "You're done. We'll see if they got your bird, then we're going home."

Daniel averted his gaze. "Look, I'm sorry I swung around. I shouldn't have, but I knew I could get him."

"I thought you didn't want to hunt."

"Changed my mind. Come on, I didn't mean to ruin this for you."

Johnny pursed his lips, thought it over, then tossed back the gun. "You do that shit again and I will stomp a mud hole in your ass."

"I won't."

Johnny glanced at the GPS. "Rookie's already got your bird and coming back. I'm glad I'm alive to see this."

"Yeah, that's the first quail I ever shot," said Daniel.

Johnny snorted. "I'm being sarcastic."

"I know, Johnny. And you know something?"

"What?"

"I like the way they feel... these man pants..."

* * *

Johnny bagged two more birds before they returned to the truck. Daniel missed an opportunity to shoot another because he had hesitated, but that was just as well. He was much calmer now, his rage gone cold like the early evening air. They were both shivering as they packed up the truck and headed out, the sun now eclipsed by the treetops.

"I'm glad we did this," Daniel said.

Johnny cocked a brow. "Really."

"Yeah, I feel better." Daniel glanced out the side window. "I've been ignoring you for years, Johnny. But you're right. It's time for me to step up to the plate. I wish dad were here to see it."

"Next thing you'll tell me, you want to buy a pistol and have Willie teach you a few things."

"Maybe I do."

* * *

They drove in silence for the next fifteen minutes until they reached Daniel's Acadian style home at the end of a cul de sac. It was an impressive country shack with four bedrooms, three baths, gabled dormers, and a wraparound porch. Behind the house lay acres of woodlands that unfurled like a mottled green carpet into the Big Shakey Swamp. Daniel and Reva had done very well for themselves. Her BMW was parked in the deep shadows spanning the paver driveway, and Daniel's Lexus was in the garage, since Johnny had met him at the house.

After pulling up, Johnny said, "If you guys want to come back to my place and grab some dinner..."

"No, I'm tired, Johnny. And I still have to go over some final grades."

"All right, then."

Daniel gave Johnny a weak grin and climbed out of the pickup.

And there it was again—a definite shift in his appearance, his head held higher, his gait longer and more purposeful. Once he mounted the porch stairs, Johnny backed out of the driveway. As he rolled the wheel, he noticed that Daniel had gone in but had forgotten to close the front door. From just inside the darkened home a pair of figures clutching each other crashed into the door jamb, then the taller, who was wearing a black balaclava over his head, dragged the shorter—who was Daniel—back into the house. Johnny was already throwing the truck in park and leaping out. He grabbed his SIG 1911 Ultra from the door pocket and wrenched the .45 from its holster.

Johnny made it across the driveway in three breaths, up in the porch in two, and was slicing past the door when a pounding of boots echoed from the back of the house. He squinted toward the main foyer, where the man with the balaclava was just turning a corner. He wore dark clothes and a backpack hung from his shoulders. Johnny could not get a shot and started after him. However, a groan to his left drove him into the formal living room, where Daniel lay on the floor, clutching his chest.

Torn between chasing the assailant and tending to his brother, Johnny swore in frustration. He banged a light switch and gasped. Daniel had sloughed off his jacket, and his blue UNC sweatshirt was now turning a deep red. He was bleeding out fast from what Johnny assumed were multiple stab wounds.

Johnny's gaze alternated between the foyer and his brother lying in agony. He reached for his smartphone and realized it was still charging inside the truck. He dropped to his knees, shoved his pistol into his waistband, and then rifled through Daniel's jacket pockets. He found his brother's phone and dialed 911. He put the call on speaker and set down the phone. After tugging off his own jacket and sweatshirt, he lifted Daniel's shirt and grimaced at the four puncture wounds. He applied pressure with his own shirt as Daniel tried to talk.

Johnny shushed him and said, "I got you, Dan. I'm here. I got you."

"I'm sorry, Johnny. It's my fault. I should have..." Daniel coughed and could not finish. His teeth were outlined in blood.

The 911 operator repeated her question for the second time. And then a third. And then she threatened to send over a police unit if no one answered. Johnny finally did, but he could barely speak. When he was finished, he regarded Daniel, whose eyes had gone vacant.

At that Johnny raced out toward the family room, where the sliding glass door had been pulled open. He stomped across the back porch and slowed to gaze across the woodlands, the pockets of darkness deepening between the trees.

He returned inside, where he spotted Reva lying on the kitchen floor, her waist-length hair splayed across the tile. She, too, had been stabbed repeatedly in the chest, while her arms and hands bore the cuts of an intense struggle. With her ashen face and blank eyes she was like an eerily beautiful porcelain doll that had fallen from atop a little girl's bookshelf. Just above her, the kitchen drawers had been tugged open, and iPods and iPads were missing from the charging station. Johnny jogged into the master bedroom, where he found more of the same: drawers pulled and searched, Reva's jewelry box empty and lying on the floor.

He hustled back to the front of the house, passing through the front door. He returned to his truck and seized his smartphone. A few seconds later he reached Josh. It took several attempts to get the entire sentence out: "Get the boys over to my brother's house right now."

"What's going on, Johnny?"

"Just get here!"

As he started back for the house, he began to hyperventilate. By the time he reached the living room, where the wood floor was now a sea of Daniel's blood, he could no longer stand. This was not one of his Marines who had gone downrange. This was the boy who was afraid to fight, the boy who shuddered as the old man had come up the stairs, the boy who wanted to become a sheepdog despite his lifelong fear. Johnny crawled over to his brother and cupped Daniel's head in his hands.

Some time later, the police arrived and were prying him free, asking him questions that seemed detached, reverberating from someone else's nightmare. There was only one voice that meant anything now.

It was 1968, and the old man was leaving for his second tour in Vietnam. Johnny was a small boy taken out for a ride and given his first lecture on manhood: *Being a man means that when I'm not home, you are in charge. You protect your little brother. You protect your family. Understand?*

"Yes, sir."

Chapter Four

"My brother was great at hiding things from the old man. One time we stole some Playboys, and we had them all over the house. The old man never caught on. Dan was always the brains behind those operations, and he knew how to keep a secret much better than me."

—Johnny Johansen (FBI interview, 23 December)

Within a few minutes, Daniel's house became a grim spectacle of flashing police lights and thrumming diesel engines that drew neighbors onto their driveways where they stood, rapt, clutching their throats. The police tape went up, the streets were cordoned off, and the WSFX-TV news crew was held at bay near the end of the block. It was a scene ripped from someone else's memoir, not Johnny's.

Fortunately, Johnny knew a few members of the Holly Ridge Police department, since they often shot with him at the outdoor range adjacent to the local VFW hall. The responding officers found their shooting pal alone, bare-chested, and covered in his brother's blood. The police chief himself, Dennis Schneider, a retired Navy senior chief petty officer who also frequented the VFW, had abandoned his dinner to get down there.

The crime scene investigators and forensic team were already in the house. Johnny sat in the passenger's seat of an F-150. The truck belonged to one of the detectives, Paul Lindquist, a hefty man in his fifties with the long sideburns and bushy mustache of a Wild West bartender. As Johnny gave his statement, Lindquist's expression teetered between a sympathetic pursing of the lips and a sudden narrowing of the eyes behind his bifocals. Johnny had already submitted to a blood-alcohol test and had allowed the police to search his truck, so long as they were careful with the dogs. His story would have to be verified, of course, and he understood that. As Lindquist slowly and methodically raised questions, Johnny struggled to answer. Moments from the hunting trip flashed like lightning in his mind's eye, while Daniel's voice boomed: *"I'm the sheepdog now!"*

Willie, Corey, and Josh reached the house before the streets were cordoned off, but Elina was delayed at one road block. She had tried to call Johnny twice, finally sending him a text while he was busy giving his statement. He hated that she was out there alone, sitting in her car after learning that her brother-in-law and sister-in-law had just been killed in a home invasion. Lindquist said he would call back and allow her to pass through.

Chief Schneider approached the truck, his eyes full of sympathy. Johnny lowered his window. "I'll share a few things," he began. "Because if it was me, I'd want to know right away, too. But don't you repeat this to anyone. Not yet, anyway."

"Thank you, Dennis."

"They already found the knife. He dumped it as he ran off the back porch. We're pretty sure it was taken from the kitchen, since there's an empty slot in the holder. Hopefully they'll get something from it. Got some boot prints out back and out yonder heading off toward the swamp. Rubber boots. I'm willing to bet they're the same size prints we found at the Cottages. Jewelry and electronics missing, maybe some cash, we don't know. Trust me, we're not ruling out anything, but so far it looks like a burglary gone bad. He hasn't killed anyone till now. I doubt the perpetrator was armed, which is why he grabbed one of Dan's knives. Sometimes these things escalate."

Johnny's breath shortened. "This whole thing ain't right. This guy would've seen Reva's car in the driveway. He would have known someone was home."

"Not necessarily," said Lindquist. "If she only had a few lights on, he could have thought the house was empty. Maybe he figured they'd gone out to dinner."

"All right, so he comes in, Reva confronts him, and he kills her," Johnny said. "Why does he stick around?"

"We don't know yet how much time passed," Lindquist pointed out. "Autopsy might help with that."

"Even if it's two minutes," said Johnny. "That's too much. But anyway, he's finishing up when Dan opens the front door. Why doesn't he run? Why does he have to kill my brother?"

"I don't know, Johnny. Maybe it was just a reaction. Instinct. We'll find out."

Schneider added that he would keep the barrier tape up even after they were finished. This would buy Johnny more time to have the place cleaned before he allowed his nieces back into the house. The forensics people had used contrasting black and white latent print powder as well as fluorescent red on the textured and brushed stainless steel surfaces in the kitchen area. All of that would have to be wiped away. The waxed wood floor would clean up well, and the ceramic tile in the kitchen area was not porous but a section of grouting was permanently stained. Schneider had the number of a local tile guy who was a master at matching grouting. While this was morbid business and not something Johnny wanted to contemplate so soon, it was an important consideration. He would spare his nieces the sight of their parents' blood.

"Now if you don't mind, we'll send you home," said Schneider. "Get showered up. Take more time to think about it, see if you can remember anything else. Then you come back down to the station so we can go over it just once more. You have the boys drive you. I don't want you behind the wheel of a car. And who knows, by then I might have some more."

"Roger," Johnny said. "But I need to call my nieces and let them know."

"You do that. And on behalf of the entire department, we're very sorry about your loss. I know you could use something to believe in right now, so I'll promise you this: *we will* catch the man who did this." Schneider squeezed Johnny's shoulder and headed back up the driveway.

Johnny faced Lindquist. "I need to make a private call."

Lindquist reached for his door handle. "Take as long as you like. And Johnny, just one more thing. You think someone would want to kill your brother or his wife?"

"No way. Daniel didn't make waves. People liked him. He was always winning awards at the college, best teacher of the year, that shit."

"What about Reva? She have any issues at work?"

"I don't know."

"Did they have any marital problems?"

"No. I mean just the usual that everyone has."

"I got the feeling while you were talking that you thought this was planned. Somebody wanted to kill your brother and his wife and make it look like a burglary."

"I'm not sure."

"You said you hadn't talked to your brother in nearly a month."

"That's right."

"So you don't know if they made enemies."

"I know he was trying to tell me something while we were out there. He was going to handle it himself, whatever that means. Could be something, could be nothing. But he wanted to tell me. He just held back."

"Why?"

Johnny glanced at his boots. "It was my fault."

"Yours?"

"He always came to me for help. This time he was trying to man up and do it himself."

"You know, I've been telling my kid brother the same thing for years. He's forty-seven and still leeching off our parents. My dad's pushing eighty for Christ's sake. The boy lives from one crisis to another."

Johnny shrugged.

Lindquist continued, "Anyway, rest assured we'll check into everything—friends, co-workers, the whole nine. I am nothing if not thorough."

"Thank you."

"And if it's any consolation, your brother's issue probably has nothing to do with this. Maybe it was just something at work. I'll find out. This is a tragedy, and while it's unprofessional to offer an opinion so early, I've been doing this for a long time. This doesn't look premeditated, Johnny. I think your brother walked in on him killing Reva. It's just terrible timing is all. I'm very sorry."

With that, Lindquist got out, leaving Johnny to stare at his smartphone. This phone call would change two young lives forever. The enormity of the moment sent a tremor into his hand as he dialed.

Daniel's daughters, Isabelle and Kate, were undergraduates at Georgia State University, where Isabelle, the sophomore, played women's soccer, and Kate, the senior, was on the cross country team. They had received considerable scholarships, and Daniel and Reva doted on them. Kate answered in a voice that sounded painfully young. "Hey, Uncle Johnny, what's going on? This is like so random, you calling me out of the blue."

"Kate, where's your sister right now."

"They're getting pizza."

"All right, you sit down. I'm going to tell you something, and then you tell her. Now you're the oldest, sweetheart, and I need you to be strong—stronger than you've ever been in your entire life. Do you understand me?"

"Yes, sir. But Uncle Johnny, you're scaring me."

"I know. And I'm so sorry to tell you this. It breaks my heart."

* * *

Times like these made Willie think about his own loved ones, and he thanked God they were all right. If anything ever happened to his sisters, to Ivonne, or to his son... Damn, he could barely entertain the thought for more than a few seconds. Instead, he reflected on how lucky he was, on the life he had built for himself, on the people who had lifted him up from the madness and frustration of war.

Back in the day, when he was still with 2nd Tank Battalion, he got into a "little trouble" (Marine-speak for pissing off the CO) and was given the option of doing a summer stint as a lifeguard on Onslow Beach, Camp Lejeune. While there, he had no choice but to gather intel on potential high value female targets. One day he locked on to this stunning blonde with a small child, but he assumed she was married. She kept coming to the beach, and Willie kept her in his sights. Through mutual friends he discovered that no, she was divorced, so he struck up a conversation and invited her to dinner. They dated for about six months, lived together for about a year, and then got married. She supported everything he did in the Corps, especially joining Force Reconnaissance, and while he was gone, she paid the bills, kept up the house, and raised their son. It takes a special kind of woman to put up with all the bullshit Marines can dish out, and it takes a wise man to appreciate those efforts and never take them for granted. While no professor of human psychology, Willie was smart enough to recognize that even those who wait also serve.

Willie and Ivonne forged on through the long deployments, the personal and financial stress, and the aches of being alone. And then, after seventeen hard years in the Marine Corps, Willie found himself at a crossroads. He had just come off a deployment, had yet to decompress, and heard through reliable scuttlebutt that he was being shipped off to Okinawa for his twilight tour before he retired.

At the same time, his father-in-law was trying to build a new business, The Sportsman's Lodge, in Jacksonville, North Carolina. The lodge would be a premiere shooting facility equipped with a pro shop, pistol and archery ranges, and a twenty-two acre paintball course that included woods and berm areas, along with an urban environment replete with a mock city. The lodge would also offer a variety of courses, from concealed carry to women-specific to the National Rifleman's Association basic pistol course.

There was no doubt that Willie's father-in-law and brother-in-law could use his help and expertise in the business, and Willie was torn between leaving the Marine Corps before retiring or doing his last three years in Okinawa so he could collect a pension. Every operator knew that Force Recon was a mistress with whom few women could compete. Indeed, the strain on his marriage was the second huge factor he took into account. It was money versus family. In the end, he realized he owed it to Ivonne and to the rest of his loved ones to remain behind and help them build that business. He had served proudly with the United States Marine Corps, and he would always be a Marine, but the time had come to move on and allow that recon mistress to go off and seduce another, younger man.

Once the Sportsman's Lodge was established and began to grow, Willie was getting offers from outside contractors who did business with the Marine Corps. They wanted to bring him on as a shooting instructor. Willie decided to further help the family by no longer drawing a salary from the lodge and volunteering his services to help when needed. Meanwhile, he would pick up paid work from these contractors. He spent a few years working for a small firm as a recon and sniper instructor at Camp Lejeune, then was hired by Professional Solutions as the lead civilian contractor at the Special Operations School for Close Quarters Battle and Explosive, Mechanical, and ballistic Breaching. This school was run by Marine Special Operations Command (MARSOC). He became the instructor and wrote curriculum for the use of Special Operations Modified (SOPMOD) equipment by MARSOC operators. From there he smoothly transitioned to Triton 6 to work with Johnny and Corey. However, he still missed the adrenaline rush of combat. The next best alternative was to continue honing his shooting skills through competitions all over the United Sates, where he could network with veteran military operators, make new friends both personal and professional, and clear all of life's stresses from his head. His preference was "3-Gun," where he would fire a rifle, handgun, and shotgun while shifting through different stages and engaging various targets in different positions. Transitioning swiftly between weapons and reaching the next shooting position without falling down were just a few of the challenges. The competitions were part of his professional development and allowed him to set personal goals, not to mention the bragging rights he earned when his aim held true.

Sadly, Willie's goal at the moment had nothing to do with shooting. He was at the wheel of Johnny's car and taking him home. During the ride, he wanted to ensure that Johnny did not blame himself, because that was a natural instinct of all sheepdogs who lost one under their protection.

They drove the first quarter mile in silence before Johnny blurted out: "I should have gone in to say hi to Reva."

"What're you talking about? She was already dead."

Johnny hesitated. "The son of a bitch never learned to fight."

Willie took a deep breath and spoke more deliberately. "Can't blame yourself."

"Want to hear something crazy? I was telling him about the break-ins at the Cottages. I said every man should own a gun. You believe that?"

"I believe you were a good brother, and you did everything you could."

Johnny looked at him strangely. "What could it be?"

"What're you talking about?"

"The thing he had to do. He was coming for help, but he changed his mind."

"He needed your help?"

"He said he did, and then he changed his mind. You know, I was always telling him to get busy. Stop whining about all the shit in your life. Get out there and shake some trees."

"Don't forget, your brother schooled his way to the top. He was running the show over there. Old Mad Dog Mattis said the most valuable real estate on the battlefield is the six inches between your ears."

"Right on."

"So don't be saying that shit. Your brother Daniel Johansen was a man. And he was a hell of a lot smarter than you and me. We're just knuckle-draggers. He needed help with something outside his envelope."

"Son, don't piss down my back and tell me it's raining."

"I'm serious, Johnny. Give him some credit."

"All right, look here, he said it was time to step up to the plate. What does that mean?"

"Good question. Maybe it had something to do with Reva? What about her?"

"I went over that with the detective. They were just bored. They didn't have any problems. He wasn't leaving her."

"What if she had a secret?"

"Like what?"

"Like we all got our homeowners and car insurance through her, right? Maybe there was a fraud case. Some kind of retaliation. Maybe she was stealing from the company? Maybe she was having an affair?"

"We talking about the same lady? You know how she was, a real classy broad, nothing crude or redneck about her. I can't imagine her doing something like that. She served us ice cream is those fancy bowls."

"She was born in India, right?"

"So?"

"So maybe this has something to do with her country. Maybe it's payback from some family member. Some shit we didn't know about."

"Look, if she was into something and got my brother killed, then our boy Columbo will be all over it. But you know, we wouldn't be sitting here with all these questions if I had called him once in a while and asked how he was doing."

"Everybody does the same thing, Johnny. We lose touch. That doesn't make us bad people."

"Every time I talked to him, I felt like I was pissing him off."

"You probably were. Because you remind him of the old man. And he had issues with the old man. So anyway, we'll keep thinking about it. And maybe the police will find something at his house."

They stopped at a light, and Willie glanced over at Johnny, whose eyes were burning. Johnny met his gaze and said, "Sorry about all this. Sorry for putting you out."

Willie frowned. "Shut up."

The light turned green, and Willie stomped on the pedal. His phone rang. "What's up, Josh?"

"He all right?"

"You want to talk to him?"

"Yeah."

Willie handed the phone to Johnny. "Hey."

Trying to give Johnny a bit of privacy, Willie focused on the days to come and the nights soaked in alcohol.

Rest in peace, Daniel and Reva Johansen. Rest in peace.

Chapter Five

"After the funeral, I caught Johnny staring at my tattoo: I am my
brother's keeper. He believed those words, and nothing would change
his mind. Thank God for that."

—Josh Eriksson (FBI interview, 23 December)

Johnny and his wife lived in a white, three-story deck house with hints of Victorian
architecture. Two staircases rose from the left and right garage doors, joined at the
center, then swept up to the grand second story entrance. Johnny had purchased the
home from a man whose grown daughters often came to visit, so each of the six bedrooms had its own en suite. Out back stood a private dock on the canal for Johnny's
twenty-one foot Kencraft Bay Rider, along with a commercial-sized flagpole atop
which Johnny proudly displayed the stars and stripes. From the second-story back
porch, where they often ate meals, Waters Bay would shimmer to the south, and they
could just catch a glimpse of Permuda Island State Reserve to the northeast.

Willie pulled into the driveway, and Johnny dragged himself out. He crossed to
the tailgate and released the dogs so they could run across the street, head down to
the canal bank, and do their business. Elina had been driving her car behind them,
and she wanted to give Johnny a long hug, but he said he needed to take a shower. He
spent nearly thirty minutes under the hot spray, staring blankly at the pink whirlpool
at his feet. He leaned on the wall several times and fought against a powerful ache that
pressed on his ribs. He would not allow himself even a moment of weakness. One
chink in his armor would be one too many. Instead he focused on the problem. On
the solution.

Something had been bothering his brother. He brought his brother home. His brother was killed. That was *not* a coincidence.

Stepping out of the shower, he found Elina on the edge of their bed, wiping tears from her eyes. He collapsed beside her and slid a wet arm over her shoulder.

"Johnny..."

"I'm all right."

"We're here."

All he could do was nod.

"I know you're not hearing this, but if we talk, it'll help. I'll wait. I don't care how long."

Elina knew him better than anyone. He dealt with grief on his own time, in his own way, and she was always there when he was ready. Was it like this between Daniel and Reva? Johnny could not be sure. His brother never shared intimate details about his marriage; in fact, Daniel had spoken more about Reva in the past twenty-fours than he had in the past ten years, making his confession about seeing her for only an hour a day and saying, *"That's no life,"* all the more troubling.

Johnny closed his eyes and thanked God he was not alone in this. He clutched Elina a little tighter. This was the woman who would get him through. This was the woman who had been with him for the better part of his life, and their story began more than twenty years ago when he was down in Key West, Florida attending the Special Forces Combat Dive Supervisors Course. After a long day of travel, he checked into the school and then headed for the ville to link up with the boys—marines who had come from other recon units. With orders to rescue some college girls from their innocence, they dropped in on the world famous Sloppy Joe's bar on Duval Street. The place was packed wall-to-wall with empty-headed blondes, none of who caught Johnny's eye. But then this exotic-looking woman with auburn hair and iridescent green eyes floated to the edge of the dance floor, and as Johnny was about to make eye contact, some other clown asked her to dance. Like any good 0321 worth his salt, Johnny waited patiently, reconnoitering the situation. When the time came, he broke from his covered and concealed position and met this woman at the bar. He asked what she was drinking. Corona. He offered to buy her the beer. She declined. He insisted, reaching into his smelly sock where he kept his money. He paid for the drink. Her name was Elina, and she was born in Finland but living in Miami. She was on vacation with her friend, Debbie, who was at her apartment nursing a hangover from a previous day's cruise. Johnny was so taken by this woman with the accent that he kept her talking and dancing until the wee hours. He created an elaborate story about having no place to go and needing to collect his gear from the airport the next day. Elina allowed him to spend the night at Debbie's place but warned that he would *not* be getting lucky.

Ironically, they stood each other up for a second date but crossed paths soon thereafter. They spent more time together, and when Johnny was away, they began writing letters. As their relationship grew, Johnny did everything he could to see her, if only for a weekend. One Friday he and his buddy packed up the car and headed from North Carolina to Miami. These were the days before cell phones, and along the way Johnny realized he had lost Elina's address and phone number. He did remember where Debbie lived in Key West, so he and his buddy drove all the way down there, just so they could find Debbie and she could put them in touch with Elina. They called Elina from Key West, and she left Miami at midnight, arriving some three hours later but shrugging off the long drive. That was when Johnny thought she was falling in love. He knew he was. A year later they stood at the altar of a small white chapel on the grounds of Camp Geiger and exchanged their vows.

During those early days of their marriage, Johnny worried a lot. Would Elina be strong enough to handle so much time alone? He made sure to stay in touch. They had to number their letters because he would receive them in bundles and wanted to read them in the correct order. He began to marvel over how independent she was—independent enough to remain happy while he was gone, but never forgetting that they were a team. She understood the challenges he faced as a Marine and the challenges they faced as a married couple. She joked that the toughest part was putting up with his stupid jokes. When he came home from a deployment, they were always nervous. He understood that the last thing she needed was him barging in to disrupt her routine. He would always ease back into it, complimenting the changes she might have made to their home and to her personal appearance. They would get used to being around each other again, and before they knew it, they were back to normal—a married couple for over twenty years who were all that and a bag of chips.

"I need to get dressed," Johnny said, rising from the bed. "I'll have the boys take me back to the station."

"Okay," she said. "You must be starving."

"Last thing on my mind, but now that you mention it."

"I'll talk to Jada and Ivonne. We'll see if we can have something ready by the time you get back." She rose and put her hands on his cheeks. "You know I love you."

"Yeah. And do me a favor when you go down there. Tell Willie I got some birds in a bag that are probably stinking up the truck."

"I'll let him know." She reached the doorway.

"Hey."

She glanced back at him.

"Love you, too."

* * *

Josh was waiting with Corey in the man cave located on the ground floor behind the garages. He had drawn a tall can of Michelob Ultra from the mini fridge and now leaned on the semi-circular bar, staring at the Claymore mine propped up on the shelving unit behind the counter. Embossed on the rectangular-shaped explosive were the words FRONT TOWARD ENEMY. Marines never needed that admonishment, Josh mused; they were always leaning toward the danger.

Above the Claymore sat a powder horn that Johnny had commissioned from a gifted artist. Carved on the horn was a map of North Carolina during the 1800s. The map included the "Johnson Land Grant," marking an area where Johnny's family had settled. The carver had done all the research and had surprised Johnny with this discovery. Along with the map was an early emblem of the Marine Corps, and below it was Johnny's name. In the center of the horn was a compass ringed by twenty-three stars, each one representing a year that Johnny had served his country. Indeed, the horn was a unique piece of art commemorating Johnny's past, but Josh knew it symbolized much more. It spoke of Johnny's generosity and of his care and concern for others, as evidenced by the tale of how he had acquired it.

Johnny had been attending a civil war reenactment with a friend who had brought along his eight year old boy. Times were tough, a divorce was on the horizon, and the boy was caught up in all of it. Feeling for the kid, Johnny slipped him a twenty dollar bill to buy a souvenir from one of the vendors. The boy had his heart set on a powder horn, the cheapest of which were 100 dollars. The boy left that tent disappointed. At the end of the day, Johnny spoke alone with the vendor and told him, "I want you to make this kid believe he negotiated you down to twenty bucks for that horn, and I'll pay you the difference." The vendor was on board, and the boy left with his powder horn, feeling like a master negotiator. Meanwhile, Johnny realized that he, too, had been struck by the artistry and craftsmanship of the horns, and he wound up ordering one for himself.

Wearing a melancholy grin, Josh lifted his gaze away from the horn to the bottles of Jack Daniels whose dusty shoulders would soon gain many fingerprints. Off to his left rose the straight limb of an oak tree mounted on a stand, the branches filed down to nubs upon which Johnny hung his ball caps and jackets. Displayed across the surrounding maple beadboard walls were various placards and scrolls, one depicting sailors' knots, another noting how Marines were your best friend or your worst nightmare. A 2nd Force Reconnaissance banner with gold fringe trim towered above the leather sofa, and mounted beside it was a gleaming Mameluke sword. Over one hundred challenge coins lined a rack near the door and were a testament to the many friends Johnny had made .

Johnny's most prized possession was a green paddle mounted on the wall across from the bar. This keepsake had been given to him at retirement during his recon sendoff ceremony. The paddle was polished to a rich luster by the men in his unit and decorated with ribbon racks, the 2nd Force emblem, and a metal plaque that noted his insert and extract dates. Below those dates was as a quote ("You're either on the train or under it") and a thank you "From the Men of Force Recon's past, present, and future." The paddle tradition among reconnaissance Marines dated back to World War II, when "Marine Raiders" engaged in clandestine raft operations to secure beaches, relying solely on their paddles for propulsion when near the shoreline. They carried these paddles everywhere, and soon the wood became worn and scarred, as did the men.

The paddles were the reason Johnny had built the man cave in the first place. He was never one to have such a room because it reminded him of people who had nothing else in their lives except for who they had been in the Corps. But then Marcus, one of Johnny's old buddies, had come and asked why his paddles were tucked away in a closet when so many men had put their hearts and souls into making them. It was then that Johnny realized how selfish he had been. Marcus was right. It was time to honor the men who had given him so much. It was time to create a room about them, not just him, and everything on display should be a gift from a warrior, with the powder horn being a very rare exception.

Like Johnny, Josh had a few paddles himself. He hung them in his office at Warrick Marine, and one in particular came from the Navy and marked a major change in his life.

After nine rigorous years in the Corps, Josh had been lured away to the Naval Amphibious Base in Little Creek, Virginia, home of the U.S. Navy Center for Anti-Terrorism and Navy Security Forces. He took all of a week off before assuming his new duties. He transitioned from wearing a uniform to wearing a suit, from being a Staff Sergeant to being a GS-12, and not long after, a GS-13—the federal employee equivalent of lieutenant colonel. He was brought in as a program manager and functional team leader. He was given just twelve months to create the entire U.S. Navy's Riverine

Program so that Navy personnel could go tear-assing around the Euphrates just like Small Craft Company had.

While in Little Creek, he met a woman named Jada, an admin intel analyst from Lake Charles, Louisiana. She possessed everything he wanted in a woman. She had a keen wit. She was an aggressive go-getter when it came to professional matters. She had movie star hair that glittered like fourteen karat gold. Best of all, she was one hell of a marksman. On the day they met, Jada knew immediately that she and Josh were soul mates. Even their names were similar. She hatched a plan to win his heart. She began by telling her female co-workers that Josh had a sexually transmitted disease so they would avoid him like the plague. Josh discovered this about a year later, at his own birthday party, and he had a good laugh. He had been working at Little Creek for a long time, unaware that his colleagues were thinking, *this guy has an STD*.

In the beginning, Jada kept her feelings for Josh a secret. Several times each week they would have lunch at Arby's. She hated Arby's. Despised it. But it was time alone with him. Back then, Josh had another girlfriend, and Jada would let down her hair and shake it out, hoping to leave behind evidence in Josh's car that might complicate that relationship. This went on for months, and Josh eventually broke up with the other girl and sensed that Jada liked him. One day out of the blue, he invited her up to their second floor offices to tour some new construction renovations. She looked at him strangely but went along. When they were finished, he grabbed her and went in for the kiss. Later that year, on Halloween, he asked her to marry him.

They exchanged vows in a simple ceremony under an old oak tree. Their "minister" was one of Josh's colleagues who had earned his ministry certification online. The wedding took place at work, while they were still wearing their 5.11 tactical boots. Jada did not care though, so long as they were together. She had known Johnny's brother very well, and had cooked up a storm with Reva during the holidays when they all came together. She rarely broke down, but after hearing the news, she had quietly wept.

"You want another one?" Corey asked as he fetched himself a beer.

Josh waved him off. "I'm good."

"So what do you think? Just a break-in?"

Before Josh could answer, Johnny came thumping down the stairs. Despite his bloodshot eyes, he looked refreshed in his sweatshirt and cargo pants. "Willie still outside?"

"Yeah, he went to get the birds and call Ivonne," Josh answered.

"Beer, Johnny?" Corey asked.

Johnny nodded, and Corey shoved one in his hand.

"I put in a call to Bryce," said Josh. "North Topsail will be all over this. We'll keep the pressure on all these guys." Bryce was one of Josh's old aft gunners and now an officer with North Topsail Beach Police. "Tomorrow I'll get with the mayor of Holly Ridge and the town council. Little political pressure wouldn't hurt, either."

"That's great," said Johnny, his voice cracking slightly.

The rear door opened and in strode Willie. "I'm leaving the birds outside. Ivonne's on her way over. She's real sorry about everything, Johnny."

"Thanks." Johnny grabbed a beer and tossed it to him. "Let's sit a minute."

"Roger that." Willie plopped down on the sofa.

"When things cool off, we need to go through this ourselves," said Josh. "We'll make sure the truth comes out."

"Well, the truth so far is this," Johnny began. "My brother wasn't acting normal. He wanted to tell me something."

"What do you mean 'not acting normal'?" Josh asked.

Willie answered for Johnny: "He had something going on, and he was going to man up and get it done."

"But it was something he was going to run by me," said Johnny. "Then he didn't."

"Whatever it is, we'll help you find out," said Corey. "You know that."

"Right on," Johnny answered. He faced them all. "Sorry for all this."

"If you apologize again, I'll crush this beer can on your head," said Willie.

"And we'll do the same," Josh promised.

Johnny climbed off the bar stool and raised his beer, bringing them to their feet. He stammered a moment, then said: "My brother was never a warrior. He didn't have that mentality. But he was a good man. And he married a good woman." Johnny's voice grew thin as he added, "May they rest in peace."

After sipping his beer, Josh tensed. He hated seeing his brothers like this. He was reminded of an old Viking proverb: "A hungry wolf is bound to wage a hard battle." The wolves had been hungry, all right, and they had taken Johnny's brother and his wife—but they had no idea who they were dealing with now.

Josh could trace his ancestry back to Norway, to some of the fiercest warriors and chieftains who had ever lived. He had studied the sagas of Icelanders that detailed events from the 10th and 11th centuries. He imagined that one of his forefathers had carried into battle the mighty Ulfberht sword, whose creation was a thousand years ahead of its time. Most swords during the medieval period were constructed of soft iron with little carbon. The steel used for the Ulfberht had been acquired in India and contained higher levels of carbon and much less slag. The sword could penetrate enemy armor and be removed much more effectively than a conventional blade. Once elite warriors began carrying the Ulfberht into battle, they realized that in their calloused hands was one of the greatest swords ever forged. While Josh might never wield such a weapon, he understood that its power was already in his heart. He understood that "the longer the vengeance is drawn out, the more satisfying it will be."

Chapter Six

"They met at the golden arches, a symbol of American culture known throughout the world. I wonder if they appreciated the irony."

—Corey McKay (FBI interview, 23 December)

The McDonald's on Main Street in Cedar Falls, Iowa was a popular haunt of employees from the car dealerships lining both sides of the street. Three mechanics from the Toyota Service Department waited patiently for their coffees and Egg McMuffins while engaging in a heated debate over the upcoming Hawkeyes game. Two portly salesmen bragged about their new diet plans while placing their order. A knot of senior citizens had staked out a table in the back, the women swiping fingers across their iPads, the men scowling at newspapers clutched in their wizened hands. The main entrance door swung open, and three teenaged girls dressed in varsity jackets rode in on a blast of cold air. They were shivering and giggling. The young men behind the counter, none of them older than nineteen, lifted their chins with recognition and began a conversation about cutting class. They ignored a young woman with an infant tucked in the crook of her arm, and it was only when the baby screamed loudly enough that she finally gained their attention.

As the sun rose higher through the front windows, and the sweet aroma of breakfast foods thickened, Rasul Abdi Yusuf finished his tea and continued sitting alone in his brown UPS uniform. His eyes left his smartphone only when the main door creaked open, and once he had inspected the new arrivals, he would return to playing *Grand Theft Auto* while breaking occasionally to surf the web. He consulted his watch: 8:14 a.m. Dr. Nazari was running late.

Rasul was a twenty-eight-year-old graduate student at the University of Northern Iowa. The Doctor of Technology degree had become a nightmare because of his Advanced Statistical Methods class, but if Allah willed it, he would pass. Rasul was an American citizen and an only child born in Michigan to parents from Saudi Arabia. He moved to Illinois when he was seven. While attending middle school, he was bullied and branded a "camel jockey." After weeks of pushing, shoving, and taunting, he finally snapped. He pummeled the fat perpetrator into a bloody pulp, screaming that he was more American than him. A change of schools was only a temporary fix. The 9/11 terror attacks were still raw, and it was impossible to escape from the scrutiny and hatred no matter how hard he and his parents tried. He lived under a cloud of suspicion all the way up through high school, where in his junior year someone spray painted the word *terrorist* across the hood of his Honda Civic.

While he was an undergraduate attending Illinois State University, he joined the Muslim Students Association and found kindred spirits there. Many had suffered the verbal and physical abuse that he had, and now their new mission was to spread the word that Muslims and non-Muslims could co-exist peacefully, despite all of the ignorance and bigotry. After all, this was their country, too, and they loved it as much as anyone else. He was an idealist back then, prepared to mount his soapbox and change the world.

By the end of his freshman year, the message was beginning to wear thin. He met new colleagues who persuaded him that the MSA's work—while necessary and important—was falling on deaf ears. These men of the Muslim Brotherhood brought Rasul to the local Islamic center. There, he connected with other young men who were as bitter and disillusioned as he was. He studied the history of the Brotherhood and its roots dating back to 1928, when Hassan al Banna, the son of a well-known imam, created The Society of Muslim Brothers in the Egyptian city of Ismailia. Rasul attended workshops that introduced him to the Brotherhood's greatest ideologue, Sayyid Qutb, who in his seminal work *Milestones* characterized the United States as the oppressor of Muslims everywhere. Qutb argued that Muslims should return to a state of complete adherence to Islamic Law and could only do so through a series of milestones. As Muslims dove deeper into their studies, they would recognize their requirement to wage jihad until the world was under Sharia law. Rasul came to realize that *Dar al-Islam* (the house of Islam) was at war with *Dar al-Harb* (all those countries like the U.S. where Sharia law was not in force, and these, collectively, made up the house of war). Arguments over how the Koran should be interpreted would continue in perpetuity, and there were many who disagreed with Qutb's contentions and chose to ignore the call. Rasul, however, was young and impressionable, and he was looking for direction. He had not recognized it then, but he had undergone the process of "progressive revelation" and had achieved milestones of enlightenment. The infidels called this radicalization. He called it an awakening. He became well-versed in the six stages of the Islamic movement put forth in Shamim Siddiqi's book *Methodology of Dawah Ilallah in American Perspective*. These stages were recruitment, organization, training, resistance, migration, and armed conflict.

By the time Rasul graduated, his destiny was clear: he would fight jihad to transform America into an Islamic State ruled under Sharia law. The Brotherhood had already established dozens of social, scientific, and health institutions in the United States, including the Islamic Medical Association and others. New Islamic centers were being constructed every year. Ground operatives in every state collected intelligence on local and federal law enforcement personnel. Brothers with doctorate degrees in Islamic culture offered their services as counterterrorism experts to many federal agencies, where they, too gathered intel for the cause. In sum, the Brotherhood was embedded in all aspects of American society, from Wawa convenience stores to the White House. Even more impressive was their capability to moderate any threat, arguing themselves that not all Muslims were terrorists. Most were tax-paying, law-abiding citizens who wanted to raise their children and pursue happiness. At the same time, these innocents served as perfect camouflage for the Brotherhood and other like-minded jihadis.

Rasul had nearly finished a level of his game when someone rapped a knuckle on his table, startling him. Dr. Nazari grinned and headed toward the restroom. The older man's face was clean-shaven, his hair closely cropped. He appeared more South American than Middle Eastern, and the graying at his temples was a recent addition in the past year. After scrutinizing the other patrons, Rasul left and joined his associate.

"*As-salam alaikum*," said the older man.

Rasul returned the greeting: "*Wa 'alaykum al-salaam*."

"How was your flight?"

"It was crowded, but otherwise not too bad. There's an envelope for you back home."

"You were discreet?"

"Of course."

"You gave him your new number?"

"I did."

"Excellent. I'm proud of you, Rasul. There are always a few who have second thoughts and lack the courage, but not you."

"Our friends in West Virginia trained me well."

"I knew they would. And you proved to the others that we can trust you."

"I'm more than just a courier."

"You are." Nazari gave him an appraising stare. "When you were a boy, you had no idea that you would grow up to become one of us, *Al-Saif*, the Sword."

"I wanted to be an engineer like my father."

"You will be."

Rasul nodded, even though his grades said otherwise. "I'm due back at the warehouse this morning."

"We'll be in touch."

"And if there's any more trouble, you'll let me know."

"Rest assured. *Baraka Allahu fika*, Rasul."

He bowed his head. "And may Allah bestow his blessings on you, too."

Chapter Seven

"It was a hard day, full of drama. I was shaking trees and nothing was happening. I felt like I was under the train. And then it got worse."

—Johnny Johansen (FBI interview, 23 December)

Corey sat on his haunches, tugged off one of his gloves, then traced a bare finger around the boot print. It was 0950, and the rich, oaky scent of burning firewood wafted over from the chimney of an old farmhouse in the distance. A cold front had come through the night before, plunging temperatures some twenty degrees below normal. There was something telling and almost sinister about the weather, but Corey shrugged off the feeling.

He and the others were out behind Daniel's house, following the perpetrator's escape route identified by the police. The prints ended at an embankment beside a dirt road stretching off through the east side of the forest. Tire tracks from at least four or five different vehicles had dug furrows in the dirt, and each would have to be analyzed, although none of them appeared fresh. The first theory was that their man had doubled back toward the swamp and had escaped to the north, using the wetlands to break up his trail; however, the teams had only discovered a few extra boot prints to support that assumption before the trail went cold across the long beds of pine needles. Theory #2 held that he reached the embankment, where someone had picked him up. While that might be possible, none of the neighbors mentioned any visitors or suspicious vehicles in the area, and again, there were no fresh tracks to support that. This was a rural town sans any traffic cameras or other high tech surveillance devices.

Human intelligence was the best they could gather, but in rural areas, HUMINT was often valuable because more people knew each other and were, in turn, a lot nosier.

What the police had confirmed was that their man had approached on foot from the woodlands; therefore, he might not have seen Reva's car in the driveway. He had used a screwdriver or similar tool to gain entry through one of the French doors on the back porch. Once inside, he encountered Reva, who had returned an hour early from work, this according to Mrs. Donna Rae Hennington, the sixty-three-year-old widower and math teacher from Dixon High School who lived next door. Mrs. Hennington had neither seen nor heard a thing after waving to Reva while collecting her mail.

Evidently, the perpetrator had caught Reva before she could flee, and instead of using his jimmying tool (which he had either pocketed or ruled out) he drew the nearest weapon of opportunity—an 8" Wusthof cook's knife from the block set on the granite countertop.

The more Corey thought about it, the more the police department's narrative made sense. A few minutes earlier, he had called Lindsey with an update, and she, too, had agreed that Daniel and Reva were such generous and unassuming people that she could never imagine someone wanting to kill them. Once again, she pleaded to join him. She was still up at her office in Charlotte, where she specialized in corporate wellness for a large insurance company and had done business with Reva. Corey told her to hold off coming down until they had firm dates for the wake and funeral. She had held it together pretty well, but by the end of the call she was crying and saying, "I need to be with you. I can't ever lose you." Those words forced him to imagine the same, a life without her, a life that had been blessed because of her.

They had met three years ago while on a friend's boat, and that meeting seemed preordained given Corey's love of watercraft. They began hanging out with mutual friends. They exchanged numbers. Their conversations grew deeper and more intense until the inevitable first date. She was in her late twenties, with hair the color of a Caribbean beach, but it wasn't just her looks that had quickened his pulse. She was light years smarter than some of the college girls he usually dated in Wilmington.

Though he never bragged, securing dates back then had not been too difficult. He had just left the Marine Corps, was in great shape, and the ladies told him he had a twinkle in his eye they could not resist. Sometimes they would ask why he left the Marines.

While Corey was definitely a gambling man, he realized after his first enlistment that if he re-upped, a guy with his experience would be rushed downrange, where he had already burned out eight of his nine lives. The thrill was gone, in part because Corey had matured and had set longer term goals for himself. Besides, he had seen more than his share of combat. The only problem was he loved the boats and working with all those great crews. Leaving them was like losing his identity.

But then fate had struck. Josh had heard about Corey's impending EAS and recruited him right out of the Marines. Cory became a civilian contractor and course supervisor in the Navy Riverine Program at the Joint Maritime Training Center, Camp Lejeune. He trained over 140 riverine sailors per fiscal year. He created and executed high risk exercises and dynamic live fire ranges. He supervised other instructors and taught various conventional and special operations units throughout the United States and abroad. At the same time, he returned to school, where he earned a bachelor's degree in Business Project Management with a minor in International Business Development and Finance from American University. After six years in the riverine program, and with his degree in hand, he was ready to branch out and help Johnny turn Triton 6 into an efficient organization fulfilling critical military and law enforcement needs. Johnny, the charming sales rep with the great sense of humor, along with Willie, the marksman and firearms expert, were like an intricate Suisse chronometer, the whole became vastly greater than the sum of its parts.

Corey pushed off his haunches and straightened with a groan. The cold had penetrated his bones, and his back cracked in protest. He squinted off toward the tree line, where in the whisper quiet of morning, Johnny and Willie were combing the area. They had the chief's permission to come out for another look, but he doubted they would find anything his investigators had missed. His people had been searching all night and were just finishing up. The chief said he would call or visit Johnny once he received the preliminary autopsy reports.

Josh's hands were jammed into his jacket pockets as he hiked up the embankment and joined Corey. "What I see... is not what Johnny wants me to see."

"What do you mean?"

"It's all obvious."

"Really?"

"I think so. I'm this guy. I've hit a few other houses in the Cottages, easy marks. I'm good at this, and I'm getting better." Josh closed his eyes as though he were reenacting the crimes. "I recon the house, I know when they come and go. I don't want any trouble. I just want to get in and get out. Easy day, like Johnny says."

"But not this time," Corey said.

"No, she's home. I didn't expect that… but why do I push it? Why don't I just leave?" Josh snapped open his eyes. "Am I *that* stupid?"

"I don't know."

"Maybe I'm not stupid. I'm desperate. I'm pawning this shit to feed my habit. Believe me, I know that mentality."

"I talked to one of the other detectives. He said the guy goes for the money, jewelry, guns… that kind of stuff. And that doesn't say much about who he is. And it's true. Most of these guys avoid a confrontation."

"Right. But not this guy. When he realizes she's home, he's pissed. He's already put work into this house, and he's committed. He can't stop."

"Because he's high and desperate."

"That's right. It's all about his fix, and she's just in the way. So was Daniel. You can't talk to people when they're like that. You can't stop them."

Corey nodded. "It all blew apart once he got that door open. While he's killing her, Daniel walks in."

Josh's expression soured. "We can run this by Johnny, but he doesn't want to hear shit right now."

"Not until he finds out what Dan wanted to tell him. But what if he doesn't? You know how he is when he gets fired up. What if this is it? Just a junkie who killed them. Maybe he won't accept it. Losing guys downrange is one thing, but this was his brother, like the most innocent guy in the world. I don't know. Maybe Johnny will go off the deep end."

"What do you mean? We all live in the deep end."

Corey's lips curled in a reluctant grin. "Yeah, I guess we do."

* * *

The VFW hall in Holly Ridge was located halfway down a rural street with a rather commanding name: Hines Stump Sound Church Road. The white, single-story building resembled a converted warehouse with a bright blue entrance canopy and hard water stains creeping up its corrugated aluminum walls. Barely larger than an average tract home, the hall stood on the periphery of some dense woodlands like a ghostly relic from another time. Every winter the grass out front turned brown, while the wind brushed the exterior in a fine layer of dust. When no cars were present, the hall seemed abandoned, yet it was anything but.

Inside, the stench of cigarette smoke, dry roasted peanuts, and drug store cologne worn by several regulars crinkled the noses of the uninitiated. The ceiling tiles were tinged yellow and blotted from leaks. An ancient jukebox sat near the door, glowing with its current selection, an old Hank Williams song that crackled through failing speakers. Seated atop the warped veneer of the counter was a fishbowl filled to the brim. Positioned at its bottom was a shot glass. The object was to drop a quarter into the bowl and see if you could land it directly into the glass. If you did, you scored a raffle ticket for a 50/50 drawing. The quarters did drunken backflips before ever nearing the shot glass, and that was all part of the fun.

Behind the bar and separated by a half wall was a kitchen where specials from chili to chicken soup were prepared. The waitress and part-time cook, Edie, wore her gray hair in a bob reminiscent of Jacqueline Kennedy. Every man in her family was a veteran, so she knew how to navigate around these boys. The regulars were from all branches of the service, although the Marines were best represented, given their proximity to Camp Lejeune. Several of the hoary chain-smokers assumed their usual formation at the bar and never removed their veteran ball caps. Their heavy eyes widened only at the sound of barstools squeaking. They would glance sidelong to scrutinize the new recruits, and then return to their croaking about politics while cradling their warming beers.

Johnny had not said much all morning, and breakfast was no more than a cup of coffee, half of which he had dumped in the sink before heading out. That was why the second beer hit him so hard, and why he abruptly marched outside alone to the adjacent shooting range with his 1911, his holster, and a hundred rounds of Winchester white box. After inserting his earplugs, he assumed his firing stance at roughly twenty-five yards. He sighted a rock seated along the berm and took a few warm up shots. Out of corner of his eye, he spotted the others gathering at one of the tables behind him. To their immediate right stood a tree that Josh and a few members of Small Craft Company had planted, along with a time capsule. The tree and capsule were a tribute to the men he had lost and to their attending families who had wept and thanked Josh for organizing the event. As far as Johnny was concerned, that area adjacent to the berm was sacred ground. As a matter of fact, this entire place was.

Willie waved to the other guys, motioning them to leave Johnny alone.

Johnny continued firing, taking three second pauses between each shot until his magazine was empty. He hit the rock he had been targeting only twice. He raised his trembling hand and scowled at it, then holstered his pistol and stood there, blaming his loose groupings on his lack of focus and the days that lay ahead. He swore and tugged out his earplugs.

"Hey, Johnny," Willie called. "Why don't you join the twenty-first century and buy a Glock?"

Anyone unaware of Johnny's relationship with Willie might deem that a callous remark, given the circumstances. But Willie was trying to cheer him up. Whenever they shot together and Johnny missed, Willie would tease him regarding his penchant for the 1911, a pistol that dated all the way back to a visionary firearms designer whose career spanned the late ninetieth and early twentieth centuries. That man's name was John Browning, and he had become synonymous with cutting edge firearms technology. Browning held over 128 patents, and his guns were copied all over the world. He was so dedicated to his craft that he literally died of a heart attack while working at his bench, designing a new self-loading gun design. His most famous weapons were his Hi Power pistol, his .50 caliber machine gun, and his automatic rifle. The U.S. Army adopted the Browning pistol design on March 29, 1911, and the weapon became known as the Model 1911. The Navy and Marine Corps adopted the M1911 two years later. Despite all of that, Willie loved to tease Johnny about his preference for an "ancient" weapon.

"Hey, stud, why don't you get down here," Johnny urged him.

Willie nodded. His Glock 34 with competition trigger spring kit was tucked in his holster. "I thought we were grabbing lunch first."

"I can't eat. They made that big dinner last night. Two bites and I was done. I don't know, I just can't sit around any more."

"Well, looks like you won't have to. We might have something." Willie lifted his chin at the sound of car tires crunching over gravel.

Chief Schneider's silver SUV with department insignia rolled up behind them. The man climbed out, removed his sunglasses, and flipped up his jacket collar. Everyone gathered around him, but he spoke directly to Johnny, "Okay to talk in front of them?"

"What do you think, Dennis?"

"All right, so I got the autopsy. Nothing surprising there. Bruising, evidence that they both struggled, and they died from their knife wounds. The guy wore gloves, so the only prints we found on the knife were Reva's."

"No prints from Daniel?" Johnny asked.

"I'm afraid not. We were hoping to find some evidence of clothing, even the smallest stuff from his jacket, his backpack, or his pants, but so far nothing. Now rest assured, we're following up on everything else, including the home computers. We have investigators at the University, too, and at Reva's job. We'll want to interview their daughters when they arrive."

"Roger that. Elina's picking them up at the airport right now."

"Good. You let me know when we can do that. You call that flooring guy I told you about?"

"Yeah, I'm supposed to meet him later. You sure you guys are all done with the house? You didn't miss anything?"

"My teams worked all night, Johnny."

"Roger, and thanks for all your help on this. We'll be in touch."

Schneider nodded. "If there's anything you need, you just call, okay?"

Johnny gritted his teeth and watched the chief leave. He stood there a moment more, and then turned to Willie. "Let's set up some targets."

* * *

A few hours later, back at the house, Johnny wanted to console his two nieces. Their eyes were swollen, their hair disheveled, their sweatshirts wrinkled from being jammed on a commercial airliner for several hours. He told them about the police interviews, but then, without thinking, he began his own series of pointed questions. Before either girl could answer, Elina cut him off, saying, "Let's save that for later, Johnny." She was right. She told him to focus on the funeral arrangements, while she worked out the details with Reva's parents. Those items would keep them busy. However, he already *was* busy going over every word of his last conversation with Daniel, trying to read between the lines and ferret out the hidden message. The realization that Johnny had only once gone to his brother for help cut deep. In trying to obey his father's wishes and protect his kid brother, Johnny had lowered Daniel's self-esteem. All he wanted was the best for his brother, and all he had done was make matters worse.

He descended to the man cave and adjoining office, where he began to make his calls. Hunting one day with his brother, discussing his death the next. Unbelievable. Johnny hit the wrong button and was thumbing through voicemails instead of contacts. He came across one dated over a month ago and tortured himself by listening. His brother's voice buzzed through the tiny speaker:

"Hey, Johnny, Reva wants to know if we can bring anything else over for dinner. Now don't play martyr again and tell me to show up with nothing. We'll do the side dishes, whatever, just call me back."

Johnny never returned the call. His brother and sister-in-law arrived for Sunday dinner with side dishes, and Elina was upset because she had made some as well.

With a deep sigh, Johnny set his elbows on the desk and rubbed the corners of his eyes. His leg began to twitch, the old wound stinging with new pain. He and Daniel had been on their way to little league practice and were taking the short cut through the swamp. Johnny slipped and bashed his leg across a sharp root. Daniel pleaded that they should go back, but Johnny screamed that he was okay. Daniel tried using a leaf to wipe off the blood, but Johnny smacked him away.

Shuddering off the memory, Johnny stood and padded over to the couch. He stretched out with Rookie tucked in beside him, and with Musket and Bomber lying on the floor. He considered a nap, but the door bell rang constantly, as neighbors and more friends stopped by to pay their respects. The ladies, thank God, were handling everything. He told Elina that he was not ready for visitors and that no one should talk to the media. He did not want their faces splashed all over the TV for some scumbag's viewing pleasure.

Meanwhile, the guys were back at the office, doing some final tweaks on the proposal. Johnny had insisted they do so, offering them a breather from all of this. He already felt guilty enough for disrupting their lives. In hindsight, that might have been a bad idea. They were probably sitting there and ignoring the proposal. They were talking about him, discussing how they could help. He knew those boys like the back of his hand. And that thought triggered a memory of something Daniel had said:

"Sometimes you think you know somebody, right? But you don't know them at all."

Who had Daniel been talking about? Himself?

Johnny bolted up, scaring the dogs. He grabbed his jacket and keys and left without telling anyone.

Chapter Eight

"Marines are relentless. And that was Johnny. Never quit. Can't spell defeat. All he wanted was the truth, and he was willing to fight to the death for it. We all were."

—Willie Parente (FBI interview, 23 December)

As Johnny proceeded onto Alumni Drive, he glanced at the passenger's seat, where the ghost of the old man sat with his arms folded over his chest. *"I'm very disappointed in you, son. You have no idea."*

"I'm sure you are."

Johnny cleared his thoughts and pulled into the parking lot in front of DePaolo Hall. He locked the truck and started off. The UNC Wilmington campus was a broad and picturesque collection of colonial style brick buildings located between Cape Fear River and the Atlantic Ocean. Over 14,000 students were taught by over 500 faculty members, according to the website and map Johnny had perused on the way over. Tugging up his collar, he followed the sidewalk until he reached King Hall, a two-story building with a wide staircase leading up to three pairs of entrance doors crowned by fanlights. Johnny hustled inside, hit the stairwell, and reached the second floor. He was out of breath but glad the place had heat. He found Suite 205, the Pre-Engineering Department, and caught the attention of a smartly dressed black woman wearing tortoise shell glasses. Her desk plate read: Mrs. Jennifer Pattel, Administrative Assistant. She glanced up, and her mouth fell open in recognition. "You're Dr. Johansen's brother..."

"Yeah, I'm Johnny."

She waved a hand across her face, trying to compose herself. "I'm sorry, I'm Jenn. I came in to work today, and they told me what happened." Her tears came fast. "You know, I've been working here for over ten years."

Johnny already had his driver's license and a picture of him and Daniel in his hand. "I was going to show you these so I could get into his office."

"The police were here this morning, just after we opened."

"I know. I wanted to come by. I just had to get out of the house, you know? Maybe I'll pack up a little bit. Is that all right?"

"I understand. They didn't put up any police tape or anything." She reached into her desk drawer and produced a large ring with color-coded keys. She escorted him through the suite and into a hallway. Daniel's office was the first door on the left, which she opened then flicked on the light, revealing a twelve-foot square room with French style windows. "Dr. Johansen used to brag about you all the time."

Johnny nodded and felt the air escape his lungs. He was ashamed to admit that after helping Daniel move into the office over a decade ago, he had never visited, not even once for a quick cup of coffee. He felt embarrassed for needing the map and website to find the building.

"Let me know when you're done, and I'll lock up after you. Oh, we close at five, so you have about an hour. And, if you would, when you have all the arrangements made, can you let us know?"

"Absolutely."

"The faculty and staff loved your brother. We'd all like to pay our respects. Our winter break just started here, but I can forward the information to them. Some of his colleagues are still in town, and I know they'd want to be there."

"I'll get your card before I go."

"Just holler if you need anything."

She nodded and left him surrounded by the artifacts of his brother's life. While Johnny had his own share of mementoes in the man cave, he had always been the more Spartan of the two. He hated clutter. If in doubt, throw it out. Conversely, Daniel saved everything with the dedication of a world-class hoarder. An entire wall was dedicated to his book collection. Hundreds of texts buckled shelves rising ten feet to the ceiling. Johnny could spend an hour just browsing the titles, from civil engineering to computer science to mathematics books with technical terms on their spines that could have been written in Chinese.

A small section of books along a lower row drew his attention: these were Daniel's *Hardy Boys Mysteries*. He had every book from the original series—all except #8 *The*

Mystery of Cabin Island, which he had given to Johnny for his twelfth birthday. The book was, in part, a token of appreciation because Johnny had protected him from their father and from bullies at their school. Daniel had urged Johnny to read the novel so he could do better in English class, but Johnny never did. He threw the book in a box of old toys and moved on, while Daniel made the honor roll.

Nearby on the same shelf were some framed black-and-white photos featuring the family, the largest of which tightened Johnny's chest. Two boys in little league uniforms leaned on a chain-link fence. Johnny wore his usual sarcastic grin. Daniel stared wide-eyed like a puppy dog. A few other pictures featured Johnny in his uniform, and there was another of him at Daniel's wedding, serving as his brother's best man.

On the wall to Johnny's left hung Daniel's degrees: a B.S. and M.I.E. in Industrial Engineering, and a Ph.D. in Industrial & Systems Engineering. He had earned all three from North Carolina State University. Daniel said they called it "academic incest" when you tried to get a job at the same school where you had done your coursework, so he had applied to many schools but wound up at UNC, which was part of the North Carolina university system but technically not the same school as NC State in Raleigh. Along with the degrees were plaques bearing the school's emblem, and these named Daniel as teacher of the year, or researcher of the year, or distinguished him as an honoree for some Greek fraternity or sorority. The old man had "not raised no dummies," but seeing all of his brother's accomplishments made Johnny feel inadequate. He had paddles on his walls. Dr. Daniel Johansen had all of this.

In the center of the office and facing the doorway was Daniel's desk, more accurately described as a landfill of dog-eared textbooks, piles of mail, and stacks of old school newspapers. Crammed beside them were leaning stacks of manila file folders with class designations written in black Sharpie. Several empty coffee mugs whose lips were stained brown sat precariously along one edge. There was an open area about the size of a cereal box where he squeezed in his laptop and worked in the glow of a dusty green banker's lamp. Johnny could not blame the entire mess on his brother. No doubt the police had rifled through the papers and all of drawers, looking for anything that might suggest he had brought death upon himself.

Johnny drifted back to the bookshelves because a title there had caught his eye, one about leadership written by a Marine Corps captain. Beside it was another soft cover on military management. Johnny estimated that Daniel had purchased over a dozen self-help books, and many of them appeared new and had been stacked horizontally in front of some older texts.

In the far corner stood a pair of steel file cabinets. Johnny opened the first few drawers. Class files, grades, course plans, student roles, and other college-related materials were all there and revealed absolutely nothing about Daniel's secret. Back at the desk, Johnny flipped through mail, an unremarkable assortment of textbook solicitations and announcements of upcoming engineering conferences. He assumed that if there were anything telling in the stack, the police had already confiscated it. Should he tell Schneider about this visit? Perhaps not. The man might find it insulting that Johnny was working behind his investigators. However, Johnny might find something telling that they, not knowing Daniel, might overlook.

A faint knock on the open door surprised him, and he whirled toward the sound, expecting to find Mrs. Pattel.

"I'm sorry to bother you, but I saw you go marching across campus like a bat out of hell, and I wanted to stop by."

The old man had the face of a well-done hamburger and the voice of a V8 engine burning oil. Describing him as five feet tall was being generous, although he added a few inches via his ball cap with its single row of embroidery—brilliant reds, yellows, and greens. These were military ribbons representing the National Defense, Vietnam Service, and Vietnam Campaign Medals. His stubbly cheeks and broad nose glowed like an alcoholic's. A wheeled travel bag half-zippered and pregnant with who knew what was clutched in his right hand. Was he some homeless vet? His newer down jacket and orthopedic shoes suggested otherwise.

"You need help old timer?" Johnny asked.

"May I come in?"

Johnny frowned. "You look familiar."

"I used to go to the VFW a lot. Haven't been there in a couple of years, though."

Johnny snapped his fingers. "That's where I know you from. You used to tell that story about the Battle of Lost Patrol. You got banged up pretty good there."

"And you told me about your old man fighting at LZ Bird."

"Yeah, I remember that."

The old timer removed his ball cap to expose his bald, freckled pate. He took a step farther into the office and proffered his hand. "I'm Norm Mack, 1st Battalion, 9th Marines, 'D' Company, 1st Platoon."

"Roger that, pop. What's going on?"

"I'm an independent book buyer here on campus. I go around and collect unwanted textbooks from professors and students. I sell them back to my company and make a small profit. I use the money to support my online gambling habit."

Johnny rolled his eyes. Norm might have been a veteran Marine, but he was also a solicitor, and dealing with him was the last thing Johnny needed now. "Well, look here, I don't know if you heard the news about my brother, but I'm not selling. And I'm a little busy right—"

"I'm not here for books, Johnny."

"You remember my name?"

"I've known your brother for years. He used to tell me all about you. That night raid in Fallujah? Man, that was some shit. He was so proud. You boys must have got along famously."

Johnny winced. "Yeah, so, uh, what do you need?"

Norm hesitated. "First, I'm very sorry for your loss."

"I appreciate that, but right now I need to start packing—"

"No, right now you need to listen to me."

"What?"

"I said listen up, Marine. Like I said, your brother and I were friends. I'm on campus two, three times a week. We spoke a lot. And I don't think what happened to him was just a robbery. I think he might've been involved in something really bad."

"Whoa, slow down there, ranger. What're you talking about?"

Norm yanked his bag out of the doorway and shut the door after him. "How well do you know your brother, Johnny?"

"Who are you?"

Norm lifted his palms. "Look, I was going to contact you. I don't want any trouble. But when I found out what happened last night, I thought no way, it can't be a coincidence."

Johnny took a step toward the old man, who began to shrink under Johnny's gaze. "Talk to me, pop."

"Did your brother ever spend any time in the middle east?"

"He traveled for work, but I don't remember him ever saying, hey now, wait a minute. What the hell are you asking me that for?"

"Daniel and I... we never talked about religion. I just always assumed he was one of those liberal academic atheist types, and I was okay with that. We got into politics a lot, but he never talked about his faith. You ever talk about that with him? He ever say he was converting to another religion?"

"Norm, do you know something about my brother? Yes? Or no?"

He hesitated, scratching nervously at the stubble on his chin. "I saw something that really bugged me. Could be nothing, but I can't stop thinking about it. I just can't. Did you brother have any Arabic friends?"

Johnny threw up his hands. "He's here, you got people coming from all over the world, foreign professors teaching classes. Maybe he did. So what?"

"Do you know if your brother reads Arabic?"

"Look here, I'll kick you out on your ass right now. Last chance, pop."

"Wait. Just please listen. I came in one day, a little later than usual. He's usually got the door open, and I stopped knocking years ago. I just roll in and take a seat. Even if he's got books to sell, we bullshit for a while. He tells me about the students or some research he's doing, or we talk about you or what's going on in the news. So I come in one day, I don't know, I think it was just after Halloween, and he's got the door cracked open. I don't think anything of it, so I push it open and walk inside. He's got some papers and pieces of unopened mail spread out all over the desk. He says hi, but I can tell he's nervous. While he's scooping up the mail and shoving it in the drawer, I see it's all written in Arabic."

"That's it?"

"Yeah."

"That's what you wanted to tell me? My brother was an engineer. You don't think he dealt with engineers from all over the world? Maybe he reads Arabic. What're you getting at?"

"Look, I'm sorry I even told you. Maybe you're right. Maybe it was nothing. But I felt like I knew your brother. Or at least I thought I did. I see his beard getting longer, I catch him reading shit in Arabic, and a month later, he's dead. What would you think?"

"I think back in 'Nam you took some shrapnel to the head, and it's making you see things."

"Johnny, do you really believe it's all a coincidence?"

"All right, pop, let's cut to the chase. You think my brother converted to Islam? Are you shitting me? He was the son of an Army Black Hat and the brother of a United States Marine. You got some pair. How dare you. Get out."

"I'm not accusing your brother of anything, Johnny. I'm just saying that from where I stand, and based on what I saw, it looks like he had some secrets. And maybe it was those secrets that got him killed." Norm reached into his inner jacket pocket and placed one of his business cards on the desk. "I haven't talked to the police yet. And I won't. Because you and I are Marines. My number's there. I'm really sorry."

Johnny glared at Norm as he moved to the door, opened it, then shuffled out. Johnny remained there, trying to catch his breath.

The beard. The Arabic. The need to tell him something. Johnny cast his mind back to a snippet of conversation from that Sunday dinner he had been thinking about earlier. Daniel had shared a story about one of his sophomore students who had just won an engineering competition. The kid's name was Abdul Azim Mohammad, and Johnny had been unable to hide his reaction.

"What? What's that look for?" Daniel had asked.

"I don't know. Be nice if just for once an American kid won something."

"The kid is American, Johnny. And he happens to be a Muslim. And he doesn't want to kill either one of us—or anyone else at this table."

"How are the sweet potatoes?" Elina had asked. "And don't forget, we also have corn, carrots, green beans, and mashed potatoes."

Pushing himself off the door, Johnny went to the desk, yanked open the drawers, and tore through the envelopes, index cards, and any other papers he could find that might be written in Arabic. He grew more frustrated as he sifted through the files. He whirled to the steel cabinets and dug through them as though searching for a bomb. By the time he got to the third drawer, he was exhausted and bleary-eyed. He faced the massive wall of books, and his heart sank. Any one of those texts could hold secrets shoved within its pages. Was he prepared to search every book? Daniel was the master at concealing things.

Johnny's phone rang. The number was unfamiliar, but he answered anyway. Shit, it was the flooring guy heading over to Daniel's house. Johnny had forgotten all about him. He said he would meet him there in thirty minutes.

As he started for the door, Johnny felt something crunch under his shoe. He stopped, looked down, and picked up a small piece of ceiling tile. Well, the police had been very thorough. They had pulled at least one of the ceiling tiles to have a peak up top. Johnny noticed the screws on the heating and cooling vent register were also freshly scratched. Then again, what if the investigators had not pulled the tile or opened the vent? What if Daniel had? No, if he had something to hide, he would pick a much less obvious place, or, he would pick a place he assumed you would look, placing the item right between your eyes so you never saw it. When he hid some of the *Playboys* they had stolen, he had removed the covers and replaced them with other magazine covers. After that, he had stacked them with other magazines right there in the living room basket. He placed them at the back of the pile where the old man would see them but assume they were issues he had already read. He only emptied the magazine basket a few times per year.

Johnny dragged one of the file cabinets away from the wall, then tipped it sideways and walked it over to the ceiling tile in question. He used Daniel's chair to mount the top of the file cabinet. He balanced himself like a broken down acrobat, ducking and extending his arms to catch his balance. He removed the tile then thrust his head into the opening. He fished out his smartphone, putting it in flashlight mode. A quick scan of the ten inch space between the concrete above and the tiles below produced nothing. The ductwork to his immediate right ran parallel with the tiles toward the far wall, where it turned up. As Johnny was about to lean down and replace the tile, he reached up and ran his fingers along the top of the duct. Sure, people hid things *inside* air ducts, but how often did they hide them *on top* of the conduit? That sounded like Daniel's MO. Lo and behold, Johnny's hand bumped into something that felt like cardboard. He groaned and reached farther into the ceiling, seizing the object and bringing it down. It was a small shipping box with the labels ripped off. There was no dust, suggesting it had not been there very long. Johnny set it near his feet, replaced the ceiling tile, then carefully climbed down.

Once on the floor, he opened the box. The first thing he found was a note hand-written in Arabic:

ىلإ ثدحتلا .نيومتلا ةكرش يكيتكتلا سنيالير ىلإ بأ اذهلا
.ةباوبلا ةقاطبو حيتافم ديرت تنأ هل لوقأ .تروبالا ىعدي لجر
.لبقملا يعاس لصتا ،عيزوتلل دادعتسا ىلع تنك امدنع

The second was a set of keys and a card with gate codes and instructions on it. The card was from a climate-controlled storage facility in Sneads Ferry called East Coast Storage.

Finally, there was a small package wrapped in heavy white paper. When he turned it over, there was a label affixed to the top. The label depicted a scorpion, and Johnny knew exactly what this was—

A block of Colombian cocaine.

Chapter Nine

"The Marine Corps brotherhood means we're never alone, but sometimes we forget. I don't blame Johnny for what he did. Those were the worst days of his life, and he was just trying to protect us."

—Josh Eriksson (FBI interview, 23 December)

Johnny left the university in a daze. Norm's card, along with Jennifer Pattel's, were in his pocket, and the shipping box he found lay on the front seat, staring back at him. He headed out of Wilmington, driving until he was on Ocean Highway, en route to Holly Ridge. Ten minutes later, he could not remember how he got there. His ringing phone startled him. Another unfamiliar number.

"Johnny, hey, it's Paul Lindquist. Where are you now?"

It took a moment for the detective's name to register. "Oh, hey, I'm out and about. Going to my brother's house to meet the flooring guy." Johnny stole another glance at the shipping box.

"Reason I ask is I swung by the house and Elina said you weren't there. She didn't know where you were, and she didn't want to call or text, but she was worried."

"That woman knows me very well."

"Well, I'm sorry to intrude, but I wanted to give you an update. We've been working very hard on this case, and to be honest, there's not much here. Phone records don't send up any red flags. I'm told forensics is still looking at the computers, but so far they're clean. I mean your brother didn't even surf porn or download pictures."

Johnny spied the package again. "Well, he was no saint."

"Who is? Anyway, we interviewed everyone at Reva's office, and we heard nothing to suggest they had any enemies. No hints of adultery. Nothing."

"Roger that."

"Your brother's colleagues are harder to pin down since the term ended. I spoke to a couple of professors on the phone, and we interviewed his assistant while we searched his office. The dean came over, and we got a chance to talk to her. She said your brother loved the university more than any faculty member she knew. He was Mr. School Spirit. And they all called him the nicest guy in the world."

"He was."

"He sure has a lot of books."

"I know."

"Well, rest assured we did a thorough search, top to bottom. I even pulled a ceiling tile and checked the air vent for you."

Johnny gasped. "I guess that's all I can ask. You're probably right. Whatever Dan wanted to tell me... it doesn't have anything to do with this."

"You know I agree, but that won't affect this investigation. I keep my bias out of it—because every once in a while I get surprised."

A police car with flashing lights came roaring by in the opposite direction. Johnny reached over, grabbed the shipping box, and shoved it under his seat.

"Johnny, you still there?"

"Yeah."

"Can you hang on for a second?"

"No problem." Johnny checked his rear view mirror, half-expecting the police car that had passed to turn around and pursue. That made no sense, but the paranoia coursed through him like a 5-hour energy drink.

"Sorry, Johnny, I just got a quick question. Were you just up at the university?"

"Yeah, yeah," Johnny answered without hesitation. "I was going to tell you. I didn't want you to think I was working behind you."

"Really."

"Yeah, sorry, just going through some of my brother's things."

"Johnny, you can't do that without telling us. We're cutting you a lot a slack here, you being a twenty-three year veteran and all. The taxpayers pay me to be Mr. Suspicious, and most violent crimes circle right back to a family member. Now I'm not saying you did anything wrong, but you have to ask yourself how this looks to the police. If you've been upfront with us, and you're not holding anything back, then you've got nothing to worry about. For now, I need you to let us do our jobs."

"Roger. I just needed to get out of the house. How did you know I was there?"

"Your brother's assistant has been helping us track down his buddies, and she mentioned that you stopped by."

"She was pretty upset. My brother had some good people around him."

"He sure did. Well, all right, Johnny, you relax and do like I said. We don't need any help. Soon as I have more, I'll be in touch."

"Thanks." Johnny let his head fall back on the seat. He blinked hard, feeling the initial shock begin to wear off. In his mind's eyes, he went through the box's contents again. A note in Arabic. Keys and instructions to a storage facility. A block of Colombian Cocaine. How was Daniel going to "step up to the plate" with these items? The possibilities formed a hollow ache that clutched his chest. He reached into his pocket and produced Norm's business card. He dialed the number.

"Hey, old timer, it's Johnny."

"Hey, Johnny, I'm glad you called. I wanted to apologize again—"

"Don't. Just listen. Is there anything else you remember?"

"I don't think so. I told you everything. I might be old, but I know what I saw, and I know what I believe."

"You didn't ask Daniel about the Arabic writing?"

"No."

"Why not?"

"I told you he was nervous, and I didn't want to push it."

"You notice anything else that was weird, out of the ordinary after that?"

"No, everything seemed normal. Johnny, do you believe me now? Did you find something?"

"Tell you what, you just keep your word, Marine. Don't talk to anyone."

"My word is my bond."

"Roger that." Johnny ended the call. He fumbled with the phone's charger cord since the battery was down to fourteen percent. He nearly ran off the road doing so, and once he reached the next red light, he began to hyperventilate. He might even throw up. His thoughts raced from supposition to supposition:

Daniel had met some jihadis at the university who had intrigued him with their soft voices and promises of inner peace. They wore him down and had him discussing his childhood under the old man's iron rule. Daniel's desire to become a true man allowed them to brainwash him into turning his back on his family. He secretly converted to Islam. From there, they radicalized him. He began smuggling cocaine for jihadis tied to a Colombian cartel. The product came up through Miami and was stored in Sneads Ferry before being distributed throughout the country. Dr. Daniel Johansen, the son of an Army Black Hat and the brother of a Marine, was helping jihadis fund terror attacks against the United States of America.

Or maybe he was being black-mailed by the jihadis? Maybe he had converted to Islam but then had second-thoughts about becoming a jihadi? Maybe he had stumbled upon their operation and had paid the ultimate price? But an innocent man would have gone immediately to the police, right? Why hide the evidence?

"What the hell?" Johnny muttered aloud. Could any of this be true?

If Johnny ran these theories past his old friend Mark Gatterton, the man would describe exactly how Daniel had been radicalized and why he had betrayed his country. Gatterton, a Naval academy graduate, had been a platoon commander, assistant operations officer, and airborne/diving officer with 2nd Force Reconnaissance Company. He had gone downrange with Johnny on several occasions and had completed the U.S. Army's Ranger Training School.

After resigning his commission, Gatterton joined the FBI and became a member of the bureau's Counterterrorism Division. He created the FBI's first program to train special agents in identifying and responding to threats posed by Islamist terror groups. With over a decade of dedicated service, he left the bureau to become an independent consultant. Through his website, his many publications, and his lectures given all over the country, he trained and educated leaders at all levels on various threats to security.

Unfortunately, Gatterton's Marine Corps background did not allow him to mince words or abide assholes and other assorted buffoons, especially those in government whose blind eyes and politically motivated inaction had already resulted in causalities at home and abroad. He pointed fingers at those in office who he believed had direct ties to jihadis or whose organizations had been infiltrated by the Muslim Brotherhood. He named names. His blog posts and interviews on Fox News incited many to label him an Islamophobe. Johnny would run into him at military trade shows, where they would reminiscence about their days in the Corps until Gatterton went off on a rant about how certain government officials were traitors and working to undermine the country. When Johnny would mention Gatterton's name to colleagues, they would grow wide-eyed and say, "Yeah, I saw that guy on the news. He's really out there. He doesn't give a shit. He calls out the entire government. And now he's got a huge target on his back." The mad liberals and the jihadis both wanted to silence him forever.

If there was any man out there who could advise Johnny on what to do, it was Gatterton. He spoke often about how jihadis actively recruited young people on college campuses, using Muslim Student Associations as fronts for their activities. The UNC Wilmington campus had an active MSA, and Daniel had worked with Muslim students like that kid who had won the engineering competition.

Johnny took a deep breath and ordered his phone to "Call Mark Gatterton."

A few seconds later came a familiar voice: "Hey, Johnny, you old rock star, what're you doing now?"

"I'm in the truck."

"What's going on?"

"Where are you?"

"Still home in Arlington. I don't fly out until next week."

"Good, I'll need you here in a day or two. We're burying my brother and his wife."

"Shit, Johnny, I'm sorry. What happened? Car accident?"

"Nah, it was a home invasion."

"You kidding me? God damn it."

"Yeah, sorry to call with the bad news."

"They catch the guys?"

"Not yet."

"If you want me to look into it—"

"No, no, the boys here are all over it."

"Well, all right then, no problem. I'll be there. You can count on it."

"Good, I'll text you the details."

Gatterton's tone softened. "How're you doing? You hanging in there?"

"Doing the best I can. We'll catch up when you get down here."

"Roger that. And Johnny, you call me if you need anything. Anything at all."

"I will. Thanks, Mark."

Johnny hung up. It was just good to hear his friend's voice, even though they could not speak openly over their phones. Gatterton's regular line was no doubt being monitored by the alphabet soup of intelligence and law enforcement agencies.

Then again, Johnny was still reluctant to tell anyone, not until he learned the truth—because what if Daniel had converted to Islam? What if he had been in bed with drug smugglers and terrorists? Generations of Johnny's family had dedicated their lives to the United States. To learn that his own flesh and blood could have done something like this... How could Johnny *ever* live that down?

* * *

The flooring guy was a gray-haired Lynyrd Skynyrd fan with a camouflage ball cap on backwards and a pony-tail swinging like an errant snake beneath the brim. At least ten different grout colors had stained his jeans and concert shirt into an abstract mosaic, yet his light brown work boots looked freshly drawn from a Wal-Mart shelf. The right side of his face was swollen from all the chewing tobacco he had jammed between his cheek and gum, and he spit occasionally into an old soda can he had cut in half and had carried with him into the house.

A cleaning crew had already done battle with the hardwood floor, lifting the blood pools and restoring the wood to a rich sheen. Now it was up to Mr. Bernard Truehall to chisel out all that stained grout in the kitchen. "Y'all know I can remove the blood," he had told Johnny. "Just wish I could do somethin' more to make ya feel better. I'm very sorry."

The home, Johnny assumed, would be left to Daniel's daughters, and he wondered if they would keep it. Were it his, he would wait a year, then put it on the market and unload it fast, before anyone remembered it was the "Holly Ridge Murder House." Of course there were always some unscrupulous real estate scumbags who could pick it up and either flip it or lease it to unsuspecting buyers or tenants. Those investor pricks could care less what had happened to the prior owners. A more radical idea would be to hang on to the property, bulldoze the place, and start fresh. He would present all these ideas to the girls... but in due time.

"You can stay or come back. This'll take me a few hours," Truehall told Johnny. "I can lock up for you, too."

"That's fine, you get going," Johnny answered. He gave the man the barest of nods, then found himself walking a little too quickly into the master bedroom, where he started on a tall chest of drawer's on Daniel's side of the room. Boxers, socks. Did anyone still wear Argyle socks? At the same time, Johnny's phone beeped with multiple text messages.

From Elina: Please call me when you can. We want to do dinner here.

From the funeral home: Mr. Johansen, we have a few more things to discuss, if you can call us back.

From Willie: You okay? Dinner's at your house, and we're all coming.

"Hey, Johnny?" called Truehall from the kitchen. "You got company."

Johnny sighed and left the bedroom, winding his way to the front door. Chief Schneider was standing there as Truehall slipped by him, bringing in some of his tools. "Bernie's an ace, Johnny. No worries there."

"Thanks for the recommendation."

"Paul tells me you were up at the university."

Johnny steeled himself. "Yeah, I'm trying to get a handle on all this. It's going to take me a year to pack up his office. Might get my nieces to help."

"I know Paul warned you about interfering, and I'll just emphasize that. I know you Marines can't leave well enough alone, but this time, I'm telling you, Johnny, you need to remember that these things are very delicate and lawyers can twist shit like you wouldn't believe. I need you on our side."

"Absolutely."

"Well, don't bullshit me, son. You need to stand down."

Sure. Easy day, no drama, Johnny thought. *I have a brick of Cocaine, the keys to a storage facility, and a note written in Arabic.*

He answered aloud, "I'm standing down, Chief. All day long."

"Good. This punk can't hide from us. We'll get him."

"I'm counting on you."

"I know it, Johnny. Now can I say, you're looking rough. You got no color. Get your ass home and eat, all right? Come on..." Schneider threw an arm over Johnny's shoulder and led him outside.

Johnny could have resisted, but it would be nice to decompress over dinner. He needed time to further appreciate the enormity of his discovery, and he needed to plot his next move a lot more carefully than his last one. Allowing the police to learn of his visit to the university was a rookie mistake. He should have remembered they were talking to Daniel's assistant.

"You can trust Bernie with everything," the chief said. "When he's done, he'll secure the place for you. He's good people."

"Roger that."

They reached Johnny's truck, and before he climbed inside, the chief lifted his chin. "Paul said there was something your brother wanted to tell you."

"Yeah, but it was probably nothing."

"Maybe he wanted to say how lucky he was."

"Lucky?"

"That's right—to have a brother like you."

Johnny snorted. "I doubt it, Dennis, but I appreciate it."

"You bet. Go eat. Get some sleep."

Johnny climbed into the cab and shut the door. He could almost feel the heat billowing off the package near his feet. What did the note say? What was inside that storage facility? What had Daniel been doing with a block of Colombian cocaine?

For just a moment, Johnny considered what would happen if he discarded the box...

...if he wrote off his brother's death as a terrible tragedy...

...if he let those secrets rest with the dead.

He could probably do that.

If he were not a Marine.

Chapter Ten

"You're asking if I think Johnny has PTSD? Dude, who doesn't have it? We used to joke that Marines don't have skeletons in their closets 'cause the bodies are always fresh. But all we really have in there is everything... everything we can't forget."

—Corey McKay (FBI interview, 23 December)

Edward Senecal and his wife Mimi held vigil in Emile's room at St. Michael's Hospital. Down below, the rush hour traffic pulsed through Toronto. Their son's attending physicians were en route to update them regarding Emile's status. Like most doctors, they were running late, and Senecal felt like a dog on a leash, tugging his way between the window and the door, his stomach churning.

Since being ruthlessly battered by those Muslim boys, Emile had yet to open his blackened eyes, and the brain swelling had continued. Senecal and his wife had not left the hospital. The nurses were pleasant and professional, offering to buy food and provide anything else they might need. While Senecal and his wife smiled politely, their eyes remained grim. Mimi stood over their son and was visibly trembling. Seeing her like that drove Senecal to the bed, where he clutched her hand, trying to offer her something firm and stable, trying to be the man she needed right now. Behind them, the doctors entered with a somber greeting.

"We need some good news," Senecal muttered. "Anything you have." This was unfamiliar territory for him. In every aspect of his life, he was in control. At work, he was always spearheading the conversation, even with potential clients. He was never at someone else's mercy.

The leonine Dr. Kamran was the taller of the two physicians, with a well-manicured beard and semi-rimless glasses. His associate, the cherubic Dr. Levin, was clean-shaven and wore his graying blond hair slicked back with gel. Kamran cleared his throat and consulted a tablet computer. "Mr. and Mrs. Senecal, we know this is an incredibly difficult time for you, and it's hard to think clearly. But we need to pause now to review your son's injuries and his response to treatment. Then we'll discuss our observations. We've made those together and independently."

"We just need to know... Will he make it?" Mimi blurted out. "Can you save him? Please, god, tell us you can. That's all we want."

Senecal squeezed her hand. "Mimi, please, let's listen."

"Emile came in with very serious injuries," Kamran said. "Critical injuries. We made sure you understood that during our first consultation."

Senecal nodded anxiously. "You made that very clear."

Kamran pursed his lips, glanced at his partner, then continued, "The trauma Emile received to his extremities, to his nose, and to his lungs were manageable, but the blunt force injuries to his brain were significant, and those injuries are irreversible."

"What does that mean?" Mimi asked.

"I'll explain," answered Kamran. "First, we have very specific guidelines to determine brain death in children, and we followed those to the letter."

Senecal flicked his gaze to Emile, his only son lying in a cocoon of tubes and wires. "My boy is brain dead?"

It was Dr. Stone's turn to speak: "Dr. Kamran's neurologic examination indicated that Emile met the legal criteria for brain death. After a shortened interval, I was able to conduct my own exam and apnea test, and I'm afraid I reached the same conclusion. We even brought in a third physician, which we don't have to do, and he concurs. While Emile feels warm to the touch and seems to be breathing, his brain isn't helping with those functions. He's in a persistent vegetative state. Without mechanical assistance, he would pass away in a day, a few days, maybe a week or two. We don't know. Of course mere words can't express how terribly sorry we are."

Mimi tore her hand out of Senecal's grip and drifted to the window. She began sobbing loudly, leaving Senecal to face the two doctors, who despite being veterans of similar conversations were both glassy-eyed and obviously moved.

"We know this will take some time," Dr. Kamran said. "And we assure you that everyone at St. Michael's understands that. But it's important that you know all the facts."

"What else is there?"

"Well, because your son will be legally classified as brain dead, we recommend that his ventilator be removed, and that we allow him to pass on naturally. I wish there was something else we could do, but there isn't."

Senecal swung around and shut his eyes. The darkness gave way to their street, to Emile screaming for help as he was clubbed to the ground. Senecal reached out, but a numbing force held him back. He wrenched open his eyes and balled his hands into fist. "Are you sure about this? I don't know anything about the kinds of tests you conduct."

Dr. Kamran softened his tone. "Mr. Senecal, the examinations were performed with great care. As Dr. Stone mentioned, we even brought in a third colleague, just to be absolutely certain."

"So my boy is not coming back."

"I'm afraid he's not."

"Mr. Senecal, I understand what you're feeling right now," said Dr. Stone.

Senecal's voice cracked. "My boy's gone, and you're telling me you understand?"

"I lost my own boy to cancer last year," Stone explained. "He was just a year older than Emile."

"I'm sorry."

This repulsive feeling, this helplessness, was completely alien. Here he was, a captain of industry, yet he was no longer at the helm of his own life. His boy had been taken, and there was nothing he could do. Emile was going to learn how to be a man. He was going to take over the businesses. And that was just the beginning...

Senecal glanced past the doctors to the armed security guards outside the door. He lifted his palms, as if to surrender. "All right, look, I'm okay."

"You will be," said Dr. Stone. "You'll get even more angry. You'll have thoughts that scare you. We've provided some recommendations for grief counseling. You should go. I did. It works."

Senecal could not mask his skepticism. "Look, I don't need to talk to anyone right now except my wife. And you're not doing anything with my boy until we say so."

"Of course," Dr. Kamran said. "And again, if you can't make the decision on your own, we can help."

"What kind of world do we live in, when something like this happens?" Senecal asked the doctors. "You tell me? What kind of a world?"

"Mr. Senecal, you're very upset right now," said Kamran.

"They killed my boy."

106

"You can't change that, but what you can do now is focus on your wife and your daughter. You'll need to make the best decision for them. This is a tragedy, and the longer you delay the inevitable, the longer you wait until the healing begins. As we've said, there's nothing more we can do. Now it's up to you."

Senecal turned to Mimi, who was kissing Emile's forehead. He studied her a moment, then faced the doctor. "They killed my boy."

Senecal's mind filled with a cold rationale for the horrors he was about to unleash.

* * *

Johnny had an eight-gun security safe in his downstairs office. The safe was equipped with a heavy green door and key lock. The door was splotched with stickers from Sig Sauer, the National Rifle Association, Reliance Tactical Supply Company, and other manufacturers of firearms and tactical gear.

With the shipping box tucked under his arm, Johnny entered the house through the garage and headed directly into the office. He opened the safe and squeezed the package onto the shelf above his rifles. Once again, the paranoia reared its ugly head. Chief Schneider handed him a search warrant, then opened the safe and lifted the block of cocaine.

"All right, son, you got something you want to tell me?"

"Not really, Chief. Want a beer?"

Johnny grabbed one from the refrigerator and headed upstairs, into the living room, where everyone had gathered around the dinner table.

After taking his chair, Johnny cleared his throat and said, "Look, I don't want any awkward stuff. Let's eat and relax. We sure as hell need it. I'm glad you're all here."

"Me, too," said Elina.

That broke the ice. Conversations began and plates were filled. During the meal, Johnny told them about the cleaning and grout replacement at Daniel's house, and his nieces said they were unsure they could ever go back. Maybe someone else could get their stuff, and they should probably sell the house. Johnny comforted them by saying he and Elina would go with them to the front door. They could decide then if they wanted to step inside or not. The girls half-heartedly agreed. While it was painful to do now, they needed to remember how Daniel and Reva lived, not how they died. That house and its contents still represented a life well-lived.

And it might also hold more secrets.

After dinner, Johnny and the others retired to the cave, where those dusty bottles of whiskey came down from the shelves. The first commandment was to get drunk, and the shot glasses were summarily filled. Johnny took his and dropped onto the sofa, but he was not there. He was at Daniel's house, searching behind pieces of art, lifting mattresses, and ransacking his brother's home office. He pulled out the desk drawers, got on his hands and knees, and strained his neck to spy anything taped onto the bottom of those drawers, like he had seen on old crime-drama TV shows. He searched the inner breast pockets of every suit jacket Daniel owned. He lifted the tank covers of each of the four toilet bowls. He shone a flashlight behind the washer and dryer.

"Hello, Johnny, you with us?" Willie asked.

"Now I am. Just went somewhere for a little while."

"Elina says the wake's tomorrow, and the funeral's the day after," Josh said. "Who'd you go with?"

"Andrews."

"They do a great job."

Johnny glanced over at the hallway, and from his position, he could barely make out his gun safe. "How's the proposal?"

"To be honest, we haven't done shit on it," Corey said. "It's hard to wrap our heads around it, you know? We'll get back."

"Roger. Any of you guys talk to Band-Aid recently? Know how he's doing?"

Josh and Corey shook their heads. Willie frowned and said, "Last I heard, he was still working over at the marina."

Johnny nodded. "I talked to him back in, what was that, August, when I brought the boat down there."

Sergeant Ashur Bandar, the interpreter attached to Johnny's platoon during that night raid in Fallujah, had been paralyzed from the waist down. He had chosen to settle in North Carolina, where his cousin had a house and where Johnny and the guys kept in touch, using his nickname, "Band-Aid." Despite having earned his college degree, Bandar took odd jobs that lasted no more than a few months before someone pissed him off and he had another of his infamous meltdowns, where he would scream, "Stop telling me you understand! You don't understand! Stop trying to make me feel grateful for the things I have! Stop turning me into your welfare project! My life is not your project!"

Johnny had helped Bandar find work at a marina in Hampstead, where the former terp had learned how to fix boat motors and where he could explode to his heart's content since the place was owned by another veteran Marine, Dominick Sattler, who understood Bandar's angst and knew where it was coming from. They joked about renaming the place "Dysfunctional Veterans Marina."

"You want me to call old Band-Aid and let him know?" Josh asked.

"No, I'll do it," said Johnny.

"It was on the news. He probably heard," Willie said. "And if he didn't see it on TV, you know how word travels."

They all nodded.

While Johnny would love to see Bandar at his brother's wake, he had another reason for asking after the man.

Ashur Bandar could read Arabic.

Johnny accepted another shot from Corey, who had just poured them all a second round. The warming in his chest took him back to a night of debauchery in the Philippines, and the pleasant numbness began around the base of his neck.

By the third shot, Johnny was lifting his finger at the boys, narrowing his gaze, and speaking like a root canal patient. "I bet you all got secrets you don't tell me. What's your secret?"

"I could tell you," said Corey. "But then I'd have to pour you another shot, and I'm too lazy to get up."

"I got nothing to hide," Willie said. "Ain't no false advertising here. What you see is what you get."

"I'm not hiding anything," said Josh. "But I ain't volunteering anything, either. You know where I'm coming from."

"You're all full of shit," Johnny said.

They replied, but his eyes had already closed, and sometime later, in the middle of night, Elina woke him and helped him upstairs and into bed.

* * *

The nightmare was different this time. Sergeant Oliver was not on the stairs, about to leap on the grenade, Daniel was. He wore Oliver's uniform and shouted that he was the sheepdog, just before—

Johnny shook awake. He lay there on the sweaty sheets, panting. He reached blindly for the night stand and grabbed his phone to check the time. 1459. Really? He glanced out the window. Sunshine. Well there it was. The exhaustion, stress, and alcohol had sent him into a twenty-hour coma that felt like twenty years. Did cars now fly and robots cut the grass? He sat up and scuffled toward the bathroom.

"Johnny, are you up?" Elina called from the hallway. She told him to get in the shower. They were taking his nieces out for an early dinner before the wake at seven. Johnny told her okay, then he returned to the night stand and called Bandar.

"Band-Aid, how you doing?"

"What's up, Johnny, I know why you're calling."

"So you coming? The wake's at The Market Street Chapel at seven. I would love for you to be there."

"You can count on me, Johnny."

"Hey, dude, you sound like you just got up."

"So do you."

"I got an excuse."

Bandar paused. "I don't."

"Well, get your ass cleaned up. I'll see you later."

* * *

The Market Street Chapel, part of Andrews Mortuary and Crematory, was an old southern home constructed in the Georgian style back in the 1920s. The grand entrance foyer and smaller anterooms were furnished with sofas and chairs covered in rich fabrics. Wainscoting and elaborate window treatments featuring heavy draperies created bold, ornate statements across the walls. Dozens of oversized floral arrangements formed a semi-circle reaching all the way to the chapel entrance. As Johnny stepped inside, he was awestruck by the outpouring of support. Dozens of people stood on line, waiting to enter the viewing room, while dozens more loitered in the foyer. Elina had coordinated with Reva's parents so that the viewings and burials were together, as they should be. Reva's father, wearing white to the wake as was customary by Hindus, grabbed Johnny by the arm and began introducing him to Reva's sisters, her cousins, their children, their cousins, and Johnny feared he would be there all night if he did not escape. He politely slipped away and wandered toward the back of the room, where Josh and Willie had convened.

Josh slapped him on the shoulder. "Look at all this. Everybody's here for you, bro. Because of who you are. Don't forget that."

"And don't run away," added Willie. "Because you have an entire battalion coming to pay their respects."

Corey and Lindsey walked up, and Lindsey gave Johnny a deep hug. "That's a really nice suit."

His cheeks warmed. "I was praying it still fit."

A dark-haired man, not quite six feet, with a day's worth of stubble on his square chin, finished signing the guest book, then shouldered his way through the crowd. Only someone like Johnny would notice the man's gait and peg him as a former operator. He took Johnny's hand in his own, then gave him a deep hug. "Very sorry about your loss."

They drew back and Johnny nodded. "Are we being recorded?"

Mark Gatterton snorted then pointed to his heart. "If you see a laser dot, hit the deck."

"No, shit."

Gatterton smiled. "It's good to see you, Johnny. Wish it wasn't like this."

"Me, too."

Gatterton already knew everyone, so the introductions were spared. Despite Willie's admonishment, Johnny excused himself for a moment, then pulled Gatterton aside and said, "You doing any research on the drug trade? Links to jihadis and coke coming out of Colombia?"

"No, but I guess you are. Where's this coming from?"

"Ah, it's work-related. Figured I'd ask you before the storm hits and I forget."

"No talking about work now."

"Just real quick."

"Look, Johnny, you got Corey and Josh over there. They were down in South America. They know Colombia better than I do. And what about your consultant working for the DEA?"

"I thought you might have some current intel."

"It ain't earth shattering, I'll tell you that. Same old shit. FARC rebels in bed with jihadis. Money pouring in from the Middle East. Coke coming up the pipe. Narco subs. The whole nine." Gatterton snorted. "You thinking about a career change?"

"No, wiseass. I'm thinking about some lost opportunities close to home."

"You phrased that very carefully."

"What do you mean?"

"You want answers, but you can't ask the right questions."

"Mark, you know I've always... I wish I could—"

"What?"

Johnny sighed.

Gatterton leaned in closer. "I don't work for the FBI anymore. You can talk to me."

"You're right. This isn't the time." Johnny squeezed Gatterton's shoulder, thanked him again for coming, and said they would catch up later or tomorrow.

"Hey, Johnny, if you need me to call in a few favors to get things moving here, you let me know. Some of my old friends from the bureau still love me. Why? Because I call out their pussy supervisors in all of my lectures!"

Johnny winked and headed off. He got ten feet before a squad of veteran Marines surrounded him; these hard chargers had flown in from all over the country. After shaking what had to be thirty hands and getting choked up, he rubbed his eyes, found Elina, and they settled down on one of the couches.

"This is a beautiful thing," she said.

"What?"

"Seeing all of our friends... and how much they care."

"You're trying to make me cry."

She smacked him on the arm. "You know what I mean."

"Yeah."

She raised her brows. "So, did you pay your respects?"

"Not yet."

"What're you waiting for?"

"I don't know."

"You need to go up there. You don't have to say anything or do anything."

"Maybe I'll wait till the end."

"That's fine."

They sat for another minute, then Elina was dragged off by Reva's mother, and Johnny did a brief recon, searching for Bandar. He asked the guys, but none of them had seen him. There were four or five disabled vets inside the chapel, but only Bandar could read that cursive script in Johnny's safe.

Johnny's nieces left the chapel, and Johnny followed. They paused on the walk-way, and Isabelle buried her head in Kate's shoulder.

"Hey, we're strong," Johnny said, marching up to them. His slid his arm around both girls and added, "We can do this."

Kate shook her head. "No, we can't Uncle Johnny. We can't. All this religion and God. It's all bullshit. Look what happens."

"You know what your dad used to tell me? He said no matter how smart he got, God was always smarter. I thought he'd go off to school and become an atheist, while I found God in a foxhole, you know? But your dad never stopped believing. That's what our parents instilled in us. We were Southern Baptists but we didn't go to church much. Didn't matter, though, because we learned to have faith in God."

"So you think God had a purpose for murdering our mom and Dad?" Kate asked, glaring at him.

Johnny lowered his voice. "God didn't do that. Some evil bastard did. And we'll catch him. And he'll pay."

"I like the way you interpret religion, Uncle Johnny."

"Sometimes you can't keep your eye on the target if you turn the other cheek. I know that sounds wrong. It's not something your dad would ever agree with, but that's the way it is for me. Your dad ever sit down and talk to you about God?"

"Not really. Mom made us learn about Hinduism, but we never got into it."

"Your dad ever mention changing his religion?"

"You mean become Hindu like mom?"

"Uh, yeah, sure."

"I don't think so."

Isabelle slid away from her sister, backhanded tears from her eyes, and said, "I thought he wanted to become a Muslim."

Johnny's jaw dropped. "Really?"

"Yeah, because he was always talking about these students and how they were like geniuses, and they all had names like Mohammed and Abdul, whatever. He used to make us feel bad because those guys were so smart. I was like, Dad, if you love them so much, why don't you go hang out at the mosque? Sometimes he didn't even ask about us. He was just talking about them."

Johnny shrugged. "Your dad was a great teacher. He was excited about his students. But you guys always came first. Don't think for a minute you didn't. He loved you more than anything. You don't forget that."

Ivonne and Jada arrived at Johnny's side, and his pleading look said it all. They took over consoling the girls, while he returned to the chapel and began catching up with more of the guests. The conversations lasted another hour, until the last of them headed off to their cars, leaving Johnny and Elina alone. The utter silence reminded him of diving, of heading down to two atmospheres, then another thirty-four feet to three, then four... the pressure mounting on his shoulders.

He walked up to his sister-in-law's casket and frowned as he studied her dress and hair. They did everything they could to accentuate her beauty, but she still resembled a wax figure. Without planning it, without even thinking about it, he whispered, "He was lucky to have you. I know we didn't get along at first, but I'm glad we both came around. You didn't deserve this."

Johnny walked over to his brother's casket. At Johnny's insistence, Daniel's beard had been trimmed to a quarter inch and his hair cut regulation short. They looked like brothers again, old Army brats, and Johnny found it hard to believe that the shipping box and its contents had ever belonged to this man who shared his blood. Maybe they did not. Maybe someone had grabbed one of Daniel's empty boxes and hid the materials in his office. But why? To frame him for something? Was someone coming back for the box? Johnny's head began to throb as a migraine took hold, another byproduct of the stress.

* * *

They were burying Daniel and Reva in the morning, and Johnny was not feeling very well, so he asked to be left alone for the night. Once he, Elina, and his nieces had returned to the house, he took a few aspirins, then sprawled out with the dogs on his living room sofa. He put on the Military Channel, then lifted his phone and scrolled through some photos. He found a picture of Daniel and zoomed in on his brother's eyes, as though he could find an encrypted message in the mottled brown reflections.

He sat up. He had time. He could drive over to that storage facility in Sneads Ferry. He could do it right now.

Or not. Maybe he should wait until after the funeral. But why? Would that really make a difference? Or was that just another excuse?

Slow down, Marine. If he made any moves, they would be planned, rehearsed, and executed to ensure success. No witnesses, no loose ends of any kind. Swift, silent, deadly.

Elina came in from the kitchen and hunkered down at the edge of the couch. She put a hand on his cheek and whispered, "You're a good man, Johnny Johansen."

"Maybe I'm not. Look here, what if one day you woke up, and you found out I was somebody else? I lied about who I was."

"I don't know. Why are you asking me that?"

"Imagine I'm this Russian spy."

"No, you're just crazy."

"So I'm this spy, and I get arrested, and now everyone knows that Johnny Johansen was no Marine. He was a traitor. How would you feel?"

Elina eyed him as though he were a teenaged boy. "What do you want me to say, Johnny? I'd feel terrible. I'd be embarrassed, I guess. Then I'd go on the talk shows and make money so I could pay all your legal bills."

"Imagine that. Would you forgive me?"

"I would have to forgive you."

"Why?"

She rolled her eyes. "Because I love you."

Johnny took enormous comfort in that, more than she would ever know. "You're a good woman, Elina Johansen."

She leaned in for a kiss.

Chapter Eleven

"Not all prisoners are behind bars. The war on terror made some Marines prisoners of their wounds or prisoners of what they saw. For them, there ain't no easy day."

—Johnny Johansen (FBI interview, 23 December)

Johnny's friend Matt Bowlin had an acoustic guitar balanced on one knee as he strummed and sang one of his original songs: "Jim Beam In My Canteen Cup." Matt's lively baritone filled the entire chapel, and everything about him, from his thick black hair to his handlebar moustache to his snakeskin boots, said cowpoke. He had already released an album that was selling well on iTunes, and he was a co-star on the PBS reality show *Utopia Joe* about an Oklahoma artist and his wife who created amazing projects.

Before his rise to music and television stardom, Matt had been a battalion ammo chief and Color Guard Sergeant who had put together shooting packages for Johnny and Willie when they took their platoons out for training. He was a real class act who had earned the battalion many awards and honors. Johnny had not seen him for years, and then one day out of the blue he ambled into Buddy's Crab House and Oyster Bar near the pier on Topsail Beach. Matt was barefoot and wearing board shorts, a rash guard, and a bandanna. He apologized for looking like a hippie and getting fat, and he reminded Johnny that he used to get his bang-boom-pow for his teams. He invited Johnny and Elina to watch him play at several local clubs, and Johnny could hardly believe that this once shy Marine was wearing a dusty white cowboy hat and aviator shades and that he could belt out tunes like Waylon Jennings, Willie Nelson, and George Strait. They rekindled their friendship and remained close ever since.

After Mass, a group of over two hundred moved in an unwieldy caravan to the gravesite next door at Sea Lawn Memorial Park. It was another unusually cold day, the temperature hovering in the upper 30s, but the sky was so clear and blue that divine intervention must be at work, or at least Johnny thought so. He glanced up, tilting his cheek toward the sun. He took in a long breath through his nose, and it smelled as though it might snow. As the caskets were lowered into the ground, Matt sang, "How Great Thou Art," his voice as thick as honey and booming above the wind.

* * *

Eight hundred miles north of Wilmington, at York Cemetery in Toronto, a much smaller casket than those used to bury Daniel and Reva was positioned above a rectangular hole. Instead of two hundred mourners, a mere twenty stood in a broken semi-circle around the gravesite. While dozens of employees, clients, and business partners had expressed their condolences and desire to attend the funeral, Edward Senecal and his wife had allowed only the immediate family.

Nicholas Dresden and his wife Victoria were there, of course, standing beneath their umbrellas in the freezing rain and listening intently to the priest:

"Lord God, source and destiny of our lives, in your loving providence you gave us Emile to grow in wisdom, age, and grace. Now you have called him to yourself. We grieve over the loss of one so young and struggle to understand your purpose. Draw him to yourself and give him full stature in Christ. May he stand with all the angels and saints, who know your love and praise your saving will. We ask this through Jesus Christ, our Lord. Amen."

Dresden could barely meet the gazes of Edward and Mimi, whose faces could not be more stricken. He had not seen his partner since that night at the hospital, and their only communication had been a few text messages regarding business or the funeral details.

Afterward, on their way back to the cars, Senecal waved him over. Dresden braced himself and crossed the wet lawn, tilting his umbrella into the wind.

Pale and with bloodshot eyes, Senecal seized Dresden's hand and said, "Nick, what can I say? This is the worst day of my life."

Dresden groped for a reply. "It was a beautiful service, and Victoria and I want to express our deepest condolences."

"Thanks. We need to talk."

"Here?"

"Absolutely. So what do we have, Nick? We have an administration running wild with executive orders. We have an election coming up that could tank our businesses. I can't click on a news site without wanting to throw my phone across the room. Everything I see and hear tells me we've made the right decision."

"Eddie, we shouldn't talk about this here, and not today."

"I just spoke with our friend in Washington. We'll need good coordination with UXD, EXSA, and Smith to keep things rolling."

Dresden's heart sank. "It was just a crazy idea. That's all it was."

"Come on, Nick, don't you remember our plan to change the world?"

"I remember. But this isn't about business anymore."

"What happened to my boy is symptomatic of the problem. And we have the will and the means to correct that problem."

"You can't use rhetoric to deny what this really is, and what's at stake."

"All we're doing is opening the public's eyes. They'll cry for us and our friends to protect them, like we always have."

"But how we get there is the problem."

Senecal raised his brows. "We both know our history. The tree of liberty must be refreshed from time to time with the blood of patriots."

"You're going to invoke Jefferson to justify this?"

"Think about it, Nick. There's no more bold statement than one written in blood."

Dresden's pulse quickened. "Eddie, you need to slow down. I want you to stay away from the office, and in a few days we'll have a long conversation about all of this, weighing our options before we do anything. It's not too late."

"You have to admire one thing," Senecal began, ignoring Dresden. "You have to admire my long term thinking. I could exact short term revenge, but I can see the big picture. I see a new America and a new Canada."

"I see the inside of a jail cell."

Senecal chuckled under his breath. "We're all prisoners of our own mortality. And so we do this for future generations."

"Eddie, I've been doing a lot of soul-searching."

"Really? I thought we'd already sold ours years go."

"Eddie, listen to me. I can't involve any of my companies in this."

"Sure you can. No more hedging those bets. You want to believe in something? Believe in this: we're the only ones audacious enough to pull this off."

"Don't do anything else without me."

"The ball's in play. We're moving fast. I don't want to hang a scandal over your head or threaten you into this. That's ridiculous. You've thought about it as much as I have. You wanted it as much as I do. And besides, I have a surprise for you."

"What's that?"

Senecal smiled tightly. "You'll see. Now come on. They're waiting for us."

Dresden fell in behind his partner, feeling the bile rise at the back of his throat. Yes, Eddie probably did have enough evidence to hang a trading scandal or two over his head, in which case he would wind up in jail anyway. And what was this surprise? Given his partner's state of mind, Dresden feared the answer. He imagined a car accident on the way to the brunch, with Senecal's limousine t-boned by a tractor-trailer, killing everyone. He shuddered over the thought and climbed into his car.

* * *

Johnny walked from the gravesite to a pair of oaks, where he and Elina shook hands with and hugged their guests. Reuniting with so many old friends reminded Johnny that his life had not been wasted, that years spent putting people together and making shit happen really meant something to them. To him. It took more than thirty minutes for him to say good-bye to those not coming back to the house for brunch, including Mark Gatterton.

"I was hoping to stay, Johnny, but I'll need to catch a flight out. My schedule for next week got messed up."

"That's okay. I appreciate you coming."

"It was good to see you."

"We've known each other for what, fifteen years, maybe more?"

"At least."

"That's a long time."

Gatterton narrowed his gaze. "I'll ask you one last time: what's going on?"

Johnny shrugged. "You still play with those prepaids?"

"I do."

"Here's my Burner number. Get one and call me on it."

Gatterton's eyes widened. "Roger that."

After a brief hug, Johnny watched the man shouldered his way through the crowd of dark suits and dress blue bravos.

* * *

Back at the house, Josh removed his jacket, rolled up his sleeves, and helped Jada, Ivonne, and Lindsey set up for the brunch. They had brought in catering orders from several different restaurants, and Josh was lighting up the Sterno with a promise that he would not set fire to the house. When he glanced up, he caught Johnny staring at the tattoo on his forearm: *I am my brother's keeper.* He smiled and asked, "You hungry, Johnny?"

"Starving."

"Me, too."

Johnny winked. "That was a good service."

"Matt did an awesome job. He's out on the pier right now, getting set up with the band. It's warming up outside."

"Yeah, it is."

Josh lowered his voice. "You hear anything else from the police? I saw Schneider there, but I didn't want to ask."

"Nothing. They're hoping the guy hits another house."

"If he's smart, he'll lay low after this. I had a theory. Guy's a junkie. That's what made him so desperate. But we don't have to talk about that now."

Johnny agreed, and then he got roped off by Elina, who wanted him to roll the beer cooler onto the porch. Willie and Corey slipped up beside Josh, and Willie asked, "How is he?"

"He seems okay, but he's got a weird look on his face."

"What do you expect?" asked Corey.

"No, his mind... you can almost see the gears grinding. Something's going on, but I don't know what."

"He'll talk when he's ready," said Willie.

* * *

By 1400 most of the guests were departing, and by 1500, it was just the immediate family and the guys. Corey and Willie were transferring bulging trash bags to the bin in the garage, while Josh went down to the man cave to collect the dozens of empty beer cans he had arranged on the bar like bowling pins because of his OCD. Josh checked the office, then went out the door and inspected the driveway. Johnny's truck was gone. He sent off a text, and Johnny replied: be right back.

Another hour went by, and Josh grew more concerned. Playing a hunch, he drove over to Daniel's house, where he found Johnny's car parked in the driveway. He tried the front door: open. He stepped in, crossed into the kitchen, then heard some scuffling from the garage. There, he found the attic staircase open. He mounted the stairs, reached the top, and found Johnny, sweaty and covered in fiberglass as he tore insulation from the roof.

"Yo, Johnny, what the hell are you doing?"

"The girls will own this house, and I guess the home inspector will check out this insulation when it comes time to sell."

"What're you talking about? Why are you pulling it away from the roof? Are you looking for something?"

"What would I find up here?"

"I don't know."

"Hey, you realize Band-Aid never showed up at the funeral?"

"Why are you changing the subject?"

"Look, I don't know what I'm doing." Johnny lowered himself onto one of the crossbeams and wiped dust from his forehead.

"You think your brother hid something?"

"Who knows?"

"Why don't you come home? You're going through some shit. Better to work it out where there's beer."

"Roger that. Let me ask you something, man to man. You be honest with me. What did you think of my brother?"

Josh opened his mouth.

"Wait," Johnny said. "I'll let you off the hook. You guys thought he was a pussy. Definitely not a warrior."

"I wouldn't call him that," Josh said. "When I first met him, I thought it was funny that you two were brothers, because you were opposites. It was like the brains and the brawn. I thought your brother was a smart man and a good father. He was very well spoken. I liked talking with him. He knew a lot about politics. He told good stories about you guys growing up. And he never made me feel dumb."

Johnny cupped a hand over his eyes.

"Aw, dude, I didn't mean to..."

"It's okay. Let's get down."

They descended into the garage, where through watery eyes Johnny glanced around and said, "You ever see a garage with no tools? He didn't fix shit. He always paid for someone to do it. I tried to teach him, but he wouldn't listen. You'd be lucky to find a goddamned screwdriver around here."

"Not everyone is mechanically inclined."

"I don't know. Some things are just man skills, and Dan didn't have a knack for any of them. He was always with his nose in a book or banging on a computer."

Josh ran a hand over Reva's BMW, which they had moved into the garage. "What are you doing with the cars?"

"Don't know. His lawyer should be calling me soon. I know he had a living will and a trust for the girls."

Josh nodded. "I'm driving up to Washington tomorrow, but I wish I wasn't."

"Why do you say that?"

"I feel like I'm bailing on you."

"You're not. We need you up there."

"Okay. So, you're not lying to me about anything?"

"What're you talking about?"

"It's me. Josh. I feel like I've known you my whole life. You know how to deal with death. You're not losing your mind. You're pulling down that insulation because you know something. You think that whatever Daniel wanted to tell you is the reason why he was killed."

"You trying to call my bluff, son, or what?"

"I just know what I see."

"Look here, I tore up this house. I even looked under all the drawers, and I didn't find anything, so there you go. My theory is shot. Imagine that."

"But if you find something, you'll let us know."

Johnny's grin was tentative at best. "Oh, yeah."

"You found something already, didn't you."

"What are you talking about?"

"That's why you're here. You got a lead."

"I got nothing, dude."

"The girls tell you something?"

"Forget it. Let's go."

Josh sighed. "Are you sure?"

"Look, if I had something, we'd be all over it like a fat kid on a cupcake, right?"

Josh allowed himself a smile. "Yes, we would."

"All right, then."

As they left the garage, Josh thought, *You're lying to me, Johnny. I wish I knew why.*

* * *

Elina came out of the bathroom and slipped into bed with Johnny. He lay there, with an arm draped over his forehead, just staring at the ceiling.

"How are you, Johnny?"

"I'm here."

"Somehow we made it through."

"We did."

"So you went back to the house..."

"Yeah, I was just looking around for anything that... I don't know."

She slipped in closer and wrapped her arms around him. "We'll be okay."

"I guess they had a good run, right? Just... God, they weren't even fifty."

"They were too young. Anyway, the girls will stay here until the end of the month. They'll go back to school in January."

"All right."

"We have an appointment tomorrow with the grief counselor."

"You know how it is. I'll go for you."

"You need to get it out."

Johnny took a long breath, then closed his eyes. "We got that big flagpole out back. It's the biggest one in the entire neighborhood. It's like a beacon. I buy the best flags. People around here, they know who I am. Twenty-three years in the Marine Corps. That shit is real."

"Yes, it is."

"Well, who knows, by tomorrow I could go from *he*-ro to *ze*-ro."

"What do you mean?"

"Ah, who knows what I'm saying anymore."

"Stop thinking so much. You're scaring me. Tomorrow, we'll stay home with the girls, and we'll go see the counselor, and we'll have a nice lunch. Maybe we'll go over to Buddy's. Or I'll twist your arm so you take us to the Thai place."

"It's all good. I just have one errand to run in the morning."

Chapter Twelve

"We own the night by limiting the number of variables. We plan, we rehearse, and we use familiar gear. You train as you fight. Even tactards like you know that. So when that shit went down in Detroit, I knew exactly what we were looking at."

—Willie Parente (FBI interview, 23 December)

Johnny drove up the gravel driveway of Sattler Marina and its neighboring dry stack facility in Hampstead. He parked and hopped out, clutching his olive drab ball cap lest it fly off his head. Black Mud Channel, which lay behind the main repair shop, churned hard in the gale, and the American and POW/MIA flags atop the tall poles out front were rattling to the high heavens. As he neared the front door, the whining, humming, and buzzing of multiple power tools rose like rock guitarists warming up before a show.

The repair shop was about 5,000 square feet, with at least six boats under simultaneous repair by as many crews. Anyone unable to tolerate the smell of diesel fuel or grease or hot wax or burning rubber for any length of time would do well to keep their visits brief. The place smelled like summer to Johnny, and he could stay there all day long. He was reminded of getting his boat repaired, of watermelon, of corn on the cob, and of flounder fishing at night. He found Dominick Sattler up to his elbows in a Mercury outboard, his forearm tattoos covered in grease, his hair tied back in a ponytail. "Hey, Johnny, long time no see."

"Yeah, not since yesterday, right? So how you doing this morning?"

"Well, thank God it's Friday. This is the second powerhead I've put in this bitch in two weeks. I've had issues with both of them. Can you believe that?"

"What the hell? Where's the quality control?"

"Yeah, right? I call the manufacturer, and they tell me installation error. I say, *bullshit*! Anyway, what brings you down? You got issues?"

"Not with the boat, no. I'm looking for my boy."

Sattler winced. "I didn't want to bring it up yesterday, but I haven't seen him since the night of your brother's wake. He said he'd be there."

"He told me the same."

"Yeah, and now today he's a no show. I thought he was doing pretty good for a while. Maybe one or two meltdowns a month, that's it. You were here back in what was it, August?"

"That's right. What do you think's going on?"

"Not sure this time."

"He willing to get any help?"

Sattler made a face. "You try to get him help, but you know how he hates the VA, just like everyone else now. They drive him nuts."

"I think they hate him just as much."

"Well, that's true. Anyway, you know I cut the guy a lot of slack. We're all here to be a positive force in his life. But I think he's taken a turn for the worse. It's not good when he disappears like this."

"Where he is now? At his cousin's house?"

"I would expect. I was planning to check on him at lunch."

"I'll head over."

"You been there, recently?"

"No."

Sattler winked. "Good luck with that."

* * *

Johnny parked in front of Bandar's three-bedroom ranch house, climbed out of his truck, and paused to thank God he was not the landlord or real estate agent trying to sell the place. The front lawn was a patchy carpet of overgrown straw with a few crushed beer cans lurking within. A late 80s Dodge pickup sat up on blocks in the driveway like the corpse of a dinosaur, its windshield covered in a thick tar of leaves and dirt. The quarter panels and bumpers of more cars lay against the side of the house, along with stacks of bald tires and a landscaper's trailer with a broken axle. Near the trailer were plastic garbage cans that had toppled over, spilling white kitchen bags shredded by the night critters. A rusting old basketball hoop with frayed net stood near the garage door, and the last time a ball had gone through that hoop there was a different president in the White House. The garage door itself had been repeatedly struck by an intoxicated driver (AKA a pissed off, disabled veteran Marine) and bent back into place. Obviously, the door no longer functioned and hung crookedly from its tracks. Furthering the home's obscene curb appeal was the front entrance, which had once featured a charming white porch. The porch had since collapsed from termite damage, the railings lying like splintered bones across the dead weeds. A makeshift path of milk crates bound together by kite string led up to the front door, whose window had cracked from top to bottom and was held together by eleven pieces of strategically positioned duct tape. In place of a welcome matt was a hand-written message scrawled on a brown bag and taped to the door. The message read: Fuck Off!

Bandar's handicap van was parked just ahead of Johnny's truck. The old GMC with rusting fenders teetered between the lawn and the street. This was a safer place to park when you could not judge distances to the aforementioned garage door. Bandar proudly displayed his Marine Corps bumper sticker and reluctantly hung his blue tag from the rear view mirror. His left front tire was low, and Johnny would remind him of that only after he tore the man a new one for the unsightly condition of the home. Where the hell was his cousin?

Wringing his hands, Johnny headed up the cracked concrete driveway, mounted the milk crate porch, then shook his head at the paper bag and tore it off the glass. He rang the doorbell and waited. No answer. He rang again. He tried the door, which was open, and thrust his head inside. "Hey, Band-Aid, it's Johnny."

Again, no reply. The air inside the house reeked of something that had burned on the stove, macaroni and cheese, perhaps. From another corner came the faint trace of urine. Johnny pushed open the door and surveyed the living room and kitchen beyond. Bandar's Rent-A-Center furniture looked like it had fallen off the truck en route and had been repaired by a team of blind monks equipped only with more duct tape. The love seat's arms and legs were practically mummified in silver. The sofa's cushions were ripped, the polyester stuffing bulging like puss. The tan rug beneath it all had not seen a vacuum in years. Against the far wall were boxes stacked haphazardly with their tops ripped off. Clothes, books, old video games, VHS tapes, and sports equipment spilled over the worn cardboard and across the floor.

Johnny called once more as he moved through the living room and toward the kitchen on his left. The tile felt gritty under his boots. A homemade ramp system of plywood and two-by-fours rendered the countertops and sink wheelchair accessible, although that no longer mattered. The linoleum countertops were hidden beneath so many pizza boxes, empty two liter bottles, and fast food bags that one had to assume a little league team met there nightly for dinner. Given this disaster, the sink should be overloaded with dirty dishes; that, however, was not the case. Bandar ate off paper plates and with plastic utensils that, along with dozens of beer cans, overflowed from the nearby trash bin. In point of fact, Bandar's sink was being used to store engine parts in various stages of degreasing.

Off to the right, in the nook area, sat a butcher block kitchen table sagging on one side as though it had had a stroke. Atop the table were two empty bottles of Jack Daniel's, an 8x12 photo album, and a yellow legal pad with a pen neatly positioned beside it. Johnny scanned the pad. This was the information he had given Bandar about the wake and funeral. Johnny turned back a few pages and found paragraphs from some essay or book Bandar was writing, the pen pressed so hard onto the paper that it almost cut through. He chose one paragraph at random and began to read:

Which brings me to my next issue, what we really are: disposable heroes. The pogues in D.C. pull us off a pegboard at Walmart, plop us on the battlefield, and let us perpetrate acts of violence they can't stomach or even imagine. Like Jack Nicholson said in the movie, they can't handle the truth. So we eat the shit while they hold their noses and look the other way, and everyone's happy. But if we survive, they're pissed. They wish we were killed in action. If we make it back home, they secretly pray that we'll cap ourselves so there's no chance of exposing their corruption. Those lucky enough and can still walk are on a goddamn tightrope, and there's no safety net. The only thing we got are battle brothers who can ease the fall and help uncover the lies that the pogues ram up the liberal media's ass. I'm so tired of it all. I'm so tired of living in a country where fat pussies sit at home playing video games and gorging themselves on Big Macs and Doritos until they vomit, a country where the media blows its nut every time some pop star gets into trouble but doesn't care about a Marine who bore a burden they can't even fathom. I grew up in war-torn nations. I grew up scared for my life every day. I kissed the ground when I got to this country. I was a patriot. I sacrificed my ability to walk. To be with a woman. To stand up like a man. And now I ask, What am I doing here?

Johnny had heard them all in their various incantations, the battle cries of the desperate, the depressed, and the disillusioned. He used to tell Bandar to "turn all that anger into rocket fuel—because rocket fuel lifts you up, and rock stars always fly first class."

Setting down the pad, Johnny stole a quick look at the photo album, mostly pictures of Bandar during his early days in the Marine Corps, boot camp, some of the admin shit he had done, and a series of pictures of him out on a patrol in Iraq. There was even a hard copy of a defense.gov article where Bandar had been interviewed about becoming an interpreter for the Corps. He discussed how proud he was to serve America and how his language skills would be an invaluable asset to his unit. He could communicate with friendly forces regarding enemy movements, booby traps, and so on. He could also help interrogate prisoners.

The photos, the empty bottles of whiskey, and the information about the funeral were the narrative of a wounded man desperately trying to make sense of his past, present, and future.

"Come on, Johnny, let me fight."

Johnny could have told Bandar, no, you're too valuable to go out there. But he understood what was in the Marine's heart: to prove himself worthy of the blood stripes than ran down the sides of his dress blue trousers. Those stripes represented the blood of Marines killed during the Mexican War, but as far as Johnny was concerned, they represented every Marine who had paid the ultimate price. All Bandar had wanted was to do his job, and Johnny, the platoon sergeant responsible for his safety, had given him the chance. The terp never blamed him. He didn't have to. Johnny spent weeks torturing himself over how Bandar saved their lives but had given so much in return.

With a deepening sense of urgency, Johnny left the kitchen and entered the hallway leading to the three bedrooms. Along the way, he counted three fist-sized holes in the drywall at wheelchair height. The master bedroom door was cracked open, with sunlight wedging through.

"Band-Aid? It's Johnny? Wake up call. I'm coming in."

As he drew closer, Johnny realized why that unholy smell was so familiar: Bandar's bedroom reeked like the men's room at the Trailer Bar. As the name suggested, the bar was literally a single-wide trailer, and it was one of Bandar's usual hangouts. Tensing, Johnny pushed open the door. His eyes were assaulted by freeways of dirty clothes connecting the closet with the bathroom; by more junk food Styrofoam and empty liquor bottles and stacks of pistol cases crammed onto both nightstands; and by the man himself, lying naked on his waterbed, with a pale yellow stain swelling across the white sheet like an abstract sunflower near his crotch. If only the horrors ended there. He had always been rather hairy, given his ancestry. Remove the razor from his cheeks for a few months, and you had a heavy woodsman's beard. His haircut, or lack thereof for several years, suggested he played backup guitar for Aerosmith. In just a short time he had gone from slightly unkempt veteran to desert island cannibal.

Grimacing, Johnny hustled into the room and threw open the windows, despite the wind and temperatures barely hitting fifty degrees. He needed to air out the ungodly odor. He leaned across the bed and shook Bandar several times by the shoulders. "Sergeant Band-Aid, did you pee in your rack again?"

"No, Gunny."

"Rise and shine. We're going to the head."

"No, Gunny."

"I'll be right back."

Johnny crossed into the bathroom, turned on the hot water, and began to fill up the tub. He found a fresh bar of soap under the sink, tore off the packaging, then drew a wash cloth from the linen closet, surprised to actually find one there. Holding his breath, he scooped up Bandar, carried him into the bathroom, then slowly lowered him into the tub. He slapped Bandar's hand onto the safety rail mounted along the wall and ordered him to hang on.

Bandar finally opened his eyes, the veins thick and glowing. He had a world class hangover. Legendary.

"Good morning, Sunshine," Johnny said.

Realizing what was going on and that Johnny was now bathing him, Bandar shook his head and raised a finger. He wanted to say something, then began to sob.

"Why you crying, son?" Johnny asked. "The water too hot?"

"Don't make me laugh."

"What're you doing here?" Johnny asked. "And where the hell is your cousin?"

"He left about six months ago. Said he couldn't take me any more. He shows up once a month when my disability check comes in—so he can get his rent."

"Well, that is some shit, isn't it? And your house looks like a dump."

Bandar chuckled under his breath, even as the tears continued. "You code enforcement?"

"How about this? How about I'm still the platoon sergeant, and you're still under my command." Johnny spoke more slowly for effect. "This train don't stop at the pity party. Are we clear on that?"

"Roger that." Bandar could have issued those words in a normal, respectable tone. The fact that he had chosen sarcasm changed their meaning entirely.

Johnny's tone grew more serious. "Hey, dude, don't tell me off—because you already did by missing my brother's wake and funeral."

Bandar covered his face with a hand. His voice cracked. "I'm so sorry, Johnny."

"A haircut. A clean shirt. It would have been a done deal. Why didn't you call me and tell me you needed a hand? I would've been down here in a second."

"I was too embarrassed. After you asked me to come, I couldn't stop thinking about that night in Fallujah. What an idiot I was. Oh, please, I want to go out there. I want to get shot and get paralyzed so some fat bitch on welfare can hold up a poster of Marines pissing on Taliban bodies while the casket of one of my buddies comes off a plane."

Johnny lowered his voice. "You know what your problem is?"

"What?"

"You're not on TV. I told you, you're a rock star, dude. You go off on these rants. You're an intellectual, you think that shit up off the top of your head. You got a gift. It's like rap or poetry or music shouting shit or something. They should put you on TV like Dennis Miller, one of those guys, you could go on and on..."

"You think Fox News would air some raghead Muslim talking about how screwed up America is?"

"Look here, son. I want you to get this through your head, because I don't want to hear this Haji or raghead crap ever again."

"Johnny, please, I know what I am—"

"No, you just listen to me. You swore an oath. The same one I did. You stood next to me and fought with everything you had. You gave your blood. You gave your legs. You are a Marine. You are my brother. That's who you are. I don't care what God you pray to. Would I watch you on TV? Hell, yes I would. I wish you had spent more time with my brother. You two smart asses could've shaken some trees."

Bandar glanced up at Johnny, his lower lip thrust out, his eyes swollen with fresh tears as he nodded. "You know what the hardest thing is, Johnny? I'm downrange the second I wake up. I'm downrange trying to get onto the toilet. I'm downrange when some asshole parks too close to my van and I can't lower the ramp. I'm downrange till the last second before I fall asleep. Some days you're just too tired to fight."

Johnny widened his eyes to a madman's proportions. "Well, I got some good news. You know what today is?"

"Let me guess..."

"You're absolutely right. It's an easy day. No drama. We're going to get you cleaned up. Then we're going to square away this house. I got a contractor I'm going to call. He'll roll down here and do some work on the outside."

"Johnny, I don't have any money. My cousin doesn't have shit, either."

"Don't worry about it."

Bandar covered his face again. "I used to think I'd never get to this point. There were a couple of years where I was just a hardcore mother, you know? I was doing good at the marina, too. But last month some redneck came in, and I heard him telling Dom he didn't want *the crippled A-rab* working on his boat. I could've blown right there. But I didn't. I just thought about how this guy summed up my whole life: crippled A-rab. And it made me think I didn't deserve to be at your brother's funeral."

Johnny tapped a finger on his temple. "You put that on yourself. All we see is a Marine we respect even more because you wear your sacrifice every day. Hell, son, if I were you, I'd go high and tight with the haircut. I'd wear a Marine Corps T-shirt to the job, and when Mr. Redneck comes in to call me a crippled A-rab, I'll ask him to bring in his wife, so I can wink at her, and she'll know what a pussy she married."

Bandar started laughing. "You stole that from General Mattis."

"He told it a little differently," Johnny admitted. "But you get the idea. You can tell that bastard you're ten feet tall when you're carried on the shoulders of your brothers, the greatest fighting force on Earth."

"You're right, Johnny."

"Okay, so now you scrub up, call me when you're done, and we'll get this easy day rolling along. I need to give Elina a shout and link up with that contractor. Be right back."

Out in the hallway, Johnny gave Elina a capsule summary of Bandar's condition, then added, "I really need to stay with him right now." Elina whole-heartedly agreed. She would take the girls to the grief counselor without him. They would try to meet up afterward for lunch. She told him to call if he needed any help. He would.

Unfortunately, this was not the first time he and Elina had discussed Bandar's situation. Bandar had some highly marketable skills, but sadly he had never exploited them. When he had been medically discharged from the Marine Corps, he should have relied upon his college degree and his fluency in four different languages to work as a civilian interpreter or government contractor for an intelligence agency. He would have been rolling around the hallways of the NSA instead of the dirt roads of the Redneck Riviera. But no, he had allowed the depression and alcoholism to destroy those opportunities, and now he could barely function at the marina. How could he throw away so much and continue along this downward spiral? It had to stop.

Once Bandar had finished bathing, Johnny told him there was a change of plans. He hired a cleaning service to come do the house, and the outside contractor would arrive in the late afternoon to haul away the debris and provide estimates for replacing the garage door and rebuilding the front porch. There was no reason for them to remain home, so they were heading out to Junior's Barbershop, where the owner himself would break out the chainsaw to do battle with Bandar's beard and locks.

During the drive over, Bandar confessed, "Okay, Johnny. I'll go high and tight. I'll get clean."

"You do that. And make it stick."

"A couple days after you're gone, when I'm sitting all by myself, I'll just fall off the wagon. It's happened a hundred times. I'm a drunk, and changing that is... man, it's a hard day."

"No one can help till you're ready. It all starts with you. You have to think you're worth it. We already think you are. We believe in you, you fool. Okay?"

"I'll remember that, Johnny. I'll remember everything."

"If you can get yourself cleaned up, and you can walk the straight and narrow and do like I told you at the marina, I might have some stuff for you at Triton 6. But you can't even go near that shit till you're sober and ready to rock star that world."

"Now you got me excited, Johnny."

"Good."

Abruptly, and before he had time to think twice, Johnny reached into his inner breast pocket and produced the note he found in Daniel's office. "Here. Do me a favor—translate it."

Bandar read the note and frowned. "Where did you get this?"

Chapter Thirteen

"In the Art of War, Sun Tzu said, 'To know your enemy, you must become your enemy.' And we did. That's how we realized that smuggling cocaine was just the tip of the iceberg."

—Josh Eriksson (FBI interview, 23 December)

Reliance Tactical Supply Company was on Highway 172 in Sneads Ferry, just a stone's throw away from the True Value Hardware store, the used car dealership, and the real estate agency. Arthur McNeil, a former Operational Detachment Alpha sergeant that Johnny had run into a few times in Iraq, co-owned the place with a few Army buddies. McNeil and his associates had purchased about an acre of land where they had constructed a 10,000 square foot manufacturing facility, offices, and an 800 square foot storefront. They offered tactical nylon gear to hunters, law enforcement, military personnel, and anyone else seeking high quality products made in the USA. McNeil told Johnny that up to seventy percent of his business was now online, but he kept the storefront open because his web customers liked to see that they were purchasing something from a brick-and-mortar shop and not some mysterious warehouse. Johnny and McNeil had discussed the possibilities of a partnership with Triton 6, wherein Reliance would supply the tactical gear on a given contract. McNeil said he would jump at such an opportunity. The right contract had yet to present itself, but Johnny had felt certain that a joint venture was definitely on the horizon.

He pulled into Reliance's dirt parking lot and consulted his watch: 1530. The place was open until five. Several other pickup trucks were parked in the lot, and a few, Johnny knew, belonged to the college-aged help. Taking a deep breath, Johnny opened the door and stepped out. He remained there with the truck door shielding him from view. He tugged his 1911 Ultra from the door pocket and clipped the pistol's holster onto his waistband, the .45 now effectively concealed inside his pants. He tugged down his shirt, zippered up his jacket, and slammed shut the door. With a chill breaking along the base of his spine, he headed toward the shop.

An electronic beep signaled his entrance, and immediately the scents of rubber and nylon and even a trace of gunpowder reached his nose. Thousands of pieces of gear were stacked on shelves or hanging from pegs jutting from the walls. An entire section of backpacks towered off to the left, with another area featuring dozens of dropleg pouches and holsters. Taco pouches, magazine pouches, and medical and ordinance pouches of every kind formed row after row, with colors ranging from black to tan to olive drab and multi-cam. Rigger and duty belts, along with gun and range bags, crammed a few more displays. Camouflage netting was festooned across the ceiling to complete the effect of being downrange.

Two silver-haired hunters dressed in orange vests stood near the gun bags, discussing one, while a knot of guys with crew cuts, off-duty cops perhaps, were at the glass counter along the back wall. They were inspecting a half dozen holsters spread out before them.

Johnny tugged down his ball cap and drifted off to the right, feigning interest in the pistol mag pouches, sifting through the triples and quads with their side release buckles. There was only one kid behind the counter, a string bean in a black polo shirt with the Reliance "RTS" logo on the breast pocket.

Five minutes later, the kid finished helping the men at the counter and approached Johnny. His name badge read: KYLE. He offered a perfunctory greeting, barely looking up from his phone. "You looking for some mag pouches?" he added, demonstrating his keen-eyed intellect, the future of America right here.

"Yeah, I was wondering if LaPorte could help me."

Kyle flinched. "You mean, Randall? He doesn't work here anymore."

"Really, when did he leave?"

"A while ago."

"How long?"

"You're not another detective, are you?"

Johnny drew back his head. "Hell no, something happen?"

"How do you know Randall?"

Johnny lifted his palms. "I was just in here before and he helped me. Seemed like a nice guy. Must've been your day off or something."

"Well, he's gone now."

"He get into trouble?"

"Who knows? Ten thousand in tactical gear missing from the inventory, and he just vanishes. We're not sure he took the stuff, but..."

"Wow, that's too bad. I didn't hear about it. Was it on the news?"

"The boss kept it quiet. Not great for business, you know?"

"I hear that. Anyway, I'm looking for some mag pouches for my brother, but I'm not sure these are the right ones. He was in here, too, maybe you helped him and you might remember him." Johnny tugged out his smartphone and showed Kyle a picture of Daniel.

"I remember him. I think Randall helped him."

"Well, that's my luck."

"Why don't you call your brother and ask him?"

"It's his birthday. I want it to be a surprise."

"Well, all right, I think the doubles are good. Not sure he'd be real comfortable carrying around four magazines unless he was planning to get real busy, you know what I mean?"

"Roger that. Tell you what, I'm going to take off, and I'll be back tomorrow. I might be able to find out what he wants instead of playing guesswork here."

"Sure."

"Thanks for your help today."

Without glancing up, Johnny left the shop and hustled back to his truck. Within thirty seconds, he was back on the road and trying to catch his breath. He played back the conversation in his head and swore that he had asked for LaPorte instead of Randall. If he had really been helped by LaPorte, then he would have known the kid by his first name, which would have been on his badge just like Kyle's. Johnny hoped that Kyle had not noticed that.

Johnny reached into his breast pocket and pulled out the paper on which Bandar had written his translation. He read it again:

Go to Reliance Tactical Supply Company. Speak to a man named LaPorte. Tell him you want the keys and gate card. When you're ready for distribution, contact the next courier.

Bandar, of course, had asked about the note, and Johnny had answered, "You never saw this. We never talked about it."

"Maybe you're the one in trouble, Johnny."

"Don't worry about me."

They had taken Bandar for his haircut, and he had entered the barbershop as Tarzan and come out looking like the Middle Eastern version of Clark Kent. Even Junior, the rotund black man who sang Stevie Wonder songs while he worked, had marveled over his own handiwork.

With the grooming complete, Bandar and Johnny had met Elina and the girls for lunch at Buddy's, after which Johnny had driven Bandar home. There, he had a quick consultation with his contractor buddy, who gave him a great deal on rebuilding the porch and replacing the garage door. Following that conversation, Johnny had driven to Reliance.

Now, as he drove away, he spoke into his smartphone, "Search the web for Randall LaPorte, North Carolina."

He found a Facebook account under that name, one with the photo blocked, along with a Twitter account that had LaPorte's picture: he had blond hair that reached his shoulders and the trace of a beard on his narrow face—or at least that was his appearance at the time of the photograph. He looked more like a guy in search of hellacious waves than hard drugs. His Facebook said he attended UNC Wilmington and could very well have been one of Daniel's students. Johnny clicked on the Twitter photo and saved it to his camera roll, then he called Norm Mack.

"Hey, it's Johnny, where are you?"

"I'm on campus."

"Look here, I'm going to text you a picture of a student. I want you to tell me if you recognize him."

"I'll try."

Johnny pulled over into a gas station and parked near the air pump. He worked his thumb over the phone and listened for the upload chime.

"I don't know, there are so many students here," Norm began. "Wait I got it now. Okay, this kid, yeah, he looks kind of familiar."

"Was he one of my brother's students?"

"I don't know. Maybe you can go online and get a hold of his records."

"Go back. You said he looks familiar?"

"That's what I'm trying to figure out. Wait. I know where I've seen him. He used to work with the professor across the hall from Daniel. I saw him in that guy's office a few times. That's where I know him from."

"Who was the other professor?"

"Tall guy. Swarthy-looking bastard. Beard. Thick accent. Not sure if he was Middle Eastern or not. I think he only worked there for a year. Not a regular. I remember trying to buy some books from him, and he was a rude son of a bitch."

"Okay, Norm, I can't go up there myself, if you know what I'm saying. I need you to gather intel on this other professor. Can you do that without making it look obvious?"

"Johnny, you're talking to the king of bullshit artists *and* a veteran Marine. I'll head over there right now. I'll call you back when I got what you need."

Before Johnny could respond, the old man hung up. There was a breathless edge in Norm's voice, one that unnerved Johnny. If that old codger made one misstep that tipped off Daniel's assistant, then all bets were off.

With his pulse mounting, Johnny pulled out of the gas station and drove until he was on highway 210 and within a quarter mile of East Coast Storage. He slowed to twenty-five mph and cruised by the facility. Business office just outside the six-foot tall rolling main gate, with a couple of golf carts parked out front. Storage units lined up in rows out back. The climate controlled building on the right. Fence and barbed wire perimeter. Security cameras. Motion-activated lights. Just your run of the mill storage facility and convenient distribution hub for the Colombian cocaine market.

* * *

Johnny returned home, where he found Kate and Isabelle in the living room, watching old episodes of the Kardashians on Netflix. He pointed to the TV and told them that these people, their friends, and the producers of the show represented everything that is wrong with America. They scowled, then Kate cleared her throat and said, "Uncle Johnny? We're ready to go back to the house now."

"Really." Johnny regarded Elina, who was at the Keurig, making herself a cup of coffee. "I guess the counseling worked."

"We wish you were there," she said. "But you did a good thing today, Johnny."

"You want to run over there now?" he asked.

"But you just got home."

"So what?" He faced his nieces. "Y'all ready?"

"Yeah," said Isabelle. "And for your information, one session with a therapist hardly changed our lives. We just decided to be brave like you."

Johnny's cheeks warmed. "Tell you what, I'm not feeling very brave right now."

"How come?"

"Oh, it's a long story."

"You hear anything from the police?" asked Kate.

"Nothing yet."

"This is bullshit! When are they going to catch the guy!"

"Whoa, Kate, watch your mouth," Johnny snapped.

"I wonder where she gets that from?" asked Elina, locking her gaze on him.

"All right, everybody out," Johnny ordered. "We'll shoot over to the house, then we'll come back and figure out dinner."

Johnny grabbed his keys from the countertop as his phone rang. "One second," he told them, heading toward the stairwell. "Just need to take this."

"Johnny, all right, get yourself something to write with," Norm said. "I have everything you need."

"You were good? She didn't suspect anything?"

"Look, are you going to trust an old Marine—or ask more stupid questions?

Johnny sighed. "All right. What do you got?"

Chapter Fourteen

"I'd be lying if I said it was an easy decision. When we were downrange, we wouldn't even think about it. You fight for your brothers. But after being away for so long and starting a whole new life, you think, I could go to jail. I could die. But then you remember who you are, who you've always been, and there's nothing that can change that."

—Corey McKay (FBI interview, 23 December)

Johnny, Elina, and the girls reached Daniel's house by twilight, and for some reason the long shadows and grainy light reminded Johnny of an old console TV he had as a kid. The TV's picture tube was beginning to fail, but the old man would not purchase a new one until the set officially died, and so for nearly a year they had squinted at the dark, low contrast images, and Johnny often speculated that his brother's eyesight had been ruined by their father and by quality control engineers at Zenith.

"You okay, Uncle Johnny?" Kate asked from the backseat.

"I'm fine. Let's go."

They neared the front door, and Johnny glanced back before inserting the key into the lock. Isabelle shifted her weight from leg to leg, and Kate shivered through a breath. "You'll smell the new grout and all the cleaning chemicals," he warned them.

"Okay," said Isabelle. "Come on, hurry up."

"I thought you guys were worried about this."

"I want to see exactly where it happened," said Kate.

"Oh, we don't need to be so morbid," Elina said.

"Uncle Johnny, tell us more about that night," said Isabelle.

Johnny shook his head. "Come on, we don't need to drag through that."

"But you never told us," she argued. "You can't remember?"

Johnny pushed opened the door. He stepped aside. "Who's first?"

Abruptly, the two brave college girls with attitudes were shaking in their running shoes. Kate's eyes were already gleaming with tears. She tugged at the collar of her jacket and stepped inside, glancing immediately to her left. "My father died in here, didn't he," she said.

"Yes." Johnny flicked on the light, then came up behind her, putting his hands on her shoulders. The wood floor shimmered.

Isabelle pressed him again. "Tell us everything, Uncle Johnny."

Johnny's throat began to tighten. "I can't."

Kate lowered her head and began to cry. Isabelle pushed past them and strode toward the kitchen, with Elina rushing up behind her.

"I guess we're not brave," Kate said, turning to face him and bury her head in his chest.

"Yes, you are. You're here, right?"

"I guess so."

Once she had composed herself, they walked back toward the kitchen, where they found Isabelle and Elina standing near the island. "I can't tell where he fixed the floor," said Elina.

"Great job, right?" asked Johnny.

"So she died in here," said Kate.

Johnny nodded.

"One of the knives is missing," said Isabelle. "See it? Right here." She pointed to the block of knives on the countertop.

"We'll get that back from the police," Johnny told them.

"Not sure we want it," said Kate.

Isabelle began to hyperventilate. She looked at them, wide-eyed, then hunched over and vomited all over the kitchen floor.

"Awesome," groaned Kate.

"I'll take her to the bathroom," said Elina.

"I got this," Johnny said, grimacing at the floor. He grabbed some paper towels and turned on the faucet.

"Don't worry, Uncle Johnny, I won't throw up like her," said Kate.

"Thank you. You never know how you'll react. You think you can handle something, but then you need more time."

"When you were in Iraq, you had friends die."

"Way too many."

"How did you deal with it?"

"There're all kinds of things you tell yourself. But in the end you just try to make your life worth their sacrifice. You try to make them proud every day, because they're looking down on you, and they're watching, okay?"

She choked up. "Okay."

"Let me ask you something. Did your father give you any gifts? You know, like a big check or something?"

"No, why?"

Johnny tasted the lie but was compelled to continue. "We were going through the bank records, just accounting for everything."

"Is there money missing?"

"No, but I did see a few big checks."

"Oh, that was probably tuition, plus they always gave us some extra food money and some fun money for clothes."

"Ah, gotcha."

"You want to go over to your room?"

She nodded. He took her over there, and she sat down on the bed and looked around. "We have to sell this place. We can't come back here anymore."

"We'll talk about that. You'll make a good decision."

"I hope so."

His phone rang. "Excuse me." He stepped onto the back porch, staring off toward the darkening edge of the forest. "Big Pat, thanks for getting back."

"Johnny, I have to tell you, hearing some of the things you called me on that voice mail made me laugh real hard."

Johnny chuckled. "Call 'em like I see 'em. So how are you?"

"Doing well. I hope you got my sympathy card."

"I did. I appreciate it."

"Well, you're lucky you caught me. I'm working some night ops. It's like zero one here. They got me subsurface a lot these days."

Pat Rugg had left behind his old digs in Florida to take a job with the Saudi Aramco oil company. He worked for the Tanjib Marine Ops Division as a diver surveying underwater installations, ships' bottoms, drilling rigs, and platforms. He identified and sometimes even made the necessary repairs to those craft and installations. He had never married and had sworn to live the playboy's life until he could no longer afford Viagra or until his body fell apart, whichever came first. The job with Saudi Aramco had already lasted about five years and was a far cry from some of the other work he had been doing, everything from plumbing to home construction to going out to Hollywood to try his hand at acting. He was offered a small part in a disaster film, playing a bum with a pet dog who is nearly killed when twisters carrying demonically possessed zoo animals ravage a small town. Pat passed on the role, holding out for something better because he had artistic integrity. He landed a Burger King commercial, then abandoned his dreams of Oscar-winning glory.

"So what's going on?" Pat asked.

"I was going to text you this, but if you can take a note..."

"At my desk now. What do you got, partner?"

"Guy's name is Dr. Ramzi Shammas." Johnny paused to spell it for Pat. "He's an engineering professor. He's from Alfaisal University in Riyadh. He came over here to UNC as a visiting professor for one year. He just left this past semester. There's a picture of him on his school's website."

"Hang on, I'll pull it up now. So is this guy a potential client? You want the whole deal on this guy or what?"

"He's not a client, but yeah, whatever you can get."

"You remember Billy Brandt? He hit that compound with us in Fallujah."

"Hell, yeah, I do. Crack shot. Excellent operator. I lost touch with him."

"Because he's working with The Agency in Riyadh. I link up with him for lunch every now and again."

"So you're thinking we can lean on him. That's outstanding. But look, for personal reasons I don't want red star clusters going off, if you know what I mean."

"I hear you. We'll take care of it quietly. I'll have Billy do his thing. Matter of fact, I've already had him do a workup on some of my bosses, and these guys are pieces of work, let me tell you."

"Right on. Let's put Billy on this guy."

"Hey, dude, it's done. I wouldn't be here if it weren't for you."

"I didn't get you the job, Pat. You earned it."

"If you say so. They don't usually hire apes."

Johnny laughed. "The next time you come home, you let me know."

"Hell, yeah. A party at Johnny Johansen's house is one you don't miss."

"Well, I have to agree."

"So yeah, I'll call you when I got something on this. You be careful, all right?"

"Always."

"Take care, Johnny."

That was a good call; it lifted Johnny's spirits. He remained there for another minute, checking his email, then Elina joined him on the porch. "Who was that?"

"Big Pat."

"You thank him for his card?"

"I did."

She took a deep breath. "I think the girls have had enough."

"You think this was good? Or was it a big mistake?"

"I'm not really sure."

"I think it was good. If they avoid it too much, their minds will start working, and then they go crazy."

"It's harder for them, Johnny. They're so young."

Kate and Isabelle joined them. "Maybe we can tear down the house," said Kate.

"Yeah," said Isabelle. "Then we can build something really cool."

"Slow down there," Johnny said. "You know, we got some of that Moose Tracks ice cream at home?"

"That sounds like a plan," said Kate.

"Maybe it'll make my stomach feel better," added Isabelle.

* * *

Elina fell asleep on the couch at about 2230. Johnny's nieces were watching a movie, and so he slipped downstairs into the man cave, took the dogs out for a walk, then returned and grabbed one of his range bags. He filled the bag with what he needed, and then he quietly exited the back door. Wincing over the grumble of his truck's engine, he pulled out.

Ten minutes later, he eased into the parking lot of the CVS Pharmacy, taking his truck around the back of the building and rolling into the last spot. He did a brief equipment check, then slipped off into the wooded area between the pharmacy and the back of East Coast Storage.

The company's perimeter fence lay about five hundred yards away, and he approached at a slow and deliberate pace, mindful of every dip in the path, fallen log, and low-hanging branch threatening to scrape his face. The Steiners hanging from their strap around his neck tugged harder as he came up a small mound and crossed a new mat of pine needles. The air grew noticeably colder, his breath coming thicker, his anticipation sending a shudder across his back.

He neared the fence, where brilliant halogen lights mounted atop tall poles illuminated the entire south side of the facility. Mounted to those same poles were the cameras and motion-sensor equipment. Johnny crouched behind a broad pine and tugged out the Steiners. He zoomed in on the Hess Express gas station across the street. It was 2313. He would have to time it perfectly. He surveyed the clerk behind the counter, a heavyset kid in his twenties with a thick beard and curly hair. The kid's gaze did not stray far from the counter, or from his phone, or from the front door. Most of the folks at the pumps Johnny pegged for retail clerks en route home from late shifts on a Friday night. A few college-aged kids were stopping off to pick up their cheap beer. The business would come in waves.

Johnny lowered the binoculars and rubbed the corners of his eyes. Now this, this right here, was reconnaissance. Toward the end of his career, he had grown frustrated by the changes imposed upon his beloved Recon Marines. They had gone from being the eyes and ears of their commanders to just an infantry platoon with a jump and dive badge. They had succumbed to the "action guy mentality," engaging in many more direct action operations than they should have. They were, at their heart, supposed to be intelligence gatherers, not door kickers sent in to clear and sweep cities on operations still referred to as "reconnaissance" when they were anything but. Infantry commanders did not know how to use them effectively or found it too difficult to plan and coordinate their missions; consequently they became straight up shooters, sometimes to the benefit of commanders competing with peers who had infantry battalions. The way to the top was having a maneuver element on the ground that did something a bit more glorious than reconnaissance. Just after leaving the Corps, Johnny had written a multi-page rant on the subject, and while he only shared it with a few friends, everyone who read it nodded and said, "This is everything that's wrong with the community, and you should have stayed in to fix it." Johnny would laugh and say, "Sorry son, I love the recon community, but that's one battle where only the stars and bars have a say." Back then, he would not have imagined himself squatting beneath a pine tree, reconnoitering a Hess gas station and a storage facility on a solo mission that he had planned and executed himself.

Earlier in the evening he had brought up Google Earth on his laptop, zooming in on the area above the facility, deciding his best avenue of approach. Johnny had assumed the gate codes were no longer good, and he had confirmed that fact by sending in Norm earlier in the day. The old man had carefully plugged in the numbers to the keypad. Access denied. That account, Johnny figured, had been closed, and the chances of finding more bricks of cocaine were not good. In fact, if there had been a shipment stored there, it had been moved just before or immediately after his brother had been killed. Nevertheless, he had to check it out.

Johnny pulled on his balaclava, concealing all but his eyes. He rose, then jogged along the tree line, breaking free near the fence. He picked up his pace along the east side, and then he dropped onto his belly near the front of the facility. He fished out his binoculars. The gas station's pumps were empty, and the clerk stood near the coffee machines like Bigfoot wielding a bottle of Windex and a wad of paper towels. With that, Johnny stowed the binoculars beneath his jacket and sprang to his feet. He raced around to the six foot tall wrought iron fence and scaled it. With a groan, he hit the ground on the other side, the impact reverberating into his knees the way it would after a HAHO—a High Altitude, High Opening parachute jump. He recalled several in the high mountain desert, where due to the altitude of the landing zones, he would strike the ground with a nearly bone crunching force.

He hustled down the row of storage units, knowing exactly where he was going. He rounded a corner, then found 31B on his left. No lock on the rolling metal door.

With gloved hands he reached down and dragged up the door until he could duck under it. He used his smartphone's flashlight to reveal an empty unit, with only a few splinters from shipping pallets littering the floor. If only he had the luxury of a forensics team that could do a thorough examination of the unit itself.

Moreover, surveillance footage might show who unloaded and loaded the cocaine; however, getting his hands on that footage without alerting the police was impossible. Instead of storing recorded data onsite, most companies had their images uploaded to a DriveHQ FTP server (or something similar) in real-time. Even if an intruder destroyed a security camera, he could not destroy the recorded data, which had been sent over wifi and stored on the web. Johnny would need a serious computer hacker to obtain a copy of that footage, which, given the camera angles and distances, might not disclose very much.

He paced around the unit, opening his thoughts to some other course of action that might present itself (other than getting the hell out of there). He was no covert operator with the country's full intelligence apparatus at his disposal. He was no "One Man National Asset," gamboling around like a super spy with a super model on his arm. He was just a good ole boy from North Carolina.

However, he had determination in spades. And like the old man said, it was never the size of the dog in the fight, but the *size of the fight* in the dog.

Chapter Fifteen

"I knew this lance corporal who used to kiss a quarter and slide it into his left breast pocket. He said it was to pay the ferry boat driver to take him across the river after he died. He said it was good luck. He got shot in the neck. Never had a chance. He didn't need a good luck charm. All he needed was his fellow Marines."

—Johnny Johansen (FBI interview, 23 December)

The trail had gone ice cold at the storage facility. Johnny stayed up until 0200, trying to learn more about Randall LaPorte and Dr. Ramzi Shammas. While they said you could discover a lot about people through simple internet searches, Johnny found little more about LaPorte. His old Twitter posts were innocuous ramblings about school and work, along with a few remarks on his relationships with girls. If he was a member of other social media websites, he had joined under fictitious user names.

A few academic articles about civil engineering and bridge-building operations that Shammas had written or co-written turned up as .pdf files, but otherwise, he too, had a very limited online presence. Johnny did a search of the Muslim Student Association at UNC Wilmington, where he found photographs of the club's leadership, including a familiar name, that of the club's vice-president: Abdul Azim Mohammad. He was Daniel's student and had won the engineering contest. LaPorte was not listed among the membership, nor was Shammas mentioned as a faculty sponsor or anything else. Exhausted and frustrated, Johnny went up to bed, where he found Elina awake.

"I couldn't sleep," she said. "You need to tell me when you're going somewhere."

"New rule?"

"Now it is."

"Wow, roger."

"Don't roger me, Johnny."

"Look, I just went over to the gas station to fill up the truck. Then I was downstairs on the computer."

"You can understand why I'm worried?"

"Yeah. Sorry."

"Well, look, the attorney was nice enough to meet us on a Saturday, so now I can finally get some sleep. Another big day, tomorrow."

"Okay." Johnny stripped down to his skivvies, went to the bathroom, brushed his teeth, then crawled back into bed. Within minutes, he was asleep.

The nightmare was different this time. Sergeant Oliver was not on the stairs, about to leap on the grenade, Willie was. *"Hey, Johnny. You know we'd follow you anywhere, right? Even if we thought you were wrong, like that night in Germany, when we got drunk and the MPs were chasing us through the snow? We ran through that kebab stand and all those backyards. We must've hiked ten miles back to the base and jumped the wire. Half the time you were going the wrong way, and I knew it, but I still had your back, you remember that?"*

Johnny whirled as the grenade went off... and he shuddered awake.

* * *

Willie took a deep breath. The thousand milligrams of Naproxen anti-inflammatory medicine had kicked in, and his joints felt loose and ready to go. Chalk up the need for meds to all those years of running, jumping, shooting, and falling down into irrigation ditches in the Marine Corps. Alas, he was no longer twenty, but now he had age, treachery, and prescription medication on his side.

The range officer lifted his voice: "The shooter is Willie Parente. On deck is Paul Kowalski. In the hole is Mitchell Deaver. Does the shooter have any questions?"

"No," Willie answered. His Glock 34 was tucked into his G-code holster. The 9mm pistol featured a seventeen round magazine, but Willie had added one of Dawson's magazine extensions, giving him twenty-two rounds in the mag and one in the chamber. His hands were held high, palms out. He had already walked the entire pistol course and could visualize it in his head. He would be "unconsciously competent" with no pauses as he ran between each array of targets, and if his weapon malfunctioned, he would handle the issue without emotion or thought. It was all muscle memory and timing.

"Make ready," said the range officer.

Willie double checked his boots. He stood squarely behind the long, thin pieces of wood painted red that marked the fault lines on the grass. "Ready," Willie said.

"The shooter is ready. Stand by."

Clipped to the range officer's waist was a blue Pro Shot timer that would record Willie's number of shots, his splits, and his overall time on the course. While the device did this, the range officer would focus his attention on safety, ensuring that Willie obeyed the 180 degree rule of not swinging his weapon back toward them, that he kept his trigger finger safe when moving between groups of targets, and that he remained within the firing zone and did not have any negligent discharges. At the same time, another man, the score keeper, would track Willie's shots to see if he missed or failed to shoot a target.

The timer beeped.

Willie spun around and leveled his pistol on the first of four steel targets, standing at a range of fifteen yards. These were white, circular plates mounted on poles and designed to fall back forty-five degrees when struck. To Willie's immediate right and left were barriers constructed of PVC piping and blue tarp material. The barriers were held up by rebar hammered into the ground, and they formed an elaborate maze through which Willie would run and shoot.

His first round toppled the target, and with the pinging steel echoing away, he fired at the others, boom, boom, boom. Even as the last target fell, he was already on the move, racing along the blue barriers, making a sharp left turn, then pausing to sight the first of five paper targets ten yards away. With his heart thundering in his chest, he released a double-tap on target #1, then he took on the rest, firing from left to right. Only his two best hits would be recorded, so he could take extra shots if he chose, although the added time would count against him. There was a trade off between accuracy and time, and that gauge needed to be adjusted on each stage of the competition. Some stages required more speed, others more accuracy. Willie felt exceedingly confident on a pistol-only stage and would sweep through this one, driving nails like a banshee.

He had started the course with twenty-two rounds in the magazine, one in the chamber. He had fired fourteen thus far. He counted his rounds because there were sixteen targets, and he would need thirty or more rounds to complete the stage. At some point he would need to reload, and he had carefully planned that moment. He would not run his pistol until empty and allow the slide to lock back. Dropping a magazine and then having to rack the slide wasted valuable time. Moreover, he would only reload while on the move.

After hammering the last paper target, he charged away, jogging parallel with the barrier to his right until he reached the end, where two more barriers positioned in a V-shape allowed only a narrow, three-foot gap of visibility. Here Willie took aim at three more steel targets, much larger silhouettes with shoulders and heads, but they were placed farther out at twenty-five yards and spread about ten yards apart. The last one required Willie to swing hard to his right. So far his marksmanship had been terrific, but he tried to ignore that. The moment he told himself, hey, you're having a great day, was the moment he screwed up. Well, that thought crossed his mind, just as he opened fire. He caught the first target dead on, panned to the second, fired, missed, squeezed off another round and *ping*—he got it. The last one took three more shots until that distinctive ring finally met his protected ears.

Twenty rounds gone.

One in the chamber, only two left in the magazine.

He turned to his left and began running, even as he ejected his magazine and slammed home a fresh one. He bolted straight down another line of barriers, these containing four different shooting positions, with large plastic barrels stacked two high on either side. He would need to take on each target separately, since they were spread so far apart and sitting about fifteen yards away. Also, standing beside or partially in front of them were white "no shoot" cardboard targets that had big Xs drawn through their centers. Their placement reminded Willie of a hostage situation, where you had to hit the shooter behind the victim. Willie arrived breathlessly at the first position and took aim. Double-tap. Nice hits. He darted about five yards to the next zone and fired again. Then on to the next one, where he unleashed his rounds. He transitioned smoothly to the final spot, freeing his last two shots and breathing a deep sigh that he had delivered lead only where he had intended.

"If you're finished, unload and show clear," said the range officer.

Willie complied.

"If you're clear, slide forward, hammer down, and holster," the officer added.

Once Willie had holstered his pistol, the officer announced, "Range is safe!"

The score keeper went to each of the paper targets to record Willie's hits. Meanwhile, the other nine guys in Willie's squad moved in behind the score keeper, resetting the metal targets, picking up brass, and pasting the paper ones with stickers so they would be ready for the next shooter. Willie helped the others with the reset, even though as the last shooter he was not obligated to do so. He received some congratulatory remarks from his buddies. He was disappointed with a few of his shots, but overall it was a solid first stage—and the competition was for a great cause.

Willie, along with about fifty other 3-Gun competitors, was raising money for the Marine Special Operations Command foundation, which supported active duty and medically retired MARSOC personnel and their families. Their hosts, the Ant Hill Shooting Range here in Bolivia, North Carolina, was owned and operated by proud supporters of the military, and because of that, many veterans attended their events.

Today's three 3-Gun competition was comprised of five stages, three of which involved shooting only one weapon at a time, either a pistol, a shotgun, or a rifle. Two stages required shooters to transition from shotgun to pistol and rifle to pistol. The group had been divided into five squads, and everyone rotated from stage to stage around the course. Ironically, Willie might only shoot for a total of three minutes across five stages, but he had to dedicate an entire day to do so. It took him ninety minutes each way to get to the range, then another five to six hours to compete (because most of the time was spent resetting the stages and waiting on other competitors). To someone on the outside, this sounded insane, but to shooters like Willie, the self-induced stress of trying to fire accurately while on the clock and with everyone watching created a rush that was just a hair's breadth away from being in an actual gunfight. Additionally, the camaraderie at these events was second to none. Everyone from all walks of life—doctors, lawyers, waitresses, mechanics, welders, kids, and housewives—was a shooter, and they all loved talking about firearms and ballistics. What was more, even the most fierce competitors would not hesitate in lending someone a gun to replace a broken one, although doing so might result in that generous shooter losing his match. No one liked to win because of someone else's equipment malfunction; that was a hollow victory to be sure. Besides, everyone had invested so much time and money that they hated seeing someone drop out. Willie had been offered weapons when his had gone down, and he had paid it forward when the need arose. This was just one of the many aspects that made 3-Gun such a great and highly addictive sport.

As he headed back to the waiting area, a familiar face emerged from behind his fellow shooters.

"Hey, Johnny, what's going on?"

Johnny grinned and said, "I've come to see how your skill sets have improved."

"Well, let's hope so. I'm shooting this one as a tune up before the Tarheel match in Raleigh. So, why didn't you tell me you were coming? We could've carpooled."

"Kind of a last minute thing."

"I thought you'd be busy today."

"Just in the morning with the lawyer. I told Elina I needed to get out and get away from it all for a few hours."

"Good deal. Next stage is shotgun and pistol."

"Right on. We'll link up later for an early dinner. It's on me."

"I'm all over that."

"Good. Now just remember one thing. You're the school bus driver."

"Roger that," said Willie with a wink. "Because I'm taking them all to school."

* * *

They drove up to Wilmington and had dinner at a barbecue place, where the conversation was mostly about Triton 6 contracts and some old buddies they had seen at the wake and funeral. Afterward, Johnny told Willie to climb into his truck, that they needed to talk for a minute.

"This sounds bad," said Willie, plopping down in the passenger's seat.

Without a word, Johnny handed Willie a block with a Scorpion label, a set of keys and card from a storage company, and a note written in Arabic.

Willie gasped. "What the hell?"

"I found these in my brother's office, up in the ceiling."

"Are you shitting me?"

"No. I've been following up, but I hit a dead end."

"What do you mean *you've* been following up?"

Johnny shrugged. "I haven't, uh, told anyone about this."

"Damn, Johnny, how long have you had this stuff?"

"I found it the day after my brother got killed."

Willie turned the block end over end. "Colombian?"

"That's right."

Willie tested the block's weight, sensing it was a little light, since he had held blocks of cocaine before while downrange in Afghanistan. He shook the block, and it seemed as though something might be loose inside. "You mind if I open it?"

"Why?"

"Because I know how these guys operate."

"All right, go ahead. Just don't get it all over the truck. I'm in enough trouble already."

Willie carefully unwrapped the block, which was already cracked in half. The block had a hollow center, and inside he found two sets of curled plastic cords with pencil-like attachments at their ends. Having been well-trained in breaching operations, Willie knew exactly what these were: mini boosters for ignition charges. They were used to ignite slurries and emulsions to full detonation. The initial shock wave traveled through the ignition line, then the detonator initiated the mini booster, giving the energy impulse necessary to initiate larger explosive charges. According to their labels, they were made by a company called EXSA.

"And you found this in your brother's office?" Willie asked again, the shock doing the talking for him.

"He was trying to tell me something, Willie. I think he was murdered for this."

There were few things in this world that frightened Willie, but the enormity of this situation was enough to set his pulse racing, his hands trembling. "So you haven't gone to the police?"

"My brother was growing out his beard. He worked with Muslims all day long. They recruit jihadis right out of the college. You know how his politics swung all over the place."

"What are you saying?"

"I'm saying I'm concerned. What if he was involved? Maybe he got scared, he backed out, and they killed him for it. Or maybe he double-crossed them for some reason. Who knows? The point is, if Daniel was a jihadi and got killed for it, man, I can't even bear that..."

"Well, you got no choice now. You need to tell everyone—the police, the FBI. You got coke and explosives coming up through North Carolina."

Johnny went on to explain how Norm Mack had tipped him off, how Bandar had translated the note, and how he had questioned a clerk at Reliance Tactical. He had found the storage unit empty and had reached the end of the trail.

"I can't hand this over," Johnny added. "Not yet. I need to know what my brother was doing. You saw how many guys came to his funeral. Can you imagine them turning on CNN and watching a story about him being a jihadi? I've spent my whole life trying to make the old man proud. I spent my whole life in the service of this country."

"I hear you, Johnny, but this is some serious shit." Willie picked up his smartphone and ran a quick web search for EXSA. They were a Peruvian company that manufactured explosives for mining operations. "They're killing two birds with the coke shipments," Willie said, after sharing the find with Johnny.

"I've got a couple of names. I called Pat Rugg. If we can find these people—"

"Stop." Willie stared emphatically at his friend. "Listen to me, if you go to the police now, it might not be too late."

"Are you kidding? They knew I was up at the university. They warned me about interfering. If they knew I was sitting on all of this—"

"Damn..." Willie sat there a moment, wrestling over what to do. Johnny was digging his own grave with a backhoe, going fast and deep. He needed help, but saying yes to something like this...

"You remember that time in Germany?" Johnny asked. "That bar fight with those Army dudes. How we were being chased by those MPs?"

"Good times."

"I had a dream about that."

Willie looked at him. "Really?"

"I didn't know where I was going, but you followed me. Right?"

"Yeah, 'cause you outranked me."

"You weren't my friend?"

Willie sighed. "I see where this is going. You don't have to play that card, Johnny. I don't agree with what you're doing. I think it's dangerous. But I understand. What do you need?"

"First, I know what I'm asking. But my back's against the wall. I got nothing. And I could use everyone's help."

"You tell Corey and Josh?"

"I'm planning on it. Josh gets back tonight."

"Why don't we go home, sleep on it, then we'll meet up tomorrow. We'll get them up to speed, then we'll see where we go from there."

"I thought about doing nothing, just throwing everything away."

"You?" Willie asked. "I don't believe it. You're one of the most stubborn bastards I know. You'll tear the shit out of this entire state till you get the truth."

"Yeah, I will. And I'm sorry for dragging you into this."

Willie nodded. "It sucks, but, oh well. If you're going to be stupid, you better be hard. And I've had a hard life."

* * *

Back home, Johnny told Elina about Willie's competition, then they watched a movie and ate some homemade chocolate chips that Kate and Isabelle had baked. Around 2200, Johnny let out Bomber, Musket, and Rookie for their walk. He waited at the edge of his driveway while the dogs ventured across the street, between the two houses, and down to the canal, where they would do their business at the water's edge. During the day, good neighbor Johnny would return with his doggie bags and clean up.

Johnny zipped up his jacket and shivered against the cold. He stared down the street, where only a few lights glowed in the windows. Some neighbors were retirees who turned in and rose early, like Brenda and Tom Shepard across the street. They were already in bed and watching the local news.

A few minutes prior Johnny had received a text message from Josh, who said he could meet in the morning. Corey had checked in and confirmed as well. Johnny wished he could explain to them how he had agonized over this, but words would not be enough.

With a deepening frown, Johnny noticed the dogs were running late. He called out, then whistled, the sound growing thin on the rising wind. Was that a truck engine off in the distance? He squinted through the darkness, toward the canal, hoping to find a silhouette. Groaning in frustration, he started across the street, already rehearsing how he would scold them. When he reached the canal, the dogs were gone. Or so he had thought.

About five yards back, off near his neighbor's house, the ground began to move. He rushed over and found all three dogs lying on their sides. They shook violently and foamed at the mouth. Had they eaten something bad? Was there something in the water? His breath quickened as he glanced around.

He turned back to Rookie, who was no longer moving. Beneath the dog's collar was a piece of paper. Johnny used his phone to illuminate words written in black marker:

Back off. Otherwise your wife and nieces are next.

Chapter Sixteen

"Joining the Marine Corps changed my life forever. Joining Johnny did the same damned thing, for better, and for worse."

—Willie Parente (FBI interview, 23 December)

The three bedroom ranch on West 4th Street in Cedar Falls, Iowa shone in the faint glow of the corner streetlight. Blue siding and beige shutters had been freshly painted just a week before Thanksgiving. The house was built in 1953, the first year of Dwight D. Eisenhower's presidency, and other than routine maintenance, not much had changed on the property since then. A white picket fence extended down to the front curb. An American flag hung from a mount beside the garage door and billowed in the cold, dry air. The Ford Fusion parked in the driveway was washed every Friday, its oxford white surfaces reflecting the towering oak tree whose roots spanned large sections of the front lawn. During the summer, one might expect a front window thrown open and an apple pie cooling on the sill. Boys would play touch football, while neighbors tended to their flower gardens and bought lemonade and cookies from girls sitting behind a cardboard stand down the street. Meanwhile, were he still alive, Norman Rockwell would have sat behind his easel and captured these images on canvas for his editors at *The Saturday Evening Post*. This was small town America, in all of its glory.

Tomorrow was trash collection day, and Dr. Mohammed Nazari rolled his bin out of the garage. As he reached the curb, he was met by his next door neighbor, Frank Austerlitz, an owl of seventy-seven whom everyone called "Frankie." With stooped shoulders and an uneven bearing, Frankie, whose ancestors had settled in Iowa in the

1830s, reached the curb, released his bin, then sighed and wobbled over to Nazari. "Good evening, neighbor."

"Hello there, Frankie. How are you feeling?"

The old man grimaced. "New meds, old meds, none of them work. They just give me constipation. And my back is still killing me."

"I'm sorry to hear that."

"Don't grow old."

Nazari smiled. "I wasn't planning on it."

Frankie glanced at Nazari's house. "That paint job looks great."

"You've told me at least four times."

He frowned. "Really? Well, you take better care of the house than Jack Dover and his alcoholic wife ever did. That's why he cheated on her and he never had time to fix up the place."

Nazari shrugged. "I still say this is a nice neighborhood with some great people. I was worried when I first moved in, but everyone's been so friendly. And I figured this house deserved a fresh coat of paint."

"Now you're making me feel bad about my place."

"Oh, your house looks fine, Frankie. If you need anything, let me know. You have a nice night."

Nazari returned to his garage. A dozen or more cardboard boxes were stacked haphazardly along the far wall, waiting to be unpacked. He had moved in nearly a year ago, but he had been so busy at the university that even his weekends were crammed with research, catching up on emails, and grading student exams. It was just as well now. The America he knew—the one his father had escaped to in 1978 during the Iranian Revolution and the one that had changed forever on 9/11—would be born again. Unfortunately, Nazari would not be here to marvel over his efforts. Allah had other plans for him. He shut the garage door and went inside to his home office, where a colonial-style desk and colossal hutch were stacked with paperwork. Sitting near the lamp was a black-and-white photograph of Nazari and his parents taken over thirty years prior, when he had been in kindergarten. He remembered the trip on the Long Island Railroad, the car clicking and clanking from the Ronkonkoma Station all the way into New York City, where his parents had taken him to visit the Central Park Zoo. Back then, his mother's thick black hair had flowed down to her waist. Her parents had emigrated from Sao Paulo, Brazil, and she had been born and raised in Miami. She was accepted to the State University of New York at Stony Brook, where in her sophomore year she had met Nazari's father. They were married before either of them graduated, and Nazari was born the year his father entered graduate school to earn a doctorate in electrical engineering.

Nazari had attended his parents' alma mater, where he earned an M.S. and Ph.D. in civil engineering. Afterward, he accepted visiting instructorships at the University of Toronto and at Alfaisal University in Riyadh. It was there in the capital city of Saudi Arabia that he befriended members of the Muslim Brotherhood. Refuge and patronage were provided to them by the House of Saud, who used them to bolster their Islamic legitimacy and gain greater influence over Arab politics. Swayed by his friends and colleagues, Nazari adopted the Brotherhood's ideology, which blended Islam with Arab nationalism to criticize and ultimately shun autocracy and the West. He agreed with the notion of empowering the people with Sharia Law to create an ideal republic. His time away from America allowed him to develop a more objective eye, and he grew frustrated over the evil he saw within a country he had once loved. Like young Rasul, his eyes fully opened. Muslim-Americans faced an increasing threat, and America was doomed if it continued along its current path.

Just last week Nazari had sent his wife, a Saudi national, along with their five-year-old son back to their apartment in Riyadh, where they would remain until called for. He told his wife that the politics in his department had become untenable and that he wanted to return to Alfaisal. He was working on that transition now. He spoke with them nightly to assure them he would arrive soon. What they did not know, and what he could not tell them, was that once he arrived in Riyadh, they would flee to the tribal lands of Waziristan in Pakistan. There, far away from the reach of the Americans and the Pakistanis, they would reside in a safe house until it was secure enough to return.

Nazari took a seat then swiveled to his hutch. He opened a bottom door and spun the combination lock on a small safe mounted inside. He withdrew the envelope Rasul had delivered, then opened and read it again. The typed, unsigned note had come from a man they knew only as "the liaison," and he was their direct connection to "the suppliers." This relationship between *Al-Saif* and both the liaison and the suppliers had been established through a third party in Africa. The note contained a list of six approved targets, their GPS coordinates, and a tentative operation date and time. Nazari and his colleagues had been studying and reconnoitering those targets and others for the past eighteen months, coming at them from every conceivable angle until they were satisfied with their plan of attack. However, they were powerless without all of the requested materials, and operations to procure those materials and logistical support were now underway.

The length and breadth of the jihadist network in the United States was staggering, even to Nazari. Sympathizers working as "consultants" within the NSA, CIA, FBI and the Department of Homeland Security provided current intel through a dedicated team of couriers. Revelations of America's intelligence gathering activities included specifics on their tactics, techniques, and procedures; in reaction, Nazari's group now relied upon hand-written messages delivered by courier or meetings at Islamic centers to pass information in person. Prepaid cell phones were used more rarely, as was the internet. He disagreed with his jihadi colleagues who organized their activities on Twitter and other social media websites. While the use of couriers often delayed communications, operational security was far superior to any online or cell phone contact. Using couriers or face-to-face meetings left law enforcement officials with little more than human intelligence to gather, and when it came to the Muslim community, not everyone was forthcoming, even those with nothing to hide.

In point of fact, the American government was either incapable or unwilling to recognize how vulnerable their intelligence and law enforcement agencies were. Hubris and politics played a large role in perpetrating the myth that Americans were much safer than they were during the days leading up to 9/11. While Islamic consultants were fully vetted within American intelligence and law enforcement agencies, there was no procedure, technique, or device (even a polygraph) that could *truly* expose the intentions in a man's heart. Consequently, these consultants engaged in denial and deception activities that kept agencies mired in false leads.

While Nazari had been reassured by his contact in Africa that he could trust both the liaison and the suppliers, he did not. He had demanded to know their identities, but that information was classified for everyone's protection. Rasul was the only person who had had direct contact with the liaison, and this much they knew: the man was a middle-aged Caucasian about six feet. He spoke English with a decidedly northeastern accent. He always wore a wool coat, a black baseball cap, and sunglasses. He was probably an American and acting as little more than a courier for the suppliers, thus he was not in any position of real power. He had warned Rasul that any attempt to gather intel on his whereabouts or identity would result in an immediate shutdown of all operations. Nazari had been instructed by his colleagues in Cairo to honor the liaison's request. Careful consideration had been given regarding their relationship with him and with these suppliers.

Therefore, Nazari was supposed to accept help—and remain unaware of its source. Only a fool would agree to those terms. If the situation presented itself, he would pursue these men, learn their identities, and eliminate any leaks in security.

Some of the materials had already been smuggled into the United States and his cells already controlled them; some were coming from within via the suppliers, and these he assumed would be procured through bribery, extortion, and other means to get men to do their bidding, or at the very least, look the other way.

Al-Saif was, indeed, the clandestine sword that would pierce the heart of America. While operating under the auspices of the Brotherhood (and keeping their name and operations out of the media, unlike ISIL), the network was led by a six-man core group directed by Nazari. Ahmed Mohammed Al-Nasser, currently employed with Transops Security in Arlington, Virginia, was in charge of forged documentation, IDs, and procuring operational funds through their contacts in Africa, the Middle East, and South America. Mahmoud Fahmi, a broker with Century 5 Properties in San Diego, California, was responsible for the rental or purchase of safe houses through-out the country. Amr Kaseb of the U.S. Islamic Group, a nonprofit created to promote Islam in the community, trained and recruited couriers. Bassem Younes owned and operated Transnational Trucking headquartered in Windsor, Connecticut. He over-saw the transport of all materials and personnel. Sameh Ismail was an international sales associate with Blue Door Arms and Ammunition of Warminster, Pennsylvania. He engaged in the legal sale of weapons abroad and the illegal smuggling of those same arms back into the United States. Every member of Nazari's leadership team was an American citizen, enjoying all the rights, privileges, and protections granted to them under the Constitution.

In the years following 9/11, *Al-Saif's* presence quietly expanded so that operational cells were now present in all fifty states. Each cell was comprised of a bomb-making support cell, a transportation cell, and a strike team. They were issued direct orders by courier and were instructed to report their status back to their nearest "friendly" organization (such as a mosque or Islamic center) by the same means. Secure strategic level communications were conducted through a broader web of couriers connected to these friendly organizations and orchestrated by Amr Kaseb. Sometimes at this level, open emails between organizations could be issued to share information using code words and phrases, and those reports would filter up through one or more asso-ciates, then finally reach Nazari.

Now, with six major targets approved, Nazari would begin the painstaking pro-cess of disseminating the information to his leadership team and down through the operational cells. He tugged open his laptop computer, and the screen blinked to life with the header and side bar menus of Adobe Creative Suite, a graphics design pro-gram he had mastered in recent years.

Chapter Seventeen

"Our enemies will gain Allah's approval and reach Paradise only if Sharia law is established around the world. They'll use any means necessary to reach their goal. When they die, their children take over, so don't let the politicians fool you. We can win battles, but the war never ends."

—Josh Eriksson (FBI interview, 23 December)

Johnny thrust his shovel into the ground and dug as though under gunpoint and ordered to finish the grave in ten seconds. Beside him, Josh did likewise, and behind them lay Rookie, Bomber, and Musket.

Earlier, a breathless call to Josh had sent the man out to procure two fifty pound bags of lime from a neighbor who worked on a small farm. By the time Josh had arrived, Johnny had already loaded the dead dogs into the back of his truck. If losing them were not excruciating enough, he had been forced to work through his tears and literally smuggle the dogs back to his truck. No one could know. No one.

As they had driven out to the game lands, Johnny found it difficult to breathe. The loss of his prized Gordon Setters, the murders of his brother and his sister-in-law, and the complete magnitude of what he had uncovered in his brother's office were unimaginable. Despite the gut-wrenching agony of it all, he would remain strong. He had to—because he must now take this fight to another level, a level that he had never imagined would take place in his own country, let alone his own town. He, like many others, had believed that fighting in far off lands kept his loved ones safe from the evil lurking outside America's borders. Oftentimes that was true. But not now. The fight had come home to his house, to his brother's house, to their entire family.

As Johnny dug, he remembered the day the dogs had come home from the breeder. They were just pups, untrained, barking and chewing up the house. Then he had sent them off to bird hunting school, and afterward, he had spent countless hours with them in the woods. Their companionship and unconditional love made them much more than just pets; they were beloved members of his family and the best lance corporals in the world, hungry and mission focused.

As expected, Josh was in shock as Johnny told him everything, but without hesitation Josh swore he would help. He would do whatever it took. He *was* his brother's keeper.

"When we get back, we need to send the girls away," Johnny told him as they continued to dig. "These jihadis, whoever they are, have been watching me from the beginning. I thought they were long gone."

"Corey and Willie are at the house now," said Josh. "So don't worry about Elina and the girls. We got that covered."

"We need to get Jada to take them down to our place in the Keys. I mean everyone. Ivonne, Lindsey, everyone. Jada's the gunslinger. She's in charge."

"You won't have to ask her twice." Josh lifted another pile of dirt, then began shaking his head. "I'm so sorry about all this, Johnny. Really."

Johnny finished his hole, then he moved on to start the third one. His eyes were watering again, but he ignored the tears and put his anger into each shovelful of dirt. "What am I doing here, Josh? I'm burying my dogs."

A mental switch was thrown, and Johnny flung the shovel into the air. With fingers digging into his palms, he lifted his head and screamed at the top of his lungs, sustaining the ragged note until he coughed. The fury made his veins feel as though they would burst through his skin. He was ready to call upon all the evil in his heart... the things he had seen during wartime... the unspeakable. He gritted his teeth. Payment was due. Payment in blood. And he wanted it now. He swung around, looked down at the dogs, and screamed again. Before he finished, the shivers took hold, and his palms were back on his face, hiding the tears.

Josh seized him by the shoulders and got in his face. "You still with me, Johnny? Because I'm with you."

"Roger that." Johnny's voice grew thin. "We didn't have any kids. Those dogs were all we had."

"I hear you, but you still have friends," Josh said. "A lot of friends."

Johnny pictured Daniel's funeral, the chapel overflowing with people who truly cared about him, the relatives and Marine Corps brothers alike. He remembered Elina saying how beautiful it all was. He glanced at Josh and nodded. Heaving a deep sigh, he walked off to fetch his shovel.

They returned to digging, finishing the last hole a few moments later. Once they had lowered each dog into his grave and poured in the lime to dissolve the remains and prevent any stench, they stood back. Johnny's lungs tightened, and the world grew dark around the edges. Josh caught him before he hit the ground, and a second later, he was blinking and asking, "What happened?"

"You almost went down."

After taking in a long breath, Johnny regained his balance and closed his eyes. "I can't tell you what this feels like."

"That's all right."

"What do I tell Elina? She loved the dogs more than I did."

"You'll know what to say."

"If I lie, it might be worse."

Josh squeezed his shoulder. "You'll be okay."

"Just give me another second."

They stood there, leaning on their shovels. "Best dogs in the world," Johnny blurted out. He looked at Josh. "I should've let it go. They'd still be alive if I didn't go up to the college and meet that old man. If I didn't keep pressing."

"You had no choice."

"I'm telling you, I should've let it go."

Josh's tone sharpened. "You knew your brother better than anyone. He wanted to tell you something. You couldn't let that go. Know why? Because that's who you are. There was *no way* you could stop. But they had a choice. They didn't have to kill your dogs."

Johnny averted his gaze and nodded. "Thanks for coming. Like I told Willie, I didn't want you guys involved. You got your own lives.—"

"Which include you and Elina. And your nieces. Don't forget that."

"I don't want you to get in trouble."

"Been there most of my life. Too late for that. Now listen up, when we get back, we need to do this calmly, by the numbers. You don't want your nieces freaking out."

"Roger that. Thanks for coming, Josh. Thank you."

* * *

The moment he entered the house, Johnny seized Elina by the hand and led her upstairs and into their bedroom. He asked her to sit on the bed.

"Johnny, what's going on? Why is everyone here? Willie and Corey are playing dumb, and I know you told them not to say anything."

"Look here, you're going with Kate and Isabelle down to the Keys. Jada's going, too. So is Ivonne and Lindsey. All of you are going to hang out down there for a while."

"What're you talking about? And where are the dogs?"

He braced himself. He knew this woman. He knew her strength. "Elina, I took the dogs for a walk, but they didn't come back. Someone poisoned them."

She looked at him as though he were speaking another language. But then, she studied his expression, as though she had misheard him. "What did you say?"

He told her again.

"Are they okay? Where are they?"

"Elina, the dogs are dead."

She frowned, took several more breaths, then bolted from the bed. "What did you say? They're dead? They were poisoned? What're you talking about?"

"Lower your voice, please."

She spoke louder. "My dogs are dead?" The first tear struck her cheek, followed by another.

Johnny raised his palms. "For the girls, please..."

She shook her head. "What's going on? Where are my dogs?"

"You need to sit down. Let me talk to you."

Her voice cracked. "Johnny, don't tell me my dogs are dead."

He hesitated. "I have to."

She collapsed to the bed, burying her face in his chest. He held her for a few moments until she glanced up and hissed, "Who killed my dogs?"

"Listen to me. Daniel and Reva weren't just stabbed in a home invasion. Someone murdered them, and it's not safe here. Those same people have threatened us."

"Are you crazy? What are you telling me?"

"It wasn't just a robbery. Someone *murdered* them."

"Did they do something bad? Did you?"

"I swear, Elina, I don't know what's going on, but I need you to be strong. We can't put Kate and Isabelle through this."

Her mouth fell open. "What's happening to us?" She grabbed him by the wrists and shook his arms. "Who killed my dogs?"

"We'll find out. I just need you to go."

"Can't the police protect us?"

"They're working the case, but they can't watch us twenty-four seven. They don't have the budget or the manpower. It's just better if you leave. Like I said, Jada, Ivonne, and Lindsey are going, too. You'll be safe."

Her gaze met his for a second, but then she stared through him. "I can't process all of this. I can't. I want to be in our home. I want our dogs back. I want this to be normal."

"I know. So do I."

She broke down again, then caught herself and asked, "What do we tell the girls?"

Johnny shrugged. "Surprise vacation. Anything to keep them happy. They can't know about this. It's too much right now."

"You're right, Johnny. You're right." She noticed all the dirt under his fingernails. "Where are my dogs?"

He took a deep breath and closed his eyes. "I buried them out in the game lands."

"Without me?"

"I'm sorry. I wanted to do it quick. People are watching us."

"Even now?"

"I don't know."

She rushed over to the window and peered through the blinds. "Are you telling me everything? I'm warning you, Johnny."

"I found something in Daniel's office. A block of cocaine, a note written in Arabic. I don't know if he was involved or spying on the group, but whatever it was, they killed him for it. At least that's what I think."

"Cocaine? Arabic writing? Your brother was a geek. He wasn't some drug smuggler."

"I know. It's crazy."

"And now they want us." She whirled from the window. "I'll talk to the girls. We'll get packed."

Johnny closed his eyes, fighting back his own tears. "We'll be okay."

He rose and kissed her on the cheek, then hustled downstairs to the man cave, where Josh, Willie, and Corey were waiting for him. He opened his gun safe and began removing his rifles and tossing them on the sofa. He added his shotgun and several pistols to the cache. Then he moved to a locked closet, keyed it open, then returned with a few ammo cans and a box filled with dozens of empty pistol and rifle magazines. He sat on the edge of the sofa and began loading magazines.

"Whoa, slow down there, Big Sarge," said Willie. "We ain't going bear hunting yet."

"Hey, they got spotters outside? We'll go get 'em," Johnny said, already losing his breath in anticipation.

Willie cursed under his breath. "Johnny, you know I'm your friend, but at this point running alone is a bad idea. We don't know who we're dealing with. We have to go to the police." Willie lifted his chin to Corey. "What do you think?"

"I don't know." He faced Johnny. "Whatever you need, you know I'm here, but Willie's right. We don't know what's going on. Then again, if you talk to the police, how do you explain all the evidence you held back? Will you go to jail for that? We should find out. I guess all this is blowing up, but we need to work it out before we do anything."

Johnny understood their reservations, yet he continued loading magazines like a machine, working unconsciously, filling one mag then inserting rounds into the next.

"Johnny," Willie said, leaning over to make eye contact. "I know you want to kill them because I do, too, but if we go off and do something half-cocked, then what? We wind up in jail? Elina loses you? Your nieces lose you? And they all need you, right?"

"Everyone, listen up," Josh began. "For now, we keep this to ourselves, and we follow up on our own. I'll tell you why."

Willie lifted his brows. "I'm listening."

"Think about it. Cops are trained to be suspicious. So Johnny gets LaPorte's name and the location of the stash. He goes over there. The cops don't know why. No matter what Johnny says, they might think he's involved. Maybe he's trying to blackmail the smugglers, maybe he *was* working with his brother. At this point, the cops might focus on Johnny—and us—and not the real killers."

"I guess that could happen," said Willie.

"And my point is, Johnny's already guilty of aiding and abetting—covering for his brother—who might've been running a drug trade on campus. We don't know. And we don't know if Daniel knew about the boosters inside the coke."

"Maybe he did," Willie said. "Maybe that's why he had a sample block hidden in his office. He was going to show someone how they were doing it. Or maybe he didn't know. The block hadn't been opened, but again, the boosters were still there."

"So now Daniel was somehow involved with smuggling drugs *and* explosives," said Josh. "And Johnny knew about it. And he didn't go to the police."

"Then he has to explain the dogs," said Corey. "And the note to back off."

"Johnny, you just tell them the truth," Willie said. "You were in shock when you found the stuff. You didn't want anyone to think your brother was smuggling drugs or God forbid he was involved with terrorists moving explosives. It was about your brother's memory, your own reputation, and hell, you can tell them you were thinking about your friends. If your reputation is ruined, that hurts our business, which hurts all of us, right?"

Josh raised a finger. "Willie, you just hit on something big. Our businesses can't afford the negative publicity of police crawling through our files. That might scare off clients and get us in trouble with the government. Shit, our security clearances could be pulled. This could go south for us *really fast*."

"That's not happening," Johnny said. "I know there's a lot at stake. Willie, I wish I could go to the police. That would be easy. But I can't. I'm sorry. When I found that stuff in my brother's office, I should've turned everything over to them. But I didn't. Now I'll accept responsibility for that decision."

"I hear you," said Willie. "But yeah, it does affect all of us."

"That's what kills me."

Josh raised his voice. "I just thought of something else. If we hand it off to the cops now, Johnny will be charged with something—obstruction of justice, I don't know. And think about it. Will there ever be any real justice for his brother? They *killed* his brother and sister-in-law. They *killed* his dogs. They've threatened his wife and nieces. They *need* to die."

"On that much we agree," said Willie. "And don't get me wrong. I'm not just thinking about myself. I spent a lot of time letting my emotions get the best of me. I don't want to see us make the same mistake."

"We won't," said Josh. "And here's something else: there's no guarantee that these guys will ever leave Johnny alone."

"That's right," added Corey. "These guys said back off. Handing it over to the cops is not backing off, and maybe they'll still want to punish Johnny for that. He'd always be looking over his shoulder—"

"And I don't live that way," Johnny said. "We let the cops do this, and I'm telling you, they will *not* work it the way we would."

"You mean they're bound by the law," said Willie. "And we're not?"

"I mean their brother wasn't murdered. And some of them have the skill sets of Barney Fife from Mayberry. Might as well be him and Opie Taylor working the case."

"But they still have assets we don't," Willie argued. "We're talking about a criminal investigation. You think four rednecks can do it alone?"

"We'll call on the Agency and the Bureau. In fact, I already have."

Willie frowned. "Now I'm confused."

"So am I," said Josh. "If we turn this over to the Feds, and these guys are linked to terrorists or they are terrorists, then operational security is blown to shit and these bastards run back into their rat holes. The jihadis have operatives everywhere just waiting to blow the alarm. Johnny, your friend Mark Gatterton will tell you that. The freaking jihadis are hard-wired into our government."

"Mark will be working with us. He knows the Bureau, knows the players. He has the friends we need. We'll get some intel through him. I told you Pat Rugg is looking into Shammas. What I didn't tell you is that one of our old buddies from Fallujah, Billy Brandt, is working for the Agency in Riyadh. He's pulling up some intel but doing it all under the radar. So you see, Willie? We have assets. They're called United States Marines. And we can trust them."

Willie's expression softened. "Right on, Kemosabe."

"So it's settled. We're *not* going to the police," said Josh, glancing around the room for the others' assent.

"I'm good," said Corey.

"I said this to Johnny, and I'll say it to the rest of you," Willie began resignedly. "If you're going to do something stupid, you better be hard."

"Amen to that," said Josh. "Now let's get down to business. Johnny, you pissed off somebody by going to Reliance then going to the storage place. Let's go back over the players."

"The old book buyer guy, Norm, I told you about? I sent him on a recon to plug in the codes at the storage place, but that's all he did. I didn't tell him anything about why. I don't think they were watching him, just me."

"What about Bandar?" asked Josh. "He translated the note."

"And he knows what it said," Corey finished.

"He sent me a text just before he checked himself into a rehab," said Johnny. "He's going to try it again. He's got no phone and no visitors for ten days. I'm glad he's there. He'll be safe."

"You tripped the wire either at the storage place or Reliance," said Willie.

"I think it was Reliance," Johnny said. "I talked to that kid Kyle. I was asking for LaPorte. I should've been asking for Randall, so that kid might've suspected something."

"Either that or someone else at the shop was watching you," said Corey. "Don't you know the owner of that place?"

Johnny nodded. "SF guy named Artie McNeil."

"You were working on a link with them," said Josh.

"Yeah. Anyway, he wasn't there—or at least I didn't see him."

"Whoa. My brother-in-law knows those guys over at Reliance," Willie said. "Are we saying they're involved in all this? No way."

"Kyle told me that ten thousand in gear got stolen from the place, and then LaPorte took off. McNeil asked the police to keep it quiet, so it wasn't on the news."

"So maybe it's just the kid working for him who's involved," said Willie.

"Kyle was the only one I talked to there. He could've tipped off the guy who killed the dogs—"

"Or maybe it was him," said Corey.

"Only one way to find out. Corey, I need you to get on that computer up on the bar and get this kid's address."

"Why don't we just go down to the shop?" asked Willie.

"Because we're going tonight," Johnny answered.

"You got a last name?" Corey asked.

"Nope."

"All right," Corey said, typing furiously on the keyboard. "Sometimes the websites show pictures of the sales associates. No luck there."

"Wait a minute. Those guys from Reliance like to compete at Tarheel and Ant Hill," said Willie. "As a matter of fact, the kid you're talking about might've been down there a few times. They post the results on a website called NC section dot org."

"Pulling it up now," said Corey.

Willie leaned in over Corey's shoulder. "They weren't there today, so go to the last 3-Gun."

Corey pulled up the long tables of results. "We're in luck. Only one Kyle... Kyle Jessup, right there." Corey did a simple Google search for "Kyle Jessup North Carolina." They found the kid's Twitter, Instagram, and Facebook accounts, and Johnny verified his picture. A white pages result yielded his home address. They brought it up on Google Earth. Cape Harbor Apartments in Wilmington.

"All right, let's go help the girls load up," said Johnny. "Then we're going over to Kyle's place."

"What if somebody tails the girls down to the Keys?" asked Corey.

"Somebody *will* be tailing them," Johnny said. "I called Matt Bowlin. He's taking his guitar and his guns. He'll be meeting up with them on the highway, two cars. He's overwatch. I'm sure he'll book himself a gig or two while he's down there."

"Right on," Corey said.

Johnny faced them and shivered through a breath. "Oorah. Let's go."

Back upstairs, Johnny loaded bulging suitcases into the back of Jada's SUV. Before they pulled out, he stole a moment with Elina. "Hopefully, this won't take long."

Her tears came fast. "This is all so crazy, Johnny."

"I know. Just please... trust me."

"You don't have to ask. But you do need to be careful."

He stared deeply into his eyes, and there she was, that sexy Finnish girl he had met at Sloppy Joe's so long ago. "I'm sorry about all this."

"No more apologies. Adjust on the fly, right? We'll go down there, and we'll be okay. I've spent a lot of years waiting for you, Johnny."

"I know. And I don't say it enough, but I love you."

He took her into his arms.

Chapter Eighteen

"We were down in Seadrift, watching some of it happen on the computer, and we couldn't believe it. The whole time I kept thinking, oh my god, here we are, four knuckle draggers in the middle of all this."

—Corey McKay (FBI interview, 23 December)

Allah, the compassionate and merciful, would take good care of Randall LaPorte; of this, he felt certain. The angel on LaPorte's left had recorded his wrongful deeds, and the angel on the right had recorded all of the great things he had done in the service of Allah. According to his math, the good outweighed the bad, and Allah would forgive him. But would anyone else? He downed the last sip of his Bud Light, crushed the can in his hand, and tossed it out the open window of his old Ram pickup. For several hours he drove aimlessly up and down Ocean Highway, grappling with his excuses and reading an imaginary news story in his head:

Randall LaPorte, twenty-two, of Raleigh, North Carolina, was found murdered yesterday at a friend's apartment in Wilmington. He was the only son of John and Beth LaPorte, both serving time in state penitentiaries for tax evasion and for a real estate scam they organized back in 2009. Described as a troubled youth by one of his faculty advisors at the University of North Carolina, Wilmington, LaPorte found solace when he converted to Islam, after which his grades dramatically improved. "He told me that the teachings of Sayyid Qutb and Shamim Siddiqi changed his entire outlook on life," said Tyrone Legacy, an academic advisor at UNC. "When I researched these men, I learned that Qutb was a harsh critic of the United States and was hung for plotting the assassination of Egypt's president. Siddiqi wrote a book back in 1989 detailing a plan for Islamists to take over the United States and establish Islamic rule. Needless to say, I was alarmed by what he was reading. However, the changes in his life were positive, and his attitude seemed much improved. I've never seen a student turn 180 degrees like this. I knew his parents were in jail and that he had used the money from the sale of their house to go to college, so there was a lot riding on him doing well, and we all wanted him to succeed. I can't believe someone would want to murder him. I do remember something he once told me. He said the United States was a country of *kafirs*. I had to go look it up. It means heathens in Arabic."

LaPorte popped open another beer, glanced at himself in the rear view mirror, then cursed and sighed. He dialed Dr. Shammas's number again. Still no answer. He beat a fist on the wheel and took a long gulp of beer. He had avoided alcohol since converting to Islam some two years ago, but tonight he was weak, and he needed something to take the edge off. He had stopped at the Hess Express across the street from the storage facility and had purchased a six pack, intent on drinking every last one.

Was he punishing himself for his failure? Was he trying to turn himself into his father, an out-of-work drunk who had become a criminal, a man who had browbeaten his wife into submission and wound up ruining her life, too? Fuck him. Dad had allowed a country full of greedy, fat infidels to poison his soul and destroy his life. He should have been stronger. He should have stood up to the bullshit instead of becoming a victim.

A phone rang; it was one of four prepaid cells on the passenger's seat. LaPorte almost drove off the road before answering. "Dr. Shammas? I've been trying to call you for the last two hours."

"I was busy. Did you finish it?"

"He won't bother us again."

"Excellent. What about the body?"

"Uh, he's still alive."

There was long pause on the other end. "What do you mean?"

"I thought the original plan was too sloppy."

"So you didn't do it?"

"I poisoned his dogs. I sent him a warning. He'll back off now."

Another pause, and LaPorte held his breath. "Randall, this is your second mistake."

"Excuse me? Mistake?"

"Yes, and I'm a fool for trusting you. We need to talk. In person. Go to the Islamic Center in Wilmington. I'll meet you there tomorrow. Go there and *don't* leave."

His second mistake. The first, according to Shammas, was stealing all that tactical gear from Reliance and outfitting dozens of operational cells by utilizing the storage facility and their distribution route through Sneads Ferry. Shammas had called it "a grave error," and that he "should have been consulted first." LaPorte thought he was doing Allah's work. After spending a year gathering intel on local law enforcement personnel who frequented the shop, the time had come for a bold move—because those who take bold steps rise higher in any organization. LaPorte had seized the opportunity, but his efforts had gone unappreciated and had triggered Shammas's wrath.

Fearing what the professor might do next, LaPorte had volunteered to take care of Johnny in order to redeem himself. Shammas was hesitant, but LaPorte had sworn he could get the job done without compromise or complication. However, when the moment came... He raised his voice now, the beer doing most of the talking: "I'm telling you, professor, I made the right decision. This guy's scared now. He won't do anything."

"You didn't have the courage, did you?"

LaPorte stammered, "I could have... I could have easily killed him, but I thought about the ramifications. One brother dies, the other goes missing..."

"I considered all of that. We'll discuss this tomorrow," Shammas said.

LaPorte flung the prepaid phone out the window, toward the woods along the shoulder. He did this in anger, yes, but the phones were used only once then tossed away. He jammed his foot on the accelerator. The truck leaped forward, the exhaust wailing.

When he was thirteen, his father had taken him deer hunting, and a majestic buck had been in his sights, but he had failed to pull the trigger. Disgusted, his father ripped the rifle out of his hands and took the shot himself. He missed. They had been waiting all day for that buck. When asked, LaPorte could not explain why he froze. Consequently, as the time had drawn near to kill Mr. Johnny Johansen, LaPorte had fixated on that hunting trip. He vowed that he would not surrender again. However, as he planned the execution in his head, a force like electricity or gravity or air pressure rendered his finger immobile, and he realized he was a prisoner until he could breach all of his fear. He convinced himself that once he received his training in Pakistan this spring, he would be a true jihadi fighter, but not until then. Resignedly, he had come up with the plan to kill Johnny's dogs.

LaPorte popped open another beer and glanced down at the speedometer: 88 mph. With a shudder, he backed off and let the truck coast down the highway. He shuddered again at the thought of going to that Islamic center. Shammas's message could not be clearer: he no longer trusted LaPorte, and given LaPorte's knowledge of their personnel and operations, he was now a terrible security threat. They would slap a pillow case over his head, tie it around his neck with an extension cord, then drive him out to the game lands. They would shove him to his knees. The report of a rifle or pistol would be the last thing he heard.

LaPorte took a more violent gulp of beer and reminded himself that there were other jihadis who would better appreciate him. He would join them, and together they would continue the Brotherhood's work. Controlling the United States was even more important than supporting the mullahs of Iran or destroying Israel, he had learned. Doing so would have a huge and positive impact on the future of Islam. The most effective way to accomplish that goal was for American Muslims to infiltrate, undermine, and ultimately seize control of the government. With the United States under Sharia law, Islam's enemies would finally be defeated. Between America's assets and its new found spiritual truth, God's Kingdom on earth would be established forever. Corruption, greed, lust, and materialism would no longer ruin people's lives. LaPorte would find a wife, settle down, have some children, and raise them in a country that was no longer a wasteland. He would never abandon them for pleasures of the flesh.

Another of the prepaid cell phones rang. He considered not answering, but then he snatched up the phone and recognized the number. "Randy? It's Kyle."

LaPorte had trouble masking his suspicious tone. "What's up, dude?"

"I think something bad's happening."

"What do you mean, something bad?"

"Artie just called me. He said the cops want to interview me again tomorrow. I think they've been watching me. Remember that guy who came into the shop, the one who was looking for you? He might've been a cop."

LaPorte tensed. "I told you he's not a cop. You know what to say."

"Hey, I'm worried, man. They're going to work me over good. I don't know what you're doing—dealing drugs, whatever, I don't care. But we need to talk."

"You mean you want more money."

"Dude, you know I do. I could go to jail. Remember my cousin's house in Murrayville?"

"Yeah."

"Why don't you meet me there? Wait outside."

"You think your cousin would let me crash for a few days?"

"Hell, yeah, dude, no worries. Just throw him a few bucks. It's late, though, so just wait outside until I get there."

"How long will you be?"

"Maybe ten minutes."

"All right, on my way."

LaPorte thumbed off the phone and made a hard U-turn, heading back to Murrayville. He could be there in five.

* * *

Johnny lowered the .45 from Kyle's forehead.

The scrawny kid thumbed off his phone.

"Now you call your cousin. You tell him LaPorte is heading over there. You tell him to stay inside. Got it?"

Kyle swallowed and dialed the number.

They were inside the kid's one-bedroom apartment, where their ever gracious host was seated at a table that had not been wiped off since spring break the previous year. Kyle had obviously been studying interior design with Ashur Bandar, and the place reeked of mold and something remotely stale. In the living room, piled before a 42" flat screen seated atop a buckling console, were hundreds of video games, with even more strewn across the glass coffee table and on the floor beside the sofa. The sink hole in the middle of that sofa was a broadening testament to Kyle's addiction.

Just as the kid hung up with his cousin, Willie came out of the bedroom holding Kyle's rifle, shotgun, and two cases containing his pistols. "Some nice toys you got here, son."

"You look familiar."

"3-Gun at Ant Hill," Willie said. "Good to see you, too."

Entering the apartment had been rudimentary. They had rung the doorbell, then had followed with a nervous knock. Johnny called out, "Kyle, dude, come on. Let me in!"

With glazed eyes and hair jutting at unwashed angles like the undead, Kyle had opened the door. Johnny had the kid's neck in his hands before either could take another breath. They spent five minutes interrogating Kyle, who remained arrogant in the face of four menacing Marines. Even Johnny's pistol did little to temper the boy's sarcasm. Maybe he thought this was all part of a video game. Johnny groaned and thought, *kids these days...*

Kyle argued that LaPorte had dragged him into everything. While LaPorte never admitted to ripping off Reliance, he had the access to the warehouse and the opportunity. Kyle assumed he was dealing drugs, and LaPorte had hired him as a spotter, keeping tabs on the customers coming into the shop. That's all Kyle knew. LaPorte had already paid him two grand for his services, and he had warned Kyle to keep his mouth shut.

"Nothing else here," said Corey, coming out of the bedroom. They were searching for anything that indicated Kyle was a jihadi.

"Wasn't jack in the closet," added Josh.

"What're you looking for?" asked Kyle.

Johnny ignored the question. "I'll take that phone. And the keys to your truck."

"You're stealing my ride?"

"Borrowing. Let's go."

Willie handed off the kid's weapons to Josh and Corey.

"I'll expect my guns back," said Kyle.

"You hear this kid?" asked Willie. "We'll hang on to them for now." He crossed to one of the video game controllers and tore free a piece of wire. He bound Kyle's wrists behind his back. The kid stood there, his collar bones protruding from beneath his t-shirt.

"This is totally illegal," Kyle said, flinching as Willie tightened the cord.

Corey snorted. "You mean like aiding and abetting a terrorist?"

"What're you talking about?"

"Is LaPorte a Muslim?" Johnny asked.

"I don't know. Who are you guys? Homeland Security?"

For the first time since they had entered his apartment, young Mr. Jessup sounded scared. It was about time. A sense of pleading came into his eyes, and his voice sounded like a broken clarinet. "Am I really in serious trouble?"

"Have you thought about converting to Islam?" Josh asked.

"*Allahu Akbar*," Corey said, wriggling his brows.

"You think I'm a terrorist? That's insane. Go look at the paper targets in my closet! I got pictures of ragheads on them!"

"Oh my god, he's a racist," said Willie.

"Look here, you do what we say, and you walk away," Johnny said. "Nobody knows about anything. We don't want you. We want your buddy."

"He's yours."

Willie grinned crookedly at the others. "He's not much on loyalty, either."

They escorted Kyle outside, where he protested about the cold and how he should be wearing his hoodie. His arms were covered in gooseflesh.

"It's even colder at the morgue," Willie quipped.

They locked up Kyle's guns inside Willie's SUV. Then they shoved the scarecrow into his crew cab Tacoma. Willie and Corey would drive Kyle's ride, leaving Willie's SUV behind. Johnny and Josh had taken their motorcycles, and the group headed off in three different directions to challenge any spotters watching Johnny's house. To the best of their knowledge none of them had picked up a tail, but they would remain vigilant.

As Johnny cruised down the highway, with the 2007 Ultra Classic purring between his legs, he considered shooting LaPorte a few times before questioning him. One in the arm, one in the leg, just to let him know they were serious. As he shivered over that, he realized he had made another mistake. He should have asked Kyle to better describe LaPorte. The photo Johnny had was a portrait from the shoulders up.

For a second, Johnny squinted through the darkness, past the road and into the main foyer of his brother's house, where the man with the balaclava was just turning a corner. He wore dark clothes and a backpack hung from his shoulders. He was taller than Daniel, at least six feet, two inches, and more broad-shouldered. Kyle was about the same height but much too lean; however, LaPorte could be their man. A punk college kid might have taken his brother's life. That seemed awfully pathetic.

Johnny's breath shortened. They were close. He could barely contain himself. Josh rolled up on his imposing sport bike, a Triumph Daytona 955i with geometry borrowed from the aerodynamic machines of some science fiction film. He nodded.

Just ahead, Willie turned off the highway. After backing off the throttle, Johnny squeezed the clutch lever and downshifted. They followed Willie into a neighborhood of mostly ranches set far back on their property lines and roosting like quail beneath dense clusters of longleaf pines and southern red oaks. There were no sidewalks, only a narrow strip of cracked chip seal leading into even more dense sections of canopy paralleled by tall fences of pampas grass. The occasional street lamp left hazy puddles on the road, and the occupations of some residents were readily apparent, as they parked their landscaping trucks or work vans with business magnets along the grassy shoulder.

Willie's brake lights flashed, and Johnny held his breath. He was downrange again, experiencing that strange mixture of intoxication... and dread.

Chapter Nineteen

"You know what the problem with you boys is? You give the jihadis a clean shot at your heads—because you're too busy covering your asses."

—Johnny Johansen (FBI interview, 23 December)

Willie pulled to the curb and thought, *okay, now we'll be charged with kidnapping. So there it is. If you're going to do something stupid...*

"It's right around the corner on Ferndale," Kyle said. "Thirty-one-twenty. Two bedroom house with a detached garage out back."

"You're being a lot more cooperative," said Corey. "We like your new attitude."

"I'm thrilled to be here," Kyle said.

Corey snickered. "I spoke too soon."

"What does Randy drive?" asked Willie.

"Dodge Ram pickup," answered Kyle. "It's white. He's got big mud tires."

Johnny and Josh ran up alongside the truck. Willie gave them the address and a description of LaPorte's truck. "You got a warning order, boss?"

"I'm thinking about it," answered Johnny. "We'll get some eyes on him first." He glanced over Willie's shoulder, toward Kyle. "How tall is your buddy?"

"I don't know. Five-eight?"

"So he's not taller than you?"

"No, pretty short guy."

Johnny looked disappointed. "All right. Be right back."

As they took off running, Willie faced Kyle. "I took another look at your scores at Ant Hill. They weren't too bad."

"What do you care?"

"You work for some good people. And you might have some talent. Be a shame to throw away your life on something like this."

"You think you're a badass because you win over there, huh?"

Willie frowned. "I win because I practice. And because I love it. The day you brag is the day you lose."

"I would crush you in any video game, you name it."

"Did you not hear what I said?"

"Any game, dude."

Willie chuckled under his breath. "A video game? Really? Son, there was a night back in Fallujah. I wish you could have been there."

* * *

Ferndale was even narrower than the perimeter streets, and that worked to their advantage. Johnny led Josh around the corner, and they sprinted from tree to tree, moving in toward the home from the east, searching for the nearest covered and concealed position. The idling pickup was parked about six doors down, with gray exhaust rising from its tailgate.

While Johnny felt his age, he was back in his element, selecting the next tree and bridging the gap like a wraith in jeans and leather biker's jacket. Still, the cold air bit hard at his lungs, and he needed extra time to recover between each tree. Sitting behind a damned desk and doing paperwork had taken its toll on his fitness. They drew within two doors of the house, then crouched behind a broad trunk, their boots slipping across the pine needles, their shoulders brushing against the scaly bark.

"We could try to take him right now," Johnny said breathlessly.

"It'll be real loud if he takes off and we need to fire," Josh pointed out, gasping and red-faced himself.

"You're right. We need to get him out of the truck."

Josh pulled up a map of the neighborhood on his smartphone. "Check it out. Willie comes right up the block, then cuts in front of his car, boxing him in. We roll in from the north, around the corner. If he realizes he's boxed in, he might surrender."

"If Willie cuts him off, he'll know something's up. Let's have Willie roll up behind him. Maybe he'll get out. Then we got him."

"Sounds a little more risky."

"Yeah, but if he doesn't get out of that truck—"

"I know, but if Willie drives up behind him—"

"There's a chance he'll see Kyle's not driving the truck," Johnny concluded. "I got you. So let's do this."

Johnny shared his plan with Josh, who mulled it over for a moment. He finally nodded and said, "One more thing. What if he's armed? Are we willing to get into a gunfight? Wake up all the neighbors? Leave behind evidence? Maybe get shot ourselves?"

Johnny swore under his breath. "I'm asking too much of you guys already. I'll go in alone. You just back me up."

"Look, I'm just bringing it up. We'll assume he's armed. Ain't no other way around it. Maybe Willie can get a bead on him before he makes a move."

"Roger that." Johnny tipped his head in the direction they had come, and they slipped away, returning to the truck a few minutes later. They went over the plan with Willie and Corey, who agreed that getting LaPorte out of his vehicle was their number once concern. Kyle would lie across the backseat, out of view. The threat of gunfire was ample persuasion for him. Corey would keep low in the passenger's seat, armed with a P226 9mm pistol. Willie had his Glock 34 in his strong hand, his weak one on the wheel.

"Call me when you get over there," said Willie.

Johnny nodded, and he and Josh mounted their bikes, fired them up, and rolled off, taking a perimeter road around the neighborhood to come in from the opposite direction. They kept far enough away so that their engines were only a faint drone at LaPorte's location. Josh was watching his GPS as they reached the corner, then pulled over to the curb. With his heart triphammering in his chest, Johnny called Willie and said, "Good to go. Let's do it."

"On our way," said Willie.

"All right," Johnny said. "Stay on the line."

* * *

LaPorte sighed with relief as headlights flared in his rearview mirror. What the hell had taken Kyle so long? The Tacoma raced by and parked in front of his truck. LaPorte was about to roll the key and shut down the engine when he looked up and stopped. Although the Tacoma's rear window was tinted, he could still discern the driver's silhouette, the head extending beyond the padded headrest. That head appeared much larger than Kyle's. Maybe LaPorte was just seeing things, the beer blurring his vision, the stress turning to paranoia.

He reached for his prepaid cell and dialed Kyle's number.

Why wasn't he getting out?

* * *

Corey looked down at the ringing phone in his lap. "It's him," he told Willie. "What do we do?"

"Let him answer it," Willie said, gesturing to Kyle.

Biting his lip, Corey reached back, thumbed the phone to answer, then held it to Kyle's mouth and ear. Corey mouthed the words *Tell him to get out!*

"Randy, hey, yeah dude, I'm here. I was just calling my cousin to wake him up first. Don't want to be rude. Come on."

Corey thumbed off the phone and motioned for Willie to open the driver's side door, as if Kyle were getting out. Willie did but held back.

"Damn, he's not getting out," said Willie. "He's waiting for us first."

Corey glared at Kyle. "What did you tell him?"

"You heard what I said!"

"Did you tip him off?"

"No. You heard it!"

"What's going on, Willie?" Johnny asked from the phone.

"Hang on," Willie told him.

* * *

LaPorte caught a glimpse of the gloved hand that had opened the door. A large hand exposed below the arm of a light brown winter jacket, probably a Carhartt similar to the one LaPorte was wearing.

The only trouble was, Kyle always wore hoodies, sometimes two at a time against the cold. He didn't like Carhartt jackets and was not a leather man, either. Sweatshirts, hoodies, no matter the weather.

So that was not him. And this... this was a police set up, and LaPorte had driven right into it like a fat bastard trying to pull off a real estate scam. He threw the truck in gear, slammed his foot on the accelerator, and rolled the wheel, racing past the Tacoma. He checked his rearview mirror as the truck fishtailed and tires screeched across the rutted road.

* * *

"Sorry, Johnny, he took off," hollered Willie. "He's on the move, heading your way!"

Were this Iraq or Afghanistan, Johnny would have ordered his men to shoot out the tires of LaPorte's truck, end of story. But now they had to apprehend their boy swiftly and silently, without leaving behind rounds in rubber tires or brass casings on the side of the road. How far was LaPorte willing to run? Or more importantly, how much gas did he have?

The punk came roaring around the corner as though he were competing in a monster truck show, the Ram a second away from rolling over. Johnny and Josh peeled off from the curb, just as LaPorte crushed their ghosts. They were in front of him now, the beams from his headlights bouncing across their path.

Josh broke left, riding along the shoulder, and Johnny darted in front of him—just as LaPorte veered across the road, forcing them toward a stand of trees. Josh braked hard, and Johnny nearly hit him before sliding out on his back wheel. They dropped behind the truck as those enormous mud tires spat gravel across their faceplates.

LaPorte hung a right and then another sharp left onto Murrayville Road, a two-lane highway spanned by power lines and cutting through swaths of dense forest. They crossed the bridge over Interstate 40 and streaked past the New Hanover Country Fire Department at speeds nearing eighty mph. Whether LaPorte was a bad driver or impaired Johnny could not be sure, but the truck wandered to the right, then the left, unable to hold a straight line as the blaring bass note of LaPorte's mud tires changed key under fierce acceleration.

They were barreling now toward the intersection of North College Road, where the light turned red, yet LaPorte held speed. Johnny and Josh rode abreast but kept several car lengths back, in case the kid took a shot at them. What would he do now? Blow the light? Turn left? Right? Johnny stiffened as they neared the corner, and LaPorte cut the wheel sharply, about a hundred feet before the intersection. He bounced off the road, the rear tires airborne as he reached a grassy section with poor runoff to their right, part of a Kangaroo Gas Station whose sign shimmered in the thick air. As the rooster tails of muck rose higher in his wake, LaPorte raced between a maze of power poles, coming too close to one on the right and snapping off his side mirror. He spun out, accelerated again, then slid almost sideways onto North College Road, leaving twin trails of mud.

Meanwhile, Johnny and Josh opted for the gas station's side entrance, and they rumbled past the empty pumps and fell in behind LaPorte before he gained any ground. North College was a four-lane road, and LaPorte exploited all that extra real estate, changing lanes haphazardly, then drifting once more to the middle.

Johnny's speedometer touched ninety, and Josh veered in closer and threw up his hand, as if to say, how long can this go on? Johnny nodded and pointed ahead. They weren't giving up. Hang on.

More gas stations, churches, and a Food Lion supermarket blurred by, and Johnny itched with the desire to draw his .45, race up, and shoot out one of LaPorte's tires to finish this. It might come to that, evidence be damned. They reached the overpass at Route 17, their engines and tires echoing loudly off the concrete rails on either side as they flew over the cars below. Given LaPorte's serpentine path, Johnny was thankful there no other vehicles on the road. However, their luck could run out fast. It did. Johnny wove into the left lane and spotted the running lights of a car about a quarter mile ahead. They swept toward that unsuspecting driver like remora trailing a white shark.

Johnny signaled to Josh, who stole a look for himself and flashed a thumb's up. They slowed a little more. The gap widened. LaPorte charged up behind the car, but at the last second the driver took a hard right, disappearing down a side street. Johnny breathed a sighed then geared up, as did Josh. They were slammed back into their seats and resumed the chase. The business district gave way to residential homes seated on acre-size lots with dirt driveways and carports like hives for piles of junk. LaPorte blew through the red light at Glen Eden Drive, narrowly missing the blue minivan that had triggered the signal. Johnny rolled to the left, whipping behind the van then leaning upright on LaPorte's tail. Josh returned to Johnny's draft.

Just ahead, the road forked where North College merged with Castle Hayne Road. LaPorte kept right, perhaps a little too far, leaping ahead at nearly one hundred miles per hour. A speed limit sign vanished beneath his truck, appearing flattened on the other end. The truck's body leaned hard as they reached Castle Hayne, where LaPorte took out a row of mailboxes before straightening his wheel. Like North College, this road was a four-lane highway with ample room and creative opportunities for LaPorte to destroy more obstacles in his path. Once again, he crossed the dotted yellow line and into the left lane. Johnny thought the kid might plow head-on into the Hardee's sign rushing toward them. Cutting the wheel, LaPorte jerked right and punched the accelerator.

The road narrowed to two lanes as they left the small town of Castle Hayne, and Johnny signaled for Josh to hold position. He blasted ahead into the oncoming traffic lane. Now riding alongside the truck, Johnny raised his arm, motioning the kid to pull over and end it now. LaPorte's face shown weirdly through the side window, half in shadow, his long hair clumped like a bundle of yarn spilling over his head. Johnny waved again.

As expected, LaPorte rolled his wheel, believing he could knock Johnny off his bike. However, Johnny had already backed off the throttle to slip in behind the truck. He felt for his pistol, aching to draw it.

The maneuver, it seemed, must have unnerved LaPorte, because he lost control, ripping off the road and clipping a pole beneath a billboard for Tim's Air Conditioning Service. The detour only cost him a few seconds, though, as he barely slowed down, and those Caterpillar-like tires chewed their way back onto the road.

Northeast Cape Fear River was a blackwater tributary lying just a mile ahead, and as they approached, guardrails indicated that the heavily wooded embankments had grown much steeper. There were no streetlamps in this more rural stretch, the darkness now enveloping them.

Headlights rose in the distance. One pair, then another. Johnny gripped his handlebars even tighter. They were still down to two lanes and would lose the shoulder as they reached the bridge. LaPorte edged to the right, coming within a foot of the guardrail. Then he turned more sharply, careening across the road and into the left side guardrail. That impact sent him caroming to the right; however, the oncoming driver had panicked over LaPorte's fluctuating headlights and had changed lanes to pass. LaPorte shifted lanes, too, and they were still locked in their game of chicken.

Johnny waved to Josh, and they slowed dramatically, just as LaPorte veered around the oncoming car, missing it by mere inches. The second car shot in behind the first, and that driver passed with a more comfortable gap and horn blaring.

Before their engines faded, LaPorte's right front tire blew out with a violent bang, catapulting the truck into the guardrail. Given the height of the Dodge, the size of the tires, the velocity of the vehicle, and the angle of approach, only one thing could happen. It was physics, pure and simple.

His mouth agape, Johnny slowed even more as the truck burst through the guardrail, sending pieces of twisted metal boomeranging toward the gloom. The pickup sailed above the steep embankment like a horse in a steeplechase, the image so surreal that Johnny glimpsed it in slow motion, as though his brain were trying to catch up. With the stench of fuel and burning rubber already filling the air, the truck's nose pitched forward—

And LaPorte plunged twenty feet toward an impenetrable wall of swamp gums, pines, and cypress. As Johnny and Josh slowed to a stop, the pickup struck the trees with the boom of an artillery shell. At once, glass shattered, wood splintered, metal buckled, engine hoses burst free and hissed liquids, and the truck slammed onto all four tires with a thundering splash into the swamp.

Johnny was already off his bike, bounding toward the section of missing guardrail, with Josh shouting for him to wait. At the rail, Johnny started down the embankment, but his footing was tenuous, the angle too steep, his heels already slipping. He paused, leaned back, and found himself clutching a clump of grass for support.

"Don't do it," Josh said.

"I have to talk to him."

"I know, but if somebody drives by, it's over."

"Is he down there?" Johnny asked. "It's too dark. I can't see."

"I'll get a light. But we need to move!"

Johnny squinted at the pickup below, its front end buckled by several trees. The engine had died, its chugging replaced by the ticking and groaning of metal as the pickup bobbed on the water. Josh returned with a flashlight from Johnny's bike. The beam exposed streaks of blood on the driver's side door and quarter panel. Josh panned a bit more, and there he was, Mr. Randall LaPorte—or at least part of him. Half his torso had gone through the windshield. Most of his skull was missing. A severed arm had wedged itself between folded sections of the hood and now jutted up like some bizarre antenna.

"He's done," said Josh. "We need to go. Somebody could've called the police."

Johnny cursed. And cursed again.

"Come on!" screamed Josh. "If they know we're here, our mission's over. Let's roll!"

Josh was right. No Recon Marine would ever let himself get compromised on an objective, and this was no different. If they were caught, a first-year prosecutor could make a manslaughter case against them in a heartbeat. Grinding his teeth in disgust, Johnny clambered up toward the road.

Back at the bikes, he told Josh they needed to contact Willie—but not here. They drove off, then Johnny signaled that they turn down a wooded side street. With their bikes tucked up close to the perimeter trees, Johnny read a text from Willie, who said they had gone to a gas station, parked, and were waiting. Johnny told him to meet back up at Kyle's apartment. They would be there in about fifteen minutes.

With their helmets tucked in the crooks of their arms, they sat there for a moment, with Johnny swearing again and Josh rubbing the stubble on his jaw, eyes creased in thought. "As far as Kyle is concerned, we lost his buddy. We don't know where he is," said Josh.

"Agreed."

"But somebody's going to find him. And if Kyle talks…"

Johnny shook his head. "The kid won't talk."

"Oh, really. What do you plan to do with him?"

"I'm going to motivate the young man."

* * *

Johnny's nose was about six inches away from Kyle's. "So when the police search this place, they'll find four hundred grams of cocaine. According to North Carolina law, you'll do about fifteen years and pay a fine of about two hundred and fifty K."

"You don't even have the drugs."

"You willing to take that chance?"

"I'll tell them you planted the stash."

Johnny lifted an evil grin. "You think anyone will believe that?"

Kyle glanced at his boots.

"Son, you have a choice. You get up tomorrow and you go to work like nothing ever happened. If the police come, you don't know us. We weren't here."

"Or what?"

Johnny cleared his throat and spoke in a rapid fire: "Or... you go running to the cops, you tell them everything. You get us involved, and like I said, we make sure they find the coke. They'll think you were working with your friend. You might even do extra time for distributing. So, to paraphrase one of my favorite Marines, I'm pleading with you—with tears in my eyes—to do the right thing."

Johnny was hardly crying. But now the kid was.

"Remember what I said?" Willie asked Kyle. "You got skills. You plan to waste your life on something stupid?"

"No. I'll go to work tomorrow. Nothing ever happened."

Corey directed an index finger into Kyle's face. "If we find out you talked—"

"I won't say anything."

"Good man," said Willie. "Your buddy's gone. You're off his payroll. You don't owe him anything."

"Except his stuff."

"What're you talking about?" asked Johnny.

Kyle took a long breath. "I let him crash here for a while. He's got some clothes in the closet. I think his backpack is still behind the couch. You know what? You can have it all. I just want it out of here."

Josh and Corey crossed to the sofa as Johnny went on:

"So let me get this straight. You let him live here for a while? Was this before or after you think he stole from your boss."

Kyle hesitated. "It was for like a week... after."

"So don't screw around with us, son. You know he stole the stuff, and you harbored a criminal."

"I needed the money, all right? You think I make a fortune at that shop? You know how much my rent and tuition cost? Do I look like I have scholarship money?"

"Johnny, check this out," said Josh. He and Corey had found LaPorte's backpack, a tan Jansport with rear pocket and suede leather bottom—not the dark-colored pack worn by the man who had killed Daniel.

Josh handed him a piece of 3x5 card stock with perforated edges and printed via laser printer. The card featured a tri-border design, and beneath large Arabic writing was a word in English: *Alhamdulillah*. Johnny recognized the word as "praise Allah" or something similar. "Prayer card? Bookmark?"

"Do they even use prayer cards?" asked Josh.

Johnny regarded Kyle. "You ever see this before?"

"No, I told you, I don't know what he did outside of work. If he was a Muslim, I didn't know or care. He didn't look like a terrorist, unless a redneck terrorist is what you're after. I just wanted his money."

"Oh, man, this is bad," said Corey. He handed Johnny a blank 9x12 manila envelope, atop of which were some black-and-white pictures printed on computer paper.

Johnny leafed through the photos, which began with a close-up of his house; another showed Elina walking to the mailbox; a third was a tight shot of her leaving with his nieces; and the last one captured Johnny on the driveway with Bomber, Musket, and Rookie. Johnny pulled the guys aside, out of Kyle's earshot. "LaPorte didn't kill Daniel and Reva, but I bet he killed my dogs."

"Why would he have these pictures in his backpack, unless someone else took them and gave them to him, so he could follow," said Willie.

"That's what I'm thinking," said Johnny.

"Well, for sure he was watching you," said Corey. "He got his, though, didn't he?"

"Anything else in there?" Johnny asked, gesturing to the backpack.

"Just a couple of textbooks."

"Have the kid show you his clothes and anything else. We'll take it all out of here for him. I want to keep that prayer card, but we'll ditch the rest." Johnny turned to Kyle. "All right, son, we're cutting you loose, trusting you to do the right thing."

Kyle's head drooped.

"Look at me," Johnny ordered. "Time to put on your man pants. Keep your mouth shut. And everything will be okay."

* * *

Exhausted, Johnny and the others drove back to his house. Josh spent thirty minutes surveying the neighborhood with a pair of Steiners, while Corey and Josh spent some time out back, reconnoitering the canal from Johnny's dock. It was 0220, and the roads were empty, with no indications of a tail or anyone else watching the house, although they would maintain watch. At first, Johnny assumed that LaPorte could not have been working alone. Then again, this group, whoever they were, knew they had a security leak, and the more spotters they had in place, the greater the risk. LaPorte might have been their last man on the field before they had pulled up stakes and left.

After reconvening in the man cave, Johnny delivered a brief and depressing after action report: "Well, boys, that kid might've been our only link to the professor. If we can't find Shammas, then that's it. I'm not sure what else do to do."

Corey, who was seated at the bar and working on the notebook computer, swiveled his chair toward Johnny. "I got an email from Steve in Colombia. He said there's a competitor down there called I-SOC out of Galveston."

"Who are they?" asked Willie.

"International Special Operations Consultants," answered Corey. "They roll like us. Josh and I bumped into them a few times when we were down there. Turns out these guys backed up some Colombian Marines during a raid on a FARC warehouse. They found some explosives stolen from EXSA in Peru. They also confiscated some drums of potassium chlorate. The stuff was manufactured in Brazil by a company called *Exportadora Selva Brasileira*."

Johnny had seen potassium chlorate before; it was an odorless white crystal or powder that, when combined with a fuel, formed an explosive mixture. Insurgents in Afghanistan were using it as a new and easier source to make their IEDs.

"Maybe we can talk to some of those I-SOC operators. See if anyone's heard of Shammas," said Josh. "I'll get on that."

Corey raised his chin at Johnny. "You said Pat was contacting Billy Brandt. Why don't you call Pat and see how they're making out? They're eight hours ahead of us."

Johnny sighed. "I figured he'd call me if he had anything."

"Maybe he does," said Willie. "He wouldn't call you at zero two."

Johnny's thumb was already tapping across his smartphone's screen. Pat answered on the second ring. "You're up late."

"Been an interesting night."

"I was going to call you later, but since we're here—"

"You got something?" Johnny asked excitedly, with the others moving around him to overhear.

"Maybe."

"Hang on. I'm with Josh, Willie, and Corey. I'll put you on speaker."

Pat greeted them, tempering his humor to account for the late hour and Johnny's tone, then he finally continued: "Okay, this is from my notes. Prior to taking the job at UNC Wilmington, this guy Shammas taught at the National University of Engineering in Lima, Peru. Apparently, he speaks very good Spanish."

Johnny's eyes lit up, as did everyone else's. "So Shammas was in Peru."

"Roger that. Got something else that might be more actionable for you."

"Talk to me, bother."

"Billy picked up some HUMINT near the university in Riyadh. Turns out Shammas has several known aliases."

"No shit."

"Yeah, he's pissed off a few people over the years, and one of them was willing to talk. Billy ran those names, and one came up hot. Mr. Ramzi Ben-Youssef is a licensed real estate broker in... wait for it... North Carolina. He owns a company called Carolina Properties. He has an office up near you in Jacksonville. Coincidence? I think not. Ben-Youssef *is* Shammas. And he's your guy."

"How long has he been up there in Jacksonville?"

"Public records show about three years."

"So he's been coming to North Carolina long before he took that teaching job."

"Roger that."

"So why's he working at the university?" Johnny asked.

"Well, it ain't for just the money, and if this is going where I think, you need to slow down. I don't want to help you get in trouble."

"You won't. This is just what we needed. You tell Billy I owe him big time, and you thank him for keeping this thing low-profile. What can I say, Pat?"

"Hey, once a Marine. You keep me posted on all this. And stay low."

"Roger that." Johnny hung up and regarded his friends.

"So why is Shammas a real estate broker?" asked Corey.

"I read about this," Josh began. "He's doing it because it's the first step in nation-building. He's doing for Muslims what some white supremacists are doing in small towns out west. I think he and his buddies are buying up cheap property, setting up Muslim enclaves, and populating them with enough registered voters to neutralize any local town councils. It's Sharia Law by democratic process."

Corey shook his head. "Well how do you like that?"

Johnny snorted. "I don't. Now saddle up. We're going to J-ville."

Chapter Twenty

"What we found in that real estate office was a game changer. Johnny had already opened Pandora's Box so to speak, but this took us to a whole new level."

—Willie Parente (FBI interview, 23 December)

Rounds buzzed over Johnny's head, a few splitting open the trunks behind him. He picked up the pace and kept on because he had steel in his back and a brother he needed to find. An AK-47 set to full automatic rattled from the adjacent field. In a matter of seconds, Johnny was at the perimeter, crouched down and counting six men converging on an irrigation ditch on the opposite end of the field. They weren't fleeing... they were *chasing...*

"Hey, Bro, wake up."

Johnny's eyes snapped open. "What's going on?" This wasn't Fallujah. He was seated in his pickup, the seat lowered all the way back, the heat humming softly, the engine idling.

"It's zero eight forty," said Willie.

Johnny raised his seat, then knuckled sleep grit from his eyes. He blinked and looked around.

The Carolina Reality office was in a strip mall called Westbrooke Village, just south of the Lowes and Best Buy on Western Boulevard. Saigon Nails, Game Stop, Wells Fargo, and a jewelry store were among the other tenants advertised on the colonial-style sign near the curb. Johnny and Josh had taken their pickup trucks, with Willie and Corey riding shotgun, respectively. They reached their target about fifty-five minutes later, after which they split up. Johnny and Willie parked at the Hardees across the street, while Josh and Corey got in closer, near a Staples office supply so they could observe the strip mall's rear exits. They took turns catching some shut-eye, although Johnny drifted off for no more than a few minutes at a time. The only significant report came from Willie, who, after spying the realty office through his binoculars, noted that a status light on an alarm panel on the wall glowed green, indicating that the alarm had not been activated, a curious fact to be sure.

"Saw some Vietnamese ladies going into the nail salon," said Willie.

Johnny yawned and said, "Text Josh. Tell him we're moving in. And just follow my lead." He threw the truck in gear, drove across the street, and parked in a spot near the bank. They climbed out, and Johnny walked right up to the reality office and tried the door. The window was a tic-tac-toe board of information and photos of local homes. Inside, several desks were cluttered with papers, files and brochures, with more cubicles arranged in the back. A conference table with six chairs and big screen television mounted on the wall nearby reminded Johnny of the Triton 6 office.

"Looks like they're still in business," he told Willie. "Come on."

They headed several doors down to the nail salon, where Johnny entered and met the gaze of the Vietnamese girl at the front desk. If she was twenty, that was being generous. Her shirt featured some weird cartoon cat, and her earrings resembled pieces of circuitry rather than jewelry. She reminded Johnny of his nights rolling around on Court Street back in the 1980's. Court Street was the home of the "buy-me-drinkie" bars in Jacksonville. Leisure ladies from all over the world would draw jarheads and sailors into the clubs, give them a little bit of affection, and allow them to buy drinks; it was like the Wild, Wild West and a great place to find trouble of all kinds.

The girl smiled, then raised an index finger with an impossibly long silver nail. "Manicure? Pedicure? Deluxe or regular?"

"Oh, I'm sorry," Johnny said, blushing. "I'm not here for that." He glanced at Willie. "You want a pedicure?"

Willie returned a fifty-caliber stare.

Johnny snorted and regarded the girl. "Anyway, we had an appointment with Mr. Ben-Youssef from the real estate company. You guys don't know him or know where he is, do you? He's never missed an appointment before."

A slightly hunch-backed woman with lightning-white streaks at her temples left one of the nail stations and raised her chin at Johnny. "Oh, you talking about Mr. Ben. Very nice man. He's not here. He had someone die in the family."

"I'm sorry to hear that. You know when he left?"

"He's gone for two weeks."

"Hey, Johnny," Willie said, pointing to a TV suspended from the ceiling. The local news was showing images of LaPorte's pickup truck being towed out of the embankment. The caption read: local man and suspected criminal found dead in crash.

Johnny held back his reaction and smiled at the woman. "Thank you very much."

She took one of his hands and examined his nails. "You come back. You need manicure. I give you discount."

"Okay, we will," Johnny lied. "Thanks."

As they left the shop, he called Josh and told him to meet out back. The alarm was off, and they would breach that door. While this would not be a standard breaching operation in typical Marine Corps fashion, , they would bypass that door one way or another.

On a lark, Johnny tried the door knob. He glanced over his shoulder at the guys. "Are you kidding me?" The door swung open, and they rushed inside.

A tangy odor hinting of lemon wafted through the narrow break room. There was a small table and chairs, coffee pot and microwave, and a countertop littered with fast food bags and a nearby garbage bin piled high with frozen food boxes and plastic containers.

Corey raised his hand, gaining their attention. He pointed to a Styrofoam cup with a teabag's string dangling over the side. Steam rose as Corey grasped the cup and mouthed the words *still hot*. He shifted to the microwave, put his hand on the back, and nodded.

They drew their pistols. While Josh and Willie headed out into the main office, Johnny aimed for the bathroom door, with Corey at his shoulder. Taking a deep breath, Johnny wrenched open the door. They sighed.

"Clear out there," said Josh, returning with Willie in tow. "But behind that last cubicle there's a cot and some blankets and pillows."

Johnny cursed. "Somebody was just here. Maybe it was him."

Corey felt the back of the 36" flat screen on the wall, then crossed to the table and thumbed the remote. The screen warmed to life, tuned to the local news. "Guy was having tea and watching this."

"Maybe he saw LaPorte's truck and took off," said Willie.

"That lady said he's been gone for two weeks," Johnny said.

Josh stepped out of the bathroom. "Well, someone's been living here. There's a bag in there with a toothbrush, toothpaste, the whole nine. If it was Shammas, maybe he would sneak around after hours."

'"How the hell did we miss him?" Corey asked.

Johnny bit back another curse. "While you were driving over."

"You're telling me we were that close?" asked Josh.

Johnny snickered. "That's our luck. He probably had some rental car parked down the street by Lowes or something. Oh, well, let's tear this place up. Just keep away from the windows."

They split up and began a methodical search of the office, going through every desk drawer, file, and sifting through stacks of papers, from contracts to hardcopy printouts of listings. There were no desktop computers, only power stations for plugging in laptops, which assumedly were with their owners. Johnny sifted through the papers on the desk nearest the cot.

He stopped for a moment and lowered his head. Every time they thought they had something, the trail went cold. Every damned time. His stomach twisted. He sprang to his feet and, in a sudden rage, swiped at the papers, sending a tornado across the room.

A sandwich wrapper from Subway hit the floor, along with something else.

Something that caught Johnny's eye.

It was a card identical to the one found in Kyle's backpack. He rushed over and grabbed it. The card had the same Arabic greeting and border on the front—but there was a notation on the back.

"Got something?" Willie asked.

Johnny handed him the card. Nothing ever surprised Willie.

This did.

Chapter Twenty-One

"It was the same in Iraq. The bad guys could be anybody—the mechanic, the shopkeeper, the woman walking down the street with two kids. You had to use your instincts. And you couldn't rule out anyone—not even the brother of a Marine."

—Josh Eriksson (FBI interview, 23 December)

The students who took advantage of office hours were the overachievers who already knew how to communicate respectfully with their professors and were simply verifying their understanding of the material. Those who truly needed one-on-one instruction told Nazari that it was impossible to see him because, in their words, "it was insane to get up that early." Instead, they would email him their verbose and grammatically challenged queries and expect article-length replies replete with external links for further reading and study. These were the students who thought they were *entitled* to a painless and convenient education because they were paying a fortune in tuition. They had no idea that they should be *earning* their degrees. They were utterly unaware that their professors were trying to facilitate their growth—not take their money and hand them diplomas like receipts for Big Macs. This is what American society had wrought upon its youth. This was one of a thousand wrongs that would be righted.

Nazari leaned back in his office chair and finished reading yet another email from a young lady who had failed his course and who now, during winter break, thought her groveling for sympathy and makeup assignments would wear him down. He deleted the email and glanced over at the welcome letter from the University of Northern Iowa's Department of Technology. He had dug through his files and found this document, rereading it this morning, the melancholy swelling in his chest. He secretly longed for another life, one in which he could remain a professor at this great institution because America had already been saved from the infidels. However, that was not Allah's will, and his days here were numbered. In his heart of hearts, he was not a warrior but a scholar. For now, though, he must be both.

He sighed, partly in resignation, partly over a restless night's sleep. It was 10:47 a.m. He opened up his graphics program and returned to work on the courier cards. The liaison and suppliers assumed there would be only six targets. Nazari closed his eyes for a moment and allowed the enormity of his undertaking to flow through him and lift his spirits. His breathing slowed, and for a moment, he glimpsed the rising dunes and oases of Paradise—until his office phone shattered the image. Was this the call he had been expecting?

He braced himself and answered. "Hello, this is Dr. Nazari."

"Hi, professor, this is Paul Lindquist. I'm a detective with the Holly Ridge Police Department here in North Carolina. I'm wondering if you can answer a few questions. This won't take long."

"Uh, yes, sure, I guess so. What's this about? Am I in trouble?"

"No, sir, we're just following up on investigation into a student at UNC Wilmington. His name was Randall LaPorte. He was doing an independent study with a colleague of yours, Dr. Ramzi Shammas. We understand you were friends."

"Professional colleagues," Nazari corrected. "We wrote several papers together, and I recall a presentation we did a few years ago."

"You wrote him a recommendation letter to get hired at UNC."

"Yes, I did."

"Do you know where he is now?"

"I haven't spoken to him in a while. We were emailing about I-E-D-E-C a few months ago. I believe that's the last time we spoke."

"What was that you mentioned?"

"Oh, that's the Interdisciplinary Engineering Design Education Conference. It's out in California."

"That's a mouthful."

"Which is why we use the acronym. May I ask what's going on?"

"Sure, I'm sorry. We had a robbery down here. Randall LaPorte might've been responsible, but he was killed last night when his truck ran off the road. We're following up with everyone who might have had contact with him."

"I see."

"Strangely enough, it's as though Dr. Shammas has dropped off the map. I even contacted his old school in Saudi Arabia, and they don't know where he is."

"That's not unusual. He likes to travel a lot, the Middle East, South America. It's winter break. I'm sure he's flown off to some exotic location. The students call it dropping off the grid, right? He was always a bit of an adventurer."

"Does he have any regular destinations? Does he frequent the same hotels? What else can you tell me about his traveling?"

"I'm really not sure. Like I said, we're just professional colleagues. I'm well aware of his research and teaching qualifications, but we've never socialized. I do know he's been a guest presenter at universities in maybe a dozen countries."

"Is there anything else you can tell me that might help us find him?"

"I'm afraid not. I assume you've sent him emails. He might take a while, but I'm sure he'll get back. I can take your number, and if something comes to me, I'll return the call."

The detective was pleased with this response, and Nazari diligently scribbled down the number then offered a polite good-bye.

When he glanced up, Rasul was standing in his office. The younger man closed the door and lowered his voice. They spoke in Arabic. "Was it the detective?"

"Lindquist. The informants in Wilmington were correct. And this man sounds... committed."

"That's not good."

"No, it's not. Dr. Shammas has done some incredible work for us with the east coast network and the dive teams, but his poor judgment now... what can I say? He's created a terrible breach that continues to widen."

"He recruited LaPorte. We kept the operation small. What could have gone wrong?" asked Rasul.

"Everything, it seems."

"Where is he now?"

Nazari rubbed the bridge of his nose. "On the road."

Rasul's tone grew ominous. "I can do whatever you need."

Nazari relaxed his shoulders. He would not act rashly. "Let him take his meeting. But I want you to meet him there. You get him to the safe house."

"Trust me, I will."

"Good. Now I have a feeling you'll get fired from UPS for taking off so much time."

"I'll call in sick again. If they give me a hard time, I'll threaten them with a discrimination lawsuit." Rasul smiled darkly.

"Now you sound like an infidel."

Rasul hoisted his brows. "Know your enemy."

"All right, then. Safe travels. Contact me when you have Shammas."

"I will. May Allah bestow his blessings on you."

"And on you."

Once Rasul had left, Nazari returned to his computer screen.

According to Islamic tradition, Muhammad invoked Allah by a number of characteristic names. Some of Nazari's preferences included Al-Muntaqim (the avenger), Al-Ḥasīb (the bringer of judgment), and Al-Mumīt (the bringer of death). The names were known as Asmaa al-Husna (the most beautiful names), and while some Muslims believed there were ninety-nine in all, the published lists were inconsistent, with names randomly appearing and dropping off without explanation. There was no single agreed upon list, and many scholars argued that no such list was ever provided by the Prophet Muhammad.

Controversy notwithstanding, Nazari had found a list he preferred, and, accordingly, he would design at least ninety-nine courier cards, each one containing one of the names for Allah and designating a specific target. Allah, in all of his names and in all of his greatness, would be there alongside the fighters. Once Nazari was finished creating the cards, he would travel up to "the hub," where they would be printed and distributed to his network of couriers.

A knock came at his door. "Dr. Nazari?"

He glanced up at a young woman with a green pixie cut and bloodshot eyes. She resembled one of those characters from a Japanese comic book. "Yes?"

"I took your class last semester? I emailed you yesterday about trying to fix my grade?"

"Oh, yes, Ms. Sumner. You're not from Iowa, are you?"

"What?"

"You're an out-of-state student."

"Uh, yeah, my parents live in Virginia."

"Near Richmond?"

"Yeah, pretty close."

"How far from the nuclear power station?"

"You mean North Anna? Maybe a few miles."

Nazari's lips curled in a grin. "I have some friends who work there. Are you going home to see your folks?"

"I plan on it."

"Excellent. I'm sure they'll be happy to see you. Now what's this about fixing your grade?"

Chapter Twenty-Two

"In the grand scheme of things it is ironic. We formed Triton 6 with pennies in our pockets, but we had big dreams. The idea was to become so successful that a firm like D&S Equities would buy us out. After that, we'd be sipping margaritas on our private yachts. Be careful what you wish for, I guess."

—Corey McKay (FBI interview, 23 December)

The Sig Sauer P220 was an effective compact pistol and preferred by one Nicholas Dresden, who whirled, drew the .45 from his waistband holster, and blew a sizable piece of Edward Senecal's head off. The elder businessman in his $2,500 suit tumbled to the board room floor, his head bouncing like a bowling ball before his body went inert. Dresden stepped over to the corpse, casting a long shadow over the man's ashen face, a face now haloed in blood. Senecal's eyes snapped open, and he shouted, "You wouldn't take the bet!"

Dresden shuddered against his twisted imagination.

He was an hour early for the board of directors meeting, not that his staff found this unusual. Be early, be over prepared—especially when you were on defense, he always told them. He stood at the panoramic window, watching the morning commuter traffic creep across the Queensboro Bridge. The corporate chopper ten floors above granted him permanent escape from being mummified in a mobile tomb. Off to the left were Central Park and The Pond lying beneath a mantle of black clouds. The forecast called for rain, with a high of only 41 degrees. The ten-day outlook called for blood.

With a huff, Dresden left the window and crossed to the mahogany table with seating for twenty. He ran a finger across the polished surface. From dorm rooms to Third Avenue, he and Senecal had won Roosevelt's glorious triumphs and built themselves an empire. They towered sixty floors above the unsuspecting minions. Swearing under his breath, Dresden tugged out a chair and flumped into the soft leather. As he leaned back, the door swung open, and in paraded Senecal. "What the hell are you doing?"

"I told you to stay away from the office."

"Not with the board breathing down our necks."

Senecal reached the table and leaned against it, folding his arms over his chest. "I talked to our friend. There's nothing going on at UXD. You didn't call?"

Dresden glanced emphatically at his partner. "This is insane."

"Insanity is our government-sanctioned arms sales to Israel followed by our government-sanctioned arms sales to her enemies."

"That's just foreign policy business. We mollify the Muslims by keeping our Middle East attack dog on a short leash—so they'll keep selling us their oil at usurious prices. But Eddie, what we're doing isn't like that at all."

"It's *exactly* like that."

"Look, if this were some kind of vigilante attack on Muslims, I could almost reconcile with it. They murdered your boy. I understand that. But this—"

"Excuse me, have you forgotten about Namibia?"

Senecal was referring to the Taliban-backed Kavango uprising in the Republic of Namibia, a country in southern Africa. He and Dresden had had a multimillion dollar deal in place with Prime Minister Ngodji, but the fat bastard would not make the leap and commit to the purchase. Back then they never hesitated in getting creative. They hired a mercenary team to supply the rebels with two dozen RPGs, over one hundred AK-47s, and thousands of rounds of ammo. When those rebels slaughtered an entire village outside the capital, Ngodji's wallet flew open. Dresden and Senecal used to laugh about it.

"This is the same deal, Nick. Only on steroids."

Dresden shivered as a realization took hold. "Is that how you got a contact here in the states? You used our merc in Namibia?"

"Of course I did. He turned us on to the major players here."

"Oh my god. Can we trust him?"

Senecal pushed off the desk, his brows narrowing in arrogance. "He's already done his job, and our money keeps his mouth shut."

"I'm not convinced."

Senecal closed his eyes and lifted a finger. He was about to say something but caught himself and eyed Dresden, his expression now weakening. "Nick, the board is about to put us on the hot seat for this drone deal. Things won't get any better. Do we agree on that?"

"We do."

"Now, because you've been my partner for over thirty years, I'm going to stand here, and I'll take you through it again." Senecal returned to the door, locked it, then resumed. "First, think of it this way. We're just speeding up history, feeding the jihadis intel and supplies. That's all we're doing. They'll attack with or without us. We just need them to do it now, before it's too late."

Much to Dresden's chagrin, Senecal paced the room and gesticulated like an impassioned defense attorney delivering his closing arguments. The attacks, he contended, would serve multiple purposes:

They would force the current administration into more aggressively going after these domestic threats, including known terror camps *inside* the United States.

They would create a resurgence in both the personal and military defense markets, which would rescue many of their companies from the brink of bankruptcy and open new doors for government contracts, including the Aero-Vista deal currently on the table.

They would foster a less tolerant political climate to help thwart Islamic dominance and Sharia Law legislation that was already encroaching upon local governments in both the United States and Canada.

They would coax congress and the nation into examining divisive issues like gun control, school violence, racial profiling, the war on drugs, immigration reform, and even health care within the newer and more influential context of a domestic terror attack that was far more deadly than 9/11.

They would renew a sense of patriotism in the nation as evidenced during the weeks following the World Trade Center collapse.

They would inspire a surge in military recruitment and retention numbers, which would both strengthen the nation and bolster their businesses.

And finally, they would allow for a small measure of revenge and closure on the injustices perpetrated against both Dresden's and Senecal's families.

"You're right about me," Senecal said. "I am a madman. I want to kill our enemies. And this is the only way to get this do-nothing government off its ass and into action. *The only way.*"

Dresden stared at the table, unable to meet his partner's gaze.

"Nick, no more stalling. They have the target list. You make that call. You get UXD on board right now."

"Has it really come to this? You sound blood-thirsty."

"Me?" He snorted loudly. "Your family has this obsession with tracking down your great grandfather's killer. And for what? Assuming he's still alive, do they really want to kill a ninety-five-year-old Muslim? What satisfaction is there in prosecuting a man that old for war crimes? He wouldn't survive the trial. So why does your family keep looking? The son, the one your grandfather saved? He wasn't responsible for your grandfather's murder, so I ask again, why is your family still on the hunt?"

"I don't know."

"Are you ready to kill an innocent man for the sins of his father?"

"I want to know more about what happened."

"You know exactly what happened. The only sticking point between us is the amount of blood we're ready to spill."

Dresden pushed back the chair and stood. "I need some coffee."

"You're not going anywhere." Senecal moved in closer. A weird light came into his eyes. "What if I told you I've located the family. The old man who killed your grandfather? Beb Ahmose? He's still alive. I have him. I'll ask again, do you want to kill him?"

"Is this the surprise you've been promising?"

"It is. It took us years, but I finally located him for you."

"Where is he?"

"Some place accessible."

"So you've been holding him for leverage."

"You haven't answered my question."

"Don't play this game, Eddie. You can't drag me into this nightmare."

"Holding out to the bitter end. That's all right. I expected nothing less."

"Eddie, do you know what I was thinking about this morning?"

"What?"

"I was thinking about killing you. That's what you've done to us. That's what you've done to this firm."

Senecal grabbed Dresden by his tie. "Our enemy believes in jihad and sacrifice. So do I. And I've sacrificed my blood. Now you grow a pair and make that call." Senecal shoved him backward, and he nearly fell.

Swallowing, Dresden drew his smartphone from his inner breast pocket. He started to dial... then stopped.

Senecal approached. "I'm warning you, Nick. When the board sits down in a little while, I'll unload. We'll go down together. I don't care anymore. Is that how you want to end your career. In disgrace? In jail?"

Dresden thought he might crush the phone in his hand. Trembling, he glanced down and finished dialing.

Chapter Twenty-Three

"Look, stud, I've traveled the world and spent a lifetime doing things most people read about. I've gone downrange, been shot at hundreds of times, done night jumps at over 30,000 feet. I've stared the grim reaper in the face on multiple occasions, but I've never experienced anything like this. No, I wasn't scared. The feeling was much worse."

—Johnny Johansen (FBI interview, 23 December)

"Where are you now, Johnny?"

He grimaced. "That's classified."

"Don't give me that."

"Elina, look here, we're all okay."

"That's what you said yesterday. Still no news?"

"The leaves are falling. We're getting closer."

"You said that yesterday, too. How long do we have to stay down here?"

He rolled his eyes. "You're complaining about a beach house in the Keys? Really? *Really*?"

"Look, you dummy, I miss you and I miss... the dogs."

The tremor in her voice tugged at his heart. "Look, just... just keep yourself busy. Take the girls shopping for Christmas presents."

"I took them to Sloppy Joe's."

"See now, that's good. They like it?"

"Yeah. Kate got the Sloppy Joe, and Isabelle ordered the blackened chicken. I didn't realize they'd never been there before."

"All right, that sounds great. Look, I have to go. I'll call you tonight or tomorrow, okay?"

"Love you, Johnny. Please be careful."

Johnny leaned forward on the bed, exhaling against the burning in his chest.

In his mind's eye, Elina lowered her cell phone and glared at the jihadi holding the pistol to her head. Behind her, the other women were stripped to their bras and panties and cuffed to chairs. Their eyes were blackened and swollen, and welts rose from their arms and legs. Another jihadi reared back with his folded belt and struck Jada across the shoulders. She cursed and spat in his face. The man with the belt moved toward Elina, who closed her eyes—

And Johnny sprang from the edge of the bed.

"Whoa, you all right?" Josh asked, pulling on a sweatshirt.

"Yeah, I'm good. Easy day." He rubbed his eyes and reminded himself that Elina and the others were fine. His G-shock watch read 0810. They had about an hour and fifty minutes until something happened. Perhaps something big. It was time to link up with Corey and Willie.

The Holiday Inn Express stood on a road fittingly named Veterans Way in Warminster, Pennsylvania. Johnny and the others had rented a pair of SUVs, had geared up, and had GPSed their way up Interstate 95 for about nine hours. They had been in town for the past two days, reconnoitering the 40,000 square foot Blue Door Firearms manufacturing facilities and adjoining offices. The company was a well-known international supplier of firearms and one of the few that produced the majority of its own components in house. Johnny was not only familiar with Blue Door, but he had met one of the company's military salespeople at the SHOT Show—a convention for commercial buyers and sellers of military, law enforcement, and tactical products and services. While at Blue Door's booth, Johnny had watched a video tour of the entire facility. The factory housed more than forty CNC machine tools, with everything from Swiss Turn CNC lathes to vertical and horizontal machining centers. The company machined, fabricated, welded, heat treated, coated, and assembled almost every component of their rifles, pistols, and suppressors. Blue Door's CEO was always looking for avenues inside the military, and even a small company like Triton 6 interested him for future partnership opportunities. In sum, Blue Door was an American owned and operated business, fully legal and legitimate, and was well-respected in the industry—

All of which made the situation even more bizarre.

The Islamic card Johnny had found at Shammas's real estate office had led them here. Scribbled on the back of the card were *Blue Door – 10 a.m.*, along with a date three days in advance. Why did Dr. Ramzi Shammas, an engineering professor and suspected jihadi, have a meeting with an American firearms manufacturer? Perhaps the card did not belong to him? Then why was it found at his real estate office?

Johnny had reminded them that Blue Door complied with International Traffic in Arms Regulations (ITAR), just like Triton 6, meaning all of their weapons were subject to the scrutiny of the Department of State and the ATF. Those deals were researched in great detail and were only approved by the government. There was no way anything illegal was happening through those channels.

However, Shammas could be engaged in legitimate purchases on behalf of a company or companies (or acting as an informal liaison or more formal broker). While the State Department recorded the serial numbers of those weapons, once they were delivered to said country, they were not tracked after that. The cache could easily be diverted to Shammas's jihadi brothers.

At one point in the conversation, Johnny had thrown up his hands and said, "We need to get this guy by the throat."

The industrial park off Mearns Road was home to other manufacturing facilities like Blue Door, thus Johnny and Willie were able to park their SUVs in the lot behind a large warehouse next door, hike through the tracts of undeveloped property, and establish a temporary observation post from within stands of oaks and bushy red cedars. Johnny marked the comings and goings of employees, the time the offices opened and closed, and he noted the locations of each of the security cameras.

Today their recon operation would be riskier. They would park in the lot opposite the main offices, ensuring they had a clean line of sight on the glass entrance doors whose frames were anodized in a brilliant blue. While they knew the company's cameras would be on them, they had little choice if they wanted to tail or intercept their target in time. High collars, ball caps, sunglasses, and tinted windshields would all help, as would facing east so that that rising sun would glint off their hoods.

"Ready?" Josh asked.

They left the room and headed down to the hotel's continental breakfast, where they prepared four coffees to go and procured enough muffins and bagels to keep a squad of famished Marines happy. Corey and Willie had spent the night in the woods with eyes on Blue Door. They were cold and hungry, and Johnny was coming to their rescue with coffee and carbs.

Just as they climbed into the SUV, Johnny's phone rang: a local number from Holly Ridge, a number he should have added to his contacts. He answered and tensed at the sound of Detective Lindquist's greeting.

"Yeah, how are you, Detective. Any news?"

"Sorry, Johnny. Seems like your brother's place was the last one they hit. No other robberies since then. Where are you now? I swung by the house this morning, and one of the neighbors told me you were all gone."

Johnny looked to Josh, who mouthed, *Tell him the truth.*

"The girls wanted to go down to the Keys. We took a little road trip up here to Pennsylvania. I have a buddy who works for Blue Door."

"Really? I have their forty-five cal Cochise with an extended fifteen round mag. It's a really nice piece."

"Yeah, anyway, we're going to pick him up and do some hunting."

"What're you going for, elk?"

That Johnny had previously hunted in Pennsylvania was a godsend—because Lindquist's question was a trick one, and Johnny recognized it immediately.

"No, no, we're not going for elk. Season's already closed on them. We have a tight window to bag a couple of whitetails, or maybe even a black bear, but that's damned hard. You should call in sick, come up here, and join us."

Lindquist chuckled under his breath. "Son, that sounds great, but the Mrs. tells me I need to work. You believe that?"

"I do."

"Johnny, before I let you go, I'd like to ask you something. We have another investigation going on, and it's got me curious. This could be a coincidence, but I don't know if you heard about that kid who crashed his pickup on Castle Hayne near the river?"

Johnny feigned ignorance, and Lindquist gave him a capsule summary of the situation, concluding with, "So he was a student of a professor right across the hall from your brother. How do you like that? Your brother ever mention that name? Shammas? Dr. Ramzi Shammas?"

"No, he did not."

"You sure? You want to think about it for a little while? We know your brother knew him pretty well. He even chaired Shammas's hiring committee."

"I'm sorry, but we didn't see each other that much, and when we did, he talked more about his students than the guys he worked with."

"But you never heard the name Randall LaPorte before?"

"No."

"What about a student named Abdul Azim Mohammad? Your brother ever talk about him?"

Johnny opened his mouth, about to say yes, that Mohammad was the kid who had won the engineering contest. He was one of Daniel's very best pupils and vice-president of the Muslim Student Association at UNC Wilmington. Instead, Johnny answered, "Honestly, I don't remember. My brother worked with so many kids, and a lot of them came from the Middle East, India, China, all over the place."

"But that name's not familiar."

"No. He's not a suspect in my brother's case, is he?"

"We're not sure. We just can't find him."

"Well, I hope you do. You'll keep me posted?"

Lindquist sighed. "We sure will. Anyway, you take care now. Good hunting."

Johnny thumbed off the phone. He remembered to breathe.

* * *

"There they are," said Corey, lowering his binoculars. "Let's get back."

As Johnny and Josh pulled into Blue Door's parking lot, Corey and Willie jogged through the woods, trailing banners of warm breath. Corey's hometown of Girard was about six hours northwest of Warminster, hence he was intimately familiar with winters in this part of the country. In fact, his bones told him it was getting colder. They reached the SUV in the warehouse lot and punched on the heater the second they climbed inside.

"All I can say is, this guy had better show up," said Willie, shivering and putting his hand up to the vent, waiting for the heat as he drove them out of the lot.

Corey did likewise and said, "It was good times, bro."

"Tell that to my back, my shoulders, and my damned foot where I got shot. Soon as I get that coffee, I need to pop my meds. Don't let me forget."

Corey smiled. "Roger that, Grandpa."

"Hey, you'll be there. And I'll be there to laugh."

"You know it. So Lindsey sounded good this morning. Better than yesterday."

"Ivonne's happy to get away from the house."

"Some place warmer, right? And hey, I didn't realize it, but they know pretty much everything."

Willie shrugged. "Johnny told Elina, and I'm sure Jada got the run down from Josh. I think they're keeping it from Johnny's nieces."

"That's a good idea. Those girls are going through a lot already." Corey took a deep breath, and, realizing he was running out of time, he spoke quickly, "You'd do anything for Johnny, wouldn't you."

"Hey, I was the skeptic here."

"And now?"

Willie grinned crookedly. "Dude, we've already crossed phase line green, just like the good old days. Might as well see it through."

Corey thought about that, then asked, "You worried about getting caught?"

"By the police? Not so much. By them? That's another story. I like to know the size and composition of my enemy before I attack, you know?"

"That's why I brought this up. I have some news. Thought I'd wait to tell everybody, but I'll let you know first. I got a text back from our boy at the FMS."

"And?"

"And he tracked down a broker in Peru. He says Blue Door is selling rifles to the local police in Lima, and they're trying to get involved with the Peruvian National Police. The interior minister is on another big push to modernize their forces, and they're hiring guys left and right and upgrading their gear. The key international sales guy from Blue Door is this Egyptian-American dude named Sameh Ismail. We need to get more intel on him. There's no obvious link to Shammas, but he could be using another alias. First the EXSA link to Peru, and now this. Our boy Shammas has his hands on firearms and explosives being smuggled in and out of that country."

"And you boys already confirmed that the stuff comes up through Colombia and works its way here," Willie added.

Corey nodded. "Like you said, the more we learn, the bigger it gets and the more we have to hold back. We're talking about international drug smuggling and gun running, a major operation for the Feds. And we're just sitting on it."

"I wouldn't feel too guilty. I'm sure they got a finger on it already. Or at least part of it And what the hell? I thought you were Mr. Go-With-The-Flow?"

"I still am. And I'm no pussy. Let's just say I'm... *concerned*."

"Hey, we all are. Better to shoot the rabbit than go down his hole."

Corey snorted. "Tell that to the tunnel rats. Oh, that's us."

"Hey, I will say this. I know Johnny. He won't sit on this forever. We've always done the right thing." Willie faced Corey, and his tone hardened. "For now, we do what he says. We stay on the train."

They pulled up beside Johnny's SUV and wrapped their greedy paws around their breakfast. Corey had never eaten two muffins and a bagel so fast. The coffee tasted like steaming heaven. Between bites, he updated Johnny, and then Willie took them to the front of the parking lot. If anyone tried to pull a Dale Earnhardt and burn rubber for the exit, they would be there for a T-boning interception.

* * *

By 1000 Corey had finished his coffee and his mouth had returned to cotton. They kept low, peering through their sunglasses at the front doors and main entrance. About ten minutes later, a lone Camry cruised into the parking lot. Johnny shot them a text: let's see what we got.

"I'm pretty good at reading lips," said Willie.

"Really? What's her name?" Corey asked

"Funny," grunted Willie. "Stand by."

Corey squinted toward the car and jotted down the tag number so they could do a reverse-tag search to identify the owner and address. There were many websites that offered these services for a fee, although the Driver's Privacy Protection Act (DPPA) noted that it was illegal to perform a search without a legal reason to do so. They were supposed to review the privacy act to ensure their reason was protected, but in the real world, search companies wanted their fee, and members could fabricate any number of "legal" reasons to justify such a search. Triton 6 already subscribed to a document search company that included tag search; however, Corey suspected that the vehicle was a rental, and a search would only lead them back to the agency, which was under no obligation to reveal personal information about any client.

With the tag info recorded, he double-checked the photo of Shammas they had copied from Alfaisal University's website. The man who emerged was taller than Corey expected, at least six feet. He wore a suit and overcoat that looked tailored, not something drawn from the rack at Kohl's. While his colleagues might don a white knit kufi on their heads, he wore no hat, and his graying black hair was gelled back away from his forehead, with a few curls dangling behind his ears. Only his long beard and closely trimmed mustache suggested he might be a Muslim. He removed his sunglasses and strode away from the car with purpose, tucking a leather portfolio beneath his arm.

The beep of an incoming text message sent Corey's gaze flicking down to the screen. That's him, Johnny confirmed. Corey agreed. He reached into a nylon bag at his boots and removed his Nikon digital camera with its 55-300 mm telephoto zoom lens. He pointed it at the door, and the autofocus purred to clarify the image. He snapped off pictures as the door opened and Shammas was greeted by two men. The first was a pot-bellied troll with a dark complexion and beard—a man who could be

Sameh Ismail. The second was an athletic-looking black man whose bald pate seemed one size too large for his body. By some small miracle of physics, he had wrestled himself into a tight white dress shirt, suspenders, and dark blue trousers. When he proffered his giant claw to Shammas, his fingers flashed with a blinding collection of gold rings that matched his cufflinks. Corey squeezed off a shot of that bling before all three disappeared behind the tinted glass doors.

"You catch what they said?" he asked Willie.

"They were just saying hello. Nothing worth our time."

Johnny phoned Willie, who put the call on speaker: "All right, boys. This shouldn't take long. We need an ID on that short guy. Call him 'Uncle Haji' for now. And the big black dude? He's 'Easy Money.' Corey, you get some good pictures?"

"I did." Corey had already attached the wifi adaptor to the camera and was uploading the images to his phone so he could text them to Johnny and his other contacts. "I'll see if our boy at the FMS can ID these guys."

"Roger that."

A few seconds later, a uniformed Blue Door security guard ventured outside. He shielded his eyes against the glare and started toward Johnny's SUV.

Chapter Twenty-Four

"So we pulled it up on the phone. Turns out New London, Connecticut is the home of a Navy submarine squadron, the Navy Submarine School, and the General Dynamics Electric Boat Division's design and engineering facility. Some might call that a target-rich environment."

—Willie Parente (FBI interview, 23 December)

There were nine women in all, each wearing *hijabs* covering their heads and chests. They sat in three neat rows, laboring behind sewing machines under the relentless scrutiny of Fatima, a thirty-year-old woman from Mali whose parents had been nomads, more specifically Tuareg people who wandered the Saharan regions of their West African country. Fatima was lithe, with deep brown skin and brightly colored beads like the rings of coral snakes in her braided hair.

Mr. Bassem Younes had gone to Mali to recruit Fatima out of the vest making facilities hidden within the tin-roofed ghettos of Bamacko. He had smuggled her into the United States with the help of his cartel contacts in Juarez, and he had trained her as a secretary to work for him at Seaboard Shipping and Storage, with its headquarters in Windsor, Connecticut.

However, Fatima's real expertise lie in her vest designs, which had caught the attention of Younes's associates in Cairo and Riyadh. They had urged him to find her, and so for her skill and knowledge of suicide bombing—her knowledge of how to kill most effectively—he had granted her a new life, and she seemed quite content living in America.

At the moment, they were a few miles away from his trucking company, inside a warehouse used primarily to stock and distribute automotive parts to various retailers. The company, C-T Auto Supply, was owned and operated by Younes's cousin. A back office now served as the vest making workshop. Younes arrived in the doorway, sipping on his tea. Fatima came around the humming and clicking machines, wiped her hands across the bottom of her blue smock, then lifted her brows at him.

"How many thus far?" he asked.

"That first batch of material caused quite a delay," she reminded him. "But the new nylon is good. Strong but still light weight, which is what we need. And to answer your question, we have about nine thus far."

"Will you finish in time?"

"Of course. I'll keep them here day and night. We won't stop until they're finished."

"And the materials from Peru?"

"They're excellent. No issues with them."

Younes walked with her into the workshop, toward rows of folding tables erected near the back wall. The finished vests with bulging pockets lay in rows, while others still under construction were piled on two chairs. The vests were fashioned from a lightweight tactical nylon and cut in rectangular patterns with holes in their centers. Cut outs for the shoulders were placed on either side of the main hole. Narrow pockets stood in vertical rows along the front and back. A pair of wooden molds matching the front and back of the vests lay on another table. Nails, screws, bolts, ball bearings, and other metal fragments were placed onto the mold, and then the plastic explosive was rolled over the shrapnel like a layer of dough. Once all the shrapnel was contained within the explosive, the roll was placed into one of the pockets, and the process was repeated. Some vests contained separate fragmentation jackets, but this method, Fatima had argued, allowed the bomber a more stealthy approach on the target by removing the possibility of rattling shrapnel and decreasing the vest's girth. The vests weighed approximately fifteen pounds after they were wired and equipped with their handheld firing devices. Their blasts were omnidirectional, and everything—even the bomber's watch, glasses, and bones—became part of the lethal shrapnel mix.

"I won't delay you any further," Younes said.

She nodded tersely, then returned to the front of the room, where she noticed a woman having a problem with her machine and leaned in to assist.

Younes headed off toward a row of shelves jammed with boxes of parts. He turned down another aisle and reached the loading dock, where off to his right lay the rolling metal door at ground level. Four white, nondescript box trucks, each seventeen feet long, had been driven inside, and each would deliver Allah's wrath to the infidels. The Americans called them Vehicle Bourne Improvised Explosive devices. Younes called them steeds of war. Their destinations were still unknown to Younes, but Nazari had assured him that the target information would arrive shortly.

While Younes's parents had been born in Dubai, he was, like his colleagues, an American citizen. Given his heritage and the nature of his work, he had become fascinated with another young American hero. On April 19, 1995, Timothy McVeigh had parked a Ryder truck loaded with 5,000 pounds of ammonium nitrate and nitromethane in front of the Alfred P. Murrah Federal building in Oklahoma City. The truck exploded, killing 168 people and injuring over 600. The attack was one of the most simple, elegant, and effective acts of domestic terrorism in United States history. McVeigh was an artist, with absolutely no regret for what he had done. Younes had studied the hand-drawn schematic of McVeigh's truck. He understood how McVeigh had aligned the barrels, what he had placed in them, and where he had stacked more bags of fertilizer. Younes saw how shock tube detonators snaked between the materials.

Of course Younes and his men were intrigued by the prospect of reproducing McVeigh's artistry. What was more, federal regulations still failed to control the sale of large quantities of commercial grade fertilizer; however, state and local regulations did exist, although they varied wildly from state to state. In many cases, shopkeepers were asked by federal and local law enforcement authorities to report anyone buying large amounts of fertilizer, although this honor system often relied upon high school or college kids working part time at farm supply stores. These social media zombies were not the most keen-eyed observers of terrorist activity. Still, Younes, Nazari, and the rest of their core group were unwilling to take that risk.

Necessity, they said, was the mother of invention. Thus, Younes and the group had unleashed a plan as cunning and elegant as McVeigh's work.

Nearly two years prior, a massive explosion at a West, Texas fertilizer plant was used by *Al-Saif* to conceal the theft of over twenty tons of ammonium nitrate. This was an inside job to be sure, with American jihadis hired as employees six months prior to the robbery. Just after closing time, Younes's teams had moved in to procure the materials. By 7:50 p.m. a tremor that residents said felt like an earthquake rocked the town, leveled the facility, and took out a large portion of the West Middle School. A two-story apartment building with about fifty units was shredded into kindling and toothpicks. When the fires died and the smoke finally cleared, a crater spanning some ninety-feet across and ten feet deep marked the epicenter of the blast. Fifteen were killed, over 160 injured.

A million dollar investigation by state and federal officials failed to find a concrete cause for the explosions. All they knew was that a fire did start in the seed room, which backed up to a storage bin containing over 150 tons of ammonium nitrate. They believed that between twenty-eight and thirty-four tons of the chemical exploded with a force equal to 15,000 pounds of dynamite. There was no accounting for missing chemicals. As the fingers began to point, none were directed at jihadis or other extremists. Liberal media pundits wrote columns about the "complete lack of oversight by state and federal agencies crippled by the GOP's war of deregulation." While officials blamed each other for the disaster, Younes and his teams stored their cache in a Connecticut warehouse, where it would remain until needed—

Until the day of judgment.

Now, because of Younes's own bold actions, their truck bombs would be TWICE as powerful as the one used by the heroic Timothy McVeigh. The ammonium nitrate had just been transferred to this warehouse, and the plans for how to arrange the materials inside the trucks was set. Their other accouterments were contained within the blocks of cocaine shipped up from North Carolina. Younes walked by the two pallets of bricks with scorpion labels, watching as men at a nearby table broke several open and removed the boosters inside. He reached the tailgate of the nearest truck and hoisted himself into the empty bay. He stole a moment to close his eyes and imagine the fire.

...prepare against them whatever you are able of power and of steeds of war by which you may terrify the enemy of Allah and your enemy and others besides them whom you do not know [but] whom Allah knows. And whatever you spend in the cause of Allah will be fully repaid to you, and you will not be wronged.

Chapter Twenty-Five

"Look at me. You think I let the past rule my life? If I did, I might be in jail or dead. You don't look back. You keep your eyes on the road. That's why windshields are big and rear view mirrors are small."

—Josh Eriksson (FBI interview, 23 December)

The security guard raked fingers through his blond hair and fixed his gaze on Johnny. The kid was in his late-twenties, a baby-faced part-timer going to college at night with, perhaps, a military background that had given him a foot in the blue door, so to speak. He tipped his head at an arrogant angle, and as he neared the SUV, Johnny lowered his window and said, "Morning, Chief."

"Morning, sir."

And with that, the kid marched by.

Johnny exchanged a look with Josh, then lowered his head onto the seat. "I just had a heart-attack." He checked the side mirror.

"What's he doing?" asked Josh.

"He's getting into his car."

"I see him now. They have security twenty-four seven. He must be coming off a night shift."

Johnny's phone rang. "Silver Buick LaCrosse inbound," Willie reported. "I couldn't get eyes on the driver, but he's heading your way. We got his tag, just in case."

"Check it out," said Johnny as the Buick rolled into the lot, the driver backing into a space about ten cars down and facing the front doors.

"Could be a client or another sales guy," Josh said.

"Roger. Still can't see his face yet. He's looking down."

Josh snorted. "Probably playing on his phone."

Johnny squinted toward the Buick. He imagined a man getting out and hurrying toward the front doors. That man was Daniel, impossibly alive and here for some clandestine meeting with Shammas. Johnny burst from the SUV, sprinted across the lot, and seized his brother by the arm. *"What're you doing?"*

"You can't stop me."

"How could you do this?"

"It's not your fault, Johnny. It's the old man's. He made me hate everything he stood for. Love, art, beauty? They meant nothing to him. It was all about power and selling your soul to get it. You know who taught me how to be a real man? Not Dad. Allah. Only he can save us now."

Johnny closed his eyes. "You're wrong."

"What?" Josh asked. "Hey, you falling asleep?"

"No, no," Johnny said, reaching for his cup of coffee. "Just... my brother had nothing to do with any of this. Nothing at all."

Josh gave him an odd look. "Then why are we here?"

"I don't know."

"Look, I get it. You want to know why Dan was killed—but you *don't* want to know."

"Exactly."

"I've been going over it myself. Maybe he was spying. Maybe they forced him to work with them. Maybe he joined them, then changed his mind. Maybe they just double-crossed him. Maybe they planned to kill him for some other reason."

Johnny nodded and sipped his coffee. "I know what I want to believe."

"Me, too."

"I had another dream last night."

"Fallujah?"

"No. I saw everyone at my brother's funeral, and they were lined up like they were waiting to get on a roller coaster. But they were waiting for me. They wanted to know why my brother was a jihadi. They wanted to know how I could let that happen. They asked what I thought about my brother's face being on the cover of *Rolling Stone* magazine, just like that other fool from the Boston bombing. They wanted me to talk about how much I hated him and how embarrassed I was. They said I should apologize to our country, the Corps, and the recon community. They said I should've killed Daniel myself."

"Whoa. You need to get that out of your head."

"I just can't."

Johnny closed his eyes and saw Daniel raise his hands to ears. "*Allahu Akbar.*" Next he placed his left hand over his navel, his right hand on top, and began to recite the opening prayer, the *Isteftah Dua*.

* * *

Forty-five minutes later, Shammas and Easy Money passed through the front doors, exchanged a few words, shook hands, then walked toward the parking lot. Easy Money shuffled off to the south side with a noticeable bounce in his step. Johnny ordered Willie and Corey to stay with him.

Before Shammas could reach his parked car, the driver of the silver Buick hopped out—

And Johnny raised his voice, "Hey, hey, hey, look here."

The driver confronted Shammas, speaking rapidly and gesturing back toward his car.

"I'll get some video," said Josh, lifting his smartphone and zooming in on the scene.

The driver was much younger than Shammas, barely thirty, and tall, over six feet. He was nondescript for a Muslim male, with dark hair parted to the side, a coffee-and-cream colored face, and a wiry beard with the hint of a moustache. His jeans and dark green jacket did little more to distinguish him.

However, something about his bearing struck Johnny as strangely familiar.

As Shammas continued the conversation, his frown deepened. At first he seemed confused, unable to comprehend whatever he was hearing, but then his lip curled in annoyance. He stroked his beard as he listened further, and then, appearing resigned, even flustered, he shook his head and stormed back to his car, where he retrieved a rolling luggage bag from his trunk. He followed the driver to the Buick and shoved his bag into the back seat. Before climbing into the car, he lifted his hands and barked something else, but the driver simply ignored him, got in, slipped on a pair of sunglasses, and the Buick rumbled off toward the exit.

"Now what's this?" Josh asked. "A pickup?"

"Hell, yeah, it is," Johnny answered. "You see the look on Shammas's face? Dude, he was not happy. So he grabs his bag. And why leave the car? Unless he was caught off guard and knows he's going away for a while."

"I agree. And that kid, the driver? He's working for the boss, whoever that is. He got orders to pick up Shammas, maybe take him back for a meeting or some place safe for a while. Either way, this could be big."

Johnny fired up the engine. "We're on them." As they left the parking lot, his phone rang. "What's up, Willie?"

"Hey, our new friend is getting on the 276 toll road, heading east into New Jersey. And by the way, some of the tags we've researched come from rental car agencies. No surprise there. We're working on Easy Money's now."

"Roger that. Don't lose him."

"No chance. We have a full tank of gas. We'll track him into Canada if we have to."

"Thanks, Willie. Keep me updated."

"Will do. You guys rolling yet?"

"Yeah, heading south."

"Roger. Talk to you soon."

Johnny glanced sidelong at Josh, whose face had drained of color and whose gaze seemed opaque. "What's wrong?"

"I was just thinking, the last time I was following someone was down in Florida. We did a good job. She never spotted us."

Johnny knew the story of Josh's exploits as a would-be assassin, and he knew how it pained his friend. "Hey, I'm glad you're riding shotgun."

"I'm on it like a fat kid on a cupcake." Josh winked then pointed ahead. "He's turning. Don't get too close."

* * *

Although Willie and Corey had taken shifts while conducting their overnight reconnaissance, Willie had barely slept during his down time; consequently, he began to drift out of his lane as they sped north up I-95, passing through New York. He caught himself, blinked, then glanced at Corey, who resembled a pistol-whipped guard from an old WWII movie. A tiny river of drool had escaped from the corner of the younger man's mouth and puddled on his shoulder.

"Are you kidding me? We can't fall asleep," Willie warned him.

Corey jerked awake and looked disoriented, as though he had never been in a car before. "Aw, dude, we've been driving forever. My butt's numb. How far is this fool going?"

Willie shrugged and cursed.

Easy Money had squeezed his gargantuan frame into a blue Chevy Spark, a car barely larger than some of the go-karts Willie had constructed as a kid. He had led them north for over 100 miles, but now he changed lanes, ready to get off at exit 83 toward New London.

"We're in Connecticut?" Corey asked.

Willie glared. "Been here for a while now."

They followed Easy Money off the exit and south, through the perimeter arteries of historical New London, once the world's third-busiest whaling port. They eventually wound up on Montauk Ave, then turned left onto Thames Street, which terminated at Pequot Ave and the New London Harbor, whose silty waters were as greenish-brown as a ripening avocado. They passed homes with sprawling lawns and broad porches affording magnificent views. Willie found his mouth falling open, and Corey could only gape and mutter curses in disbelief. Damned Yankees knew how to live.

Near the corner of Glenwood and Pequot rose a colonial-style house with steeply pitched roof and dormers gleaming in the afternoon sun. The pale-white home had become the Pequot Inn and Marina, with its dock and facilities located across the street. Easy Money turned up the gravel drive and into the adjacent covered parking lot, choosing a space designated number six by a small, hand-painted sign shaped like a whale.

Meanwhile, Willie turned sharply into the marina's parking lot, exploiting another SUV for cover. They hopped out and double timed toward the marina's entrance so they could watch the big man strut across the brick path, mount the porch, and vanish into the house.

Shielding his eyes from the sun, Willie faced north, where dozens of anchored sailboats dotted the waves like gulls resting between airborne assaults. That tang in the wind reminded him of being deployed aboard ship or "on float" with his fellow Marines. From walking like drunks down the p-ways during heavy seas to the head overflowing with raw sewage, you could not beat those five star accommodations. He smiled inwardly and gazed farther out to where the Gold Star Memorial Bridge spanned the Thames River. If he squinted hard enough, he could see the traffic flowing over the bridge and the handful of fishing boats lying below like minions paying homage to a god of concrete and iron.

Corey was already on the phone, updating Johnny. When he finished, he looked at Willie and said, "We're not following this guy anymore."

"Why not?"

"I mean we are, but let's slow him down. You notice one of his tires going flat?"

Willie shook his head.

"You will in a second. Get me up there."

219

"Whoa, let's hold off. Let our boy get settled in. I like the plan, just not the timing. Where's Johnny at?'

"They're still on the road. South on eighty-one, past D.C. already."

"Damn. Where's Shammas taking them?"

Corey shrugged, and they headed back to the SUV. Willie pulled out and drove to the next corner. "That fence next door is good cover," he said. "Not sure where to park. I bet the marina's lot empties out overnight."

"Look down there," Corey said, pointing toward the riprap along the shoreline. A backhoe and two dump trucks sent powerful reverberations through the ground as they cleared and hauled away sand. "Let's see where they go. Could use them for cover. We might have a good view of the lot and the house."

"Worth a shot."

"So what's this guy doing here?" Corey asked.

Willie remembered being on float and bumping into a lance corporal from Connecticut who told him that the Navy had some serious operations in and around New London. "Hey, Corey, why don't you check the map?"

Corey's thumb worked overtime on his smartphone's screen. Meanwhile, Willie made a U-turn and steered back toward the marina, searching for a discreet place to leave the SUV.

"Damn, bro. Listen to this." Corey ticked off a list of facilities.

"Submarine squadron, school, shipbuilding," Willie repeated. "I thought so."

"Yeah. And did you know there are only two places in the U.S. where they build nuclear subs? Newport News in Virginia, and right here..."

"So what do you think?"

"I think everything's on the table. If these guys are jihadis, which we believe they are, then they don't *just happen to be here.*"

"All right, so we'll go there," Willie began. "We'll assume they're all targets. But do you think these guys could pull it off? With all the security in place? It would have to be a massive inside job, something they've been planning for years. It just seems impossible."

Corey snickered. "You mean like hijacking four planes—all on the same day?"

"Look, this ain't that big. We're just getting paranoid. It's just drug smugglers and maybe some small explosive stuff for lone wolf bombers."

"Okay, Willie. Whatever makes you feel better."

"Think big or go home, huh?"

* * *

The bayonets piercing Johnny's back were imaginary, but the pain was not. He had trouble focusing on anything else, his thoughts cooling and congealing, then lique-fying to evaporate again. There was the ache, along with an eternity of yellow lines tattooed across the whites of his mind's eye. Seven hours of driving with only one pit stop to get gas and use the head had taken its toll. The sun had set more than an hour ago, and they were cruising on a narrow road through the back woods of Raleigh County, West Virginia. According to Josh's map, they were just north of the Blue Ridge Mountains. The striking reds and yellows of the fall foliage season were long gone, with the headlights paring away the darkness to reveal only drab shades of brown, the portents of more winter death to come. Thankfully, there were several cars between them and the Buick, but Johnny feared that if the roads grew any more rural, they might lose that cover and have to run with lights out. They had packed a pair of night vision binoculars they used while hunting, but Johnny found them cumbersome to hold while driving. An old pair of NODs would have been perfect.

In the meantime, Josh was already two steps ahead of him. One of Warrick Marine's clients, Datron World Communications, was a supplier of military and pub-lic safety radio equipment to over eighty countries. The company's CEO wanted to put one of the drones they distributed, the Aeryon Skyranger UAV, into the hands of Riverine Patrol Boat crews all over the world. Josh was helping the company con-nect with potential clients and was in possession of several of the quad-rotors, two of which he had gathered from the office, one of which he was unfolding now, with the drone's tablet computer balanced on his lap.

The SkyRanger resembled a miniature lunar module with curving legs and four short arms that folded up and locked into place. At the end of each arm was a rotor, and the combination reminded Josh of the pinwheels he had played with as a kid. Beneath the pentagon-shaped main housing hung a globe containing a dual elec-tro-optical (EO) and infra-red (IR) payload. The drone could relay live HD video and still images from up to five kilometers away while flying to an altitude of up to 1,500 meters. The system's encrypted, low latency, and all digital network allowed real time video streaming to multiple devices.

"Will they hear it?" Johnny asked.

"They have the windows up, the heat on. And this bird is small and virtually silent. Anyone behind us? No? Good. Slow down for a minute." Josh opened his own window, then touched his stylus on the computer's screen. He held the drone out the window, waiting as the rotors buzzed and pulsed. A breath later, he touched another part of the screen, tossed the drone, then shut the window.

"Got the altitude set. Live video feed's looking good." Josh consulted his screen once more, then glanced up. "All right, you can really back off now. I have the Buick in sight. The IR on this thing is great. I can see the hot engine and the outline of the car."

Johnny nodded. "I feel like we're in the game now."

"Hey, whoa, slow down."

"What?"

"Hit the brakes!"

"What?"

"They're off the road, on the shoulder. The other cars are passing. Shit, let me see if I can land." Josh worked the stylus over the screen.

"They stop to take a leak?"

"Don't know yet. Hang on. All right, I got the bird on the ground, and we still have the feed. Rotors switching off."

Johnny leaned toward the computer screen. The Buick's rear bumper was printed negative by the drone's infrared. Trees stood like a bulwark constructed from dinosaur bones. The passenger's side door opened, and Shammas stepped out, just a pale orange figure who slammed the door after himself and ventured off into the woods.

"No drama. Just a piss break," Johnny groaned.

But then the driver's side door opened, and out stepped the younger man. He crossed to the trunk, opened it, then fumbled through a bag or suit case. When he turned to face the drone's camera, he was clutching a pistol with a long suppressor screwed onto the barrel. Leaving the trunk open, the man jogged off, disappearing into the woods.

"What's going on?" Josh asked.

Johnny threw the truck in gear. "We're heading over there."

"No, Johnny, don't!"

With his boot hovering over the accelerator pedal, Johnny glared at Josh. "We can't lose Shammas."

"You saw how that guy surprised him back at Blue Door. Maybe he faked taking a leak and just ran off. That's why the driver's chasing him now. We need to let this play out. If we don't, we blow our cover."

Johnny clutched the wheel as though he were bracing for impact with a tractor trailer, his ribs feeling as though they might crack any second. He fought for breath, the adrenaline surging. "All right. We still got the drone out there." He swore and put the SUV in park.

From the tablet computer's speaker came a faint crack, perhaps static in the transmission. Perhaps a suppressed gunshot.

* * *

The hissing of snakes—a sound not unlike air escaping from a car tire—always gave Corey the chills, and for good reason. During a hunting trip at the age of fourteen, he had come face to face with a Timber rattlesnake. Only his father's quick thinking and reflexive trigger response had saved Corey from a vicious bite. The shotgun blast had torn the snake to ribbons, and Corey had kept the rattle as a souvenir.

He finished with Easy Money's tire, and then he stole his way across the lawn and hopped the picket fence. Willie was there with a pair of Steiners, panning across the house and zooming in the side windows.

"We're good to go," Corey reported. "Let's hope he goes out to dinner."

"Roger. So what happened to the good old days, when people left their blinds or their curtains open, and women used to strip down to their bras right near the windows?"

"Are you kidding?"

"No. I just need something to keep warm."

Corey widened his gaze. "Well, don't look at me."

They returned their attention to the inn and the covered parking lot, waiting another fifteen minutes in silence while the cold settled in and the stench of low tide, a gag-inducing smell akin to rotting seafood, wafted over from across the street.

Corey chanced a quick look at Willie, and then it struck him again, as it had when they had been reconnoitering Blue Door. This time, however, the sensation was far greater, as though he were jerry-rigged to a runaway reactor producing adrenaline.

"*Drifter, thirty seconds to mark. Standby.*"

He was back in Iraq, and they were downrange. Close to the water. To the boats. To his life.

"*Hell, yeah! If it ain't wet, it ain't worth it!*"

They were always Marines. That part they had never forgotten, but the thrill of clandestine operations had been replaced by real world obligations and responsibilities, by training others to do the fun jobs, by spending more time on theory than on practice. But now he was back. They were back.

Before Corey could regale himself any further, Easy Money exited through the front door, lifting the collar of his overcoat. He hastened along the brick path, his polished leather oxfords flashing in the walkway lights as though they were drawing current. He was money, all right. Money, money.

"Let's go," said Willie, shoving a balaclava into Corey's hands.

"What're we doing now?"

"New plan. We're going to roll this guy."

* * *

The old man was an avid subscriber to *Popular Science*, and nowadays Johnny often perused the magazine's website, scanning articles about military technology such as how squids were inspiring better camouflage for soldiers and how new condensation technology captured drinkable water from diesel exhaust. In some of the more pointed articles, he learned that one of the smallest subatomic particles in the known universe was called a "quark." However, while sitting there in the idling SUV, he realized he had just discovered a new particle, one even smaller, one he dubbed "his patience" because it was infinitesimally small, arguably nonexistent. For every second that the driver and Shammas spent in the woods, Johnny lost a year of his life.

He was eighty-seven now, a hunchbacked wizard with wild white hair. He sat on the front porch of his Smoky Mountain cabin and apologized to his nieces for his failures. *"I don't know what happened to your father. I don't know who killed him."*

While they cried, he clambered to his feet and smashed his rocking chair across the porch. He screamed and shook his wizened fists at the storm clouds.

Johnny shook his head at that image and willed himself away, back home, back to Elina. She soothed him with her musical voice and with that pearlescent sheen in her eyes that had never faded, even after all these years. Being married to a Recon Marine was no picnic (not that we would truly know). He reflected on that John Milton quote he liked to paraphrase: those who wait also serve. Elina had reminded him of all the time he had spent away, and the pangs of guilt and longing struck hard. It was Daniel who always told him how lucky he was, that he had found a woman who could put up with his over the top personality, his locker room antics, and his child-like spontaneity. Johnny might be preaching the good word of "Easy day, no drama," but living with him was only for the few, the proud—and not for the faint of heart. When he was younger, he never felt guilty about his service. Elina knew what she had signed on for, but now, as they grew older together, the enormity of her sacrifices became clear, no longer clouded by his unyielding sense of duty and ego. If the trail ended here, he would return home, and she would be there for him, his rock. She would say he had tried his best. She would urge him to be thankful for what he had, and not focus on what he had lost. His brother was never coming back.

"I'm the sheepdog now!"

Johnny banged his fist on the steering wheel. "I can't take this any more," he told Josh. "We're going."

"Maybe you're right," Josh answered, studying the table computer. "Wait. Movement near the trees."

"Oh, no," Johnny gasped. "Is this... is this really happening?"

During his final year in the Corps, Johnny had been an Assistant Operations Chief with 2nd Force Reconnaissance Company. He had been responsible for directing staff members and platoons in target development, mission analysis, operational planning, and the execution of anti-terrorism operations. He had gone downrange to Al Anbar province, Iraq, where he developed unit training management curriculums, operational plans, procedures, and the tactical employment of combat supporting units. That was the Marine Corps description of serious planning, of putting people together and making shit happen. After twenty-three years in the Corps, Johnny understood that plans needed to be flexible and rewritten on the fly to account for an asymmetric enemy.

Nevertheless, this driver had completely surprised him. The kid had tucked his arms beneath the pits of a body and was struggling to drag it from the woods, moving in short bursts between which he caught his breath. He reached the grassy shoulder and picked up his pace, plowing through a bed of fallen leaves that marked his path. As he neared the Buick, he waited a moment to check for cars, then lifted the body higher and made one last dash.

Josh zoomed in with the drone's camera, and there he was, Shammas, his heels dragging, his forehead torn apart from an exit wound the size of a golf ball. A Mardi Gras mask of blood obscured half his face. The driver reached the tailgate, hauled Shammas higher, and then, in a final heave, dumped him into the trunk.

Once Shammas's legs were folded inside, the driver slammed shut the lid and climbed into the vehicle. His brake lights flashed before he sped away.

Chapter Twenty-Six

"I remember one night in Iraq when we took these Army Special Forces guys upriver. They drove their ATVs right onto the boats. We dropped them off, and four hours later they came back. Rumor was they were on a mission to get these two insurgent leaders to kill each other. I never forgot that. And that's how I came up with the plan to tie up our loose ends in New London."

—Corey McKay (FBI interview, 23 December)

The darkness materialized to life and rose behind Easy Money's car. That darkness was Corey, moving with the practiced ease of a veteran Marine, once a boat captain, now a crimson-eyed reaper behind his balaclava. The brawny man took one look at the business end of Corey's pistol, threw up his hands, then whirled—

Coming face to face with Willie's Glock.

As he opened his mouth to scream, Willie shoved a glove into that gaping maw, then jammed the barrel of his pistol into Easy Money's forehead. A shudder of empathetic pain had Corey flinching his brows.

"Shhh, big boy," Willie said. "You scream, I shoot. We're just here for a little cash. You chew on that glove and keep quiet."

In the next instant, Corey was down at the man's oxfords, wrenching free a lace he would use to bind the brawny man's arms behind his back. Back in the good old days, they would have a roll of duct tape or a pair of zipper cuffs—or even a pair of handcuffs—because in every squad there had always been some tactard who over packed for every operation. This plan, however, had been devised on the fly, and Corey had realized during the sprint over that they had nothing with which to bind the man. Then he had considered Easy Money's mirror-like oxfords—foot wear worn by the Donald Trumps and Warren Buffets of the world.

With the lace in hand, Corey followed Willie as he forced the man behind the car, toward one of the carport's brick columns that would shield them from the inn's front door and windows. Corey bound the man's arms behind his back, then got to work, rifling through Easy Money's pockets, snatching his wallet, keys, phone, and another prayer card similar to the two they had already found. He carried no weapons and was armed only with a coupon for dinner at On The Waterfront, a local seafood place. Corey thumbed the key fob, unlocking the car. In the glove box, he found the vehicle's registration and insurance information, along with the owner's manual. He scanned the documents, then nodded to Willie and came around, opening the hatchback and folding down the back seats.

"Get inside," Willie ordered.

The menace in Easy Money's eyes was impressive, even reptilian, a toxin that could both immobilize and help digest his prey. His large head shifted between Willie and the car, and Corey sensed the gears grinding in his head: *make a break now... or obey.* A man as well-dressed as him, a man of his comportment—a man of his size— was not used to being ordered around, let alone mugged.

For his hesitation and defiance, Corey rewarded Easy Money with a gloved punch to the head, a few inches west of his temple. Stunned by the blow and more docile, Easy Money barely fought back as they wrestled him into the hatchback. Corey used Easy Money's remaining shoelace to bind his legs. They rolled him onto his belly, then closed the hatchback and raced off. In their minds, they were a pair of Olympic sprinters bounding for the SUV. In reality, they were light years slower.

They had left their vehicle near the backhoe they had IDed earlier, and once across the street and back inside, Willie started the engine and guided them up a service road and back onto Pequot Avenue. "What did we get?" he asked.

In the bluish glow of the LED cabin light, Corey examined the documents. "Well, the registration and insurance confirm what we saw online with the tag search: his car is registered to the Islamic Center in Shelton, Connecticut."

"Roger that."

"Got another one of these," he said, holding up the Islamic card. "Nothing written on the back. Just the praise Allah text."

"What's up with these cards? What're they doing with them?"

Corey shrugged. "Maybe we should have questioned him."

"Not worth the risk," Willie said. "We want him to think he got mugged. Just something random. Nothing else. If he goes back to his buddies and says he was questioned—"

"Yeah, I know, that blows the alarm."

Willie nodded. "Did he have a driver's license? Any credit cards?"

Corey opened the wallet and dug through it. "No credit cards. Just some cash, couple hundred bucks at least. And here's the license. State of Connecticut. Says his name is Jerome Buttler. Lives in Windsor."

"Outstanding. We'll use the money for gas. And we'll hang on to the license, but it's probably a fake. What about the phone?"

Corey lifted the prepaid, compact flip phone from his lap. "No calls recorded, no numbers saved, no messages. He might have an app that erases everything."

"He probably does. And guess who pays the phone bill?"

"The Islamic Center in Shelton."

"No doubt."

Corey sighed. "Be nice if we could get into his room and search it."

"For all we know, the whole place could be run by jihadis. And who knows, this guy could be a player or just a courier. Do we want to take that risk?"

"He's dealing with Shammas and Blue Door," Corey reminded him. "And he's tall enough to have killed Johnny's brother."

"That's true. And there's no telling how far up the chain of command he could get us." Willie began making a U-turn.

"What're we doing now? Going back?"

"Hell, yeah. We can't leave him."

* * *

Those thugs had taken his wallet and phone. How would he explain this to his colleagues here and to those in Namibia? And what about his primary responsibilities? The phone call he was supposed to make? He spat out the glove, tugged against the shoelace digging into his wrists, then turned to Allah:

The dua' of any one of you will be answered so long as he does not seek to hasten it, and does not say, 'I made dua' but I had no answer.

The lie came like a murmur at first, then fully announced itself. He would say he had lost his jacket, and inside were the wallet and phone. He would commit to this story—because if they learned the truth, he would not live to see another day.

Given who they were.

And what they were about to do.

* * *

The GPS indicated they were on Sullivan Road, crossing the bridge over I-64. Josh divided his attention between the SkyRanger's computer screen, the nav display on the dash, and his window, where the valley unfurled like a roll of frieze carpet pinpricked with light. Soon, the two-lane road burrowed beneath a dense canopy, following a tortuous path along the ridge lines. The Buick was now eight hundred meters ahead, the driver over compensating for curves, suggesting he was not familiar with the corners and switchbacks. As a precaution, Johnny resorted to only the running lights and had reduced their speed to 25 mph.

They had been shadowing the kid for the past thirty minutes. Shammas's death had rendered both of them mute and listening absently to the engine's hum, along with the soft whir of heat through the vents. Josh had never been very superstitious, but he had an eerie feeling that they should turn back, that their deaths had already been predetermined on the day they were born, that this hunt had no part in the narrative of their lives. They were challenging fate, enraging Odin and the other gods, and recompense would be exacted with the blood of their friends and loved ones.

To combat the feeling, he checked the drone's systems time and again, wishing he had a shot of whiskey to dull the edge. Meanwhile, Johnny sat there inert, allowing his life force to drain into the seat. Even Corey's text updating them on their mugging of Easy Money had elicited no response from him. He was, Josh knew, hell bent on intercepting the driver and drawing equal amounts of intel and blood. Here was where they differed. While Johnny wore his heart on his sleeve, Josh kept his stowed aboard a Riverine Patrol Boat crewed by ogres in olive drab. Good luck getting near it. The truth was his father had taught him to guard his emotions, especially when lying supine on the double-wide's linoleum floor as though crucified against his own future. Now Josh committed himself to remaining calm and observing the enemy while trying to assess his motivation—yet another survival ritual.

Had the driver been ordered to kill Shammas? Then why had Shammas left the car? It seemed he had gone off to take a leak, and, perhaps the driver had seized the opportunity to shoot him, either because Shammas was trying to escape or because he had orders in hand. What had Shammas done to warrant his execution? Perhaps he had failed to do something. Johnny's prying represented a security leak, and maybe Shammas had paid the price for his inaction. Josh rewound the questions and reviewed them again, the suppositions flashing but as quickly dying, leaving behind smoke coiled with mystery.

Josh adjusted the drone's course, skimming the treetops as the Buick slowed, the driver hesitated, then finally turned left. Shady Oaks Road was shaped like a whip in mid-stroke and terminated about 1.5 miles ahead at the crest of a broad hill, the tallest among several shoulders of rock. Frowning, Josh worked the tablet computer, gaining more altitude. He cleared his throat. "Johnny, stop at the next corner. Don't turn."

"Roger." Johnny pulled off the road, switched off the running lights, and parked. "What do we got?"

"Check it out." Josh pointed to the navigation screen. "Looks like a dead end."

"What's up there?"

"I don't see anything yet. Maybe you can check it on your phone."

"I will. I think we got him, Josh."

The SUV's cabin, now cast in the warming glow of the tablet, adopted a new air, as though all of the pessimism, so pervasive just moments ago, had fled through a crack in the window. It was easy to assume that Johnny had lost all hope, but he had not. His was an undying hope that had raised his shoulders for twenty-three years in the Marine Corps, a hope sometimes camouflaged by setbacks and despair but one that would rise like a sniper in a ghillie suit to remind him, Josh, and every Marine that it had not forsaken them, that it was always there, as pure and clean as mountain air.

While Johnny brought up Google Earth on his smartphone, Josh tracked the Buick until it neared the end of the road, arriving at the clearing, with the little towns of Beaver and Daniels lying to the northeast like collections of candles in a darkened cathedral.

With a daring that quickened his pulse, Josh piloted the SkyRanger even closer to the clearing, toward the rough hewn perimeter of trees. He slowed to a hover, then buzzed straight up for a wider view. As the clearing grew more distinct in the white-hot display, he and Johnny exchanged a curious look.

The clearing was paddle-shaped, with the bulbous end spanned by six or seven intersecting dirt roads forming a capillary between an assortment of structures, some resembling trailers, others more barn-, garage-, or warehouse-like from above. There were fourteen in all, with as many cars parked around them—sedans, SUVs, pickup trucks. Near the more narrow top of the clearing lay several long dirt courses with tall berms like those found on shooting ranges. Over on the southwest side stood a fenced off area with tilled ground, perhaps a makeshift farm or corral. Encompassing the entire enclave was a chain-link fence crowned with concertina wire, a fence whose main gate lay beside the berms.

The Buick paused at the gate, and a figure came from the nearest trailer and stopped to unlock it. Once the gate was dragged aside, the Buick passed through, with the figure locking up after the new arrival.

"I have to bring in the drone," said Josh. "Fifty minute run time on the battery, and it's getting low. I'll send up number two while the first one's charging. Looks like only one way in or out, unless he hikes down the other side the mountain. In that case, I'll spot him with the second drone."

"Sounds good," Johnny replied. "But Josh, what're we looking at here? I can see it on Google Earth, but there's no name for it, no nothing."

"It's like some kind of private trailer park."

"Or a commune."

Josh ran a quick web search for Islam, Raleigh County, West Virginia. He clicked on the first link. "Whoa, Johnny, look at this."

Johnny scanned the headline and immediately called Willie, his voice freighted with tension. "You still up there?"

"Yeah. We're watching him. He's tied up in the car."

"I need you down here."

"You want us to leave? That's a big loose end, Johnny. I hate to say this, but what if he's the guy who killed your brother?"

"He's tall enough, but I think he's too big. He's not the guy. Get down here A-SAP. I'll drop a pin for you on the map."

* * *

Willie ended the call, then faced Corey, wearing an expression that left no room for argument. "You got the first shift."

"And it's an all night drive," Corey added, his enthusiasm knowing no bounds. He punctuated his reminder with several epithets as they both got out in the marina's parking lot and traded places, Willie now riding shotgun.

Corey sat in the driver's seat like a wax figure, scrutinizing the inn, the grounds, and the carport. "What about our boy?" He lifted his chin at the Chevy parked across the street. "Do we just leave him there?"

"Yeah, just like the first time. That's what Johnny wants."

In a matter of seconds, Corey's mood transformed from exhaustion and dread to near-breathless excitement. He eyed Willie, then stared back at the car. He began shaking his head, then flipped open Easy Money's phone and dialed a number.

"Who're you calling?"

"911."

"Are you nuts?"

"Yes." Corey grinned like a man who had spent the afternoon munching on tablets of Percocet as though they were M&Ms.

Willie raised his voice. "Dude, I'm serious, who are you calling?"

"Just wait." Corey lifted his index finger. "Yes, my friend and I were walking by the Pequot Inn and Marina in New London, and we heard some noises coming from a car there. It sounded like someone groaning inside. The vehicle is a Chevy Spark. It's parked under the carport. Here's the address..."

When he was finished with the 911 operator, Corey said, "So hear me out, Willie. We took his wallet, his phone, his license. Once his buddies realize he's been talking to the cops, he's screwed. He's another security risk. They'll want to kill him more than we do."

Willie considered that, then chuckled under his breath. "Right on."

* * *

A scant three miles up river, near the bridge and where the calming waters had transformed into a diaphanous gown with tulle glittering in the moonlight, one of the men on the fishing boats lowered his binoculars and regarded his partner. "No call tonight?" he asked in Arabic.

"Not yet. I wonder why he's late?"

"He always calls after dinner."

"I'm sure he will. I'm eager to share the good news."

Chapter Twenty-Seven

"The mountain wasn't in the way. The mountain was the way. And we didn't come down like Moses; we came down like maniacs."

—Johnny Johansen (FBI interview, 23 December)

"The West Virginia Muslims of Peace" (WVMP) claimed to be an offshoot of the American Muslim Society, although no administrator at the latter would vouch for any official connection to the former. The Raleigh County Sheriff's Department and the Beckley City Police stated in interviews that the camp was "on their radar" and that the FBI had documented its existence for the past three years. The sheriff estimated that between twenty and forty people lived in the small community, and according to public records, one Mahmoud Fahmi, a real estate broker and American citizen who resided in Richmond and San Diego, owned the land and had gone to great lengths to have public utilities brought up to the mountain.

Since the enclave's founding, not a single resident had broken the law, not so much as a speeding or parking ticket. They worked in the neighboring towns at a number of businesses and institutions: gas stations, fast food chains, daycares, and one resident was a code enforcement officer for the city of Beckley. A branch campus of Concord University employed an administrative assistant and a professor teaching business classes who were WVMP residents. An investigative report conducted by an incendiary right wing website concluded that the commune was one of thirty-five or more known terrorist training camps in the United States. The authors put forth a simple thesis: Islamic radicals were in the country and preparing for jihad on American soil while the current administration did absolutely nothing to stop them.

During late afternoons and on weekends, gunfire resounded from within the enclave. In one interview the sheriff confirmed that the residents had constructed both rifle and pistol ranges but again, they were within their legal rights to do so. West Virginia was one of the most gun-friendly states in America, and so long as the residents kept five hundred feet away from their own dwellings when practicing, they were fine. The sheriff had been asked if he believed the enclave was a terror camp. "I can tell you what I think, and I'll tell you what I can do. What I think is that there are Islamists up there engaged in military-style training. What I can do is nothing. Again, they're not breaking the law, and they're protected under the Constitution."

With that irony stuck in his throat, Johnny leaned back and massaged his temples. He was waiting for the shaggy-haired, vacant-eyed clerk at the McDonald's drive-thru to hand him his order. The town of Beaver was only a fifteen minute drive from the enclave, and Johnny had just sent Josh a text, assuring him that he would return soon with hot coffee and breakfast sandwiches. He had left his friend up in the woods, hunkered down in the frost-covered trees to monitor a feed from the second drone, which they had boldly landed on the roof of a trailer, exploiting the double-wide's satellite dish for cover. What was more, the Buick was parked just outside and had remained there all night, despite a seven AM bristle of activity. Women wearing hijabs and men in suits or work uniforms had ducked into the cars and left, raising dust clouds into the faces of the two men in parkas manning the gate. If they were carrying any weapons, they kept them concealed. A few other groups, young families with children hopping about, rounded the little ones into minivans and drove off to daycares or schools. Five or six old men in ManJams and sandals crossed from several trailers toward the barn near the corral, a barn that might have been serving as a mosque, since they were carrying their prayer rugs. They seemed strangely unaffected by the cold, shuffling slowly, almost reverently, across the rutted path. They gathered into a knot outside the barn door, then entered carefully, one after another.

With the interminable wait over and his "Mc-order" in hand, Johnny returned to the road and called Elina, putting her on the speakerphone. "Good morning, Johnny."

Her formality was no act. Elina's dignity was one of her most important possessions, and she clung to it fiercely, never allowing incorrigible men like Johnny Johansen to wrest it from her. The boys called her a woman of class, while others deemed her sense of decorum a "European thing," but to Johnny, her elegance was akin to his own sense of duty and desire to be "squared away" in all aspects of his life—no matter the situation.

"What're you doing?" he asked.

"No 'good morning?'" she challenged.

He grinned and spoke with deliberateness, "Good morning, Ms. Elina. How are you?"

"Waking up. Do you know what time it is? Or are you in some other time zone?"

"I'm in West Virginia."

"What're you doing there?"

"Talking to you. I was thinking about some puppies."

He could almost hear her frown. "Not yet, Johnny. It's too soon. We can't forget about them with puppies."

"All right. You let me know. What's the plan for today?"

"Well, Matt's taking us shooting."

"He's what?"

"There's a gun range down here."

"Yeah, I know it, Big Coppitt. It's on Palmetto, over by the Navy Station. What do the girls think about that?"

"They're excited. Neither one of them has handled a gun before. It might help them with the stress. Kate started having nightmares, and now Isabelle is saying that if Kate doesn't stop talking about the nightmares, she'll start having them, too."

"Well, it's good you're keeping them busy. And tell Matt I said thanks. Some shooting might help you, too."

"You know that's not one of my favorite things."

"But you're still a good shot. You hit the target when you picked me for a husband."

"Johnny, I have to go. You just made me nauseous."

He chuckled, then his tone grew more serious. "Hey, one more thing. I need to ask you for some advice?"

"Really? This is a first..."

"We have a chance to find out what happened to Daniel, but it won't be easy."

"Okay."

"When I say it won't be easy, I mean"—he hesitated—"it might be dangerous."

"Illegal?"

"I don't know."

"And you want me to tell you if you should go or not?"

"What would you do?"

"You already made up your mind. You want me to make you feel better about it."

"I don't know. I just want—"

"Johnny..." her voice cracked. "You know I love you. Just go. You know what to do."

"Thank you." He waited for her to say something. "Elina?"

She had already hung up. He reached for the phone but thought better of it. The rift in her voice got under his skin and raised his hackles.

"Just go."

He grabbed his coffee and drove on, the terrain filtered through a new and grimmer lens. Rolling hills walled in both sides of the road, and the power cables draped from ancient poles seemed to gravitate toward him, threatening to collapse. He passed a mom-and-pop sports bar with a tattered banner flapping from the gabled roof. The windows and doors had been boarded up against an economic hurricane that had already ravaged the area. Down the road lay a hapless transmission shop whose bays remained open like empty mausoleums. The used car lot next door featured dust-caked compacts whose bumpers frowned beneath prices no higher than three grand. Across the street was a ramshackle strip mall, its windows stained gray as though from radioactive ash. Only two of the six available spaces were occupied by accounting and printing services, their pathetic placards as weather-worn as the bar's. He neared the Walgreens and CVS pharmacies, erected at the intersection like modern day monuments radiating promise to a town whose arthritic hands clung weakly to life.

Josh's observation post was just off Sullivan Road, beyond the turn off at Shady Oaks. The tree-ringed hollow shielded them from the enclave's traffic. At two minutes out, Johnny received a text from Willie, who apologized for being late. They had grabbed a bite and had admittedly overshot the exit.

As Johnny was reading that text, his phone rang. "Hey, Mark, thanks for getting back."

"I got your message, Johnny. What're you doing up there?"

Gatterton's tone cornered Johnny into an explanation. "Like I said, I'm following up on a lead."

"What about the police?"

"Somebody needs to write speeding tickets."

"But you're wearing the man pants."

"Right on. So tell me about this jihadi camp. Can you tap any of your contacts?"

"You know me, buddy. I don't call unless I have intel."

"And you know me. I'm listening."

"I have four friends up in West Virginia who're in serious trouble."

Johnny sighed in disgust. "Oh, here we go..."

"Hey, I'm not kidding. You need to get out of there. No more playing cop."

"You never worry about me."

"I know, but the Bureau has eyes on that enclave. It's an ongoing investigation. You make an *aggressive* move, and you could be interfering with that investigation."

"What exactly are they investigating?"

"I don't have a case file, just heard they have something going on."

Johnny snorted. "So they look at satellite imagery once a week and check in with the local L-E-Os, is that what you're telling me?"

"I'm telling you as a friend to let this go. It's not worth it."

"You don't know the whole story."

Johnny summarized his findings in Daniel's office, the trail up to West Virginia, and his desire to learn the truth about Daniel's death.

"It's worse than I thought," said Gatterton. "More than just revenge. Damn, Johnny, for a guy who preaches 'Easy day, no drama,' you're anything but."

"Look here, I don't want to drag you into this."

"There's no dragging involved. I'm just worried about you. What's your plan?"

"I'm not sure yet."

Gatterton snickered. "Master Sergeant Johansen? No plan? Ha! You never were a good liar. You got a plan. You're just not sure if it'll fly with the boys."

Johnny winced over his transparency. "All right, you got me. It's just that we're close, Mark. We lost two in a row. I need to interrogate that guy up there. I won't lose him."

"When do you plan on moving?"

"Tonight."

"Damn. All right, I'll see what I can do."

"I need details on the Bureau's investigation."

"Roger that. And do me a favor: text me before you pull the trigger."

"I will."

"And don't shake too many trees."

Johnny smiled weakly. "Too late for that."

* * *

The Skyranger drone had a 1.9 mile range beyond line of sight, but it was no electronic soothsayer. It could not detail what secrets Johnny might uncover up on the mountain and what truths might free or burden his heart. For those answers, he would have to venture up there, and he wondered if he should go alone.

He picked up Josh, then drove about a quarter mile southwest where he and Willie linked up and found a single-lane path through the woods. They edged forward about ten yards, flattening twigs and cones with appreciable snaps. A long ridge rising crookedly like a spine suffering from scoliosis appeared to their left, and Johnny maneuvered the SUV behind it. The mound, along with the shortleaf yellow pines and tall brown grasses hissing in the wind, screened them from the road. Josh said they were 1.4 miles away from the drone and that signal strength was in the green.

Willie and Corey climbed into the back of Johnny's SUV, letting in a blast of pine-scented air. Their sore eyes had sunken into the deeper plains of their unshaven faces, and their once glowing skin had faded to a matte finish. Their expressions suggested they had hiked down on foot from Connecticut, all the while cursing the maniacal jarhead who had sentenced them to become dead men walking toward a West Virginia mountain.

"I know it's been a long night," Johnny began. "But here's where we're at. You already got the head's up on Shammas, and the driver is still up there. Not sure what he's doing. They might've moved the body out of the trunk while we were switching drones."

Willie's face grew more dubious. "Johnny, I've been going over this. You guys have now witnessed a murder."

"We witnessed the transfer of a body, but I hear you, Willie. We have drugs, explosive materials... Blue Door is somehow involved. That driver killed Shammas and came here to an Islamic training camp. We can't let this go. We need to interrogate him."

"You're sure?" asked Willie. "No chance of going to the police?"

"We're back to that?" asked Josh.

Willie cocked a brow. "Our operation's got mission creep written all over it now. Snoopin' and poopin' is one thing. That's what we do, and for the most part we can stay out of trouble. But now we're talking about something else—because Johnny, I already know what you have in mind. Precision raid. Reliving the days of Fallujah."

Johnny's cheeks warmed. "I won't lie to you, Willie."

"Listen to me, all of you," Josh snapped. "We go to the cops now, they lock us up. We're not law enforcement. We're not bail bondsman, but we've been crossing state lines, following people, and we witnessed a murder we didn't report."

"Let's make an anonymous call," Willie said. "I mean, look, Corey and I already mugged a guy and we made that call."

"And you'll confess to the mugging?" asked Josh.

"I would," said Corey. "I'll take my licks."

Willie shrugged. "Dude, it keeps ramping up until what? One of us gets—"

"Hold on now," Johnny said. "You know the deal. Admit to nothing, deny everything, and make counter accusations. But hey, Willie, you're right. It *is* ramping up, and we're running out of time. Shammas took that meeting, and the wheels are spinning. I don't know how long we can wait on that driver. I want to get up there, get in tight, survey that place and pick our infil and exfil. Josh, you're down here, in the car, working the drone. You'll be ready to go in case our boy drives off. If he stays up there, we'll snatch him tonight. I'm done with high speed chases and trailing people."

Willie raised his brows. "So I was right. Direct action. We're going offensive."

"Unless you have a better plan?"

"I do not."

"Johnny, you researched this place, and I did some digging on the drive down," said Corey. "The FBI knows about it, and even if they can't do anything, they have eyes on."

Johnny forced a nod. He was hoping Mark Gatterton's reservations would not arise, yet he appreciated Corey's relentless attention to detail. "The Bureau's hands are tied, just like the sheriff's and the city police chief's. It's a very small group up there with a track record for being peaceful. Hell, they're so remote hardly anyone has harassed them, except for a few reporters. If the Bureau's monitoring them, it's not twenty-four seven surveillance. Their budget would never allow that. They'll take a peak at satellite intel, but they'll rely more on the local boys, who probably drive by, maybe head up there once in a while, and they talk to the mail lady, the UPS guy, and so on."

"But it's still a training camp," Corey said.

"And they're armed," added Willie.

Corey's tone grew more insistent. "Johnny, what if we're wrong? What if there's an agent working up there? He's been undercover for a few years. Or maybe they've actively recruited a civilian, one of the actual residents. We raid the camp, that blows their investigation, and we're left holding the bag."

"We can test that theory," said Johnny. "We'll get up there and watch the place. A man arrived last night with a body in his trunk. If your undercover agent is doing his job, the Feds should be raiding the place, right? Hell, they should've been here already."

"Maybe they're hiding the body," Corey pointed out. "Maybe his cover's been blown, and he doesn't know it."

Josh threw up his hands. "We can talk ourselves into this or out of it. I'm like Johnny. I'm done losing witnesses."

"I understand that," said Willie. "I'm just making sure we're clear on this. We know the target and understand the risks. We know the size and composition of the enemy."

"I agree," Corey said. "If we go up there, we're outnumbered and outgunned. We're trespassing, and they'll shoot us, kill us, and walk away."

"You boys are forgetting a few things," said Josh. "Number one: we're Marines. They won't get their sights on us. Number two: we're Marines. And number three: we're Marines."

"They've got women and children up there," Willie blurted out. "If the op goes south, collateral damage could be bad."

Johnny held up a palm. "Guys, this is as serious as it gets. I understand that. But if we walk away now, we'll never know what Daniel was doing and what these bastards are planning. To me, it's worth the risk, but I understand if you want to leave now."

None of them would meet his gaze, as each pondered his own decision.

Johnny's chest swelled with guilt. Was he asking too much? What if he lost one of them? Could he live with himself after that? "You're my friends," he finally added. "Nothing will ever change that, and what you've done already... I don't have words."

He choked up, and in that moment, the lightning that bound them together shone in the whites of their eyes. They were back in a riverine patrol boat with a deck washed in blood.

"We're not quitters," said Willie.

Johnny swallowed. "No, we're not."

"Then let's get this done," said Corey.

"Amen," said Josh.

Johnny nodded and collected his thoughts. "I've been in touch with Gatterton. I'll try to get us more intel before we move. Willie, you and Corey go into town. Get us some wire cutters and supplies. We'll be up on that mountain for a while."

"Roger that," said Willie.

Corey glanced up from his phone. "Have you guys checked the weather?"

Chapter Twenty-Eight

"You decide if it's ironic or not, but my first job in the Marines was as an 0352 TOW gunner, meaning I know exactly what that missile system can do—and now, so do you."

—Willie Parente (FBI interview, 23 December)

Parker, Colorado was an upper middle-class commuter town southeast of the Denver metropolitan area. Its twenty square miles of subdivisions resembled sunflowers and peonies blossoming across the map. Known for its Western-Victorian downtown area, Parker was no different from thousands of suburbs that sprawled across America; therefore, El-Najjar had no desire to sightsee. His visit to the house on Newbury Court was strictly business.

From the corner of his eye he spied the two-story homes on either side of the street, the late model cars parked in the driveways, the lawns turned brown from the frost. He imagined summers here, with children skateboarding in the streets, grass being cut, cars being washed, teenaged girls walking toy poodles on pink leashes. Their happiness was born of ignorance. These infidels lived in a prison of their own making, a society whose bodies were poisoned by supersized soft drinks and junk food and whose intellects were quashed by the fashionably stupid who promoted their ignorance on social media. They had abandoned their god in favor of reality television and a chance to become morally bankrupt celebrities whose self-indulgence and scandals were worshipped by the masses. They raised narcissistic children whose sense of entitlement swelled along with their waistlines.

For his part, El-Najjar was a fifty-nine-year old imam who had spent the better part of his life in the refuge of his own Islamic community in Paterson, New Jersey, where immigrants from across the Arab world, along with Turks and African-Americans, bonded together to form a barrier against the hatred and persecution. Even as some Christians and Jews joined with Muslims to promote unity, the government recruited informants and other spies to monitor El-Najjar's mosque, never forgetting that two of the 9/11 hijackers who commandeered American Airlines flight 77 had leased an apartment in Paterson. *Al-Saif's* jihad would save everyone from the government's tyranny and open the eyes of infidels seeking the truth, those who would finally answer Allah's calling.

After tugging down his simple woolen cap, El Najjar pulled to the curb and parked. Air travel did not suit him very well. Any flight over one hour wreaked havoc with his back, as did the rental car's cheap seat with its inadequate lumbar support. Levering himself from the rolling crypt took all of his effort, and he groaned against the sudden fingers of cold air that throttled his exposed neck and throat.

The neighborhood lay in an arctic silence, the school busses having roared through an hour prior, leaving behind backpacked students and blasts of diesel fumes. A dozen or more crows kept vigil on a sagging power line beneath a lowering gray sky. El-Najjar ambled up the concrete driveway, mounted the stoop, and rang the bell.

Before he could turn to stare idly at the homes across the street, the door swung open. Tabesh's beard was longer, his hair grayer, his glasses thicker than El-Najjar remembered, but his childhood friend was still there, beaming behind his aging veneer.

"*Ahlan sadiqi,*" El-Najjar said, embracing his friend.

Tabesh returned the greeting and drew him immediately into the house. "It's been over ten years, my friend. Maybe more."

El-Najjar nodded. "I wish we had time for tea."

"Me, too. But I understand. You'll bring the truck tonight?"

"Yes. You've already moved out the furniture?"

"Just yesterday. And the family, too, of course."

"Any issue with security?"

"None. The neighbors believe we're heading back to Dearborn, and I'm sure some are happy to see us go."

El-Najjar's expression soured as Tabesh led him through the empty living room, where holes in the walls and carpet dents like crop circles were all that remained of the home's décor. They passed through the kitchen and toward a door leading to the basement. Tabesh flicked on a light, then warned El-Najjar to be careful on the narrow wooden steps, each groaning in protest as they descended into the colder, mustier air, their nostrils flaring.

The cinder block walls were unpainted, and wires and pipes pierced the exposed trusses overhead like aggressive vines. Their footfalls echoed loudly as they continued toward a finished wall at the far end. Set into the middle of the wall was a commercial grade steel door with key lock and deadbolt.

"They built this when we first moved in," said Tabesh, passing into the glare of an exposed bulb.

"I've forgotten to ask, but how long have you had them?"

"Over three years now. I thought someone would come sooner." Tabesh produced a set of keys and fumbled with the first lock. Once the deadbolt clunked aside, he glanced back at El-Najjar. "Are you frightened?"

"No."

"Not even a little?"

"I am prepared to fight and die in the service of Allah."

Tabesh nodded and swung open the door to reveal—

A room about ten feet square and lined with stacks of heavy anvil cases the size of refrigerator boxes. Tabesh reached to the inside wall and threw a light switch. Small stickers on the sides of each case bore numbers ranging from one to twelve, with the nearest cases stacked two high so that El-Najjar could reach out and touch the combination lock jutting from its side. Tabesh handed him a small card upon which he had written a list of numbers and combination codes. After matching the case number to the combination, El-Najjar opened the lock. Tabesh helped him release all eight of the heavy latches, and they pried back the lid. Although they knew what was inside, they still widened their eyes in awe.

Packed in heavy gray foam was a long tube resembling a telescope, a tripod with bulky legs, a box-shaped sight with three holes, and four projectiles with stabilizing fins folded down for packing. To the uninitiated, this was a military weapon. To those in the know like El-Najjar, this was jihad in the form of the Baktar-Shikan wire-guided anti-tank missile system. The unit was manufactured by the Kahuta Research labs in Pakistan and was the Chinese/Pakistan equivalent of an American TOW missile system. Aiming was accomplished through the Goniometer sight. The operator would simply press the firing trigger and keep the crosshairs on target. The rest was performed by the system itself, which automatically guided the missile to fly along the line of sight for up to 3,000 meters until it struck the target. The missile could penetrate armor up to 500 mm thick, and tandem warheads reached depths of over 600 mm. Two operators were required to haul around and assemble the weapon, but that was of no great concern to El-Najjar.

He removed his glove and touched one of the missiles, its lethality running up his arm and into his head.

"Sometimes late at night, I would come here and open one of the boxes," Tabesh confessed.

El-Najjar stepped back from the case and frowned. "Why would you do that?"

"If someone passed a remark to me or my wife, or if the kids at school bullied my sons, I would stand here and pray and reassure myself that our day would come."

Gritting his teeth over this, El-Najjar clutched Tabesh by the shoulders. "Your prayers have been answered, my friend."

* * *

The freezing rain began at dusk, pinging through the pine needles and branches to alight on Johnny's shoulders. He checked his phone, swearing at the current temperature, just twenty-eight degrees. Willie and Corey were equally miserable, no doubt, but Josh had it made, monitoring the drone's feed from inside their SUV.

After acquiring two sets of wire cutters and some snacks and drinks to last them through the night, if necessary, they had collected their gear, hiked up the mountain, and spread out to conduct reconnaissance and surveillance operations. They grew more attentive now as residents arrived home from work. Updates were shared via text. As the rain fell harder, Johnny moved in for more cover and a closer look.

Lying now on his belly about three meters away from the perimeter fence and buried beneath some shrubs and piles of leaves, he lifted his binoculars as a Nissan Maxima rolled up and parked in front of the trailer next door to their target's. Even before the car door opened, their target rushed out of his trailer, hopped down the steps, and jogged to the car.

Johnny smiled as a woman climbed out of the Nissan, removed her headscarf, glanced around, then kissed their target before he dragged her back to his place. Muslims refrained from sex before marriage. Tell that to their target, a backslider, indeed, whose extended stay at the enclave included an age-old form of cardiovascular training.

A text from Josh indicated that he had captured the greeting on video. Willie, who was stationed along the fence behind the trailer, reported several findings. First, the curtains on one of the windows was open, and as best as he could tell, there were only two occupants inside the trailer: their target and the woman. Second, several men had gathered at the shooting ranges across the compound but the rainfall had nixed their plans. He had zoomed in and confirmed that many of their weapons were manufactured by Blue Door.

Corey continued creating his own map, accounting for each trailer and its occupants as they returned home. Johnny had instructed him to identify those trailers where children resided. They might be able to select their approach while keeping their backs to those homes. They needed to not only account for their targets but what lay *behind* those targets. Of course, if they executed the operation correctly, no shots would be fired.

The radar map on Johnny's phone showed a major storm front with a southeast track, ready to bear down on them. The breeze kicked into a gale, with the oaks swaying and groaning, the fence rattling, and leaves swirling down from the canopy. He tucked himself in deeper and peered through his binoculars. Two pickup trucks parked near a pair of trailers positioned in an L-shape. Given the vehicles, Johnny half-expected men dressed in flannel and donning trucker caps to hop out. Two bearded men in business suits rose, waved good-bye to each other, and returned to their respective homes. Johnny asked the others for a headcount. The numbers fell between twenty-four and twenty-nine residents, but they needed to include the old men they had identified earlier.

Oddly enough, the wind died and the rain thinned to a drizzle. He lay there for several minutes, as though frozen between radar sweeps, his gaze flicking curiously to the sky for answers. Soon, the air around the enclave filled with static, and the thunderheads led the charge, ushering in an armored corps of undulating black clouds drawing lightning from the slopes. The limbs shook violently, and the NO TRESPASSING – PRIVATE PROPERTY signs posted at twenty-foot intervals along the fence clanged against the chain links and their loosened ties. Johnny ordered the men to stay low. The few cars that entered the enclave now high-tailed toward the trailers, residents running from the vehicles to seek cover, stopping only to reclaim little ones who strayed away beneath the angry heavens.

The seconds between a flash of lightning and the subsequent crack of thunder could be used to calculate the distance of a lightning strike, the so called "flash to bang," method. Every five seconds equaled one mile. However, the next bolt required no accounting—because it struck just outside the fence, a jagged seam of silvery God's blood dividing the world in half. The ground reverberated, and the thunder was so loud that its concussion slammed Johnny into the dirt. He lost his breath, grimaced, then glanced up through the rain at his phone, where another text from Josh popped on the screen: It's coming through now! Johnny tucked deeper into his hunting jacket and pulled his cap over his brows.

* * *

By midnight, the clouds had thinned to long tendrils connecting the stars. There was an almost silicone sheen to the darkness, with the rain dripping off everything in a cold yet serene soundtrack. Windows glowed from the two trailers nearest the main gate, but the others had gone either dark or shone with the flickering light of televisions, as though they were replaying highlights of the storm. Johnny cupped his gloved hand around his face to warm his runny nose. After meeting with only mild success, he eased himself back and away, finally sitting up behind the shrubs. When he turned his head, he found Daniel standing near a broad trunk, dressed in ManJams and with a prayer rug tucked under his arm. His eyes were black pools, like a shark's or snake's, the pupils having receded into that same abyss that had captured the little boy too afraid to fight.

He spoke fervently, the words in Arabic, his face contorting as he seemed to chastise Johnny for what he was doing to himself and to his friends. Johnny felt unhinged and could only sit there, rapt, his brother's robe growing translucent to expose roiling flames within. The flames licked up Daniel's neck, got under his cheeks, then raged high from his head.

And just as suddenly, he was gone. Johnny checked his watch. It was nearly 0200. Had he fallen asleep? Where had the time gone? On his phone were seven unanswered texts from the boys. With a start, he seized his binoculars.

The trailers near the main gate shone in the tight beams of halogen spotlights, but their windows were otherwise dark. There were no guards visible. The enclave slept. Johnny ordered Willie to start cutting the fence and for Corey to rally on Willie's position.

Shivering and with bones cracking, Johnny crawled to the fence and worked the wire cutters, his pectoral muscles flexing as he drew a three-foot tall opening between the links. He pried back the fence like a tent flap and secured one side, then the other with zip ties. Willie reported that he was good to go, as was Corey.

An earlier text from Mark Gatterton said he could not confirm if the Bureau had an agent inside the enclave. His contacts were hitting the proverbial brick wall as they attempted to access files on the investigation. For some reason, even they were locked out. He urged Johnny to abandon his plan. Gatterton was a great friend and an outstanding Marine, but he did not fully comprehend the agony and the aggression in Johnny's heart.

There was nothing left to do. It was time to issue the order.

Johnny drew in a long, icy breath, rubbed his jowls, then shut his eyes, squeezing them as though he could blink off his fears. Decades had passed since he had sought God's help for anything. He felt like a hypocrite who attended church on Christmas and Easter and spent the rest of the year drinking and whoring. Why would God help and protect him now? He had no answer; nevertheless, he asked for forgiveness and for protection.

All right. He was ready.

Chapter Twenty-Nine

"An old Greek once said that in war, the first casualty is the truth. He must have been drinking with an old pirate, who said that dead men tell no tales. Honestly, I'd like to shoot both of those bastards."

—Josh Eriksson (FBI interview, 23 December)

One57 in Midtown Manhattan soared some ninety stories into the night sky, marking it as the newest and tallest residential building in New York City. Two years before the tower opened, Nicholas Dresden purchased a 10,923 square foot duplex penthouse on the 89th and 90th floors for a record $89.9 million dollars. The skyscraper's exterior was designed by famed French architect Christian de Portzamparc, who chose dark and light glass to create vertical stripes that manipulated sunlight and maximized views. New York-based designer Thomas Juul-Hansen, known for his contemporary and luxurious interiors, created for Dresden a stunning living space that captured the awe and imagination of every visitor, with soaring glass juxtaposed against ultra modern and functional decors.

Dresden stood at his living room window, the multicolored city lights going nova as his focus waned. He blinked and gazed across the monoliths, toward the dreamlike expanse of Central Park, where trees wore shimmering aureoles cast from beneath their limbs. This was a fresco experienced by only the chosen few, the sons and daughters of finance, the captains of industry and real estate... the job creators, the powerful who could, in one fell swoop, decide a new course for the nation. For now, though, the city lay stock-still, like a *tableau vivant* caught between a day that had changed the world... and another soon to come.

Minutes before two a.m. Dresden had snapped awake, risen to use the bathroom, and then had padded out here, rubbing his eyes and wearing the dregs of a bad dream that had taken him to the frenzied streets of Berlin, some seventy years ago.

As a reward for selling his soul, Dresden would confront the man who had murdered his great grandfather. Beb Ahmose had been flown in from Canada where Senecal had found him. He was being kept somewhere in the city. Senecal had arranged everything, including full documentation of Ahmose's identity, a translator, and limousine ride in the morning. The knots that bound Dresden to this great injustice had tightened. Now, in less than twelve hours, a lifetime of searching—several lifetimes if he included his father and grandfather into the equation—would end. Finally end.

What would he ask the man? He had fallen asleep with that question hovering in his thoughts and found himself bleeding to death without answers. But then, accompanied by a chill of consciousness, came a revelation. There was nothing he needed to ask the old man. Beb Ahmose was avoiding capture. He had sought revenge for the death of his wife. His motivation was visceral and uncomplicated.

So, to be clear, why was he confronting him? To kill him? Senecal had forced the issue, and it seemed *he* was garnering amusement from the whole affair. He wanted to prove that Dresden was just as blood-thirsty as he was, and he would, Dresden believed, provide the opportunity and the means for Dresden to commit murder.

But what if he took a different tack?

Dresden would shake Ahmose's hand, share the story as he knew it, and tell the old man that the conflict between them was over. Dresden would not seek an apology. He would simply ask that they let the incident go. Closure through mutual understanding. Make peace with the past. Surely Ahmose had been tortured by the death of his wife and haunted by the killing of the doctor who had saved his boy. Dresden would have his resolution, even if Beb Ahmose remained silent. And most of all, Dresden would deny his partner the circus of blood he was orchestrating.

"Is something wrong?"

Her voice was thinner and higher than Victoria's, and for a moment it surprised him. She materialized from the gloom, her body flexing in a kind of primitive dance as she swung the hair out of her eyes. The lights from outside reflected off the sweat on her breasts, and she stood there, shifting her weight between legs like a school girl, biting a nail the way he had taught her.

He wasted no time drawing her into his chest. "I'm sorry to wake you. I have a lot on my mind. A big meeting tomorrow."

"We had a big meeting tonight," she cooed.

"We did."

"When does your wife come back?"

"Tomorrow night."

"Do you think she knows?"

He snorted. "I don't think she cares."

"Good. So, I've single-handedly restructured your public relations department and your sex life. I think my work here is finished."

"You're quitting already?"

She shook her head. "Say my name?"

He frowned. "Susannah."

"Now say, Susannah, you were the greatest partner I ever had."

He repeated the words.

"Say: I like the way you punish me."

He did.

She laughed. "Yes, I know you do."

"You're taking notes on all this. You're thinking this will be the greatest piece of journalism you've ever written."

Now it was her turn to snort. "I'm not here to report on your life. I'm here to be in your life. And to learn everything I can, so that one day I can dare mighty things."

"Sweetheart, you already are. Now in the days to come, I want you to remember one thing. When you try to characterize a man and his life, you can't focus on the failures or some final act of defiance. You have to examine a man's life in its entirety. If you do that, you'll discover what really lies in his heart. If you do that, you'll finally get the truth."

* * *

Rasul's orders had been to intercept Dr. Ramzi Shammas after the professor's meeting at Blue Door. He was to deliver Shammas to the enclave in West Virginia. Killing Shammas had never been part of the plan.

However, during the drive down from Pennsylvania, Shammas had argued against those orders, demanding to see Nazari. He said that if Rasul did not comply, he would reveal to everyone at the camp that Rasul was having a relationship with Zerina. Because Zerina was having sex outside of marriage (the crime of "zina"), her punishment would be most severe. She would be buried up to her neck and stoned to death.

Reeling over the news, Rasul wanted to know how Shammas knew of the relationship, and Shammas revealed that he had his own watchful eyes at the enclave. Rasul said that once they reached the camp, he would contact Nazari and share the request. As a driver and courier, that was all he could do now. When Shammas had asked for him to pull over so he could relieve himself, Rasul had seized the opportunity to silence the man forever.

When he arrived at the camp, he explained that Shammas had been a security leak, that he had failed his mission in North Carolina, and that he had tried to escape and Rasul had been forced to shoot him. Four of the men had collected the body from the trunk of Rasul's car and disposed of it deep within the mountains.

Now, he and Zerina were safe. She was twenty-six, an administrative assistant at Concord University, with long, black hair that shone like steel buffed to a high luster. Her skin was fair, nearly cream-colored, making her arched brows appear all the more striking. Light brown eyes flecked with gold shortened his breath and reminded him of the rolling fields in Iowa, an alluring countryside that made the construct of his life as an engineer seem artificial and insignificant. He wished he could dedicate his life to the exploration of her body, to the unraveling of the secrets that wafted up like jasmine from her neck and shoulders.

During his training at the camp, they had rapidly fallen in love, and he swore that one day he would marry her. Their impatience, though, along with the tempestuous influence of western culture, had driven them too soon into his bed.

The storm had kept him awake, and when it had passed, she had rolled over and slid her hand down his thigh. They made love time and again, and he marveled over the solidity of her back, the way she arched it, answering his every move. They lay there, exhausted, and some time before she drifted off, he made sure that his smartphone's alarm was set, ensuring her return to her trailer before sunrise... before anyone knew. Then again, someone did. He had not told her about Shammas's revelation. He had decided, though, that when he discovered who knew about them, that person would be confronted and most assuredly killed. He would do it with a knife, working down into the clavicle to ensure a more immediate and discreet end.

Rasul draped an arm over his head and allowed the darkness to carry him away from the trailer and toward a mountain range whose every summit glowed and pulsated in a deep saffron. The fires rose five hundred feet, the flames enveloping aircraft that exploded and tumbled into thick blankets of smoke. And from there he flew to the cities, their skylines equally ablaze above streets pockmarked with debris, streets leading out toward the highways where miles of cars became the scales of a mechanical serpent who had offered the infidels their apple, and they, of course, had taken their gluttonous bite.

He flew along the length of the serpent toward the next cityscape, where the fires now raged on every corner, roaring from the cars, the building windows, even from the manhole covers that had been blown off.

Settling to the ground, he glanced up—just as a building collapsed on top of him, the pressure from all the glass and concrete feeling more like a hand clutching his shoulder.

"Rasul, wake up!" Zerina cried. "There's smoke! The trailer's on fire!"

* * *

Johnny had drawn the gasoline in two canteens, and Willie had gathered the kindling. Corey had quipped that he had forgotten the marshmallows. Josh had commented that a smoke grenade would have required less preparation but was hardly as clandestine. At the moment, Johnny was under the trailer, fanning the flames, when the front door creaked open, and the young woman wearing her bra and panties and clutching the rest of her clothes to her chest, came dashing down the wooden stairs.

Johnny spotted her through the burning latticework that concealed the trailer's undercarriage and wheels. "Who are you?" she cried. "Rasul!"

A second later, Corey was on her, strangling the next cry.

While Johnny shifted backward on his hands and knees, the trailer's rear door flung open, and their target leaped to the ground, barefoot, wearing only his boxer shorts. A drop point folding knife jutted from the bottom of his left fist, with tongues of firelight reflected in the blade's cheek. The pistol in his right hand lacked a suppressor like the one he had used on Shammas; it was more compact, a concealed carry weapon to be sure, with a smaller magazine of seven, maybe ten rounds, depending upon the caliber. He must have rushed to the front door, seen Corey grappling with his girlfriend, then swung back to fetch his weapons. Now, in his haste, he failed to spy Johnny crawling out from beneath the trailer.

Realizing he could not make a dash for his car, or that he had forgotten his keys, their target spotted the gaping hole they had cut in the fence and sprinted over the mud. Johnny drew his 1911 from his holster and bounded off—with a chill of déjà vu splitting across his back. Behind him, the Skyranger's four rotors spun up as Josh maneuvered it off the trailer's roof. The drone soared overhead, tracking their target and escaping before being spotted by the jihadis.

* * *

Willie had packed his Barnes Precision Machine Match Carbine with the Leupold 1x6 scope. His magazines were loaded with 77 grain Black Hills Sierra Match King ammo. While he usually reserved this rifle for competitions like Ant Hill, the weapon felt right in his hands, and given their situation, he wanted nothing to interfere with his ability to put lead on target. It was better to choose a rifle he knew and had trained on than something bigger, louder, but unfamiliar. Train as you fight.

As Johnny had been setting the fire, Willie had fallen back about twenty meters away from the fence, where he had scaled a rock pile about three meters above the forest floor. There, he had settled down and could observe the trailer and the others nearby, with only a few blind spots caused by the trees. He was down on one knee, staring through the scope, as this bearded lunatic in his skivvies came charging into the forest with Johnny about five yards back in his draft. A weak buzzing from above the trees indicated that Willie and Johnny were not the only ones with eyes on the target.

Drawing upon his seventeen years in the Corps and his more recent hardcore training for competitions, he tracked the man and easily had the shot, but he was not sure what Johnny wanted him to do. If it became clear that the man might escape, Willie might go for a round to the leg, and that would certainly test his marksmanship if the target kept moving.

A gunshot rang out, startling him. He pulled back from the scope and saw two more flashes an instant before Johnny threw himself behind a tree.

* * *

Corey wrestled the woman's wrists together and used some long zip ties they had bought at Home Depot to bind her. Then he duct-taped shut her mouth and jogged with her back to her trailer, where he forced her onto the ground, then zip tied her ankles.

He felt guilty over being so rough, especially since she smelled like expensive perfume and had an extremely hot body. She was nothing like the Muslim women he had encountered in Fallujah, and he could not help but ogle her cleavage from behind his mask.

What she saw, he guessed, was a violent man, probably a redneck Islamophobe who would exploit the anonymity of his disguise to rape and/or kill her. But wait a minute. For all he knew, she could be a black widow suicide bomber in training.

Screw her! He stole another look before sprinting toward the fence. Off to his left, lights from the trailers winked on, and more gun shots came with echoing cracks from the forest.

* * *

Johnny had slammed shoulder-first into the pine tree as two more rounds drilled into the bark. Shavings and sap exploded in all directions. He counted seven rounds thus far. He rolled away and took off toward a gauntlet of shrubs and trunks ahead. The sticky-looking shadows deepened as the compound lit up like a Bangkok bazaar, tossing flashes into the trees.

With LaPorte's death and Shammas's murder replaying like an old double-feature in his head, Johnny picked up the pace, homing in on the man as he rounded the next tree. Once more Johnny blinked through a needling wave of déjà vu.

Just as the target slowed and rolled back to fire, Johnny threw himself forward, slamming onto a leaf bed draped in a layer of ice. His arms were forced back, and he skidded as though lying face-forward on a sled, competing in a skeleton race. Another double-tap tore through his ghost above, followed by a third round that punched the dirt, blasting particles of sand and ice into his eyes.

Were it not for the massive wave of adrenaline that throbbed through his limbs and dampened the impact, he might have surrendered right there. He dug in with the tip of his boot and launched himself back to his feet, his teeth bared, his pistol raised, his breath like dragon's smoke in his face.

Within the next twenty meters, the exposed roots and pine needles gave way to scabs of rock. Soon, in probably a hundred meters, they would break into a sharp descent, leaving the summit to plunge across gardens of sandstone, shifting sideways, skidding from tree to tree, wary of patches of ice that would send them tumbling. Johnny knew their target had a better chance of escape if he reached that descent, and their boy knew it, too, veering to the north to lose Johnny before they reached the drop.

As they drew farther away from the camp, their man grew harder to see, and for a moment, the shimmer of his bare back vanished. Johnny reached the next tree, the air warmed by his target's passage. He froze and pricked up his ears. No footfalls. Just his own panting and more distant cries from the camp. Perhaps someone else running? He was not sure. The acrid smoke billowing from the trailer finally reached him, and the stench bolstered his sense of urgency. And then... the drone approached and hovered, suggesting Johnny was still close because Josh was using infrared to pick up the man's heat signature.

Off to Johnny's right, something caught his eye, a dark mass, the lines too even for a pine cone or rock. He drifted a few steps toward the next tree, and there it was, abandoned in the dirt, a pistol with its slide locked back, indicating the magazine was empty.

A man's ferocious scream broke from the trees, and Johnny whirled in that direction. He cursed as a shadow that better resembled a black bear with claws gleaming sprang from a raft of sandstone and arced in the air.

Johnny lifted his pistol, clutching it with both hands to stabilize the weapon. The man's face shown through the woven darkness, his eyes glowing as though caught in headlights, his mouth twisted around his canines. The knife, now in his right hand and clutched in a reverse grip, was all of those bear claws forged into a single point homing in on Johnny's chest. At the same time, Johnny had a clean shot, center of mass.

The bear shape shifted again, his muzzle lengthening, his coat growing long and shaggy. Now he was a rabid sheepdog who had turned on his loved ones. The dog's face became Daniel's.

And no, Johnny could not shoot his own brother.

As his finger came off the trigger, Daniel's face narrowed, his beard darkened, and his eyes resumed that eerie glow. He was the jihadi again, the only man left with answers.

And once more, Johnny could not fire.

In the next instant, he was flat on his back, his hand striking a rock and knocking free his pistol. A guttural hiss spewed from the man's throat as he straddled Johnny and reared back, the blade framed by a kaleidoscope of tangled limbs. Johnny hands went reflexively for the man's arm, but it was out of reach, and when he tried to lift his legs and throw off his assailant, pain seared across his back.

The man must have sensed that Johnny wore Kevlar plates beneath his jacket, because as he brought down the knife, his aim scrolled to Johnny's head. With a grunt, Johnny seized the man's wrist with both hands; now the quivering blade hung a few inches from Johnny's forehead. As their arms shook against each other, the man suddenly reached forward with his free hand, groping for Johnny's neck.

In one concerted effort, and with muscles burning like lava, Johnny placed a palm on the man's bare chest. He sat up, catapulting the man backward.

Before the jihadi landed on his rump, a shot cracked, and blood sprayed from the man's hip. He collapsed, dropping the knife, his hands reaching toward his leg. He rocked to and fro and began wailing in agony.

Johnny clambered up, grabbed his pistol, then crawled to the knife, folded it up, and shoved it in his pocket. He slammed the man onto his back, wrapped a hand around his throat, then pressed his .45 to the kid's head. And yes, from this distance it was quite clear—he was just a kid, his gaze bearing a youthful innocence despite his terror.

"What's your name?" Johnny demanded.

The kid kept moaning. Blood poured out from between his fingers, his body shaking violently against the cold.

"Answer me!"

"I'm bleeding! I'm dying!"

"Yeah, and there're no virgins where you're going. Now who are you?"

"My name's Rasul!"

"You look familiar. Were you in Holly Ridge? Did you kill my brother?"

The kid's face loosened into a weird smile. "You're Johnny Johansen. I know all about you. Easy day, no drama."

Johnny's mouth fell open.

"And your brother," Rasul continued. "He was a martyr for the cause. He loved Allah more than me." The kid sneered, his teeth sketched in blood.

"My brother was no jihadi!" Johnny shouted.

Rasul pushed up against Johnny's grip, but then he coughed and went limp, his eyes rolling back in his head. Johnny released him and stared wide-eyed at the puddle of blood around his leg. He checked the kid's carotid artery for a pulse.

"I'm sorry, Johnny."

The apology came from Willie, who had been standing there with a pained look on his face. "It's all right," Johnny told him. "Thanks."

"Hey, guys, it's Corey," came a shout from behind them. "I'm coming up. We need to exfil now. They're in the woods!"

Shouts in Arabic echoed Corey's warning, and for a second, Johnny was back on the blood-soaked shores of the Euphrates, grimacing over the smell of burning cars instead of a smoldering trailer.

Willie rushed to examine Rasul's leg, reporting an entry and exit wound. Willie's spent brass casing had tumbled away, falling deep into the rocks, and he felt pretty sure that it, along with the bullet, would never be found.

At the same time, Johnny called Josh and told him to recall the drone and rally on the other side of the mountain. He stole a final glance at Rasul, a bloodless brown skeleton draped across the earth. Johnny shuddered with anger, and then he signaled everyone to leave.

For thirty more minutes he trekked unconsciously across the rock gardens and down to the valley, remembering only bits and pieces of how they reached the SUV. It was impossible to focus on anything but the glower on Rasul's face and the accusations that had poured from his chapped lips: *He was a martyr for the cause. He loved Allah more than me.*

Those were lies. Weren't they?

Chapter Thirty

"When Josh told me what those Islamic cards really were, it all made sense. The jihadis were forced to go old school, but we had no idea how literally they'd take that."

—Corey McKay (FBI interview, 23 December)

They parked the SUVs in a garbage-strewn alley behind a BP gas station in nearby Beckley. A warehouse-sized furniture store abutted the lot, with a Rent-A-Center's blue neon sign beckoning the have-nots from across the street. Josh was at the wheel of the SUV, and Corey and Willie had joined them in the backseat. The rain and cold had seeped into their skin, rendering them crimson-faced and shivering. Johnny said they should lay low for a while and avoid the highways, where their out of state plates might draw the attention of law enforcement. Corey found a website that provided a live stream of the Raleigh County Police, Bradley Fire, and West Virginia State Police radio communications. Wearing his earbuds, he listened intently for any mention of a shooting or fire at the compound. None so far.

The events of the past day turned end over end in Johnny's mind, as though they were trapped within fragments of broken glass, each one flipping enough so that he could glimpse it for just a second imagery from the drone, the storm coming in, the fence rattling, the lightning, the visit from Daniel, and then... the fire.

Chills accompanied the images, and the guilt came in jolts every few seconds as though he were wired to a car battery and being tortured by jihadis. He would glance around at his friends, then jerk again.

He raised his hand to see if it were still trembling, then cursed and glanced back to Willie. "I owe you."

"No, I owed you. From Fallujah. I bet you thought I wouldn't pay you back, but I had to, because you still carry around that old piece of shit 1911, and you probably would've had a malfunction before you could shoot the guy."

With barely the energy to smile, Johnny managed one. Willie was a good man, trying to make him feel better, even as he appeared sick himself, as though he might vomit over the ramifications of his actions.

Johnny steeled himself and said, "Now that we have a minute to calm down, let's go over it again, for Josh's sake."

"You told me the kid's name was Rasul. You didn't get a last name?" asked Josh.

"He wasn't exactly cooperative," said Willie. "And we barely had time to breathe, let alone interrogate him."

Johnny held up a palm, and Willie nodded and pursed his lips. "Josh, the kid knew me. He even knew I say 'easy day, no drama.' They were *that* close."

"You didn't tell me that," said Josh.

"Well they were."

Corey lifted his voice: "I think Rasul was lying about your brother, Johnny. He just said that to piss you off. I bet he was the one who killed Daniel. That's why he looked so familiar. We don't know why, but he was the guy who did it."

"I agree," said Willie. "Now it's too bad we can't ask him. Unfortunately, I murdered him, which is why I've been calling you guys out on all this—because I knew once you cut me loose, someone would die. Now here we are. And guess who's going to jail? Me."

"Nobody's going to jail," said Johnny.

"Are you sweating forensics?" Josh asked Willie. "You need a cadaver for forensics. Do you think they'll leave Rasul's body out there to be found? That's probable cause for the Feds to come in and take over their enclave. Won't happen."

Willie hardened his voice. "I hope you're right. We need to ditch the upper receiver of my rifle. We'll find a lake or something."

"Roger that," said Johnny.

"So what's the plan?" Corey asked. "I mean what else do we have? That guy Rasul, he was it, right? We can't go back up there."

"Maybe we should go to Blue Door and trail that sales guy, Sameh Ismail?" asked Josh.

"Look here, we..." Johnny could barely get the words out. "We can't do this anymore. We're done. It's way too hot for us. We need to... I don't know. Tell you what? Let me call Mark. See what he thinks."

"It's zero five," said Willie, checking his watch. "You calling him now?"

Johnny had already dialed the number, and Gatterton answered on the second ring. Johnny put him on speaker. "Hey, Johnny."

"I wake you?"

"Hell, no, I couldn't sleep, thinking about you guys down there. You all right?"

"We're okay. Well, to be honest, we're not exactly okay. Our witness, the guy whose name turned out to be Rasul, he, uh, he didn't make it."

"Aw, shit. You clean up?"

"As best we could."

"We never talked about this."

"No, we did not."

"Okay, listen to me. You need to stop now."

"I agree."

Gatterton hesitated. "You do?"

"That's why I called. Somebody needs to follow up on this. I want to hand over everything, but I'm afraid we'll get arrested."

"Do me a favor. Get over to the Richmond field office. I've got a friend there, a WM who's the Special Agent in Charge. She was an intel analyst with II MEF."

MEF stood for Marine Expeditionary Force, meaning Gatterton's contact in Richmond was a WM, a Woman Marine.

He continued, "She did a tour then decided to pull chocks and become one of us. I'll get you in there to see her."

"That sounds good, Mark. But you can't make any promises. If we talk to her, we could still wind up in jail."

"You need to be careful what you say. You give them what they need—but not enough to incriminate you."

"That won't be easy."

"I know, but don't be a fool, either. I'll prep the zone with her and call you after. Do not roll in there until we talk."

"Roger that, solid copy."

"Thank you, Mark."

"Don't thank me, Johnny. I'm used to this, just like the good old days. You're shaking trees, and I'm raking leaves."

"You've done that better than anyone, and the boys appreciate it."

* * *

Nicholas Dresden had chosen a grey, single-breasted wool suit to reflect his mood. He climbed into the limousine and sat beside Senecal, who wriggled his brows once, then returned to his Starbucks skinny vanilla latte. Dresden had already consumed two cups of coffee, but despite that and the anticipation of confronting Beb Ahmose, his sleepless night made his overcoat feel more like a straightjacket. Within five minutes, he fought to keep his eyes open and his head upright.

"You seem very relaxed for a man who's about to confront his family's past."

The comment jarred him to consciousness. "It was a long night," he confessed.

"For me as well. My boy came to me in my dreams, and you know what he said?"

"I'm afraid to ask."

"He said, avenge me, Daddy. Avenge me."

Dresden shook his head. "Eddie, where are we going?"

"Take a look."

He realized they were already on Fifth Avenue, and the limousine had pulled up outside The Plaza, arguably one of the most lavish hotels in the entire city, a landmark for over one hundred years in all of its Beaux Arts magnificence. To this day, its 152 *pied-à-terres* were booked by business leaders, politicians, celebrities of every ilk, and socialites from around the globe. The building rose nineteen-stories, which at the turn of the twentieth century was considered a skyscraper.

In truth, this was not the meeting place Dresden had in mind. He had envisioned an abandoned warehouse, with the old man gagged and bound to a chair, his nose bleeding, his eyes blackened while Senecal's henchman hovered like vultures nearby, waiting for him to expire. Whether he had been watching too many films or had simply deemed Beb Ahmose an aging thug who deserved interrogation and torture Dresden could not be sure, but The Plaza... *The Plaza*... took him aback.

Somehow he exited the limousine and reached the carpeted stairs, clutching the gold railing as he ascended. They entered the lobby of soaring ceilings and ornate chandeliers, and Senecal led him to an elevator. Once inside, his partner pressed for the fourth floor, then glanced up and said, "Are you all right?"

"Yes."

"Really? You look pale, my old friend."

"Wouldn't you be?"

Senecal shrugged. "What do you feel right now?"

"Is this an interview?"

"No, I'm not that slut you're sleeping with."

"Excuse me?"

"I'm sorry. That was out of line."

"You're watching me now? Having me followed?"

"I'm sorry, Nick. These are delicate times. We can't afford any mistakes."

"What if you've made a mistake? What if this isn't Beb Ahmose?"

Senecal smiled crookedly in disgust. "You've read the documents we collected from Cairo. You've looked over the corroborating evidence, the witness accounts, the journal entries, the nearly one thousand files my team collected on this subject—and you still don't believe?"

Dresden's breath floated away and was unwilling to return. He swallowed, clutched the wall, then steadied himself and finally inhaled deeply.

"Easy there, old man." Senecal seized his elbow. "You'll make it."

Dresden yanked free of the man's grip, brought his shoulders to full height, then brushed off his jacket as the bell chimed and the doors parted. Fourth floor. A sign pointed them toward the meeting rooms. As they turned into the corridor, the walls closed in and white caps rose from the carpeting.

* * *

Johnny and the others headed East on 64 from Beckley. En route, they exited near the town of Low Moor and tossed the upper receiver of Willie's rifle into a water retention canal running parallel to the highway. After a laborious four-hour drive, they neared the Richmond exit, and Johnny signaled that he wanted to stop, fill up the tanks, and grab some coffee. They found an Exxon on West Broad Street, and while Johnny stood at the pump, he eyed an old Cadillac parked on the other side. The windows were down, and in the passenger's seat sat a hoary old Yankees fan with a bushy moustache and fading ball cap. He held a paperback book up high, toward the dash, and read it with a large magnifying glass.

A magnifying glass. That image struck deep in the back of Johnny's mind, triggering a number of memories from childhood... and something else... something that gnawed at him.

When he finished filling the tank, he reached into his inner coat pocket where he kept the three Islamic cards they had gathered: LaPorte's, Shammas's, and Easy Money's. He lifted Shammas's closer to his eyes, but the card went out of focus. He glanced back at the old man with the magnifying glass, then stepped around the pump.

"Hey, Chief."

The old man scowled at Johnny for the interruption. "What do you want?"

"Can I borrow your magnifying glass for a second?"

"You going to steal it?"

"Here," Johnny said, pulling ten bucks out of his wallet. "Rental fee."

The old man drew his head back, then snatched up the cash with a veinous hand. "You only got a few seconds till my daughter comes back."

"Roger." Johnny turned and put his back to the sun. He squinted at Shammas's card, now glowing and fully magnified. He shifted the glass to the bottom—

And he saw it.

Josh ambled over with the coffee and was about to hand off one to Johnny. "What're you doing?"

Johnny lost his breath and could barely answer. "Look!"

* * *

The conference room was as richly appointed as the rest of the hotel, with seating for ten around the black ash burl table beneath a crystal chandelier. Seated at the head was a gaunt-faced old man, his eyes all but gone under Neanderthal brows. He seemed hollow-chested and barely filled his suit. A veil of thinning hair spanned the sides of his freckled pate, and his porcelain-white beard showed signs of being freshly trimmed. Two other men stood behind him, the first about Dresden's age, perhaps a few years older, wearing a tailored suit and polished loafers. Only his long, gray beard suggested he might be a Muslim. The other man was much younger, in his thirties, and assumedly Middle-Eastern with a black beard and broad nose.

Senecal introduced the younger man as Max, saying he would translate for them. He introduced the other man as Omar, and for some reason he failed to provide a surname.

"Nicholas Dresden, I'd like you to meet a man your family has been searching for since the end of World War II. This, sir, is Mr. Beb Ahmose."

The younger man translated Senecal's introduction into Arabic, while Dresden, still feeling light-headed, proffered his hand.

Ahmose widened his eyes and squinted up toward Dresden. He looked at the hand, and then finally, as though the effort caused him considerable pain, he raised his arm and offered a surprisingly firm grip.

"If you'll speak slowly, and not for too long at any one time, I'll translate everything you say," instructed the young man. "He's still very lucid, so you can ask anything you want."

"Have a seat," Senecal said, pulling out a chair.

Dresden nodded, and with a racing pulse, lowered himself down and said, "Ask him if he remembers being helped by a doctor while he was in Berlin. A doctor who saved his son's life."

The translator spoke softly.

Ahmose nodded slowly.

"Does he know who I am?"

"He doesn't," Senecal said before the interpreter could answer. "All he knows is that he was brought here for a meeting of great historical importance. And yes, he's come willingly—all expenses paid, of course."

Dresden leaned forward in his chair and said, "Tell him the doctor who saved his son's life was my great grandfather."

After hearing the translation, Ahmose's wide-eyed curiosity retreated back into the recesses of his weathered face.

Omar leaned down and whispered something in the old man's ear. Shielding his mouth from Dresden's view, Ahmose muttered a reply. Omar straightened and said, "My father is very fatigued, and he would like to leave now."

"Your father?" Dresden said, losing his breath. "You're the boy. You're the boy my great grandfather saved."

"I guess I am," said Omar.

"Then both of you, please listen to me. My father and grandfather were obsessed with finding you and making you pay for the murder of Franz Dresden. I understand what happened. I know about your wife. I know that my great grandfather was going to turn you in as a spy and courier for the Nazis. I know why you killed him. And I'm here, not because I expect some kind of apology, but because I want to let it go. There's nothing we can do to change the past. We can only accept it. And that's all I want now. Let's make peace with the past."

As the translator took a deep breath and began, Ahmose lifted a spiny finger and rasped in perfect English, "Quiet. I understood him. And now, Mr. Dresden, you will listen to me."

* * *

Johnny raised the card and magnifying glass so that Josh could glimpse his discovery. Within the inner line of the card's tri-border frame were a series of dots and dashes running along the bottom—a series only visible under this higher magnification. To the naked eye they blended almost perfectly into the background.

The dots and dashes were Morse code.

"These are courier cards, and this is how they're passing information," said Josh. "Even the couriers don't know what's on them. Only the people who know what to look for."

"Exactly. Give these to Corey. Get him to translate."

"Roger, but damn, Johnny, how'd you figure this out?"

"It's weird. The cards were bothering me, just sitting in the back of my head."

"So it just came to you?"

"No, I've been thinking a lot about Daniel, the stuff we did as kids, like the way he disguised the Playboy magazines and how we'd send secret messages. I kept thinking how the cards might be something more, but it wasn't until I saw the old man with the magnifying glass that I thought, hey, maybe we're not looking closely enough."

Josh stared in awe. "Wow, now you're like a fat kid with a magnifying glass!"

"Hell, yeah, and we're setting ants on fire."

While Josh left to hand off the cards, Johnny crossed back to the Cadillac and lifted his chin. "I need to buy your magnifying glass. How much you want for it?"

The old man snickered. "Christ, I'm in the middle of my book."

"How much you want?"

"Hundred bucks."

"I'll give you twenty."

The old man smiled. "Just give me another ten."

Johnny withdrew the bill. "You could've had twenty."

"Why you want it so badly?"

"If I told you, you'd never believe me."

* * *

Despite his fragility, Beb Ahmose had spoken in a commanding tone, his accent a slight but peculiar blend of Canadian and Middle-Eastern. His cheeks had ripened, and his finger was brought to bear on Dresden. He took a long moment before he spoke again, and right there, before Dresden's eyes, he transformed into an ancient Egyptian, a pharaoh with cobras rearing from his head and a red armband with swastika fitted over his suit. His ocher-colored teeth surfaced from beneath his beard, and finally his words, framed in fiery whispers, escaped from the back of his throat:

"Our people have been at war with each other for over a thousand years. Let me be clear. We hate Christianity and every other religion that does not worship Allah. That will never change. We will never change. Your government has declared us terrorists, and your own pentagon admits that your war against us will never end." Ahmose lowered his finger and nodded. "I must agree, Mr. Dresden. The war will never end.

And please, let me be blunt. I hate you. I hate your western values and everything you stand for. Your soldiers murdered my wife and laughed about it. I've lived with that for over seventy years. You thought I would forget? And now, you come here, and you sit down, and you ask a ninety-five-year old man to make peace with the past?" Ahmose leaned forward, his gaze even more poisonous. "No, Mr. Dresden. You ask the impossible. This is a war. There is no reconciliation. Ever. Do you understand?"

Dresden felt too stunned to answer. His gaze drifted up to find Senecal, now at his shoulder and reveling in the moment, as though he knew exactly what Ahmose would say, as though he had interviewed the man prior to the meeting, as though he were using this entire event to stoke Dresden's hatred and win him back into the fold.

Unable to bear any more, Dresden stormed out of the conference room, and, out in the hall, Senecal chased him down and said, "I'm sorry, Nick."

"Another lie."

"All right, but listen. What would you like me to do with them?"

"What're you talking about?"

"You heard the old man. This is a war, and as far as I'm concerned, they're POWs."

Dresden gritted his teeth and dug nails into his palms. All round him, the wallpaper and wainscoting turned black as though under flames. "I guess you're right, Eddie. You've been right all along."

"That doesn't matter. Now let me end this for you."

Dresden could almost taste the blood. "Do it."

Senecal nodded. "I know it's been difficult, but you've finally accepted the truth, and I'm proud of you."

"What truth? That they hate us?"

"No, that's a given. The truth is... you and I are exactly the same now. No more hedging your bets... and always daring to do mighty things." Senecal squeezed his shoulder. "Welcome home, Nick."

Chapter Thirty-One

"It was the phone call from Pat Rugg while we were up in Detroit that changed everything. He was the wild card the jihadis never expected."

—Johnny Johansen (FBI interview, 23 December)

After leaving the Exxon Station, Johnny found a SmartStop Self Storage on West Williamsburg Road. He secured a 5' x 5' air conditioned storage space and paid cash. There, they stored most of their gear, their rifles, and the drones. The card Corey had collected from Easy Money, along with the knife Johnny had taken from Rasul, were tucked into the side pocket of an old range bag and hidden with everything else.

Gatterton had cautioned them about giving the Feds enough evidence without incriminating themselves. They believed they were ready to do so. Next stop? The FBI.

The Richmond field office included more than just Richmond Headquarters City. The Bureau had agencies across the state in Bristol, Charlottesville, Fredericksburg, Lynchburg, Roanoke, and Winchester, with over two hundred agents and support staff. The office was a nondescript, three-story standalone building with a gated perimeter.

Before heading across the parking lot, Johnny motioned for Josh to pull over. "Look, guys, no matter what happens in there, I want you to know, well, I just want to say thanks again. For everything."

"It's been one hell of a ride," Willie said curtly.

Josh sighed. "And it's cool, Johnny. We'll be okay."

"Let's do this," said Corey.

Johnny nodded, then gave Josh the high sign. They drove up to the booth, where Johnny told the guard they had an appointment with Special Agent in Charge (SAC)

Donna Lindhower. The guard called the receptionist, who confirmed. They were taken through a security protocol that included a thorough search of their persons and the vehicle. They showed the guards their concealed carry permits and turned over their weapons. They were allowed to park and venture inside, where they endured yet another security check by the guards before being greeted by the receptionist.

After a thirty second wait, a tall, athletic woman in a black, two-piece pants suit strode into the lobby, her low heels clicking across the tile. She was in her forties, with shoulder length hair whose shades ranged from diamond to caramel. She exuded an air of confidence and conservatism, and when she opened her mouth, the precision of her speech betrayed her military background. "Hello, gentlemen, I'm Donna Lindhower. Mark brought your situation to my attention. We agreed that, moving forward, we're going to keep any input from him as well as his identity out of these discussions. As far as we're concerned, you gentlemen came in off the street. Now please, follow me."

Johnny glanced at the boys; they appeared as uneasy as he felt.

Lindhower ushered them into one of the secure interview rooms on the first floor. They took seats around a table. She stood near a digital recorder no larger than a smartphone. Johnny studied her expression, searching for a line, a crease, or curve suggesting some sympathy for them and their plight, but she eyed them with the indifference of a government employee who had already decided that they were just another case, and this was just another day on the job, despite her connection to Gatterton.

She cleared her throat. "All right, so here's what's going to happen. I'm required to record this interview. There's a camera up there near the ceiling, and I have another recorder right here. I'll start by stating the date. What is today, anyway?"

"December 17th," said Willie, consulting his watch.

"Thank you. So we'll record the date, the time, followed by the names of everyone present, including Agent Fred Seibert seated back there by the door. Once we have your initial statements, we'll take a short break and reconvene in separate rooms, where agents from our Joint Terrorism Task Force will interview you individually."

"We understand," said Johnny. "I just want you to know that I put these boys up to everything. It all falls on me."

"They're Marines," she said. "And I don't believe that."

"No really, I forced them to do it," Johnny said, wincing under her scrutiny.

"Relax, Johnny. You're not under oath. However, there's a particular section and title of the United States Code that prohibits knowingly and willfully making false or fraudulent statements, or concealing information, in any matter within the jurisdiction of the Federal Government of the United States—even by mere denial."

Johnny pursed his lips and glanced at the others. Their expressions remained stolid. One FBI special agent had nothing on some of the Marine Corps officers they had faced, men with deranged eyes who drooled over the slightest misstep in a report.

Satisfied that his friends understood the risks, Johnny faced Lindhower and said, "Easy day, Ma'am. No drama. We're on the same side."

"I know. Mark's a good friend. He told me you were all that and a bag of chips."

Johnny's cheeks warmed. "He said that about you."

She grinned for the first time then continued. "We're here to help. And maybe the intel you have can get us rolling on this."

"Speaking of which..." Johnny dug into his jacket and produced the two Islamic cards and the magnifying glass.

"What are they?" asked Lindhower.

"We think the jihadis use them to pass messages. We found them on two different individuals. If you magnify sections of the border, you'll see Morse code embedded in the dark line."

"Are you serious?"

"Have a look yourself."

She did. "Well, there it is."

"We translated the code, and they turn out to be phone numbers. We think one is for a prepaid. The other one with the handwriting on the back has the number to a McDonald's in Cedar Falls, Iowa."

"Interesting. So we'll need to hear in minute detail how you came in possession of these cards. Now, let me start the recording, and we'll go back to the beginning, as in, why you decided to launch your own murder investigation."

* * *

Nazari had parked his Ford Fusion in one of three lots at Waterloo Regional Airport, just a few miles from his home in Cedar Falls. He had received an unprecedented communication from his associates in West Virginia, and the news could not have been more grim.

Dr. Ramzi Shammas's security leak had become a runaway reactor, poisoning couriers and threatening to expose the entire network. Rasul had murdered him, and then, someone had attacked the enclave and shot the poor boy, leaving his body on the mountainside. Nazari's associates had sworn they had secured and sanitized the area and that no law enforcement entities had been notified or had visited the enclave.

There were at least two masked attackers, and they had set a trailer on fire before chasing Rasul into the woods and shooting him.

As a result, Nazari decided that the time table must be stepped up, that the longer they waited, the greater the risk for another catastrophic leak—because whoever had attacked the enclave was still out there. In turn, the suppliers needed to deliver the rest of the materials as soon as possible. Rasul had been the primary contact with the liaison, but now Nazari would assume his place and ensure an unobstructed line of communications. He had made the call, and the liaison had instructed him to say nothing and meet him in the airport parking lot at exactly 4:40 p.m. local time.

A compact rental car rolled up beside his, facing in the opposite direction. The driver's side window lowered to reveal a woolen coat. A black baseball cap. A pair of sunglasses on a cloudy day.

"Where's Rasul?"

"Dead. One of my cells was compromised," Nazari began.

"Where?"

"North Carolina. Then up at the enclave in West Virginia."

The liaison glanced away, muttering something to himself. Abruptly, he lifted his voice and asked, "What are you doing about it?"

"Everything I can."

"What do you need?"

"Tell the suppliers I need the rest of the shipments—as soon as possible. We're moving up by forty-eight hours. My people will be ready. Will they?"

"I'll make sure of it. And don't call again—unless absolutely necessary."

"I understand."

The window scrolled up, and the rental car lurched away.

With nerves fraying like wires, Nazari left the airport and drove to the Islamic center, where he met with Ahmed Mohammed Al-Nasser, his core group's money and documentation expert. Al-Nasser had requested a meeting, though he had been careful to exclude the details from his call.

"A problem in New London," he began in Arabic. "A lost wallet. An operative speaking to the police, trying to explain why he was left tied up in his car."

Nazari spoke through his teeth. "We can't afford any more of this."

"I understand. I'll resolve this issue—permanently."

"Get the truth out of him first."

"I will."

"Who will be the new contact with the fishermen?"

Al-Nasser sighed deeply. "For now, me."

"Very well. Have you heard from El-Najjar?"

Al-Nasser's expression softened. "I have. And finally a victory there. He's already on the road, and the cache is secure."

"Excellent. I've heard back from Younes. His vests and trucks will be ready."

"Now, if I understand you correctly, the suppliers believe we're striking only six targets. Once they discover it's many more, at least ninety-nine, what then?"

"Then they experience Allah's fiery will across this horrible and godless land."

"And where will we be?"

"I'm working on that. I'll be driving up to the hub this evening. It seems our friends in Colombia and Peru have presented an interesting idea. It involves the Port of Houston, and a Panamax container ship. Her schedule is opportune for our purposes."

* * *

After spending most of the day at the field office, with only a short break for lunch, Johnny and the others were sent back to their first interview room.

"They've got that camera on us right now," said Corey. "They want to see if we'll confide in each other."

Willie rolled his eyes. "I don't care. I'm so tired of talking. Never talked so much in my life. Explain it again. Are you sure? Can you be more specific? Why do you say that? Are you sure that was the name you heard?"

"I know, right?" Corey asked.

"You boys act like you've never been around an interrogation," said Josh. "You know how we grilled them back in Iraq? How does it feel to be on the other end?"

The door swung open, and Donna Lindhower shuffled inside. Her expression bore something new, something unwelcome. Fear. "We're in the process of verifying your story. In the meantime, the E-A-D for National Security wants to meet with all of you tomorrow morning, zero eight sharp."

"E-A-D?" asked Johnny.

"The Executive Assistant Director for National Security."

Johnny recoiled. "Whoa."

Willie raised his hand. "Ma'am? Are we in trouble?"

"If you bail on me, you will be. Book yourselves some hotel rooms. We can do this two ways: with or without the babysitter. You promise to be good and come back tomorrow?"

"We'll be here," said Johnny. "Can I ask why this had to go so far up the chain of command?"

"I'm sorry, Johnny, but this isn't something I can contain, nor would I want to. We need as many eyes on this as possible."

"We're just trying to do the right thing," Josh insisted.

Lindhower's expression softened a notch. "You came in here on your own, without attorneys. You didn't ask for anything. You're willing to help. I'm sure my boss will take all of that into consideration."

They rose, and Johnny thanked Lindhower for her help.

"I'm very sorry about your brother and sister-in-law," she said.

The ache rushed into Johnny's eyes. "I appreciate that. I really do. We'll see you in the morning."

* * *

They checked into an Embassy Suites on the west end, then headed down to the hotel's restaurant, The Atrium Grill, where they sat at the bar and splurged on locally brewed craft beer instead of the usual Michelob Ultra. The waitress boasted about the menu featuring European and Asian cuisines, but all Johnny wanted was the biggest cheeseburger the chef could make, as in "give me a pound of beef," he told the waitress. She tried to convince him to go fancy with Swiss or provolone cheese.

"American," he said firmly.

"Make that four," Willie said. "And fries, too."

Johnny stared absently at the battalion of bottles standing in formation behind the bar while the others watched the local news on a flat screen. Here they were again, hurry up and wait, just like being back in the Corps. Victims of bureaucratic BS. Johnny left the counter and found a private spot near the back of the restaurant. He dialed Elina.

She answered breathlessly. "Johnny? Johnny?"

"Are you okay? Oh, wait. Hello, Elina. It's Johnny. Your husband. How are you doing this fine evening?"

"Oh, shut up. Tell me what's going on."

"We're in Richmond. I should be home soon. I think it's over. Unless we get arrested."

"What?"

"Relax, we don't know anything yet. I think we're about to cut a deal with the FBI."

"You're scaring me again. I can't do this for much longer. Did you... I mean the guy who..."

"Yes. I think that's behind us now."

"Thank God."

"How did the girls like their range time?"

"I wish you were there. I think they shoot better than you."

"Damn, I bet they do."

"I wish I was with you right now."

"Me too. But I'll be back soon."

"How're the guys?"

"They've been burning the midnight oil. I think they're about ready to call it a day."

"So just call me, then. And we'll meet back there, okay?"

"Okay. But if something does happen... I don't know... if we get charged with something... I want you to know that everything we've done so far was just to get at the truth. That's all."

"You don't have to convince me, Johnny. Sounds like you need to convince yourself."

"I put everyone out on this. But hey, I need to go. Mark Gatterton's calling me."

"I love you, Johnny. Just tell us when to come back."

"I will."

Johnny fumbled with his phone, finally accepting Gatterton's incoming call. "Mark..."

"Hey, Johnny, I just got off the phone with Donna. She told me Plesner's flying down to see you."

"Who?"

"Charles Plesner, the E-A-D of National Security. I need to be honest, Johnny, I wasn't expecting this and neither was Donna."

"What do you mean?"

"I mean this guy Plesner is a first-rate ball buster who stabbed a lot of folks in the back to get where he is now. If he drops the hammer, I'm not sure I can help."

Johnny cursed under his breath. "I was just trying to find out who killed my brother and his wife. I didn't realize this would turn into a national security nightmare."

Chapter Thirty-Two

"Because I'm a Glock fan, I knew the Glock 22 was the service issue pistol of the FBI. I didn't need Plesner's reminder that he carried one. And like I've said, we always train as we fight. You take your most familiar weapons downrange."

—Willie Parente (FBI interview, 23 December)

Johnny suffered another restless night plagued by dreams of Sergeant Oliver on that staircase in Fallujah and of Daniel bowing toward Mecca. At one point, lying on the evaporating border between consciousness and some darker realm that reeked of rubbing alcohol and latex gloves, Johnny found himself on an operating table, his chest being cracked open by surgeons who tugged down their masks. They wore malicious grins and introduced themselves as Dr. Rasul and Dr. Shammas. Johnny should not worry about a thing; they would only remove his infidel heart, which resembled a hunk of blackened beef, and his soul, which, much to their amusement, they were still trying to locate.

"So the only thing you found in your brother's office was a note written in Arabic and the keys to the storage facility?" asked Plesner, peering over the rims of his bifocals.

"That's correct, sir."

Johnny glanced up at the slight man in his late fifties. He was clean-shaven, with thinning hair gone silver at the temples and skin like a drought-riddled plain. He seemed dwarfed by his own chair and overcompensated by leaning toward the table.

"Mr. Johansen, you expect us to believe that the local police examined your brother's office and didn't find those items?"

"I know my brother. He used to hide things when we were kids. I knew where to look."

Plesner steepled his fingers and smirked at SAC Lindhower, who was seated beside him. He faced Johnny, and his expression shifted once more, caught between accepting the explanation and wanting to pry further. He set his lips and glanced down at their statements. "And you say you followed up on those items, found the storage unit empty, went to Reliance Tactical, questioned a clerk named Kyle Jessup, and used him to lure LaPorte into a trap."

"Not exactly a trap, sir. We only wanted to talk to LaPorte. But for some reason, he took off, we gave chase, and he lost us. We found out later he crashed."

"I can read, Mr. Johansen. And next you say you found a card with Arabic writing in Mr. LaPorte's backpack. You also state that Mr. Jessup told you about Mr. Shammas's real estate office in Jacksonville."

"That's correct."

"Any reason for him to deny he said that?"

"Not that I know of, sir."

"Well he's denying he ever told you."

"You've interviewed him already?"

Plesner consulted another report. "Mr. Johansen, I find it remarkable that you've already forgotten where you are. We're the Federal Bureau of Investigation. We interviewed Mr. Jessup yesterday at 8:14 p.m. Eastern time."

Johnny shrugged as convincingly as he could. He needed this lie in place to protect Pat Rugg and Billy Brandt, two Marine Corps brothers he was unwilling to give up. "Sir, I'm not sure why Kyle's lying about that. Maybe he's afraid of retribution. The fact is, he sent us up there, and that's where we found the second card."

"And the writing on the back sent you up to Pennsylvania. To Blue Door."

"Yes, sir."

"They make some fine weapons."

"They do, sir."

"Not as good as Sig Sauer, though. I like my P226 much better than anything Blue Door produces. I like it even more than my service issue Glock 22."

Johnny glanced at Willie, as if to say, *Imagine that.* Willie just shook his head.

"We questioned the security officers at Blue Door. There's no record of anyone named Shammas taking a meeting there, although the team did identify the men in the photos and video you provided. We believe they were operating under aliases. The sales person you named, Sameh Ismail, flew out last night to Peru. We'll track him down there."

"Thank you, sir," Johnny said.

"So at this point, you and Mr. Eriksson go after a man you're calling Rasul because you heard his girl friend scream his name while you were inside the compound."

"That's correct."

"And Mr. Parente? You and Mr. McKay tracked a man you nicknamed Easy Money up to New London, Connecticut. You observed this man go into the Pequot Inn and Marina. While you were there, Mr. Johansen called you to rendezvous in West Virginia, and you left."

"That's correct," answered Willie.

Plesner hardened his gaze. "So you're unaware of an anonymous phone call placed to the local police? You have no idea who tied up Easy Money and left him in his car?"

"No, sir."

"A glove was found in the man's car. Only one glove. For some strange reason, he tried to explain away the incident as a practical joke played by some old friends and said the glove belonged to one of them. You're not one of his old friends, are you, Mr. Parente?"

"No, sir. Guy sounds like some O.J. Simpson wannabe."

"Do you believe that glove would fit either your hand or Mr. McKay's?"

"If it did, sir, that'd be a coincidence."

"I see. And if your DNA matched DNA found on the glove?"

"That would be impossible, sir."

"What about you, Mr. McKay?"

"Sir?"

"Do you concur with Mr. Parente's statements?"

"Absolutely, sir."

Plesner grinned and shook his head. Surprisingly, he allowed their lies to thicken the air without comment. "So, if I read your statements correctly, you gentlemen linked up in West Virginia and trespassed on private property with the intent of kidnapping this individual you're calling Rasul."

"No, sir," answered Johnny. "We only wanted to talk to him."

"Why didn't you go to the gate and knock?"

"We worried that if we did that, he'd run. So we figured we'd sneak in there and just corner him and have a little talk."

"But that didn't work out so well, did it?"

"Not really."

"Recon Marines, huh? What happened to swift, silent, and deadly?"

Willie cocked his brow and leaned forward in his chair, ready to return fire.

Johnny shot him a look.

Plesner went on: "So you're saying that you were spotted, that shots were fired, and that the man you call Rasul was accidentally hit by his own people, but you're not sure if he's alive or dead. You just got out of there A-SAP."

"That's correct, sir," Johnny said.

"Which brings you here," Plesner finished. He gave them the once over, seized his jaw, closed his eyes, then sighed deeply in dramatic fashion. "I need some time alone with these gentlemen."

Lindhower gave a look to Agent Seibert, and they quickly exited.

Plesner switched off the recorder, then turned back to the ceiling-mounted camera and motioned to stop recording. The camera's green status light turned to red. "All right, boys. As veteran Marines you're used to following orders."

"Yes, sir," answered Johnny

"Good." Without warning, Plesner slammed his fist on the table. "Now stop lying to me!" His shout hung for a long and uncomfortable moment while he returned to his reports. "The police down in North Carolina found rat poison inside LaPorte's truck. You know anything about that?"

Johnny's mouth went dry, and he fought to maintain his composure. "No, sir."

"Mr. Johansen, are you taking any medication that might affect your memory?"

"No, sir."

"So you're naturally full of shit?"

"Maybe LaPorte was thinking about killing himself," Willie blurted out.

"Well, he put his mind to it, didn't he," Plesner snapped.

Willie snorted. "He sure did."

Plesner continued. "The police also found some Styrofoam plates and wrappers from lean ground beef, the kind you find in the supermarket. Another interesting find. You know what I think? I think Mr. LaPorte was going to poison someone... or some thing... maybe an animal. A dog, perhaps? Is there anything else you'd like to tell me, Mr. Johansen?"

"Look here, they killed my brother and sister-in-law. I wanted to know why. That's what got us here. Now it seems like everyone who knows what happened is gone or dead. See what I'm getting at? Is the FBI willing to take this on and help me out? These guys are jihadis. There's something going on. It's not isolated to a small county in

North Carolina. It crosses state lines, so isn't that when you guys take over? Like you said, you're the Federal Bureau of Investigation."

"Indeed we are. But if you took the law into your own hands, then it's my job to help you go to jail. But like I said, we're off the record. So let's talk like men. That bastard killed your dogs, didn't he? Where did you bury them?"

"You think I killed LaPorte," Johnny said. "Well, I didn't."

"We can check for body paint transfer against every vehicle you own. Maybe you just forced him off the road. That would complicate matters, Johnny, wouldn't it? And in a way, I don't blame you. But I want you to understand that you can't lie anymore—because when we dig, we dig deep, and we don't stop. Not ever."

Johnny's cheeks swelled, and he puffed air. "Roger that."

"Good. Did your brother convert to Islam?"

"No."

"But you're not sure."

"I know my brother."

"You have no doubts?"

"None," Johnny snapped.

Plesner's lip twisted. "We just had a very pointed conversation about lying. Is English your first language?"

"Sir, all right, I have a few doubts. Why does it matter?"

"Good. We're making progress. Now, Corey? Willie? Who came up with the idea to use Easy Money's shoelaces to tie him up?"

"We don't know, sir," said Willie.

Plesner lifted a finger. "I'll bet it was you, Corey. You have an innovative look in your eyes."

Corey lowered his gaze.

"You find anything else on that guy? His phone? Maybe that's the phone you used to call the police?"

Willie gave an exaggerated shrug.

Plesner leaned back and pillowed his head in his hands. "You see, gentlemen, I can use my position to scare up a lot of information. You don't get to be me by asking for permission. Around here my suggestions are considered commands. I don't make recommendations. I issue edicts. But you know what my problem is? This administration has turned my beloved agency into a bunch of pussies. Case in point: I can use your statements to get a warrant to search that enclave, but I'll get a lot of push back from my own people. They'll say we need to be careful so we're not accused of racially profiling them. We need to respect all of their rights. We need to leave them alone so they can teach each other how to kill us."

Johnny snickered. "That's insane."

"Sitting right here in this room, we all agree. But it doesn't matter if we go up there now, does it? We wouldn't find anything... maybe a few traces of blood, but any bodies are long gone, and those jihadis will never admit there was any problem. In a strange way, they're your allies now. I mean, you guys could have shot and killed someone, and no one up there would talk, right?"

Johnny realized he had a white-knuckled grip on his chair and relaxed. He would not dare look in Willie's direction.

Plesner retrieved his briefcase from the floor and set it on the table. From inside he extracted a fistful of files and gestured with them. "These come from the DOD on short notice. This is everything we know about the four of you. It made for some interesting reading on the plane. And the truth is, I'm glad you're on our side. I know I ragged on you about your Marine backgrounds, but honestly, they paid off because your experience drove you closer to the truth. I value that, I value your security clearances, but there's something else I value even more."

"What's that, sir?" Johnny asked.

"We'll get there. First let me say that like every other government agency, at some level, the FBI's been infiltrated by jihadi operatives, people you'd never suspect—even converts who look like you and me. If you don't believe that, then you're a naïve fool or a leftwing nut job. The fact is, we recruit translators, specialists, and consultants from the Muslim American communities, and while we vet the crap out of them, there's no guarantee that in their heart of hearts they're all loyal to America. Our intelligence organizations are lumbering beasts, and they're not as secure as politicians would have you think. If I had to pick one group that does a great job of maintaining its operational security, despite its diversity, that'd be our Joint Terrorism Task Forces."

"We already talked to some of those people."

"I'm aware of that. But things are different now, Johnny."

"What do you mean?"

"I mean as I'm sitting here, listening to you, I realize I've had a bad case of tunnel vision. You boys operate as a team and stay locked on target no matter what. The Corps taught you that."

"That's right," said Josh.

"You're four veteran Marines who've uncovered a terrorist operation that we didn't know existed." Plesner spoke more emphatically. "How the hell does that happen?"

Johnny glanced at the others; no one was answering.

"I'll tell you how," Plesner continued. "You four are nobodies. You're outside the system, and no one has eyes on you. Between this administration, the spineless bastards in my own agency, and the jihadis leaking our secrets, I can't move on these people. Let me tell you something: this country will fall if men like you and me are not free to act."

Johnny leaned toward Plesner. "I couldn't agree more, sir."

"Good. Now before I do anything, I need a promise from you, Johnny. If you find out your brother was a jihadi, you can't let that interfere with this mission."

"What mission?"

"Look, I run the Counterterrorism Division, the Counter Intelligence Division, the Directorate of Intelligence, and the Weapons of Mass Destruction Directorate. I oversee a lot of people, but no one like you guys. Despite severe limitations you sons of bitches identified a threat to the United States. I'd be a fool not to take advantage of the current situation. With direction and oversight, who better than you? You're a four man special recon and tactics team. You're being contracted as outside consultants to the Counterterrorism Division. We'll do it under your company name, Triton 6. You report only to me. You mention this to no one—and that includes my colleagues in the FBI. We'll finally get something done around here without congressmen breathing down our necks."

"Sir, I'm not sure I'm hearing you correctly," said Corey. "Are you saying you want to hire us?"

"Exactly. Come on, Mr. McKay I know what you've been doing these past couple of weeks. I need you to keep on doing it, and we'll catch these bastards."

Willie raised his hand again. "Do we get badges?"

Josh elbowed him in the ribs.

"Sir, is this legal?" asked Johnny.

Plesner chuckled. "I'm flattered you think I'm a cowboy like you boys. Of course it's legal. We hire consultants all the time Hell, all the big defense contractors and security companies hired by the government are staffed by former military folks."

"I see how we're playing this. And if you've read our files, then you know this won't be the first time we've done contract work for the government, mostly for the DOD. I'm just looking for the red tape."

"Red tape is what got us into this mess. You won't find that shit here."

"Outstanding."

"Sir, what kind of support do we get?" asked Josh.

"You'll need to run whatever you need through me, and I'll decide if we can risk that asset and if doing so might compromise operational security. I'll draw from our JTTFs, but I'd prefer you keep this as compartmentalized as possible. We don't know who's looking over our shoulders. Nevertheless, I'll try to provide you with whatever you need. No promises, though."

"Roger that," said Josh.

Plesner rose. "Gentlemen, welcome to the FBI."

Chapter Thirty-Three

"Yes, you must look at the world through the eyes of your enemy—but you must never forget that your enemy is doing the same."

—Josh Eriksson (FBI interview, 23 December)

After a vigorous workout on his stationary bike in which he completed a series of threshold intervals designed by his personal trainer, Nicholas Dresden retired to his living room, where he reclined on the sofa with a cup of coffee and a notebook computer glowing on his lap. The call from Senecal at 6:45 a.m. confirming that Beb Ahmose and his son were "taken care of" had left Dresden feeling equally lifeless, as though a thread had been pulled, and now his entire life was unspooling into an abyss. The workout had provided a temporary distraction, but he wound up back on the computer and unconsciously scouring the web for articles about the Muslim Brotherhood and its relationship with the Nazis and Hitler. His motivation was pathetically clear: he needed to reassure himself that Beb Ahmose and his ilk were evil men who deserved to die.

In truth, Ahmose was in Berlin because the Nazis and Muslims shared a hatred of Jews. He had not sought justice against the soldiers who killed his wife and injured his son. He had exacted retribution by killing an innocent, unarmed soldier in the Medical Corps, a man who had saved his son's life. Yes, he had felt threatened. Yes, Franz Dresden was going to report him, but Franz Dresden did not deserve to die—

And extending an olive branch to a murderer who was licking the blood off his fingers for seventy years was an ineffable mistake.

Senecal did not mention exactly how he had taken care of the problem, nor did Dresden ask. An accident, perhaps. Something low key and discreet. Dresden did know that Ahmose and his son were taken back to Canada, and he assumed their lives ended there. He should not feel these splinters of remorse. He should close his eyes and purge decades of obsession from his system. That door had been closed forever, and the infidels had won. He would allow this victory to fill a void in his heart and surge through his veins.

Dresden's phone rang. The call was from Tom Barryman, Executive Director of Shipping at UXD in Texas and the man who had given Dresden and Susannah a tour of the company's static detonation chamber. Barryman was the most loyal employee Dresden had at UXD and a man with whom he had wanted to become better friends; however, Dresden's wealth and influence raised barriers of awkwardness between them, and, over the years, Barryman had politely declined many of the free ski trips and visits to Arizona spas Dresden had offered with the excuse that he would take what was due like any other worker because his father had taught him that they were independent men who did not accept handouts. While that might be true, Dresden sensed that Barryman considered himself a "simple man," and was unnerved by the prospect of socializing with the ultra rich. That was a shame, because Dresden truly admired his dedication and commitment to excellence, and he wished he could express that he and Senecal had come from the same stock.

With bated breath, he answered. "Tommy, how are you? Don't tell me you've reconsidered that trip up here? Like I said, we'd love to have you and Jenn stay with us. We'll show you New York like you've never seen it before."

"I'm sorry, sir, but I'm not calling about that. And I'm sorry to bother you."

"It's no bother. What do you need?"

"Well, you know me, sir. Twenty years as a cop, eighteen for you. I'm a straight shooter. I don't lie or try to cover up anything. I run a very tight ship here. Nothing gets by me. Nothing except this."

Dresden braced himself. "What do you mean?"

* * *

Tom Barryman had never been diagnosed with Obsessive-Compulsive Disorder, nor did he believe his insatiable desire for organization was anything more than a method to bring structure and order into his life. Two college-aged daughters and an opinionated wife had turned his home into a disorganized dungeon run by females. He would make up Bible quotes just to get their goat, saying things like "a house run by women is a house in chaos." His wife had tried in vain to find that quote, while he sipped his beer.

A place for everything, and everything in its place. What was wrong with that? Being organized brought peace. And along with peace came closure, which was why he had grown frustrated with the Dallas Police Department. There had been too many unsolved crimes and not enough resources to pursue them. Loose ends drove him insane. UXD was different. Shipments of expired explosives and munitions arrived. Shipments of recycled material left. They met their quotas, followed their strict security guidelines, and by five p.m. every week day, Barryman trundled off to his pickup truck, feeling like a hero.

This particular day had begun routinely enough. A frosty morning of forty degrees in Columbus, with enough electricity in the air to shock him as he left his pickup. As always, he walked past the yard, counting the trucks in his fleet and noting which ones belonged to his subcontractors. He had a feeling he had miscounted, so he stopped and repeated. He came up two shy. Unusual. And annoying. Before grabbing his coffee, he arrowed straight for his office and pulled up yesterday's shipping reports. The two trucks in question had left the facility at 9:41 p.m., bound for the Port of Houston. They had not returned. And worse, the paperwork for those shipments was no longer in the system, as though the inventory and the delivery had never existed— or had been deliberately erased. Barryman had inspected those trucks himself. He knew their ID numbers. He called the customs broker at the port, who said they had no record of the shipments, let alone any confirmation that he had received them.

While he was on the phone, a group of supervisors, led by the head safety inspector, came by, doing their weekly walk around and safety check. The company had prided itself on zero accidents and zero shipping errors in the past five years, and prior to that, the only employee accident was a back injury and the only shipping mistake had been a shortage to a client who had changed his order at the last moment, before the new software had been put in place.

After double-checking the files and questioning Carlos, one of the forklift operators who had loaded the trucks and had confirmed that the load was in there and that everyone had signed off accordingly, Barryman was at a loss.

He stood there in the middle of the warehouse, feeling as though the walls were expanding into a universe without laws. Everything was random and chaotic now. He was but a lonely and meaningless spec pitted against forces that obeyed no rules and who served no masters. He was losing it. The goddamned trucks had been there! He had seen them! He closed his eyes and swore to himself.

No, a security breach like this could not be kept a secret. Mr. Dresden had treated him like family and was always offering gifts. He deserved to know immediately about this.

"Tommy, do me a favor, just keep this to yourself for now," Dresden instructed. "Because if those trucks are really missing—and this is an inside job—then the people who did this may still be there, watching you."

"Are you serious?"

"We've had security breaches at some of our other companies, and it's sad to say, but most of them were perpetrated by employees."

"Not on my watch, sir."

"I understand how you feel."

"Okay. What should I do now?"

"Nothing. Lay low. I'll follow up on my end with security and with our DOD liaisons."

"Are you sure? We need to move quickly on this."

"Trust me. Business as usual for you, Tommy. I need you to be safe. I'll take care of everything."

* * *

Dresden was already in tears as he ended the call and used the prepaid phone they had given him to dial another number. "It's Tom Barryman. Yes, the one you thought might be a problem."

"We'll take care of it," answered a man whose Middle-Eastern accent was unmistakable.

After hurling the phone across the living room and listening to it smash across the tile, Dresden bolted from the sofa and faced Victoria, who scowled at him. "If it's about money, we already have enough," she said. "If it's about business, it's not worth the pain. Now stop with your ridiculous tantrum and come have breakfast."

Dresden sprang across the room, clutched her by the shoulders, and began shaking her, screaming, "You don't know *anything*!"

* * *

The last thing Tom Barryman remembered was heading into the rest room. Even though Mr. Dresden had told him to shut down his investigation, he could not help himself and planned to consult with the plant's overnight security chief, who he had summoned back to the plant to see if he knew anything. The man was on his way.

Barryman flickered open his eyes. Searing pain throbbed at his temples. The nape of his neck ached and felt swollen. The world tipped twice on its axis before he realized he was lying on his side, his arms and legs bound with what felt like electrical cord. His mouth had been taped closed, and he wet his lips against the adhesive. They had done nothing to clog his ears, nothing to hide that steady and agonizingly familiar hum and reverberation of the static detonation chamber, fully online.

He realized he was lying on a crate inside the loading room. The conveyor carried him into the first airlock, and the heavy, reinforced door dropped behind him like a guillotine. He could already feel the heat pressing down as the conveyor rattled on, moving him into the second airlock and then into the elevator that carried him up toward the feeding chamber. It took only four seconds to reach the top, during which time Barryman recalled his wife's smile, his daughters graduating from high school, and his old Labrador retriever's sigh as he balanced his head on Barryman's knee while Barryman read his Sunday paper.

Another conveyor led to the chamber, and he glimpsed the security cameras mounted around the machine, realizing with tearing eyes that they had been turned off. His murderers were not as detail-oriented as he was—because they had chosen an imperfect way to dispose of him and his body. In exactly six more seconds, he would plunge into the chamber and be cooked alive at 1,022 degrees Fahrenheit. Neither his bones nor his teeth would be fully destroyed because that would require temperatures in excess of 1,400 degrees, a number he was familiar with after having his uncle cremated. However, if his remains were mixed with munitions parts, they might be hidden from discovery. Perhaps that did not matter. Perhaps everyone in his department was in on the plan. Carlos had given him a strange look when he had asked about the trucks. Even Mr. Dresden had told him to stop investigating. Was that because he was afraid for Barryman's life? Or because of something else?

Remarkably, Barryman was able to consider these facts as the chamber doors opened. This was a testament to his prevailing calm born during his eight years in the Marine Corps and nurtured on the streets of Dallas. His was a life of absolute joy, absolute despair, and everything in between. A good run. A life worth living. He thrust out his chest in defiance.

But then... survival instincts took over.

He writhed and screamed behind the tape—

As he plunged into the fires.

Chapter Thirty-Four

"An unquestioning belief in the chain of command can be even more dangerous than the enemy."

—Corey McKay (FBI interview, 23 December)

Johnny had requested the police reports from North Carolina, the ones cited during their interrogation/interview. He noted how Detective Paul Lindquist from Holly Ridge had been following up on the LaPorte-Shammas connection. Lindquist had called one of Shammas's colleagues, Dr. Mohammad Nazari, an American citizen who taught at the University of Northern Iowa. The campus was within a mile of the McDonald's in Cedar Falls, the number enumerated in Morse code on Shammas's courier card. That card, along with the second one, was under biometric analysis by the Federal DNA Database unit. Furthermore, Nazari's personal residence was also in Cedar Falls, on West 4th Street.

Plesner agreed that they needed to follow up, but he remained skeptical because their raid on the enclave had sounded the alarm. If Nazari was involved, he might be long gone by now. Nevertheless, Lindquist's report and the McDonald's connection were the best leads they had, so they hopped on a plane and flew to Chicago, where they made their connection for Waterloo. The Bureau provided them with lock boxes for their pistols and ammunition so they could check them through. While they kept their personal smartphones, Plesner provided several throwaways that they could use at their discretion.

Johnny tried to explain his current situation to Elina without telling her they were now contractors for the FBI. He emphasized that they were much safer now and

287

had more help. She seemed suspicious and argued that she was tired of the Keys and wanted to come home. He shut his eyes and whispered, "Soon."

While they were flying up from Richmond, Plesner had moved full-speed ahead with the investigation. The Bureau's Omaha, Nebraska field office covered all counties in Iowa, and two special agents handpicked by Plesner drove up and conducted surveillance on the McDonald's. They met privately with the store's manager and showed him photos of Shammas, Rasul, and Nazari. He confirmed that the latter two were regulars. He denied ever allowing them to use the restaurant's phone to make or receive personal calls. However, the restaurant employed over twenty people, and each would have to be interviewed.

Plesner also provided more background on Rasul, whose full name was Rasul Abdi Yusuf. His parents had emigrated from Saudi Arabia, but he was an American citizen and graduate student at the university with a full assistantship in the Department of Technology. In addition, he had worked part-time for UPS as a package handler in their Cedar Falls warehouse. With a warrant in hand, special agents paid a visit to Rasul's one bedroom apartment and found it completely cleared out. A forensic team was still examining the place. Those agents also searched Nazari's office at the university but came up empty.

Meanwhile, Nazari's car, a white Ford Fusion with Iowa tags, had already been flagged and added to a highly classified case file drawing information from multiple law enforcement databases, including the National Crime Information Center. If Nazari attempted to cross the border into Canada or Mexico, license plate readers at those checkpoints would instantly ID his vehicle. Of course, Nazari need only use a rental, one provided by jihadi colleagues masquerading as prophets of peace and hiding behind innocent Muslims in Islamic centers like the one in Cedar Falls. Another special agent, was, in fact, posted outside that location. Plesner said she was armed with an IMSI catcher or International Mobile Subscriber Identity device called a "Stingray." The Stingray mimicked a cell phone tower and could locate a particular device, interfere with its signal, or even intercept calls and texts. While the jihadi leadership was aware of the Stingray's existence via numerous articles published on the web, Plesner maintained that just one call placed by an uninformed or naïve individual could establish probable cause to raid the center.

As Plesner had shared the work of those agents, the enormity of their task finally registered with Johnny: here they were spearheading a major FBI investigation. Just a few hours prior, Corey was sitting on the plane and expressing how dumbfounded he was over Plesner's change of heart. They all shared that sentiment and agreed with

Plesner's frustration regarding the Bureau's inability to do what it did best. Johnny knew exactly why Plesner had hired them; however, he still found it mind-blowing that a pogue at his level had the audacity to improvise like this. Those guys usually spent more time covering their butts than shaking trees.

Johnny had yet to inform Mark Gatterton of their new contract, and he was hesitant to do so, given Plesner's orders for their work to remain strictly confidential. As far as they knew, Plesner was the only one aware of their operation, and this, Willie had pointed out, was both a blessing and a curse. Yes, security would remain tight; however, they would only learn what Plesner knew, and if intel was miscommunicated or incomplete, then they had no other way to vet the information. This, Willie had contended, was a weak link in their chain. Josh had stressed that security was more important. Willie agreed but said that if something went south, Plesner could use them as the perfect fall guys—which reminded Johnny that Plesner may have already covered his ass—by hiring them in the first place.

Local time in Cedar Falls was 2014, with an overcast and oppressive sky, along with temperatures hovering in the forties. Johnny and Corey had been dropped off a block away from Nazari's three bedroom ranch and, slipping through shadows clinging to backyard fences, they closed with the residence, approaching from the rear. Meanwhile, Josh and Willie would advance from the east side, securing the front door and garage. Earlier in the evening, while they had been reconnoitering the neighborhood and searching for potential spotters, Johnny had shaken his head at Nazari's American flag and white picket fence. They made his stomach turn.

Once he and Corey arrived at that aforementioned fence, they bounded over it, then raced across Nazari's yard. Leaves and acorns crunched beneath their boots. An atmosphere of utter calm settled across the yard as they reached the back door and hunkered down on either side. Johnny fought for breath as the scent of burning oak from a neighbor's fireplace ushered him back to the morning after his brother's death. Without warning, he choked up. This burst of emotion surprised him. Downrange meant downrange; there should be nothing else on his mind.

"You're Johnny Johansen. I know all about you. Easy day, no drama."

Corey cast a worried glance, and Johnny rose with a reassuring look. He tipped his head toward the windows, where the blinds were open, and the house lay in utter darkness. Johnny fired up a penlight, then edged forward. A hand swipe across the dusty glass exposed an empty den with adjoining kitchen. No furniture, as though the place had gone into foreclosure a year ago. He directed the light inside for a better look, then motioned to Corey to check the other window. Seconds later, Corey turned and shook his head.

Johnny sent Willie a text message, telling him and Josh to move up and check the front windows. Meanwhile, he and Corey split up to peak through the side windows. Johnny smudged the glass and spied another empty bedroom.

They met up at the front door with weapons drawn. On a lark, Johnny turned the handle. Open.

"Wait," whispered Josh. "Alarm?"

"Let's see," said Johnny, pushing open the door.

"Well that's too easy," said Willie.

"What does he care about locking up?" asked Corey. "He took off with everything."

The front door had a mail slot beneath a pair of frosted glass windows. Envelopes and flyers were splayed across the tile, directly in their path. They ignored them for now, moving swiftly to clear the house, relying on their old "fill, flow, and go" tactics from the Marine Corps. When they were finished, they linked up in the foyer, where they sifted through the mail. Johnny shone his light on the envelopes: junk from the local Ford dealership, flyers from the supermarkets, and insurance companies advertising via official-looking letterhead to fool residents into opening their garbage.

There was, however, a blank, letter-sized envelope that had been sealed. Johnny tore it open and found a hand-written note in Arabic, one very similar to the instructions he had found in Daniel's office.

* * *

Ashur Bandar had spent nearly two weeks in rehab, tunneling his way through the highs and lows, his face smeared in the camouflage paint of despair.

But when he checked out, he swore to himself he would not backslide. He focused on what Johnny had done for him, and he returned to work with a new haircut, a clean and newly repaired home, and a fresh attitude. He was lifting weights again. Brushing his teeth. Looking people squarely in the eye. Rising above. Dominick and the rest of the guys at the Marina were thrilled—dubious that it would last—but thrilled, nonetheless.

He was at home, sipping on some hot chocolate and watching television, when a text message from Johnny lit his phone's screen.

Bandar studied the photograph and request to translate the message into English. After reading the note, he began a reply but stopped. There he was, caught in the electronic glare of helping a friend—or more accurately—helping a friend get himself killed.

* * *

He said his name was Frank Austerlitz, the next door neighbor, and he had lost his war against gravity over a decade ago. He had been standing crookedly at the front gate, scowling as Johnny and the others had filed out of Nazari's house.

"I say again, who are you people?"

"My name's Johnny. That's all I can tell you, though. We work for the government."

"Oh, yeah? You got ID?"

"You see?" Willie hollered. "We should have badges."

"Ignore them," Johnny said. He draped an arm around Frank's shoulder and said, "Look, old timer, anything you can tell us about your neighbor would really help. You'd be doing a great service to your country."

"Who the hell are you?"

"Look at me." Johnny quirked a brow. "I was a Marine for twenty-three years, and I'm still protecting that flag back there, the one your neighbor was hiding behind."

"Lots of people impersonate military folks. I see that on YouTube."

Johnny shrugged, thought a moment, then drew from his wallet a Second Force Reconnaissance Company challenge coin. "This is all I have. I wish I could tell you more. I'm a good guy. And I think you are, too."

Frank snorted. "Maybe I should call the police."

"Go ahead. Won't matter either way."

Frank scrutinized Johnny a moment more. He glanced away, heaved a great sigh as though disgusted by his own gullibility, then said, "Well, I guess I'll tell you this. We all trusted him. This whole neighborhood. Took him in with open arms because we're trying to be fair, be inclusive, you know? This is a country of immigrants. But then I see a bunch of moving trucks here, and these guys I don't know. They empty the whole place like he's a drug dealer or something. No warning. He was just telling me how much he loved it here. I mean, look at the paint job on that house."

Johnny glanced back over his shoulder; it *was* a nice paint job. "Anything else?"

"Not really. He took better care of the house than Jack Dover and his alcoholic wife ever did. Her drinking was why he cheated on her. He never bothered to fix up the place."

"I'm sorry to hear that. You see anyone else besides the movers?"

"Not since then. And I don't miss much."

"Roger that. Did your neighbor live alone? Did he have a lot of guests?"

"He was alone. Said he was never married. Very few guests."

Johnny used his phone to show the old man pictures of Shammas and Rasul. "You recognize any of these men?"

"That guy," Frank said, pointing at Rasul's photo. "He's a student. He'd come here once in a while. Sometimes he just dropped off papers."

"Gotcha."

"You think Nazari's a terrorist?"

Johnny smiled guiltily. "Just because he's a Muslim?"

"No, because he skipped town so fast. When he first moved in here, people joked about that, but I convinced them to give the guy a chance. We're all immigrants."

"Yeah, well, let's just say your neighbor is a person of interest. Now after we leave, can I ask a favor?"

"What's that?"

"I'd like to recruit you. You'll be my eyes and ears. I'll give you my phone number, and you call me if you see something."

"Shit. Really? I'm on a fixed income—and I still need to help the government catch bad guys? Dear God."

Johnny almost chuckled. "If you can get something to write with and a piece of paper, I'll give you my number. Now if you'll excuse me..." Johnny drifted away from Frank and toward Corey, who tightened his lips in disappointment.

"Damn, I was hoping we'd find more," he said. "Those courier cards had perforated edges, and I'm positive someone used a laser printer to make them. My guess is the guy who's in charge makes and sends out the cards. We just need to know where he does it and how they're distributed—then we'll have a gold mine of intel and we can disrupt their communications."

"Roger that." Johnny's phone rang.

"Hey, Johnny," Plesner began. "We just had that message translated. You boys are heading up to Detroit."

Johnny told Plesner to hold on while he glanced down at a text message reply from Bandar, who confirmed the Bureau's findings. The message included the time, date, and address for a meeting at 2300 the following evening. Whether Nazari would be there or not remained a mystery, but his associates might know his whereabouts, and any one of them could be a high value target. Capturing an operative became the next priority. Johnny confirmed their new travel plans, then regarded the group. "Anybody like Motown? 'Cause we're going..."

"Detroit?" asked Willie. "One of my 3-Gun buddies, a guy named Salvatore Rocco, lives there. Retired cop. Good guy."

"Hey, I just thought of something," Corey said. "Why didn't they drop off a courier card? Why the note? Doesn't seem very secure."

"Good question," said Johnny.

"They used a note to hook up with LaPorte," said Willie. "Maybe they don't use the cards for everything? They write notes for less secure communications? Probably faster and easier that way."

"Look, Nazari couldn't stop the mail," Josh said. "And these cells are cut off from each other. So it's likely some courier dropped this off and never realized he was gone. If they're communicating with cards and notes, the time delays are huge. Like Willie said, they only use the cards for the most secure stuff. Or maybe they didn't have time or access to the guy who makes the cards? Who knows? Point is, we're still on the hunt."

"Roger that," said Johnny. "And maybe we can catch them while they're still on the roost."

Chapter Thirty-Five

"I didn't care if they believed me or not. All I needed was for them to get down there, remain vigilant, and they would find out for themselves."

—Johnny Johansen (FBI interview, 23 December)

Ghostly workers of an old industrial age seemed to glimmer behind the chessboard pattern of windows of the Packard Automotive Plant on East Grand Boulevard and Concord Street. Once an iconic symbol of American manufacturing, the deserted factory was now a 3.5 million-square-foot billboard advertising Detroit's decades old decline and bankruptcy. Graffiti stitched across its paint-chipped walls like multicolored moss from another planet. Vain attempts at boarding up the ground floor sections left pieces of plywood strewn across fields of brown weeds. The plant's sturdy bones of reinforced concrete stood tall against the vandals, auto scrappers, paint ballers, and other assorted tourists who ventured illegally into the labyrinth of buildings to make a few bucks, snap pictures, or act out some post-apocalyptic fantasy.

More recently, the plant had been purchased by a new developer who made rousing promises of rebirth and revitalization of the lot, even as homes in the surrounding area were auctioned off with starting bids as low as one thousand dollars. The developer had hired a private security firm to patrol the grounds and force out the dozen or so vagrants living there. He had erected a chain-link fence around the perimeter and intended to demolish every structure; however, asbestos removal had presented a major snafu. If he did not first remove the asbestos, then every load would be treated as though contaminated. His twenty million dollar demolition budget would skyrocket.

"What time is it?" Willie asked.

Johnny pressed a button on his watch, illuminating the screen. "Twenty-two forty-five."

They had parked the black 1989 Jeep Cherokee between two trees on a vacant lot between Canton and Medbury Streets, one block east of the plant. The Jeep belched smoke and burned oil, while the air coming through the vents felt hot one minute, cold the next. A web of cracks spanned the windshield, and the passenger's side mirror had been busted off, the wires hanging. Rust ringed the fenders like sleep grit, and the grooves in the rear tires were all but gone, burned away by the nineteen-year-old owner who floored it through every yellow light. A trace of marijuana smoke lingered in the carpeting, and Johnny felt certain something had died under the front passenger's seat.

After arriving in Detroit, they had rented a new Nissan SUV, but after observing the location of the meeting on Google Earth, Johnny told the others that they would be sticking out like a sore thumb with that nice ride. Willie had called his retired cop friend Salvatore Rocco and had made the arrangements. The Jeep belonged to a neighbor's son who was more than happy to accept a hundred dollar rental fee for the night.

One block south at the corner of East Grand Boulevard and Canton lay the Packard Motel, a grimy two-story affair with a tin roof, brick walls faded to a light taupe, and a buckling and stained parking lot accommodating only eight vehicles for its dozen or so rooms. The motel's dimly lit sign, its windows protected by burglar bars, and its cash-only policy with five dollar key deposit seemed at odds with the handful of five star reviews Johnny had read online. Guests wrote of the surprisingly clean accommodations, new showerheads, and retro style carpeting. Johnny had imagined bejeweled pimps and bony crack whores loitering on the balconies as though the motel were a last stop before entering the underworld. Across the street, cops dressed in sweatshirts and jeans worked the overnight shift in their unmarked sedan, slugging down Cokes and devouring burgers and fries, their attention divided between money exchanges and packets of mustard and ketchup.

Those musings were incorrect, though, because on this night the motel lay mostly dormant, its denizens scattered by the cold in search of more opportunistic alleyways downtown. Still, with a few windows lit, and a pair of pockmarked sedans outside, the building maintained a thready but discernible pulse that was about to rise. The jihadi meeting would take place here in less than fifteen minutes.

Earlier, Johnny and the others had reconnoitered the plant and it environs, marking avenues of approach and exit, picking out the most probable locations of spotters, and selecting covered and concealed positions, along with lines of fire in and around the motel. They were ready. Except for one thing.

The gear bag they had ordered from Plesner had not arrived. No rifles, no protective vests, no night vision, no problem. They had flashlights, smartphones, and pistols. Josh had used his own money to pick up a pair of Steiner binoculars and some balaclavas while they were still in Iowa. Johnny had called Plesner twice, wondering about the drop off, and the man had assured him they would be contacted by someone. So much for depending upon the bureaucracy. They were out of time.

Josh and Corey were already outside, lying catlike in the brambles and taller grass of a vacant lot now a cemetery of trash between the plant and motel. They conducted surveillance from the far west side, facing the factory.

A rusting fence wandered along the east side of the street and served as a leaning trellis for dying weeds and vines creeping in and out its links. That fence provided an excellent cover position from which to observe the motel; consequently, Willie and Johnny left the Jeep, heading there. They pushed through warrens of browning foliage, the vines brushing across their balaclavas as they came in behind the fence and settled down.

The unknowns coiled tighter around Johnny's spine. Would Nazari show? How many other jihadis planned to attend? Would they be armed? Intel regarding the size and composition of the enemy was important if you planned on surviving the night—a lesson they had learned the hard way in Fallujah. At the moment, they had little more than guns and good intentions. If the situation grew too unstable, they could fall back and observe, perhaps follow one jihadi as he left. Of course that jihadi would succumb to Murphy's Law and die before they learned anything, just like all the others had.

Johnny drew his pistol and decided that no, they would not play that losing game again. They would go on the offensive—because they needed answers. Tonight.

* * *

Josh zoomed in across Concord Street, panning along the fifth story roofline of a building whose walls resembled a sheet of graph paper blotted by coffee stains. He examined every curve, hanging piece of wood, and jagged tooth of concrete from the intersections of East Grand all the way to Lambert Avenue. He shifted down to the fourth story and continued his sweep, searching between those windows covered by warped plywood and aluminum siding. He probed the gaping holes where the cracked ceilings and framework appeared either scorched by firebombs or bedecked in the crude hieroglyphics of spray paint.

"Hey, over there," said Corey. "Thought I saw movement." He pointed toward the south end of the building, near where a small bridge spanned the boulevard.

Josh redirected the binoculars. Despite the absence of thermal images, he was able to pick out a man on the fifth floor who was lowering himself to the ledge with a rifle and attached scope. The sniper wore a woolen cap and heavy coat, his face partially eclipsed by his weapon and too grainy to discern.

"Good catch," Josh said. "But aw, dude, he ain't alone."

The second sniper had tucked himself into a corner of a missing window on the fourth floor. Josh counted eleven windows from the bridge where the first man had set up shop. Sharpshooter #2 was already propped on his elbows behind his rifle's bipod, the scope and muzzle like a pair of disembodied eyes floating in zero gravity.

Josh's breath shortened as he continued scanning and froze at the intersection of Medbury Street, where another man on the fourth floor had found a static position about a meter back from the ledge, beside a mound of broken concrete. Were it not for the pale yellow light filtering through the dust motes behind him, Josh would have missed his silhouette.

"I don't get it," he stage-whispered to Corey. "Three snipers drawing beads on the motel."

"Just security?"

"I don't know."

Corey swore under his breath. "They're tough to reach. Can't get up there without making a lot of noise. Looks like they've got a thousand ways to escape."

"Why not spotters and some bodyguards in close?" Josh asked.

"I'm not sure. But maybe this isn't a meeting."

Josh nodded. "You know what it looks like to me?"

A rustling sound along the fence stole Josh's breath. He lowered the binoculars and signaled to Corey. They crawled deeper into the shrubs and listened beyond the whirring breeze and a distant car horn, beyond the creaking fence and sawing of vines on vines. Listening even more intently, Josh heard it: the barely perceptible thump of rubber on sand, on rock, on leaves, and finally on broken glass. The footfalls drew closer.

* * *

Willie had already rehearsed exactly how he would engage targets in and around the motel with his Glock 19 compact. He carried the pistol in a G-Code INCOG holster and had a fifteen-round flush mount magazine loaded with Hornady critical defense ammo. The pistol's barrel was over an inch shorter than his 34's and presented a challenge for putting lead on targets in non-lethal spots such as the arms or lower legs. At this point, though, Willie was up for anything. He had thrown caution to the wind and had roller coastered his way into a job working for the FBI. Could life get any stranger than this? He was afraid to ask.

The Glock's Trijicon night sights shone harlequin green against the motel's brick walls. Bands of shadows cast by the street and starlight hid several of the doors from view, but Willie would run and gun if necessary to cover those areas. The fence was not unlike one of the barriers at Ant Hill, and range out to the motel doors was just shy of thirty yards, similar to what he shot on the course. Repressing a chill, he lowered the pistol and rubbed his eyes, allowing his thoughts to ebb and flow back to his last conversation with Ivonne, the sense of longing and guilt magnified now that he had no idea when he was coming home.

Johnny, who was at the fence a few yards to the right, eased his way back and whispered, "Text from Josh. Three snipers at the plant. Fourth and fifth floors. Plus there's somebody on the lot. Very close. You cover the motel. I'll circle back and see what we got."

Willie gave a curt nod.

As Johnny left, the air grew magnetic, drawing out Willie's senses, his instincts, his intuition. He refocused on the motel but found himself stealing glimpses through the trees and across the lot, to where Josh and Corey lie in wait. He double-checked the phone in his pocket, making sure it was set to vibrate and remained wary of an incoming message. He shook off the tingling across his neck, and then he held his breath as headlights swiped across the corner and picked out the motel.

* * *

The cold front and its accompanying winds concealed Johnny's advance toward the north side of the lot, where the oaks and shrubs grew so dense that they concealed the entire street from view. He drew behind a man in a dark jacket and ski cap who leaned on a tree with his rifle held at his hip. The jihadi checked his watch, then lowered himself onto his haunches. The snipers above had no doubt marked the jihadi's entry, so any commotion near those trees would be detected by them. Moreover, reaching the jihadi past five yards of rutted dirt and weeds required a more violent gust of wind and a bounding stride that was sure to attract attention. For the time being they would mark this jihadi's position and continue with their surveillance. Johnny sent a text to Josh: I'm coming over. Wincing as his boots pressed on some glass, he fell back into the woods and hiked along the fence line, linking up with Josh and Corey near another stand of trees.

"I'm confused," Josh whispered. "Are these guys working security for some big meeting—or are they here for us?"

"For us?"

"Maybe we picked up a tail."

Johnny's phone vibrated. He withdrew it from his pocket and read a text from Willie: car pulling up at the motel. "I need to go," he told Josh. "Hold here."

"Roger that."

Johnny hustled off, working his way along the perimeter, keeping his distance from their friendly neighborhood jihadi posted on the north side. He reached Willie and gathered his breath before muttering, "Talk to me."

Willie pointed at the motel. "That little Honda pulled up. Tall guy, looks like a young bin Laden, got out. He went inside the office, door on the far left. Still in there."

Johnny checked his watch: 2301. "This ain't no meeting," he told Willie. "Josh thinks we picked up a tail. Maybe they came for us."

"Or they're waiting for someone else? Maybe the plan was to lure Nazari here and take him out. They're still trying to plug their security leak."

"That's possible."

"You got orders, Master Sergeant?"

Johnny grabbed his phone. "I'm texting Josh and Corey. There's a guy on the north side. He's theirs."

"Roger that. What about us?"

"You cover me."

"Cover you? What're you doing?"

"I'm calling their bluff."

"We're even, Johnny. Don't make me save your ass again."

"Not part of the plan." He pocketed his phone and took a deep breath. Clutching the fence with both gloved hands, he climbed over it, hopped down, then sprinted across the street toward the hotel.

Knowing the snipers were tracking him, he juked right, then left—the first shots coming in succession, punching a hole in the Honda's rear window at his shoulder and flattening the driver's side rear tire with a whoosh and hiss.

In three more strides, Johnny was at the motel's office door, reaching for the handle as his shoulder made contact. The door swung open—

But Johnny rolled away, ducking back outside.

A round from a shotgun blasted through the doorway, peppering the Honda to release a detonation of glass. Johnny spun forward in his counter-attack.

The jihadi stood there, a gaunt-faced demon with yellowing teeth and a matted beard. His eyes radiated a profound hatred as the shotgun's smoking barrel came to bear. The motel disintegrated around him like buildings in those old nuclear test films. Improbably, he and Johnny remained, squaring off within the embers of a charcoal landscape. All of this happened in Johnny's imagination, within one one-hundredth of a second before he pulled the trigger.

His first round pasted a red star on the jihadi's brow. The second caught him in the neck and tore free a ragged chunk. Blood spewed as he tumbled backward and the shotgun went off again, blasting into the popcorn ceiling to unleash a torrent of debris.

Before Johnny could steal another breath, sniper fire burrowed into the door-jamb. As the splinters flew, he threw himself inside the office, collapsing into the dust. He crawled over the dead man and around the counter. The stench of gunpowder clogged the air as he scrambled to his feet, his ears ringing.

In a hallway behind the counter he found a heavyset black man, the concierge, lying on the blood-soaked carpeting, his arms and hands sliced open, his chest riddled with wounds. Johnny grimaced and charged past him, searching for another way out.

* * *

Corey was halfway across the field, drawing within a few yards of the man near the trees, when shots boomed from the plant behind him and the man sprang like a buck, rushing toward the motel.

With the sound of his own ragged breath raging in his ears, Corey followed, breaking into a hard sprint that woke tremors in his knees.

Detecting Corey's approach, the jihadi spun back at the next cluster of trees and raised his rifle. As Corey threw himself toward the dirt, a gun shot exploded to his right. That was Josh, who followed with three more rounds. So much for taking a prisoner.

As Corey landed with a breath-robbing thud, so too did their assailant, his luck poor against Josh's superior marksmanship. Josh rushed to the man, grabbed him by the shoulders, and dragged him around the broadest tree trunk for cover. At the same time, Corey struggled back to his feet and high-tailed it for those trees.

More shots from the plant sent dirt and broken glass fountaining into his path as he rounded the tree and dropped onto all fours. Josh had already torn off the man's cap to reveal a shock of black hair. His long beard and the absence of a mustache suggested a lot. The jihadi's vacant eyes stared back at him, and for a moment, Corey sensed something in the man's expression, something released only after he had died, an emotion darker and more unsettling than just hatred, a venomous and contagious thing that Corey could not describe.

Josh finished rifling through the jihadi's pockets and cursed. "No ID, nothing," he said. "Get a close up of this guy."

"Roger that." Corey fished out his phone and felt pangs of disgust as he thumbed off two photos of the corpse's face.

After that, Josh said they would keep to the fence line, driving north and remaining within the denser undergrowth. Corey nodded, understanding Josh's plan. They were returning to the factory to go after those snipers.

* * *

Johnny slammed through the door at the end of the hall and staggered into an alley alongside the motel. Keeping tight to the row of trees on his right, he jogged toward the street, reaching a trio of plastic trash cans at the curb. The cans dropped like bowling pins under a sudden hailstorm of sniper fire.

Cursing, Johnny darted to the right and sprinted across the road, rounds literally paralleling his steps or striking like tiny meteors into the asphalt ahead. He reached the fence, where Willie proffered a hand and helped haul him over.

"Guy on the north side's dead," Johnny reported. "We need to get one of those snipers at the plant. Let's go!"

Johnny chose the south side fence, veering off the lot and onto the broken sidewalk to save time. They could not see the snipers from their angle, meaning they too were concealed. Only when they rounded the corner, searching for a gap in the first floor walls, did they come back under fire.

"I'll check for a car out back," Willie said, cocking a thumb up the boulevard.

"Do it," Johnny said.

As Willie hauled ass under the bridge, beating a serpentine path through a gauntlet of abandoned tires, Johnny threw himself toward the building as a round cracked directly above and pinged off the fence. "Oh, I'm coming for you," he muttered.

Gritting his teeth, he bounded across the uneven sidewalk, passing under the wooden power poles, that, quite fittingly, were rowed up like Orthodox crosses beside the building. With his 1911 in one hand and a flashlight in the other, he scaled some plywood and reached a small opening. As he entered, the cold air shimmered with dust, and the gigantic letters of some graffiti artist seemingly detached themselves from the wall and glided toward him. Some forty yards away to his left, concrete stairs once surrounded by a stairwell towered in the gloom. He aimed for them, the flashlight's beam slashing across gaping cracks in the floor.

He reached the foot of the stairs and scowled. A motley crew of Michelangelos had left their messages on the face of each step: *Risk failed. This is America. Burn this place. Cars killed the earth.*

More "artwork" covered the water-stained walls as he ascended, moving between concrete stairs and sections of rotting wood that coughed as he booted by. The wind whistled through windows fringed by teeth of glass, and soon, he traversed landings where the rest of that glass had been trampled into glittering mats that crackled like corn under his feet.

The rumbling boots of the jihadi's exit panned overhead, and Johnny quickened his pace, reaching the fifth floor and shining his light on another stairwell, at the far end, where he caught a fluctuating silhouette, along with a rifle barrel.

Johnny fired, the pistol's muzzle flashing saffron, the round chewing into the wall at the sniper's shoulder as he shrank into a cloak of darkness.

Wincing over the miss, Johnny forged on, narrowly avoiding a mountain of concrete and tarpaper from the collapsed ceiling. With the sky exposed, the light turned silvery and cold, his breath heavier, his nose running. He nearly tripped as he reached the second stairwell, double-timed down to the next floor, then let his beam play across piles of green garbage bags that had weathered down into clumps like seaweed. He stiffened as gunfire thundered to the south. That was Corey and Josh engaging another sniper.

A crash from below had him descending again, his legs wobbly from the exertion, his balance faltering despite the surge of adrenaline. He reached the third level, then the second, where he spotted the jihadi skirting a pole with a circumference that could hide two men. Johnny aimed both the light and pistol, tracking the sniper as he left the pole and, for a few seconds, appeared in the open—an apparition leaping across carpets of rubble and slowing as though Johnny's light were draining him of power.

Anticipating the man's turn toward the staircase, Johnny dropped the flashlight and clutched the pistol with both hands to control the recoil. Now relying upon his night sights, he squeezed the trigger, and the barrel kicked up slightly in his hands. The jihadi lurched and clutched his leg, but he dragged on toward yet another staircase to their left, near a broad bank of glassless windows.

As though smelling the blood, Johnny fetched his flashlight and returned to the pursuit, so caught up in the electricity of the chase that he failed to see a piece of concrete jutting up like a traffic cone. His knee brushed across the rock a second before his boot latched on.

He hit the floor like a refrigerator, losing the flashlight but maintaining his grip on the pistol. Swearing against the stinging pain in his leg, he pushed forward, seized the light, and groaned as he stood. The bleeding jihadi had already disappeared into the stairwell, leaving a trail of glittering rubies.

Johnny shuffled down another flight, slamming into the wall as his ankle twisted on a broken board. A curse reached his lips but escaped no farther. They were at the north end of the building now, past Lambert Ave, where the windows and doors were more heavily fortified against looters. The only way out was through a narrow doorway on the south side. Street lights drew a crooked shadow from that opening toward a heap of red bricks that seemed blasted from the wall by tank fire.

A scraping of shoes and ragged breathing sent Johnny's light veering toward the wall, where the jihadi lumbered like a hunchback, exploiting waist-high mounds of ruptured flooring and corroded steel beams for cover. But then he stopped, craned his head, and met Johnny's gaze. In the next second he was gone behind a dorsal fin of concrete.

Johnny hit the deck just as the first shot blasted into the wall behind him and echoed away. He pushed up on his elbows. A second round punched the floor near his right arm and ricocheted up and away. Johnny barrel rolled to the left, drawing himself to the nearest pole. He wormed his way behind it, then rose to his haunches.

As he leaned out, the sniper's rifle spoke again, and Johnny could feel that round chiseling into the stone near his shoulder.

With all those gunshots still hammering in his ears, Johnny added his pistol to the conversation. His .45 caliber double tap would, he hoped, give the jihadi pause. Unfortunately, it had the opposite effect.

Just as his second round clanged and sparked across a steel girder only inches above the man's head, the jihadi dashed off, no longer limping but raging against the horror of his wound in a last ditch effort for the doorway.

Fearing that another round might kill the man, Johnny held fire and tore off. He reached the girders and vaulted onto one, doing a two second high-wire act, then leaping to the floor and falling in behind the jihadi, drawing within a meter. As he launched forward to tackle the man, they crossed onto a section of plywood about five-feet square. The sheets were neatly arranged but waterlogged and sagging at the center.

If Johnny had the time, he might have looked up to spy the gaping hole extending through every floor and allowing rainwater to filter inside—but he was locked on to the target, programmed to win, and ready to celebrate with a beer and a bag of chips.

Under the weight of both men, the plywood boards buckled then snapped. He and his prey plunged through a hole hidden beneath the boards.

By the time Johnny lowered his flashlight, it was too late. They had fallen some twelve feet and were a gasp away from splashing into a garbage-filled swamp that had collected in the basement. Old shoes, bags, pieces of wood, signs, swollen newspapers, and a thousand other articles like the wreckage from an airliner bobbed on the surface. A thin layer of ice, along with the almost furry scent of mildew, foretold of the shock to come.

The last thing Johnny remembered was a cold rip—like a zipper—rising from his ankles to his face. The sludge enveloped his head just as his brow made contact with a hard surface. His neck snapped back, and all of his aches sloughed off into a cold and impenetrable darkness.

Chapter Thirty-Six

"I had no idea that my time spent as a lifeguard on Onslow Beach would come in handy up in Detroit, a city not exactly known for its beaches."

—Willie Parente (FBI interview, 23 December)

Willie craned his head toward a curious and muffled splash from inside the plant.

At the same time, a figure carrying a rifle skulked across the rooftop, drawing close to the parapet.

Raising his Glock, Willie targeted the silhouette. The man leaped down onto the skeletal framework of a bridge between buildings, superimposing him against the icy stars.

Judging the sniper's speed, Willie squeezed off a round, intent on striking the jihadi's leg. The bullet chipped into the ledge, issuing a white-hot spark. What occurred next was even more disappointing.

While glancing up to search for the source of that incoming fire, the jihadi lost his balance, tripped, and launched into an unintentional Olympic-style high dive. He shrieked as he dropped some five stories, spinning like a broken boomerang before striking the rubble with a deadening thud.

Swearing over the loss, Willie raced across the moonscape of crumbling concrete. He reached the sniper, lowered himself to one knee, and dug for his flashlight. He removed the man's ski cap to reveal a tangle of bloody hair, with more blood seeping across the rocks like paint from a leaky can. His dark complexion had gone ashen, and his long beard was now plastered against his neck. Willie dug through that beard to check for a carotid pulse. No sign. He worked his light across the man's face. Pupils dilated and clear fluid leaking from his ears, indicating massive head trauma. A quick search of the jihadi's pockets produced nothing but a box of ammo. Other than that, he had only his rifle: a Blue Door bolt action chambered in .300 Win Mag, a rifle similar to a Remington 700.

A nearby gunshot sent a jolt up Willie's spine. He glanced once more at the building where he had detected the splash.

Gathering up the man's rifle and the box of ammo, Willie hustled across the lot. He turned sideways to pry himself into an opening in the plywood, then panned his light across the floor toward a jagged hole near the center. Steam fog unfurled over the edges as though from a cauldron. He held the light there—just as another round struck like an echoing timpani drum from below.

Willie approached swiftly, leading with his Glock. He reached the edge, then held his breath and aimed his flashlight down into the hole. The light's beam grew thicker as it reached the near-black water. He probed a surface of flickering reflections cast off from broken glass and garbage bags and the eyelets of old high top sneakers, along with clothing so swollen and mangled that it resembled pieces of cancer-laced intestine growing with mold.

"Hey..." came a voice almost unrecognizable, more a rasp than an actual word.

Willie shifted the light—

And there, floating within this nightmare soup was Johnny, his arm raised, his 1911 clutched in his hand. He had torn off his balaclava, and his forehead looked swollen and bleeding. He squinted like a vampire and tried in vain to shield his eyes. Beside him, bobbing face down like a piece of flotsam, was another man, assumedly one of the snipers.

"What the hell? Was that you firing?"

"Yeah. Little help," he managed. "I'm real dizzy."

"Hang in there. I'll find a way down." Willie spun around, raking the light across the walls and locking onto a staircase about twenty yards to his rear. He hurried over and descended until the stairs vanished beneath the murky waves. He sighed and looked around. The plant had transformed into an ancient city cast into the sea by a massive earthquake.

Shaking his head and shivering in anticipation, Willie removed his own balaclava and his jacket, setting them down on a dry stair. He placed the rifle, his Glock, and the contents of his pockets on top of his jacket. Holding his breath, he pushed forward into the flooded basement, gasping against the cold, the water viscous in spots as though some tanker had sprung a fuel leak.

Soon he was at chest-height then lost his footing as he neared Johnny. He had decided to keep his boots on because who knew what lay beneath the surface—perhaps the rusting teeth of some steel girder or a razor-sharp piece of aluminum. He spat and emptied a path between the trash, reaching Johnny in less than sixty seconds. He came in behind his friend, latched an arm beneath his chin, and began hauling him back toward the stairs. To distract himself from the terrible stench, Willie imagined that a crowd of bikini-clad women were now witnessing his heroism. He shivered and grinned to himself before Johnny ruined the image.

"Thanks, Willie."

"Yeah," Willie groaned. "Some plan you got. Didn't I tell you I wasn't doing this again?"

"Bastard ran across some boards that collapsed."

"And he took you for a nice swim, didn't he. Easy day, huh? I don't believe this—" Willie cut himself off as he came onto the stairs and drove Johnny forward, getting him up onto the first step, then helping him maneuver two steps higher.

Eventually, he guided Johnny up and onto the dry staircase, where the palsy of ice cold water meeting ice cold air seized their arms and legs. With hands he could barely control, Willie removed Johnny's jacket and wrapped his dry one over the man. Swallowing and fighting once more against the tremors, he took up his smartphone and called Josh, who answered on the first ring. Willie gave them a situation report, proud that he only swore once.

"All right, hold there," Josh said. "We're on our way."

"Hey, wait, you get your guy?"

"No, we lost him. You?"

"No luck." Willie ended the call, then turned on the phone's flashlight app and held it toward Johnny's forehead. "You got a nice lump and a gash. Doesn't look like it needs stitches. You nauseous?"

"Not really."

Johnny's pupils were equal and reactive to light, a damned good sign. "Can you stand?"

"Yeah, I think so."

Willie grabbed his arm, then, when he was certain Johnny was up and using the wall for support, he turned back and gathered his flashlight and pistol, then slung the rifle over his shoulder. He wrung out Johnny's wet jacket and took it as well. No sense in leaving behind any more evidence than necessary.

They started up the stairs like World War II veterans, trailing thick breath and wondering if their skin might rattle off their creaking bones. The temperature was dropping even more rapidly. Down into the thirties, Willie guessed. Maybe even colder. They reached the ground floor as Josh and Corey ventured into the building, their lights lacerating a full column of steam rising from the broad rupture in the floor. As they neared and removed their balaclavas, they resembled participants in a séance, their faces lit from below, their eyes widening at the sight of Johnny's forehead. Their fearless leader now sported a bloodshot third eye that seemed weirdly mystical to Willie, as though Johnny could use that eye to finally glimpse the truth.

"Let's get him back to the Jeep," said Josh. He lifted his chin at Willie. "And you, too."

"I wasn't in there as long as him."

"Willie, your face is blue," said Corey, removing his own jacket. "And you smell like a five dollar whore." He thrust the jacket into Willie's arms.

"Our guy might still be out there," said Josh. "Let's head back across the lot. We'll get to Canton that way."

"I can't believe the cops aren't here yet," Corey said.

Willie snickered. "I read somewhere that average response time in Detroit is fifty-eight minutes—that's if someone actually made the call."

* * *

With Johnny injured and Willie freezing, Josh assumed leadership of the group. He gave Corey the binoculars and recruited him as a scout who would text back the letter K, indicating the path was clear.

While they were waiting for Corey to check in, Willie showed them the rifle he had collected from the dead jihadi. Serial numbers on the gun could be run through the Bureau of Alcohol, Tobacco, and Firearms' National Tracing Center. Their eTrace system provided an online portal to the Firearm Tracing System, where the origin of the rifle and associated paperwork could be researched. Plesner would handle that end of things, Josh assumed.

Corey signaled from the opposite end of the field; he had paused along a break in the old fence where it had collapsed under the weight a fallen tree. They dashed across the street, then kept to the trees whose roots busted through the sidewalk like the veins of weightlifters. Only then did a police siren rise in the distance. They kept on, shuffling through piles of dead leaves. They paused once more, Corey moved up, then after thirty seconds, Josh's phone vibrated.

Corey's text sounded ominous: *I need you here.*

Josh signaled for Johnny and Willie to wait. He wove between the trees and shrubs, reaching a wide oak just a meter off the curb. Corey huddled tightly behind that tree, peering up and down the street with Josh's binoculars. He muttered something to himself, his tone suggesting he was surprised by what he saw.

As Josh slipped up behind Corey, he glimpsed the object of his partner's attention: a two story warehouse of approximately 10,000 square feet with the requisite broken windows and colorful splashes of graffiti across its dingy walls.

"Hey, what's up?" Josh asked.

"Take a look. On the roof."

After accepting the binoculars, Josh zoomed in on a man wearing a black leather jacket and balaclava like their own. The man was crouched low behind the ledge, his attention riveted across the street. "That's not our sniper."

"No, it's not."

"What's that in his hand?" Josh asked, squinting into the lens.

"Looks like a remote detonator to me."

"And what's he looking at?" Josh added, although he already knew the answer.

"He's looking at our car."

Just then a text from Willie and Johnny indicated they were too cold to wait anymore and were moving up. Once they arrived, Josh adopted a hard and even tone to share the news. Willie had a look for himself, as did Johnny, although he could barely keep the binoculars on target. The group's morale dropped to funereal depths.

"Nazari set this all up," said Johnny. "He planted the note, lured us here, and hoped we'd take the bait. That last guy is his insurance man, in case the snipers failed. We can confirm that by capturing him."

"You might be right, Johnny, but we need to get you warm," said Josh. "You need to get back in that Jeep—"

"Which our buddy has rigged to blow," Willie finished. "I'm cold, but I'm good. Josh, let's get inside the building and up on the roof. Corey, you hold here with Johnny. We get this guy, we'll call you."

"I'm good to go," said Corey.

Johnny nodded. "Easy day." But then an odd look washed over his face. He coughed, leaned over, and expelled the contents of his stomach.

* * *

After five minutes of painstaking progression, shifting as stealthily as they could through the warehouse's back door, a door that had been jimmied open with a crowbar, Willie led Corey through a vast space whose floor was covered in a layer of dust and rocks akin to lunar regolith. Whatever they made in this place, some sort of concrete product perhaps, rose in gray clouds at their ankles. They reached a flight of metal stairs leading up to another door marked Rooftop Access.

With his pulse throbbing in his ears, Willie slammed open the door and ran across the roof. The jihadi in the leather jacket was hunkered down twenty yards ahead. Willie and Josh screamed for the man to freeze as they broke off from each other, advancing from the flanks to divide the man's attention.

The jihadi whirled from the ledge, brought himself to full height, then raised his arms, maintaining his grip on the remote. While his other hand was empty, he could easily reach for a pistol in his pocket or holster beneath his jacket. Reaching for that weapon would be unwise, though, and the sheen in the man's eyes suggested he knew that.

Relief flooded into Willie's head, producing a welcoming buzz like alcohol, like lovemaking turned liquid, and he imagined that this journey, this onerous march up the coast and into the Midwest, was about to end. Even the stars suggested a denouement as they grew dimmer, veiled in clouds. This tall jihadi would sit behind a table and lay it all out for Johnny. He would name names and establish a truth that Johnny could carve in stone. He would give up the entire network of jihadis. Plesner and his JTTFs would conduct raids and make hundreds of arrests. Willie and the others would be touted as heroes and dragged through the studios of morning news shows so they could be interviewed by women so attractive that his knees would buckle. There would be agents, publicists, new sponsors for his 3-Gun competitions, book and film deals, and country songs written about their exploits. But man, he hated all that celebrity crap, didn't he? He would take the new 3-Gun sponsors and that's about it. Or maybe there would be nothing. Maybe this would all go to hell again—because as much as Johnny said it, there was no easy day for Marines. Not today. Not tomorrow. Not ever.

Willie drew in a long breath. "Take that remote and put it on the ground."

The man nodded and began to move his arm.

In the next breath, their jihadi's head exploded, the impact blasting the rest of his body clear off the roof. The shot boomed a half second later from at least four hundred yards away, maybe farther.

As Willie and Josh ducked and ran to the edge, the jihadi bounced like a marionette across the sidewalk, his arms flailing at improbable angles. The remote struck once, skittered over the concrete, then landed face down.

Willie could almost hear the detonator's *click*.

With a sudden whoosh and tremendous kaboom, the Jeep Cherokee exploded in a fireball spanned by twinkling glass and shards of rocketing shrapnel. The flames writhed up to the overhanging limbs and set them ablaze. At the same time, the vehicle's chassis, heaved some six feet off the ground, collapsed with a metallic crunch onto its side, striking a mere second before one of its doors spun down to impale the warehouse wall. Smaller pieces of the Jeep struck in a meteor shower, casting the narrow road in a volcanic and primordial glow.

"Get down!" Willie shouted, turning back toward the sniper fire.

At the far end of the Packard Plant, the remaining sniper rose from the ledge and jogged away, carrying his rifle and no doubt reveling over his remarkable shot. He was no amateur, no young jihadi recruit.

"Come on," Josh urged Willie. They ran back toward the rooftop door, double-timed down the stairs, and fled outside to the sidewalk where they were bathed in heat and a flickering white-orange blaze. Willie's body seemed instinctively drawn toward the fires.

Corey was already there, and he had torn off the jihadi's balaclava to expose a blonde-haired man, or least what was left of his hair and head. "Found this," he said, handing a pistol to Willie. "Nothing else."

"Back to the woods down the street," Josh ordered. "If the cops don't come to check this out, the gangs will."

Johnny, who had been standing behind them, ambled over to the fire and lifted his palms for a moment, savoring the heat. Willie shouted to him, and he joined the others as they rallied on the denser cover near the end of the block, past an open field gilded in firelight.

Out of breath, they rested a moment while Willie inspected the pistol, a well-worn .40 caliber Glock 22.

"I figured he'd have a pistol from Blue Door," Josh said.

"Me, too," Willie answered.

"Was he a cop?" asked Corey. "A lot of police carry the twenty-two, right?"

"They used to around here," said Willie. "I remember Sal bragging how five or six years ago Detroit switched over to the Smith & Wesson MP40, the gun he prefers.

The pistols were free in exchange for their Glocks. Of course, as a Glock man, I think that's insane."

"Well, if that guy wasn't a cop then—"

Willie held up a finger, cutting off Josh. "The Glock 22 is also the service issue pistol of the FBI."

"You think he was an FBI agent?" Corey asked. "No way."

Willie lifted his brows. "You carry your most comfortable and familiar weapon. Train as we fight, right? Guy was a Caucasian. He look like a jihadi to you?"

Corey shrugged. "Maybe he converted."

"Bullshit."

"Why would an FBI agent want to kill us?" asked Josh.

"Not him per se," said Johnny. "He was taking orders from someone else, the only guy who knew we'd be here."

* * *

Charles Plesner was seated in the office of his six bedroom home on Division Street in Falls Church, Virginia. On the wall opposite his desk hung an antique cuckoo clock he had bought while traveling through the Black Forest in Germany. The current time was 12:17 a.m., and Janice had drifted by in her robe to query why he was up so late.

"Just paying the mortgage," he snapped.

"It's just a question, not an interrogation."

"I'm sorry."

"You've been nasty and rude for weeks, and then you apologize and pretend everything is okay. What's going on?"

"We're under a lot of pressure."

"Same old story. Aren't you tired of this? Can't someone else save the world?" She threw up her hands and flitted back toward their bedroom.

"I am saving the world," he called after her.

He glanced down at the phone, cursed, then dialed Johnny's number for the fourth time. He was ready to smash the phone across his desk when another of his prepaids began to ring.

The caller's voice sounded like a diesel engine with a South African accent: "Everyone's dead except me. They had Schneider cornered on the roof, so I took him out."

"What are you saying? I recruited those guys in Dearborn for you. I paid you for a clean operation."

"You're lucky I got your babysitter before they did. He would've talked. You flew me all the way here from Namibia, and what did I tell you? I said this was a job for mercs. A job for my whole team. But you forced me to drag along your guy and your amateur jihadis. Now they're dead. And your targets are still out there."

"Are you tracking them?"

"I'm off my contract. And I'm done with you. I'm going back home."

"Oh, no, you're not."

The man snorted. "You keep the rest of your money. I told you how to play. You didn't listen. I'm sorry, but I only work with professionals."

"Professionals?" Plesner bolted to his feet. "Do you know who I am?"

Of course, Plesner had never told him, but none of that mattered now. The mercenary had already hung up.

Plesner slumped to his chair, panting and trembling. He needed to call the Detroit Police. He would claim FBI jurisdiction over the scene and state there was possible terrorist activity by individuals associated with the Wayne State University Islamic Center of Detroit. An agent was down. The area needed to be cordoned off.

All right. He would do that. The next call would be to Nazari during which he would resume his role as the liaison and caution the man to step up his own security. If Dresden and Senecal learned of these leaks, they would consider Plesner a failure and have him take the fall. They had entrusted him with protecting the entire operation, and he had used his position to run interference, ensuring that Nazari and his people were lost in a plethora of misinformation and outdated intelligence.

While Plesner lacked the economic clout of men like Dresden and Senecal, he shared their undying belief that America was doomed unless agencies like his own were free to take action. He was "their friend in Washington," their liaison, their brother in arms.

Soon the world would change—but only if he could locate those four jarheads and shut them down in time.

* * *

Willie's 3-Gun buddy, Salvatore Rocco, had a crew cut the color of fluorocarbon fishing line. His beer keg torso bounced behind the wheel of his F-150 crew cab. When he spoke, Johnny had difficulty placing his accent—somewhere short of upper Midwest and leaning toward Hoboken. He gave Johnny and the others a ride back to his house, where they picked up the rental car, dry clothes, and some bandages for Johnny's head. They discussed how the police would come looking for the Jeep's owner. The story would be simple. The Jeep was stolen right off the neighbor's driveway while the kid had run inside and left the car idling. Given the city's reputation for crime, the tale was hardly farfetched. Johnny said he would pay book value plus an extra grand to replace the car, even though the kid had insurance. Salvatore would convey the news and ensure that everyone kept quiet. Besides, he still had goombas on the force who would look the other way if needed. His neighbors were good people. The kid would be thrilled to buy a new ride, one much nicer than his old one.

Johnny retired to Salvatore's garage to call Mark Gatterton. He also needed to return a call to Pat Rugg, who had left a message for him at about the same time Johnny was confronting the jihadi with the shotgun. Pat was a great guy with monumentally bad timing.

Thanks to his waterproof case, Johnny's smartphone had survived his dip into the lake of hell, although he did not use it to call Gatterton. He borrowed Salvatore's smartphone and spent five minutes delivering a rapid fire synopsis of them being hired by Plesner then subsequently set up. By the time he was finished, Gatterton sounded wide awake. "You're positive about this, Johnny?"

"He was the only guy who knew."

"What about the terp? Your friend Bandar. You said you had him read the note to verify Plesner's translation."

"Trust me, Mark, he's the last guy in the world who'd be involved."

"What if Plesner shared intel with someone else?"

"This was all his idea, and we were flying under the radar—so he could do the same."

"I don't know, Johnny."

"You're defending this guy?"

Gatterton raised his voice. "He's the goddamned E-A-D of National Security. And you want me to believe he's in bed with jihadis?"

"That's right. And he's got an agenda. And oh, I forgot to mention we had a sniper pull off a miracle shot. This was not some clown practicing in his backyard."

Gatterton groaned through a sigh. "Why would Plesner hire you, then try to kill you?"

"He was keeping his enemies close and controlled."

"Why are you the enemy?"

"Think about it, Mark. We exposed his friends."

Dead silence on the other end.

"Mark, you there?"

"Yeah, Johnny. I'm just thinking about those brain cells of yours, the ones that got blown up in Iraq, the ones coming back to haunt you. Unless you got hard proof—"

"Look, I would've sent you a picture of the dead agent, but there wasn't much left of his head. We got his gun. I'll text you the serial number. You can get somebody to run it. That'll be hard proof right there."

"You talk to anybody else about this? Donna? Anybody?"

"No. And I need another favor."

"Dear God, what else?"

"Just listen to me. Everything Plesner told us is bullshit. He didn't send any agents to the McDonald's. They never searched Rasul's apartment. They never even went to Nazari's office. There was no DNA test of the courier cards. There *was* no FBI investigation. In fact, when I wanted to see the police files from Holly Ridge, he gave me a funny look. I was the one who saw the connection between Shammas, Nazari, and the McDonald's in Cedar Falls—*not him*. I got us up there. All Plesner did was have someone plant a note at Nazari's house. He sent us up to the Packard Plant, where the risk of collateral damage was low. He walked us into an ambush, then he could say he hired some contractors on a job that went south. Done deal. He walks away—and whoever he's protecting is safe. You see, Mark, that also explains why four good ole boys uncovered all this shit when the FBI couldn't—not with Plesner obstructing his own people. I might be an old redneck, but I ain't that dumb."

"Johnny, are you listening to yourself?"

"Just check it out."

"You're a crazy bastard, but—"

"Look here, for all I know, Plesner could've hired someone to kill my brother. It could go that far. All I'm asking for is a little time. You get to your people. Please..."

"If you would've let me finish, I was about to say I'd do it. Maybe Donna can look into this without raising any brows. How do I reach you?"

"I'll call you in the morning. You won't recognize the number."

"Roger that, Johnny. Cash only. No credit cards."

"I know the drill."

"You need money?"

"I'm good. We'll work it out. You just follow up for me."

Johnny hung up, then pulled out a slip of paper with the Glock's serial numbers. He typed them into a text message for Gatterton. Next he dialed the voicemail on his own phone, listened to the update from Pat Rugg, then called the boys into the garage. "I talked to Mark. He's following up to see how much of what Plesner told us is bullshit. And I got a message from Pat. He might have another lead. I'm calling him right now. But first, switch off your phones, especially the ones Plesner gave us. We'll FedEx them back to my house so that son of a bitch can't track us."

Chapter Thirty-Seven

"The largest sea evacuation in history was conducted by ferryboat captains, coast guardsmen, and civilian boaters on 9/11. They rescued over 500,000 people from the piers and seawalls of Lower Manhattan. Boats were an invaluable asset for escape."

—Josh Eriksson (FBI interview, 23 December)

Mesquite, Nevada was a sleepy little gambling town eighty miles northeast of Las Vegas and a long way from El-Najjar's home in Paterson, New Jersey. The potholes had been substituted by ribbons of sand blown over the highways, and the locals rasped like cowboys instead of mobsters. El-Najjar vowed that once Sharia Law was in place, the first thing he would do was tear down these casinos like the CasaBlanca with their garish neon signs and palm trees swaying like pole-dancing whores. He would replace them with mosques and Islamic centers so that Allah could be properly worshipped. These infidels would know true peace and happiness—instead of the crime and misery propagated by games of chance.

El-Najjar rubbed his weary eyes as he pulled into the warehouse-sized collision shop on Riverside Road. His colleagues tugged down the rolling metal door after his rental truck. It was 10:20 p.m. local time, and he was about thirty minutes ahead of schedule.

With a wince and groan, he climbed out of the truck and greeted the teams waiting for him, nearly twenty jihadis in all. He tossed his keys to one man, who opened the truck's rear door, while another fitted a metal ramp to the open bay. A moment later, men rolled hand trucks up and into the bay. The anti-tank missile systems that

El-Najjar, Tabesh, and two other jihadis had loaded back in Colorado were divided into sets of four and placed aboard three other nondescript trucks owned by Bassem Younes' Seaboard Shipping and Storage. Each driver had received his courier card and the GPS coordinates of his destination:

One truck was bound for Virginia.

Another for Louisiana.

And the third would head south toward Arizona.

For his part, El-Najjar would switch vehicles and drive southwest in an SUV whose cargo compartment was loaded with masks, snorkels, regulators, pressure gauges, buoyancy compensators, air tanks, fins, booties, and dive computers.

He checked his watch again, and within ten more minutes, the metal door lifted to allow another truck inside. Once that vehicle was opened, its contents were confirmed: a shipment of slurry explosives from UXD in Texas that had been bound for the Port of Houston. The truck's driver had been replaced, its cargo and destination stripped from the logs. The boxes of explosives would be split between the truck bound for Arizona and El-Najjar's SUV. A second truck from UXD had recently arrived in New London, Connecticut, where its contents were received and secured.

Instead of leaving in a large convoy that would attract attention, the trucks departed one at a time in six-to-ten minute intervals. When it was El-Najjar's turn, he took a sip of the hot tea one of the men had prepared for him, then he glanced down at the courier card in his hand. He muttered, "Allahu Akbar," and headed out toward glory.

* * *

Young platoon commanders sometimes made combat operations sound like an exact science, and that always amused Johnny. Non-commissioned officers like himself knew that accurate intelligence, good equipment, and proper training were mandatory for successful missions, yes, but even the most flexible plan could not account for the volatility of human beings. Some argued that dumb luck—or fate, or God, or the divine universe—had a hand in orchestrating events, and there was nothing they could do about that.

Consequently, those men become paranoid about their tours, especially during the old man's time, where the art of survival became a religion and infantrymen became deacons anointed with the ashes of their adversaries. NCOs were the high priests of the rice paddies, carrying rabbit's feet in their pockets and tucking magic playing cards into their helmet's straps. Danger was communicated within the hiss of falling rain and through montages in the shadows between trees. They could predict it. Taste it like an old copper penny. And all around them miracles occurred: unexplained lapses in gunfire, bizarre withdrawals of superior enemy forces, grenades that failed to detonate. Some glimpsed Jesus within crowns of palms, others gaped at UFOs—strange aliens who swept down in spaceships shaped like President Lyndon B. Johnson's head to save them from the Vietcong. Some men dropped a lot of acid.

Attempts were made to quantify these supernatural patrols into charts and terms that made sense because attributing mission success to "mysticism" or a "merciful universe" or "little green men" had no place in any after action report.

Of course, the hardest of hardcore operators dismissed all of this as nonsense, as scared men putting faith in exterior forces because they were too frightened to believe in themselves and trust in their brothers. Still, unexplained phenomena occurred in all wars, especially in Iraq and Afghanistan, and Johnny had listened to the tales, shaken his head, and ordered another round because thinking about it too much gave him a headache. "Those guys just caught a lucky break," he would say.

Ironically, he believed that you made your own luck. He acknowledged that dumb luck existed but decided he would not subscribe to that magazine. Thus, when Pat Rugg characterized his lead as a bizarre coincidence, Johnny frowned and gave less credence to the intel even before Pat shared it.

"I was talking with a buddy at work who scored some extra bucks during one of his vacations last year," Pat began. "He got flown to the states to give private diving lessons to a group of college kids. It was all part of some engineering project, and I wouldn't have thought twice about it until my buddy mentioned the guy who hired him. Wait for it."

"I got you on speaker," Johnny said. "We're all waiting..."

"Dr. Ramzi Shammas, the guy you had me and Billy Brandt chasing down. What're the odds? I know it's a small world and my company does have some affiliation with the university through work-study programs, but what are the odds that I'd be chatting with my buddy and he'd bring that up and name your guy?"

"And that's it?" Johnny asked, about to roll his eyes.

"Well, I was going to tell you that my buddy taught those kids in a town called, hang on, let me look at it, I got it right there. Town is called Arnolds Park. It's in Iowa. He worked out of the Iowa Dive Shop and School. You may want to check it out."

Johnny glanced at the others, who began to nod. "Big Pat? You're a rock star."

"No, Johnny, that's you. I'm a movie star in training disguised as a commercial diver who's addicted to sex and alcohol."

"Could be worse. You could be Willie." Johnny cocked a brow at his friend while Corey and Josh chuckled.

"All right, you bastards, I need to go," said Pat. "Oorah, talk to you soon."

Johnny faced the others, wanting to let them off the hook because they were back on their own. "Plesner's left two messages on my voice mail already. He's running scared now, and he might send another team after us."

"So we haul ass to Iowa right now," said Josh.

Johnny pursed his lips and bowed his head. "I don't know. I can't ask you to do this anymore."

"What're you talking about?" asked Willie. "As my boy would say, shit just got real, son. We ain't doing this for you anymore."

"That's right," said Corey. "And we're not stopping until we find out what's going on."

Johnny sighed. "Well, I guess we got trees to shake. First thing, Josh, you call Jada. Tell her to move the girls over to Debbie's house. Elina will know where it is, and she'll tell Matt what's going on. Next thing, we need to ditch that rental and get another car. Sal's offered, but that's no good. We know anyone else between here and Iowa?"

"One of my old bow gunners came from Ann Arbor," said Corey. "His parents might still live there. I'll give him a call."

"Outstanding. So let's talk cash. Each one of us draws the max out of the ATM. We'll do that here in Detroit, because we know that bastard is watching."

"Hey, there's a twenty-four FedEx place in Ann Arbor," Josh said, having searched for it on an iPad loaned to him by Salvatore. "We can mail back the phones there."

"And we'll hit a Wal-Mart to get some new ones," said Willie. "Plus some ammo for the rifle."

"Are you kidding?" said Josh. "I'll call some boys from Sig and Warrick Marine. We'll be loaded for bear by the time I'm done talking to them."

"Look, we'll go over to Iowa and see what we got," Johnny said. "But like Pat said, it could be just a coincidence."

"It's not," said Josh.

Johnny snickered. "What makes you say that?"

"Everything happens for a reason, Johnny. My old man messed up. The Marine Corps saved my life. I met you. Here we are."

Johnny slapped a palm on Josh's shoulder. "I won't argue with that. But now we make our own luck."

Chapter Thirty-Eight

"I'm not the funniest guy, and I didn't descend from Vikings. But apparently I have some pretty good detective skills. When we got to the dive shop, I realized that what we needed was right in front of us."

—Corey McKay (FBI interview, 23 December)

Arnolds Park, Iowa was a resort community rising from the shores of West Okoboji Lake, whose 3,800 acres presented a perfect sheet of blue tourmaline stitched against the horizon. Johnny marveled over photographs of the waterfront properties he had viewed on the iPad they borrowed from Salvatore. He had plenty of time to do so. It took nearly twelve-hours to reach the Iowa Dive Shop and School on Minnewashta Beach Road, but they had driven in style since Corey's old bow gunner had come through. The friend's parents did, indeed, still live in Ann Arbor, and they had loaned them a 2007 Buick Lucerne. They were a sweet old couple in their seventies and proud veterans of the United States Army.

After arriving at 1530, Johnny and the others remained in the Buick and reconnoitered the dive shop from a parking lot adjacent to a boat launch. The shop was a standalone, single-story building of approximately 2,000 square feet, with entrance doors beneath an awning that reminded Johnny of the one at the VFW hall in Holly Ridge. The storefront glass was cluttered with so many logos vying for attention that they blurred into a mosaic of arctic blues and jungle greens. More windows along the building's east and west sides suggested entry and/or exit points. Assumedly, the shop's owner had installed an alarm system that was being monitored, although Johnny and the others would verify that once they conducted their interior surveillance.

Despite everyone's exhaustion, the mission tempo was high, in part because Mark Gatterton had called earlier to confirm Johnny's suspicions. He had spoken with Donna Lindhower, who did some discreet checking into Plesner's story and discovered that there was no investigation being conducted out of the Omaha field office and that the courier cards Johnny had given them had never been sent for analysis. In fact, they were missing. Lindhower was deeply troubled and promised to investigate the matter without confronting Plesner.

"So here we are," began Corey. "A dive shop in Iowa. Beginning of winter. I'm surprised they're even open."

"I saw on their website that the dive school's open all year because they use an indoor pool," Josh said. "And don't forget that places like this do a lot of internet sales, so they might as well be around for the occasional drop-in while they're packing stuff in the back."

"I bet they supply the first responders here, too," said Willie.

"And the jihadis," Johnny added bitterly. He tipped his head toward Corey. "Come on." They left the Buick and crossed the street, with Johnny thinking of the 1911 tucked in his concealed holster. An electronic beeping announced their entrance as they carried in a blast of cold air.

The kid behind the counter, a scruffy-faced monk in his early twenties, smiled and said, "Hey, guys." He lumbered toward them wearing a purple University of Northern Iowa Panthers sweatshirt with fading logo. If he had exercised in the past decade, there was no clear evidence. His man boobs assumed a life of their own as he shivered and said, "Wow, it's cold out there."

"Yeah, it is," said Johnny. "Wondering if you can help me out. Got a big fishing and diving trip down in Florida over the holiday break, and I'm thinking about replacing my old regulators. Also, my buddy needs help with a new wet suit."

"I can help you both."

"Anyone else here? We're a little short on time."

"No, I'm sorry the boss has already gone home for the day. It's just me."

"Hey, it's cool," Corey said. "I'll look around until you're ready." He gave Johnny a quick flick of his brows.

Johnny understood and threw his arm over the young man's shoulders. "I'm really excited about this trip. Do you carry any spear guns, Hawaiian slings, and heavy duty stringers? I'm also looking to pick up some new regulators."

* * *

After a furtive glance to be sure he was clear, Corey slipped around the counter and behind a rear door that was cracked open. He found himself in an office/stock room with several desks, an old iMac with twenty-inch screen, and a large commercial grade laser printer. A small, three-shelf cabinet was crammed with office supplies. He crossed to that shelf and spotted a box of card stock matching the size and type of the courier cards. His breath shortened. Beyond the desks, shelving units lined the perimeter and housed inventory in multicolored boxes stacked like a game of Tetris. The keypad for an alarm system had been mounted just inside the doorway. Motion sensors? Yes. Monitored? Yes. Cameras? No. He spied the magnetic strips on two of the windows and a set of wires above the shop's rear door marked with an exit sign and note to "keep locked at all times." A heavy deadbolt was fitted above the regular latch lock.

Situation report: The kid was alone. The parking lot was empty. He would close shop in less than thirty minutes.

Corey and the others could wait until after the kid left, but bypassing that alarm system would be difficult. They could slip by the magnetic strips by hitting them with a strong enough magnetic field. Once inside, they could trick the motion sensors by shielding themselves with large pieces of Styrofoam and/or hitting those sensors with certain wavelengths of light, either infrared or near infrared. That worked well in theory, but without the gear or experience to conduct such a surreptitious entry, they might trip the alarm. At that point they would resort to smashing in a window and rushing around like drunk sailors on their first shore leave, trying to find anything they could before local law enforcement arrived.

No, attempting to breech the alarm would fail. They needed a better plan, and Corey had one, but the timing would be crucial. He needed to make an executive decision without consulting the others, or as Johnny had once told him, he needed to start cooking with hot sauce.

After a final moment's hesitation, he rushed toward the back door and called Willie. "Okay, here's the plan..."

* * *

Johnny frowned at the kid, who had introduced himself as Aaron. "Son, are you kidding me? These are the only regulators you carry? Really? I've spent a lot of time underwater, and I know this stuff is garbage and way overpriced."

The kid drew back his head because Johnny had just criticized the Atomic Aquatics T3 titanium regulator, one of the best pieces of dive gear money could buy.

Johnny knew it. The kid knew it. But Johnny wanted to be that know-it-all jerk customer looking for something for nothing and putting the kid on the defensive.

As Aaron opened his mouth, the door sounded and in walked Willie, chatting on his cell phone. Josh came in behind him, feigning amazement over the rows of colorful tanks, fins, and goggles. Willie hung up and met Aaron's gaze. "How you doing, Chief? Can we get some help over here?"

* * *

Corey had timed it perfectly. First, he had thrown open the rear door's deadbolt and turned the switch on the doorknob. The moment Willie had entered through the front door, Corey had opened the back. He knew if he simply opened the rear door without Willie's help, a beep would alert the kid. Admittedly, there was a slight double-beep but hardly enough to raise suspicion. Next, Corey had slid a piece of cardboard into the gap, covering up the striker plate and holding the door slightly ajar. Now with the door propped open just enough to avoid activating the alarm, he crouched over and returned to the sales floor. He came up behind Johnny, realizing they had to move fast because cold air was seeping through the cracks of that open door, and the kid seemed hypersensitive to the chill.

"She's calling me again," Corey said with a groan. "We need to go." He widened his eyes.

Johnny took the cue. "Hey, sorry about that," he told Aaron. "We'll have to catch you tomorrow or something."

"Yeah, okay," said the kid. "Don't rule out those regulators. Go look them up online. You'll see what I'm talking about."

"I will. Thanks."

As they headed for the door, Josh lifted his voice. "Hey, bro, we're going on our first diving trip to Cozumel, and we need a lot of gear and advice. I hope you work on commission, too, because we'll be your big sale for the day, trust me."

Corey led Johnny out of the shop and around the side of the building.

"Did you call those guys?" Johnny asked

"Yeah, we could waste half the night trying to bypass the alarm, or we can get the show on the road."

"Roger that."

They reached the rear door, and Corey held up his palm. "There's a computer, printer, and I found card stock that matches the courier cards. I need time on that computer."

"Let's do it."

Literally holding their breaths, they ghosted across stock room and reached the desks. Corey settled into a chair while Johnny kept watch on the sales floor from behind the cracked door.

The computer was password protected, but Corey knew a simple hack to bypass that. Within thirty seconds, he had access to the desktop. Within a minute he swore under his breath in excitement.

* * *

Johnny had worn the colorful insignia of Master Bullshit Artist for many years, but he wondered now if that honor should go to Josh or Willie. They read the kid's body language, his tone, his desire to impress them with his broad range of diving experience, and they expertly exploited his ego, turning it against him. While he rattled on about his past adventures and how those trips had taught him so much about diving, Corey typed and occasionally traced an index finger along the computer's screen. This went on for another five minutes, with Corey using his phone to snap a few photographs of his discoveries.

At one point, Aaron swung toward the counter, and his gaze drifted up to the door. Johnny edged back and signaled to Corey. After playing mannequin for several seconds, he stole another glance and saw how Willie had maneuvered himself between the kid and the counter, firing questions like shotgun shells.

Meanwhile, Corey was out of his chair, digging behind the laser printer, which he had tipped onto its side. Johnny looked his question, and Corey just waved him off and returned to work with a small pocket knife he kept on his keychain. Within another minute, he tugged free a circuit board-looking thing with a ribbon cable hanging from the side. He shook it in his raised fist like a trophy, then set it down and replaced the printer's panels. Johnny checked the door once more before Corey whispered for them to leave. They slinked to the back of the stock room. Corey called Josh, and they timed another opening and closing of the doors to avoid a second beep.

Once outside, Johnny asked, "What did you get?"

Corey leaned back on the wall, awestruck and fighting for breath. His eyes finally met Johnny's, and while he opened his mouth, the words seemed beyond him, scattered in the enormity of the moment. The best he could muster was, "Come on."

* * *

Once they had all rallied back on the car, with young Aaron none the wiser, Johnny nodded at Corey, who had finally collected his thoughts.

"All right, guys, listen up," Corey said. "I got into that computer and hacked into a private Google account. Someone was updating another person about quote 'the dive training.' The dates coincide with the story Pat was telling us. We can assume Shammas was reporting to Nazari from that computer."

"Good ole Pat came through," Johnny said. "What else?"

"So I checked the browser's cache. Someone's been doing a lot of searches for cargo ships coming into the Port of Houston. They downloaded a list of expected arrivals and saved it as a pdf file right there on the desktop. I snapped a picture of it. Someone highlighted the arrival day and time of a ship called *M/V Mawsitsit*. I searched the name. She's a 950-foot-long Panamax Container Ship registered in Panama."

"What's Panamax?" asked Willie.

"Panamax means the largest ship capable of transiting the Panama Canal," Corey explained, reading more data from his phone's screen. "The American President Line names many of its ships after gems: garnet, jade, and so on. Mawsitsit is a special type of jade—bright green with intense black iron streaks."

"What do they want with that ship?" Johnny asked.

"Could be smuggling something—or someone—in or out of the country. Either way she'll reach the port some time tomorrow night."

"What do you think?" Josh asked Corey.

"I think we should go down there, but that ship's not the only reason."

"You got more?" Johnny asked.

"Yeah, I pulled up their inventory system, and there was a lot of back and forth between the dive shop and a place called the Blackberry Island Marina. I even saw a name on one of the invoice's that looked familiar. Mahmoud Fahmi. He's the same guy who owns the land down in West Virginia where they built the camp."

"Imagine that," said Johnny. "So where's this marina?"

"It's in Port O'Connor, Texas, only a hundred miles away from the Port of Houston."

Johnny grinned. "Easy day."

"Yeah, and guess what? Port O'Connor is a tourist destination. Lots of sport fishing going on there. Charter boats, the whole nine. It's a place where guys like Nazari and his jihadi buddies wouldn't stand out."

"How you'd get to be so smart?" Willie asked Corey.

"Drinking beer and hanging out with knuckle draggers like you."

Willie snorted. "Right on."

"So what did you take out of that printer?" Johnny asked.

"Well I got to thinking, wouldn't it be cool if we could see every print job? Every courier card? We'd know exactly what he was doing, wouldn't we."

"How would we do that?" asked Josh. "I assume our guy went in there, printed his cards, and went home. There's no record of what he did."

Corey shook his head, his voice now quavering with excitement. "That's a business printer. Customer data is valuable. They back it up in the cloud, yeah, but the printer has its own hard drive and keeps a backup of every print job."

"Yeah, but, wouldn't they erase that data?" asked Josh. "Use some program that does that automatically once a month or something?"

"They might, but you have to go into the software and turn off that function. The default setting was on, so I assume our guy never turned it off."

"Maybe he didn't know to turn it off," Johnny said. "He just borrowed the printer and thought if he didn't save anything there wouldn't be any record. Like me, he never thought about the printer having a hard drive."

"Or at the very least he knew the data was password protected," Corey said. "We could be wrong, but I think it's worth a shot. Only problem is, I can't get into the hard drive. I know a few basic hacks, but I'm not that good. That's why I pulled it out of the printer."

"Now we can see what's on it?" Johnny asked.

"It's not that easy. The data on this thing is AES encrypted, and without the key, we can't see shit. We'll send it over to Jon Mellot at the Athena Group in Gainesville, just like we did when we helped those Brazilians figure out who hacked into their computers, remember? The guys at Athena can scan the chip with the right equipment and retrieve the key."

"Josh, find us the nearest FedEx office," Johnny said. "Willie, how're we doing on gas?"

"Still got half a tank."

"Hey, I got it already," said Josh, pointing at the iPad's screen. "FedEx office in Estherville. They close at 1700. We have time."

"Good," Johnny answered.

"Question for you, Corey," Willie began. "You pulled that hard drive. When will the guys at the shop realize it's gone?"

"I'm not sure. Probably the next time he goes to print something. He'll probably get an error message that the hard drive is not found."

"Hopefully the kid won't try printing anything, close up shop, and we'll be good to go until at least tomorrow. After that, who knows?" said Johnny. "Best we could ask for, though. Excellent work, Corey. I'm putting you in for a nickel raise."

"Thanks, Boss." As they left the parking lot, Corey added, "So the good news is, we'll get this hard drive shipped down to Athena."

"And the bad news?" asked Johnny.

Corey frowned. "We'll never reach Texas in time."

"Why not?"

"It's over a thousand miles away. Sixteen, maybe eighteen hour drive, with stops for gas and bathroom breaks. And that means leaving now with no detours. That also means no mechanical issues with the car."

"Well, damn, we need to fly," Johnny concluded.

"How do we fly without tipping off Plesner?" asked Josh.

"What about using cash?" Willie suggested.

"That still won't work," Corey said. "The airline reps have orders to hit the panic button when they see that. One way cash tickets are red flags to the Feds."

"Wait a second, what about old Lance?" Johnny asked them all. "He came to the funeral. I was bullshitting with him. He's in Kansas City now. When he got out, he got all into flying. He was telling me about this plane he's got. But damn, I don't have my contacts list. They were in my phone that we mailed back home."

"Your contacts are backed up online," Corey said. "All we need to do is log into your account, and we'll get you Lance's number."

"That's great. I bet Lance can give us a ride down to Texas."

"We'll head there right after the FedEx," said Willie.

"Hey, Johnny, your phone's ringing," Corey said.

Johnny recognized the number and held his breath. "What do you got for me, Mark?"

Gatterton hesitated. "A buddy of mine from Richmond called..."

"Mark, you still there?"

"Yeah, Johnny. Donna Lindhower is dead."

"What're you talking about?"

"She was walking back to her car after lunch, and some bastard hit her, dragged her body for a quarter mile."

"Oh, no..."

"Yeah, hit and run. Then her husband left me a message. She confided in him, said she was digging into some corruption at work. I told him not to say anything, but I don't know what he'll do. It'll probably be on the news. I should've never doubted you, Johnny. Plesner had her killed. I just know it."

"I'm sorry, Mark. I feel like it's my fault."

"It's not. And whatever you're doing, don't stop."

"Hell, no, we won't. We're fat kids on cupcakes, right?"

"That's right—and that's why I'm going after Plesner."

"So now it's my turn to talk you out of it?"

"Good luck with that."

"All right, Mark, you hit 'em from that end. But talk to me... what's Plesner's deal? He can't be a jihadi, can he?"

"No, but there's a reason why he's covering for them."

"Yeah, a reason so important that he's willing to kill anyone in his way."

Chapter Thirty-Nine

"There was always a Marine willing to take the shirt off his back for us. That wasn't a coincidence. We used to joke that we're the Marine Corps mafia, but it's more serious than that. Even sacred. And it's the only reason why I'm still alive and talking to you."

—Johnny Johansen (FBI interview, 23 December)

By 0900 the next morning, Johnny and the others were crammed aboard a Cessna T210N Turbo Centurion II. They cruised at over 200 mph and at an altitude just shy of 10,000 feet. Although Lance Wertmuller had followed in his father's footsteps to become a Marine, he had spent most of his teen years wishing he were a pilot. After eight years in the Corps, he earned his undergraduate degree in Aeronautical Science and networked his way up the corporate ladder. Nowadays, the blocky German with the boyish haircut and easygoing demeanor sat in the cockpit of Gulfstream jets, shuttling rich entrepreneurs around the country. He often told the story of the billionaire businessman he had been flying to New York. The man had confronted Lance with a Styrofoam cup filled with urine, explaining that he had peed in the cup because the lavatory was too narrow and he could not get the "proper angle." Lance had rolled his eyes and explained that yes, the lavatory was narrow, but that the man should have simply sat on the bowl and gone about his business that way. The billionaire had blushed with embarrassment but still foisted the cup on Lance.

When not dealing with the fabulously rich and clueless, Lance took short hops in his own plane, picking up women between airports. "I use my toy to become their toy," he joked. Even at fifty-two, he waltzed through Neverland like a man half his age and was the envy of POMs (Prisoners of Marriage) everywhere.

The previous evening, Willie had driven them 355 miles from the dive shop to Kansas City, where they had linked up with their friendly neighborhood aviator. Lance had balked about the weather along the route, arguing that it was safer and faster to depart in the morning. He convinced them to remain at his house in Blue Springs, where he treated them like royalty, ordering takeout from the most expensive steakhouse in town. Johnny had pulled him aside and shared an abridged and somewhat vague version of their investigation, emphasizing that they needed to reach Texas as discreetly as possible. Lance agreed to ask no further questions and had refused to accept money for fuel. "It's on me."

Given the plane's range and cruising speed, Lance estimated they would arrive at Tanner's Airport (located about twenty miles northwest of Port O'Connor) between 1300 and 1400, leaving them ample time to conduct reconnaissance and reach the Port of Houston.

Meanwhile, Josh was coordinating with his colleagues from Warrick Marine, who had a warehouse and testing facility in Corpus Christi, about eighty miles southwest of the Blackberry Marina. His aim was to secure gear, but after talking to them, he hinted at something even more impressive but needed Warrick to confirm. Corey reported that his friends at the Athena Group had received the hard drive. He had stressed the time-sensitive nature of obtaining that key and searching for files matching the courier cards, which he had described to them in detail.

With plans moving forward and Johnny's impatience mounting, he glanced across the patchworks of farmland below, ranging from the deepest browns to palest ivory. He imagined the old man seated beside him, wearing his black cap and scowling at the small plane when C-130s were his usual ride.

"What am I doing up here?"

"I just wanted you to know I haven't given up."

"Well, good for you."

"Dad, I'll find out what happened. I swear I will."

* * *

Charles Plesner climbed into his BMW and pulled out of his driveway, unaware that he was being watched. Mark Gatterton had parked his rented Hyundai across the street and a few doors down behind several other cars in this upper-middle class neighborhood. He waited until Plesner reached the first intersection, then kept loosely on his tail. They left the suburbs, heading west on I-66 for about fifteen minutes, transiting the Roosevelt Bridge and arriving moments later at the storied National Press Club building on 14th Street. Plesner chose the subterranean PMI garage on the north side of G street between 14th and 13th Streets. Gatterton kept more tightly behind, finding a spot just a few cars down; however, Plesner was already heading across the garage. Gatterton double-timed into his path, reaching the elevator doors as they were about to close. Plesner shoved his hand between the doors, allowing Gatterton to enter.

"Timing is everything," Plesner quipped.

"Yes, it is," Gatterton muttered, then glanced away.

They had met only once before, several years ago, and Gatterton was betting on the fact that a self-absorbed asshole like Plesner would not remember him, despite Gatterton's media presence. Unkempt hair and three days' worth of beard contributed to Gatterton's anonymity; nevertheless, he avoided direct eye contact.

Now, here they were, alone, Gatterton catching his breath and glancing furtively over toward the slight man peering over the rim of his bifocals. Something he read on his smartphone made him sigh in disgust. He flicked his glance toward Gatterton, frowned, then returned to his phone. Was something there? Familiarity? Recognition?

Gatterton balled his hands into fists and shut his eyes. In that speckled darkness, every sensation of committing murder struck him at once:

Plesner's throat felt warm and rough like sandpaper between his fingers. As Gatterton tightened his grip, Plesner's eyes bulged, and his glasses tumbled away. He clawed at Gatterton's hands, but they were a steel vice clamping down. Clamping. Clamping. A hiss came from the back of Plesner's throat before the final tethers of life snapped. Gatterton screamed and slammed Plesner's body onto the floor.

That could all happen. Right here. Right now. Gatterton held his breath, trying to decide. He considered Johnny's brother and sister-in-law and his dear friend Donna. He owed them the truth, a truth that would be lost if Plesner died prematurely.

Gatterton opened his eyes and tanked down air. He would exact revenge on this piece of shit standing next to him. But not here. Not now.

The elevator doors parted with a whoosh and chime, and Plesner strode into the lobby, past a sign atop an easel announcing this year's World BORDERPOL Congress—the annual gathering of border patrol management and security industries from around the globe. According to the sign, the Congress included a series of workshops and debates focusing on securing borders from cross border crime, illegal immigration, narcotics smuggling, human trafficking, and other illicit activities. Gatterton had attended the conference once before and had lectured on the FBI's relationship with border patrol agencies in the United States and abroad.

Plesner reached the elevators well before Gatterton could. He remained there, anxiously waiting for another ride up to the thirteenth floor. Within a minute he emerged, winding his way through the knots of attendees, heading toward the Holeman Lounge, where he spotted Plesner having a conversation with a tall, leonine man whose 8 x10 glossy was featured on a placard that read, "How Can the Private Sector Best Support Border Patrol Agencies." Guest Speaker: Nicholas Dresden, Co-founder, D&S Equities Group. Another man, slightly less gray and more birdlike, joined them. Gatterton drifted to the wall and noted how Plesner led the talk, gesticulating forcefully, Dresden and his cohort nodding and approving of what they were hearing, then yet another man, probably the workshop's moderator, waved his hand, beckoning for Dresden and the others to come inside.

Gatterton used his smartphone to pull up the wiki page on Dresden and Senecal Equities Group. His mouth fell open as he read the summary and list of companies that fell under D&S's umbrella, a portfolio that boggled the mind and reached across all sectors of the defense and law enforcement industries.

* * *

Charles Plesner had recognized Mark Gatterton in the elevator, and he was well aware of Gatterton's record as both a former FBI agent and Recon Marine. While Dresden droned on about border issues, Plesner sat in the back row and consulted his private Dropbox account, where he had stored electronic copies of all of Johnny Johansen's records.

After a brief scroll through the documents, he found Johnny's resume and reviewed the various Marine Corps units, comparing them to Gatterton's resume, which the man had proudly posted on his website. Yes, Johnny and Gatterton had served together in Second Force Reconnaissance Company, as Plesner had suspected. Moreover, Plesner already knew that Gatterton was friends with Donna Lindhower, because she, too, had served with him.

Using one of his prepaid phones, Plesner sent off a text to a man who could help: Yes, I have an issue. He's in Arlington. I'll forward his home address.

* * *

While Lance was out paying the landing fee to Bob Tanner, the airport's owner, the group met up with two of Josh's partners from Warrick Marine. The men arrived in a pair of black Suburbans. They left one SUV for Johnny, Willie, and Corey, while the other would cart them and Josh back to Corpus Christi. Josh said he would return soon with a few surprises, just in case. They each received new prepaid phones per Josh's request, and the guys at Warrick joked that they would have added them to the company's cell phone "family plan" were it not for their particular security needs. In the cargo hold of their Suburban lay a small arsenal of weapons, holsters, plate carriers, and other gear, courtesy of their friends at Sig Sauer in New Hampshire.

Included in the cache were four of Sig's latest prototype rifle: the MCX, a weapon featuring the barrier penetration and stopping power of an AK-47 while using many standard AR-15 parts. The rifle was extremely quiet, registering with the long Sig Sauer silencer at only 118 decibels. Sig's willingness to provide the epitome of clandestine weapons and several thousand rounds of their recently developed 300 black out ammunition was a testament to Triton 6's favored contractor status with that company.

In addition to the weapons, Johnny and the others were now equipped with regular and night vision binoculars, along with Motorola two-way radios and headsets.

They spent about fifteen minutes doing radio checks and test firing each and every weapon. Since all were suppressed and the airport was out in the middle of nowhere, they accomplished this with impunity. At the same time, Lance had instructions to stall the airport's owner until Johnny sent word.

Once Lance did return, Johnny gave him a firm handshake and affectionate pat on the back. "You sure I can't do anything for you?"

"Other than leading me to hell and back and keeping me alive?"

"You know what I'm saying."

"Like I said, Johnny, I'm happy to help out a brother. And don't worry, I'll have that nice Buick shipped back to Ann Arbor for you. If there's anything I need right now, it's more time. If you got any of that, I'll take it, otherwise, oorah, on your way."

"Easy day. Thanks again."

"Be careful, all right?"

"You know we will."

As Lance hiked back to his plane, Johnny and the others seized the chance to gear up, and then, with Corey at the wheel, they drove onto State Highway 238. From there they would head south down Farm to Market Road 1289 toward Adam's Street some eleven miles away. After hanging a left, they would take Adams east for just two more miles to reach the marina. They would be on the target in less than twenty minutes.

The forecast high was sixty-six degrees, a far cry from the meat locker of northern Iowa. Johnny left the window open and brought up Google Earth images of the marina on a notebook computer loaned to them by Warrick. The east side of the port faced the pristine waters of Matagorda Bay, a nutrient-rich estuary and renowned fishing destination for oyster, blue crab, and shrimp. On the south side lay a cluster of smaller islands jutting up like the bones of some predator's talon half submerged in the blue-gray water. Separating them from the shoreline was a long, mocha-colored pinstripe of land called Blackberry Island.

Johnny zoomed in on the marina. He counted nine boat slips with hookups, a refueling station, and a small, two-story bait and tackle shop/convenience store with several rental apartments accessed by an exterior staircase, balcony, and separate entrance doors. Beside the shop stood a tin-roofed boat storage facility with room for about a dozen fishing boats.

"What do you think?" Johnny asked.

"Intel seems good. Who knows about the timing," said Willie. "Like we said, the only way the alarm will sound is when they realize the hard drive's gone at the dive shop. And who knows what'll happen then. If they're worried about using phones, they might send a courier or maybe email. Time could be on our side."

"Willie's right," said Corey. "The same jihadi owns the enclave land, the dive shop, and the marina. The courier cards were printed at the shop. We'll find something. I just know it."

* * *

They parked the Suburban in the lot of the First National Bank on the corner of Adams and Trevor Streets. Corey remained with the vehicle, keeping his eye on Trevor Street, which served as the main access and exit road for the marina.

Once the highway was clear of traffic, Johnny and Willie rushed away from the SUV, heading down an embankment and into rolling hills of butter-colored grass. They aimed for the stands of oaks rising sporadically on the north side of the marina. To their right and left lay roughhewn barrens between oases of more forested land. There were no structures or development of any kind. A northeast breeze carried rich pockets of salt, and as they advanced the smell grew stronger, filling Johnny's lungs and making him feel younger and even more alive. In a moment of weakness, he wondered what Elina was doing today and why she had put up with him for all these years. If he got himself killed, he would never hear the end of it, once she joined him in heaven. Then again, she might have to bail him out of hell first, which would irritate her even more.

With sand in their boots, they reached the trees, then spread out, straying only a handful of meters from each other. The bait and tackle shop faced south, toward the channel, but the parking lot was around back, with a dirt road that returned to Trevor Street. A Lexus, a BMW, and an Audi stood in sharp juxtaposition against the two old pickups with blistering paint and blemishes of rust along their wheel wells.

Willie's voice buzzed in Johnny's ear as they reached the last cluster of trees. "I'll get the tag numbers off those cars, and we'll have Corey run them."

"That wouldn't hurt," answered Johnny.

"Also, I can see some people in one of the apartments upstairs. Nothing too clear through the window, but I saw a couple walk by."

"What do you guys think? Should one of us take a peak inside?" Johnny asked.

"Pretty risky," said Corey. "By now Plesner could've circulated pictures of us to these guys. Maybe they'd ID us."

"Roger that. Let's sit tight for now." Johnny checked his watch. "Maybe they'll go out for lunch." He tucked himself tighter against the tree and focused on the concrete walk wrapping around the marina's west side.

Out in the channel, about five hundred yards off, several fishing boats cruised by, their wakes coalescing like bubbling curtains. A crow squawked in the distance, and the sun broke through a long barge of clouds. Shafts of clean-looking light fell across the channel now, the wavelets flashing as the water settled down. Johnny's boot pressed a little deeper into the leaves and sand, the crunching controlled by the amount of pressure he put on that foot. His senses were beginning to extend themselves, reaching out like the feelers of some giant African beetle, the tiniest sound or movement amplified ten times over.

Within the next hour he had fully surrendered himself to the landscape, to the bark at his shoulder and the bed of gray earth beneath his cargo pants. He alternated between the binoculars and Willie at his flank, consumed by their target. He thought of calling Gatterton for an update, but knowing Johnny's luck, he would be on the phone and miss something important.

The gurgling came first, accompanied by an asthmatic wheezing. And then it appeared: a twenty-foot long Tran Sport fishing boat limping toward the marina, its outboard Suzuki billowing smoke. The two middle-aged men wearing ball caps reached the dock, tied off the boat, and then shut down the engine. They hurried toward the tackle shop, bickering with each other. One removed his cap and beat the other over the head with it. Johnny took them for locals not having a very good morning. The fumes from their ailing boat motor reached the woods, making him grimace.

Ten minutes later, a third man joined them at the dock and began inspecting their outboard. He was a Santa Claus in grey coveralls, hardly a jihadi at first blush, but they could never be sure.

The repairs went on for another fifteen minutes, and as they did, Johnny felt something tighten in his gut. Not a hunger pang or spasm or hernia but a premonition—a coming together of forces both controllable and uncontrollable. The feeling grew stronger, his hackles literally rising as silhouettes appeared in one of the second story windows.

Abruptly, a door opened and three men stepped onto the balcony. They had dark hair and dusky complexions. Two were dressed in suits, while the third, the tallest and oldest with a bit of ash at his temples, wore Dockers, a collared shirt, and a pullover sweater. Recognition came as a jolt, and before Johnny could open his mouth, Willie spoke for him over the radio:

"That's him. That's Nazari."

Chapter Forty

"I'm not ashamed to admit it. When we realized what they were doing, I closed my eyes and prayed—because at that point, I thought there was absolutely no way to stop them."

—Willie Parente (FBI interview, 23 December)

Mark Gatterton waited two hours for Charles Plesner to come out of his workshop at the National Press Club. After speaking once more with Nicholas Dresden and Edward Senecal, Plesner proceeded directly to work on Pennsylvania Avenue, where he currently remained. With a GPS tracker placed beneath his car (one of several Gatterton had "procured" during his tenure with the FBI), Plesner was now on a short leash. Eager to do more research on D&S Equities and satisfied that his tracker was functioning properly, Gatterton returned to his small brick home on North Monroe Street in Arlington, where he sat, hunched over his computer, his pulse mounting at every click.

Scattered on the desk were notes taken during his phone calls with Johnny. As he picked up the nearest one scratched with the name of a Peruvian mining company called EXSA, he realized he was trembling. The name EXSA was on the mini boosters Johnny had found inside the block of cocaine. A sales representative Johnny had IDed at Blue Door had a relationship with the Peruvian government, selling arms to their local police. Now Gatterton had discovered yet another connection:

A munitions recycling company in Columbus, Texas called UXD was owned and operated by Nicholas Dresden. EXSA in Peru was one of the company's primary customers. A secondary search of the name UXD produced a recent news article detailing the bizarre disappearance of Mr. Tom Barryman, the company's Executive Director of Shipping. He had come to work and gone missing, as though recycled into thin air. A thorough search of the plant by law enforcement had produced no evidence linked to his disappearance. Witnesses had seen him arrive, but none could recall him ever leaving.

Fact: Dresden and Senecal were working closely with Plesner, but what were they doing? Why would they cover for jihadis, unless they wanted certain targets within the United States destroyed and jihadis to take the fall? What did they hope to gain?

Gatterton recalled one of the articles he had just read, an interview with Dresden published in *Wired* magazine. The journalist had painted a very flattering portrait of him and his company, but there was a moment when Dresden ranted about the inadequate policies of the current administration, the downsizing of the military, the gaping holes in intelligence, and most of all, the general public's naïve view that they were safe. He had argued that yes, many of his companies were suffering because of false assurances and the administration's over-reliance on technology to fight its "new kind of war." He admitted that post 9/11 America had been a real boon for all of his businesses, but now many in the defense industry were suffering while America grew less secure.

And then there was Plesner, who Gatterton knew shared his own point of view. He hated the Bureau's weakening power and its supervisors hired for their politically correct ideas instead of their ability as investigators. He agreed that jihadis and other informants had penetrated the inner circle. Plesner was an old school administrator whose heroes were Theodore Roosevelt and Ronald Reagan. But now, in many respects, his hands were tied by cowardly politicians, by the endless criticism of a liberal media, and by citizens with smartphones hoping to capture law enforcement brutality and corruption on camera.

What would it take to win back the hearts and minds of the current administration, along with the hearts and minds of every American citizen?

There had been a flicker of it after the marathon bombing. Boston Strong.

How could they become "America Strong"?

They would need something big, something at least as big as 9/11, a jihad on American soil the likes of which the country had never seen.

And what would that require? Rainmakers of industry. Men like Dresden and Senecal, and men like Plesner with the connections and power to protect their interests. America would die and be reborn, fertilized in her own blood. Meanwhile, this unholy trinity would be there to reap the political and financial benefits. The defense industry would surge. Plesner could set free the dogs of war and fight the jihadis as aggressively as he wanted.

Gatterton reached for his phone. Johnny had no idea what he had stumbled upon, no idea that it did not stop at Plesner. And Johnny deserved to know everything before he made a move. This was—no shit—way beyond their pay grade.

Before Gatterton finished dialing, someone kicked in his back door, the crash reverberating through the entire house. With a start, he crossed the room, wrenched open a drawer below his hutch, and produced his old Glock 22, always stored with a full magazine and one in the chamber. As he drew the gun from its holster, a figure wearing a balaclava rolled into the doorway, raising his pistol.

Gatterton fired, but so too did his assailant, striking him in the right shoulder and knocking him back, into the window, glass shattering onto the concrete walk outside. Gatterton squeezed off two more rounds, striking the man in the head and neck.

While the thug collapsed onto the wall, two more rounds punched into the window frame, and Gatterton threw himself onto the floor. White hot pain seared across his chest, emanating from a spot just beneath his collar bone, and he was not sure he could move his arm.

He gazed at boots shuffling toward the doorway, reached out with one hand, took aim, and fired, striking this second attacker in the foot. The man shrieked like some nightmare creature behind his mask. Gatterton sprang to his feet, burst into the doorway, and caught him unaware, all owl's eyes behind his mask. Two rounds to the head leveled him, the blood spewing in a tie-dye pattern, the image growing opaque in the haze of gunfire.

Gatterton reeled back, into the office, dropping to one knee, his shoulder bleeding profusely now, his hands shaking as he tried to steady his pistol. He sensed his heart racing, but the thump in his ears barely rose above the intense ringing of close quarters fire. He waited a few more seconds, then slowly backed away, toward his desk, where he reached into the drawer and seized a box of ammo and his holster. He rose, grimacing through the flames that now reached down into his abdomen. Fighting for breath, he slammed shut his laptop, gathered his notes, and shoved everything into a backpack sitting on the floor. Groaning, he left the office, with his Glock leading the way.

As he reached his rental car parked alongside the house, two of the neighbors from across the street were running toward him, calling out.

"Call the police," he shouted. "They just tried to rob me. I'm driving myself to the hospital."

But those were hardly his intentions. He knew where he could get help: a place where Plesner would never find him.

* * *

As Nazari climbed into the Lexus with his associates, Johnny called Corey and told him to stay with the Lexus. Willie gave Johnny a hand signal, and they took off running through the trees, trailing the Lexus as it churned up a dust trail and reached the paved road.

Corey would not wait for them, so once they reached the embankment, they dove into the dirt and held there.

"Okay, we're about a mile east down Adams," Corey reported over the radio. "Still moving. Going slow, like they plan to turn off. I'm dropping back a little."

Twenty seconds later, Corey issued another report, "All right about two miles now. They're slowing. Turning right onto Byers Drive, heading south. Now making a left onto Maple Street. Oh, man. Some nice houses here. Mansions, really. Turning into one house. It's got a long paver driveway. Damn. Nice place. I'll keep driving. There's some scrub... a bunch of undeveloped land across the street. Good cover positions in there. Okay, I'm turning around to pick you up."

"Make sure you get that street address. We'll check public records for the owner."

"Johnny, you know who owns that house. And by the way, the cars? All registered to an Islamic center in Houston."

"Of course they are."

Johnny checked his prepaid cell phone, discovering a voicemail from Gatterton. "Johnny, you need to call me... call me back as soon as you can. This thing has blown apart, dude. Please. Call me."

"Who is it?" asked Willie.

Johnny told him and added, "Mark didn't sound good." He dialed Gatterton's number, waited, but the call went straight to voicemail. "Mark, got your message. I'm here."

* * *

Ten minutes later, they returned to Maple Street and veered off road to park behind a rampart of mesquite trees and sedge swaying in the wind. From there, they advanced to the perimeter, where they settled down into static positions to observe the house, with Corey remaining closest to the Suburban in case Nazari left.

The sprawling mansion included at least 10,000 square feet of living space, with a tiled roof, private tennis court, infinity pool overlooking the channel, and a covered dock with two boat slips. This was a compound worthy of a celebrity, not a real estate

341

mogul with delusions of jihad. Indeed, Corey's suspicions about the home's owner were correct; in fact, Mahmoud Fahmi and his company also owned the neighboring properties, three waterfront estates in all. The Lexus was parked just outside a four car detached garage on the east side of the property. Just inside one of the open garage doors stood a bearded man with dark pants and a sandstone-colored jacket with attached hood. He was barely thirty and drifting in and out of the shadows. For a few seconds he resembled an ancient Bedouin, his modern day garb blurring into dusty robes, his boots melting into sandals made from gazelle hide. He raised a pair of binoculars, bringing them to bear on the channel.

Panning to the right, Johnny observed another man seated at the dock, his beard shorter and thinner, his hair lighter, his binoculars identical to his partner's. His jacket was open, and just inside was a pistol, a Glock most likely, holstered at his side. "Picked up two spotters," Johnny reported.

"I have two guys watching from the house to the right," said Willie.

"Two to the left as well, out on the dock over there," Corey said. "You see 'em? Over near that fishing boat?"

"Oh, yeah, we're on to something here boys," said Johnny. "Six jihadis on watch in broad daylight."

Willie snorted. "And who knows how many inside."

* * *

After reconnoitering all three estates for most of the afternoon and early evening, Johnny concluded that this, too, was another jihadi enclave, albeit a retreat for the network's upper echelon. Throughout the day, men had relieved each other on watch. Several had climbed into a Mercedes SUV and returned thirty minutes later carrying bags of groceries. Willie confirmed that Nazari, along with a half dozen other men, had gathered around a formal dinning room table with laptops and what he suspected were hardcopy maps. Willie had observed them through a broad window until one of the men snapped shut the blinds.

At 1835 the smartphone provided by Warrick Marine buzzed in Johnny's pocket. Josh was finally checking in. His friends were sending a car. They needed Johnny up in Seadrift, a waterside community about twelve miles south of their location, out past Grass Island, then north around the coast. With Willie and Corey continuing their surveillance, and Corey reporting that *Mawsitsit's* arrival time at the Port of Houston now stood at approximately 0105, Johnny figured he had time to see what Josh and his boys had put together.

Meanwhile, Corey's friends at the Athena Group were working diligently on getting into that printer's hard drive, but they had encountered a few time-consuming issues that according to Corey were hard to explain because IT guys had a language all their own, a cross between Klingon and the high nerdspeak of silicon valley.

Finally, there was still no word from Mark Gatterton. Johnny had left a second message, and he had tried calling a few more times. Deeply concerned now, Johnny could only wait on his friend. He was unsure what else to do and who else to call. He thought of Donna Lindhower and swore that if Gatterton were harmed, he would go after Plesner himself, no matter the consequences.

After hiking about a quarter mile up the road to avoid detection, Johnny met up with Josh and his Warrick buddies. Josh would not answer questions. He wore a silly grin and told Johnny to remain patient.

They drove directly to Seadrift, where at least a score of shrimp boats lay on the east side docks, their outriggers cutting like steely teeth across the stars. Guide boats with names like "Just for Eddy" and "Caught Today, Gone Tomorrow," were moored to the west. Beyond them, the San Antonio Bay lay like a sheet of granite reaching out toward the ship channel jetty to vanish beneath a waning moon.

Johnny followed the group of four men through a newly constructed warehouse with dozens of fishing and sport boats stacked three high on colossal rack systems that touched the thirty-foot ceiling. Adjacent to the rear doors and concrete driveway leading down to the launch was a separate office building about the size of a double-wide trailer. Placards on the door and above the warehouse read Seadrift Dry Storage. The owner, a pot-bellied old cowboy named Sooner, emerged from the office, spat chew into an old convenience store cup, and thanked Johnny for his service in the Marines. With a chuckle, he asked if Johnny was the owner of that "beast" down there. Johnny shrugged and frowned at Josh, who wriggled his brows.

They hiked down the driveway to the boat launch, where, shimmering in the halogen lights strung between the wooden pilings, floated the leviathan in question, her twin diesel engines growling.

"Check her out," Josh said breathlessly. "They call her *The Marauder*."

* * *

Out in the Gulf of Mexico, shrouded in the gloom of night, another vessel weighing 54,000 tons and cruising at a service speed of twenty-four knots was approaching the coast of Texas. She was 950 feet long with a beam of 106 feet, and her deck was jammed five high with hundreds of intermodal containers in shades of dark blue, red, and gray. Third Officer Luis Nando knew quite well that the U.S. Coast guard lacked the resources to keep all commercial vessels under constant visual surveillance unless they had intel suggesting they do so. At best, they monitored traffic via radar. *M/V Mawsitsit* was now showing a vertical pattern of two red lights with a white light at the center indicating restricted maneuverability as she slowed to within two knots. If a Coast Guard cutter were close enough to see those breakdown lights, its captain would call regarding assistance and receive a simple explanation: a momentary rudder control problem required a pause in order to switch to the backup control system. After that, *Mawsitsit* would be underway.

From a perch atop a section of containers located amidships, Nando and his three men watched as the crane operator climbed into his booth, then signaled with a flashlight that he was ready. Nando gave the order to begin untying the thick ropes that held down the tarpaulin stretched between two lines of containers. That tarpaulin had ensured that their most precious cargo could not be seen from the air.

As the tarp fell away, Nando leaned back and directed his own light into the void. He had served aboard *Mawsitsit* for over fifteen years, once a bright-eyed able seaman, now a jaded Third Officer whose beard was coiled with winter. He and his men had transported thousands and thousands of containers, but this... this was something new, something that required their secrecy, something that required significant payment, which had already been made to the entire ship's complement to ensure the utmost operational security. Each of them had earned an entire year's worth of salary for one night's work. What troubled Nando the most, though, was not the object gleaming in his light but the group of men who had come along to oversee the operation, six Arabs with their own special cargo and their own agenda. Six Arabs who were not to be questioned. Six Arabs heading toward the Port of Houston.

The crane coughed twice before firing up, and the operator swung the boom around. The main hoist line descended so that Nando's men could attach the lift harness straps to the hook and block. At the same time, a crew of three more Arabs arrived, mounting a rope ladder strung from the top of the forward most container and lowering themselves into the gap.

Once the straps were pulled taught, the crane operator waited until Nando gave him the all aboard signal of two flashes. The latticework boom creaked, and from the cavernous depths came a submarine surfacing improbably in midair. She was seventy-four-feet long and Kevlar coated. Her streamlined sail and bow were painted a deep aquamarine.

Nando had spoken to the sub's captain, whose Spanish was remarkably good and who had boasted about her capabilities. She could run submerged for eighteen continuous hours at a depth of sixty feet. Her twin screws driven by a pair of diesel engines were capable of six knots in short bursts. Her 1,500 gallon fuel tanks gave her a range of 2,000 miles. When fully submerged, her 249 Chinese-made batteries were her sole means of propulsion. Once those batteries were depleted she would either snorkel or surface to recharge using her engines. Ordinarily, the captain and his two-man crew hauled cocaine up from Colombia, but tonight's mission was different.

As the submarine was lowered into the churning depths, her radar echo return was masked by the much larger container ship. Nando and his men tugged on a secondary line, releasing the lift harness. Moonlight played over the submarine's hull as she submerged like a dolphin playing in the ship's wake... and then... she whispered away.

Nando turned toward the shuffling of boots across the containers. Three of the Arabs had come up from below. Nando's heart sank.

They were brandishing AK-47s. Gunfire boomed from the bridge, and as Nando's men screamed, the Arabs opened fire.

Bribery was one thing. Assuring full control of the ship was quite another.

Nando thought of the son he had not seen in over a decade as he slumped to the wet steel.

Chapter Forty-One

"I thought if I die tonight, I die helping a brother. There's no better way to go."

—Josh Eriksson (FBI interview, 23 December)

The gnarled limbs of mesquites studding Blackberry Island shone like bands of thorns in Johnny's night vision goggles. Beneath them lay drifts of white sand along the desolate shoreline. Off to the right, past rows of guano-stained posts, stood the palisades of cordgrass reflected in the murmuring channel. Somewhere within that grass was a sixteen-foot aluminum fishing boat. Near that boat lay Willie, cloaked by brooms of undergrowth and staring back at Johnny through the scope of his Sig MCX MR .308 caliber sniper rifle. The MCX MR was a mission configurable .308 platform that delivered lethality out to 800 yards. Hours earlier they had borrowed the boat from Sooner up in Seadrift, and Willie had set out across the channel to establish an observation post from which he could survey Nazari's entire backyard, along with the adjacent properties.

Meanwhile, Josh remained in a holding position at the southern tip of the island, near Ferry Channel Cut, waiting for his signal to move. The interceptor boat loaned to them from Warrick Marine was the modern day equivalent of the Riverine Patrol Boats they had brought to Iraq. The biggest difference, though, was that *The Marauder's* control station and deck were fully enclosed so that its passengers and crew were protected behind heavy armor and ballistic glass. A multipurpose compartment below deck was accessed through the bow ramp, and her full length protruding keel allowed for beaching on rugged coastlines. She blasted over the waves via twin 825 horsepower engines and twin 400-425 mm waterjets. Up to five crew-served weapons mounts allowed for multiple configurations that included the venerable M134 minigun, which Josh had mounted at the port station, courtesy of their partners at Dillon Aero. The aft stations featured an M240 and an M2 .50 caliber heavy machine gun.

Johnny assumed that Nazari and his group would travel to the Port of Houston to link up with that container ship. For their part, Johnny and the others would board *The Marauder* and arrive at the port ahead of them. However, it was already 0110 local time, and according to Corey, the ship was now arriving. Johnny and Corey had returned to their posts across the street and detected no reaction from anyone near or inside the mansion.

"What now, Johnny?" Willie asked over the radio.

"Let's hold a little longer," he responded. "If they don't leave by zero one thirty, we'll move up. Then, at say zero three thirty, we'll raid the house. Nazari's the target, and we'll take him alive."

"Even though we're outnumbered and have no QRF?" Willie pointed out.

Johnny hesitated. "Easy day."

"You mean, if you're going to do something stupid—"

"Hey, Johnny, the guys at Athena finally called back," Corey said. "They've been working all night on our hard drive—and they finally got something."

"Wait, wait, wait, hold that thought," Johnny answered as a white sedan came barreling down the road and swung into Nazari's driveway.

* * *

Mark Gatterton shuddered awake. A grid of elongated shadows shone across the ceiling, and for a second, he wondered if he were in prison. He craned his neck toward a window behind the bed, where a streetlight glared through sheer curtains. His breath steadied as he touched the bandage on his shoulder and realized his arm was still numb. He shut his eyes, saw his office, the attacker, the flash from a barrel. He trembled as gunshots rang in his head, and then... his thoughts congealed. He remembered the call to Marlene, the drive down to Fredericksburg, Virginia, the shocked look on her face as she helped him into the basement, toward a reinforced steel door with multiple locks. Behind that door lay a concrete bunker, and inside was a rudimentary but functional operating room jammed with supplies and powered by its own generator.

Dr. Marlene Heloise was a board-certified ER physician employed at Spotsylvania Regional Medical Center or "Spotsy" as she called it. She grew up in Queens, New York, and had attended medical school at New York University. Unbeknownst to her employers and most of her friends, she and her husband were active members in the VFF—the Virginia Freedom Fighters, a covert militia group whose members were frequent attendees at Gatterton's seminars regarding jihadi infiltration of the government. He had met Marlene several years prior and been impressed with her commitment to the cause. Her husband Bill was a local firefighter deeply concerned about the direction of the country. Make no mistake: their group was not hell-bent on overthrowing the government; they were, however, survivalists or "preppers" anticipating a government collapse, as evidenced by Marlene's makeshift hospital. At last count the VFF had over 6,500 members and was growing.

Gatterton seized his phone from the nightstand and gasped. It was nearly two-fifteen in the morning his time. He had yet to update Johnny. Marlene must have sedated him before removing shards of lead and copper from his shoulder, and the drugs had finally worn off.

He dialed, and when Johnny answered he spoke softly so as not to wake up his hosts. "Sorry I haven't called you sooner—but Plesner sent two assholes after me. I got shot, but I'm okay. Now just listen, Johnny. You have no idea what you've uncovered."

* * *

Johnny was trying to focus on what Gatterton was telling him—something about a firm named D&S Equities and Plesner's involvement with them—even as he watched a bearded kid who could easily be the local pizza guy leap out of the white sedan and race toward Nazari's front door. He rang the bell and shifted impatiently.

"Not good. Not good," Corey said over the radio. "Maybe he's a courier. Maybe they realized the hard drive at the dive shop is missing."

"Mark," Johnny said. "I need to call you back. This number?"

"Yeah, call me."

"Hey, Johnny, you didn't let me finish telling you about Athena," Corey said.

"You got ten seconds," Johnny told him, just as Nazari's door opened, and the courier slipped inside.

"Okay, so they found thirteen pages of courier cards. Each page has eight cards—except for the last one, which only has three, so ninety-three cards in all. They're emailing me the files right now. Here's the thing. They translated some of the names on the cards, and it seems like whoever made them is using the ninety-nine names for God in Islam. But if that's the case, then there's still six cards missing, because like I said, we only got ninety-three. I got the boys from Athena looking for the other six."

"What's on the cards? More phone numbers?"

"I told those guys about the Morse Code and had them translate the first two. They found GPS coordinates, along with a date—today's date."

"Today?"

"Yeah, and one set of coordinates line up with a Starbucks in Seattle. The other points to a high school in Indiana."

"Meeting places?"

"No, Johnny. I think they're targets."

"What if you're wrong?"

"I'm not. These are places. We have a date. Come on..."

Johnny shut his eyes. He could barely navigate through this meteor show of intel, all hitting him at once. "So... we need to know what's on every one of those cards."

"I know, but we have to translate all that Morse Code into GPS numbers, then ID the locations. That takes time."

Before Johnny could react, the windows around Nazari's house glowed, and not a heartbeat later, a mass and panic-stricken exodus began, with armed men flooding outside and sprinting around the house toward the detached garage. Others fled from the houses next door, and Willie chipped in that at least four guards now carrying rifles were running toward the fishing boat docked out back. The Lexus screeched around to the front of the house, where Nazari and his two jihadi cronies climbed inside.

"Corey, let's get back," Johnny ordered. "Willie, don't lose those guys."

Johnny broke from cover and charged toward the Suburban hidden beneath the tree canopy. Behind them, a chorus of car engines reached a crescendo. Headlights wiped across the street. Tires squealed.

"Cars are heading west," Willie reported. "They are *not* going to the port. Maybe heading back to the marina."

"Hey, guys, Josh here. I'm ready when you are."

"Boat's taking off now," Willie said.

Johnny tensed. Nazari's entourage was much too large and needed thinning, otherwise they would never get near him. It was not an easy order to give, but they had no choice; it was time to go on the offensive. He lifted his voice. "Willie, stop that boat."

"Roger."

＊ ＊ ＊

Willie had been cut loose. Men would die.

The jihadis came from the right, their bow rising as they throttled up. Willie sighted the bushy haired man at the wheel, accounting for the wind, the distance, and the boat's speed. *Steady pressure on the trigger. Wait. And... Fire!*

The man slumped. A second later, his three companions turned their rifles toward the island and fired haphazardly into the dunes.

Willie targeted the scrawny guy at the stern and fired once more. The round's impact swept the little skeleton over the side and into the murky channel. In the next second, another of his colleagues dove for the control station, while yet another unleashed a salvo, the AK-47 popping, the rounds thumping and chipping into the trees at Willie's flank.

The jihadi's muzzle flash gave up his position, and Willie struck him center of mass. He caromed off the gunwale and slammed face-forward onto the deck.

Willie's last target abandoned the wheel to cower behind the captain's chair. Willie sighed and took aim at the fishing boat's outboard, hammering it twice until the motor coughed and issued streamers of blue-gray smoke. The boat slowed and veered toward the shoreline as though it had been attacked and plundered by pirates.

In a last ditch effort, the remaining jihadi sprang up from behind the chair and reached toward a rifle lying across the deck.

Willie was waiting for him.

And no, this young man could not escape from Willie's thousands of hours behind a long gun. For just a second, he flicked his glance in Willie's direction as hot lead pierced his heart. A pleading look gripped his face, and his arm seemed to hang there, indefinitely, as though in a final wave before he dropped.

Satisfied with his marksmanship, Willie rose and sliced his way through the cordgrass. He shoved the boat off the bank and leaped aboard, the bow rocking as he reached the motor. "Willie here. Targets down. On my way."

* * *

A fleet of seven or eight vehicles had roared away from Nazari's mansion and the neighboring estates, with Nazari's Lexus positioned somewhere in the middle. The caravan was reaching speeds of ninety mph, with a Mercedes SUV bringing up the rear. Wearing his night vision goggles and with the Suburban's lights switched off, Johnny glimpsed the driver in the Mercedes' side view mirror, and that driver, in turn, locked gazes with him. Damn, he was following too closely.

A moment later, a jihadi in the forward passenger's seat hung out the window with an MP5 and opened fire, the little machine gun spitting a wave of bullets across the Suburban's hood. Two rounds punctured the windshield, leaving plasma ball patterns in their wake.

Ducking and cursing, Johnny veered into the oncoming traffic lane to avoid the shooter's bead. Seeing an opportunity, Corey lowered his window and leaned outside with his rifle, sending a triplet of suppressed fire into the driver's side window. A web-work of cracks spanned the glass, and blood flashed across the inside of the Mercedes's windshield.

Without warning, the SUV cut across Johnny's path. Shouting for Corey to hang on, he plowed into the rear quarter panel, booting the Mercedes aside and falling in behind the next car, a black crew cab pickup truck whose machine-gun toting jihadis were already hanging from the windows like gargoyles.

Corey fired again—even as they did, the cacophony of rounds whisking Johnny back to the Middle East, to that compound along the river. Blinking hard, he juked left, while Corey adjusted his bead, striking one of the truck's tires. The pickup fish-tailed to the right, the tire thumping loudly as it neared the rim.

Johnny rolled the wheel, peeling off and around the truck to accelerate. At the same time, he lowered his window, and with one hand he drew his 1911. He emptied the magazine into the truck only seconds before it spun off the road, swallowed by a dust cloud.

He glanced at Corey, whose eyes were bugging out as he gulped down air. "Holy shit!"

"No kidding. They can't shoot or drive."

"They'll get lucky."

"Eventually. I'll hold back a little." Johnny placed his pistol in the center console's cup holder, allowing the barrel to cool. He drifted away from the caravan. "Willie, where are you?"

"Coming up the channel, about five minutes away from the marina—if that's where they're headed."

"Josh?"

"I'm already here but laying low on the south side. Got about six guys on one of the docks. Four fishing boats just pulled up. They look like Intrepid 37s, Johnny, with triple Mercury Verados. They're fast."

"They spot you?"

"Not yet, but hurry. I bet these guys will pick up Nazari."

"Roger. Our boy should be there soon. We're on Adams now."

"Johnny, Willie here. If you want, I can hold back. As they pull out, I'll give them a reason to slow down."

"No, don't take that chance. Let's give them a little line. Let 'em run for now."

One after another the cars ahead made a hard left turn onto Trevor Street, confirming their final destination.

"You smell that?" asked Corey.

"Don't remind me."

A mixture of gasoline and coolant was wafting into the cabin. The Suburban was bleeding badly. A glance at the gauges suggested she would not last much longer.

"We'll make it," Johnny said, squeezing the wheel even harder. "Just give me another mile. That's all I ask."

* * *

Talib Wakim, AKA "The Syrian," pulled the last of the divers safely onboard his houseboat. They were temporarily anchored on Lake Meade approximately two miles northeast from the Hoover Dam in an area known as Painter's Cove. Surrounded by deep canyons, dry washes, and sheer cliffs hanging above water as bluish black as a catfish, the cove was cloaked by an extinct volcano known as Fortification Hill.

Fifty to seventy-five feet long houseboats like Wakim's were a common sight along the waterways leading away from the dam; in fact, whole armadas crowded with vacationers puttered between the Boulder, Temple and Virgin basins, even when water levels dropped as much as nineteen feet by the end of the season, since at its deepest point, the lake was over 450 feet deep. The houseboats were not only necessary for Wakim's operation, but they made for perfect cover.

Wakim stroked his gray beard as the young diver tugged off his mask. "Any problems?"

"None." The boy's eyes shone in the moonlight, and his beard glistened with water. "It was even easier than when we practiced in Iowa."

"We're proud of you," said Wakim. "Allah is proud."

The boy nodded. "I wish Dr. Shammas were here."

"We all do. Now get changed. We'll eat something on the way back."

Nearly five weeks of work carried out by twelve divers and twenty more brothers from a nearby enclave had drawn to a close.

Four thousand pounds of slurry explosives stolen from UXD in Texas had been packed into hundred pound satchels. Those satchels had been hiked overland to pre-arranged locations around the lake. Once the explosives had been transferred to one of the three houseboats they had rented, the boats sailed to within a mile of the dam. Under the cover of darkness, each satchel was transported underwater by a pair of divers wearing rebreathers that emitted no bubbles or signature on the surface. To account for the added weight of the explosives and to cut transport time nearly in half, each diver wore a pair of Jet Boots—battery powered propulsion devices that included small thrusters strapped to each man's thighs. These, too, allowed for clandestine passage. Meanwhile, the boats retreated to the cove and waited.

Destroying the Hoover Dam would require a nuclear weapon, but Wakim and his brothers had something more tactical and creative in mind, something within the realm of their capabilities that would have an equal if not more severe effect.

The idea had come to him based upon the discovery of the quagga mussel in Lake Meade. The infidels would never recognize the relationship between a seemingly innocuous mussel and what they had in mind.

* * *

Johnny guided them over the rutted dirt road. Nazari's caravan had churned up a dust cloud that swelled like the haboobs Johnny had witnessed in Iraq. For a few seconds, visibility was down to a meter, and then as abruptly, the road reappeared, with the marina lying about hundred meters ahead. Johnny pulled over. They seized their rifles, hopped out, then stole their way into the trees. The big Mercury outboards hummed a collective bass note as he and Corey reached the building, jogged along the wall, then crouched tightly at the corner.

Nazari and his men divided themselves between the four Intrepid 37s, with Nazari climbing aboard the boat with the dark blue hull. Beyond them, near the docks about fifty meters to the left, came Willie's fishing boat, drifting soundlessly between two shrimp boats and disappearing from view.

The last of the men boarded, and Nazari's boat took the lead, blasting away from the marina, with the other three boats falling in behind him like obedient bodyguards. Johnny counted at least five men aboard each craft, perhaps twenty combatants in all. Nearly in unison, they rolled left, heading northeast up the channel toward Matagorda Bay. The chalky lines they drew across the water faded as Johnny and Corey rose cautiously from the building.

On cue, Josh came tear-assing around the docks, *The Marauder's* waterjets blaring, its camouflage pattern hull suggesting it was more than just an interceptor boat but a living, breathing predator with offensive and defensive mechanisms spawned over thousands of years. She was difficult to see, highly maneuverable, and spat venomous lead.

Willie came charging down the dock to join them as Josh slowed. All three hopped on board, gathering behind Josh inside the wheelhouse. Josh throttled up, and Johnny's head jerked back as they entered the channel, their wake crashing in fountains against the shoreline.

"Where's he headed now?" Willie asked.

"Maybe back to the port," answered Johnny. "Maybe that container ship's his ride out."

"Hey, Johnny," Corey interrupted. "Just got a text back from Athena. They still haven't found the missing cards, but they decoded a few more for us. They said some of the cards have both a date and time: zero eight hundred Eastern Standard."

"What time is it now?"

"About zero two, but we're an hour behind, so we got five hours till something happens," said Corey.

"Damn, all right, boys, listen up. I talked to Gatterton. He told me that Plesner's working with the guys from D&S Equities. I know one of those guys, Nicholas Dresden. He did a big presentation at the Ordnance Disposal Conference down in Florida last year. One of his companies recycles explosives and works with EXSA down in Peru—and that's no coincidence. Whatever they're doing with these jihadis is huge."

Chapter Forty-Two

"As we added more targets to the list, I realized we were the only good guys in America who knew the attack was coming—just four rednecks with the world on our shoulders."

—Corey McKay (FBI interview, 23 December)

The container ship *Mawsitsit* had docked at the Port of Houston and was assigned to berth T5 at the Bayport Container Piers, where she would conduct drayage, offloading her containers with the assistance of Tropic Breeze Drayage Limited. Operations would begin within the hour.

This berth assignment—which was quite deliberate—put *Mawsitsit* approximately 6,800 feet from LML Oil Gas & Chemicals Tank Farm, which Abdul Satar Rostami now observed through the compass bridge's panoramic windows.

The farm resembled some weirdly futuristic moon colony cordoned off by walls of pipes stacked like ribs between dozens of white, cylindrical tanks with flat tops. Each of the farm's eight sections housed a dozen or more tanks of a particular size, and by Rostami's count there were over two hundred arranged in neat formations. To the north lay ribbons of railroad tracks and highways sliding into the gloom.

Behind him, the ship's captain was bound and being held at gunpoint, along with the first officer, while the rest of the complement had been murdered, their bodies jettisoned into the gulf. Once more, the captain demanded his release, and once more Rostami reared back and punched him in the left eye, which had already swollen shut.

After shaking the pain from his knuckles, Rostami sighed. In a few short hours and before sunrise, the Baktar-Shikan missile systems stored below would be delivered to the deck. Those missiles were part of a much larger cache that had been smuggled out of Pakistan years ago. Though only a rumor, Rostami heard that some of those systems had found their way through border tunnels along the Mexican-American border and had wound up somewhere out west, where they had been hidden... until now.

Allah's righteous wrath would once more be unloosed upon the United States. The sword would be delivered to their black hearts, and Sharia Law would descend upon them like a storm at first, and then, like the gentle rains to cleanse them of their impurities and prepare them for new lives in the service of Allah. For this, Rostami was ready to martyr himself, as were his men. The rewards in the afterlife were great. With a chill of anticipation, he left the bridge, heading below deck, where they would review the operation one last time.

Ironically, this was Rostami's thirtieth birthday, and he was honored to spend it here, leading his fighters in jihad.

The men grinned as he entered the crew quarters.

"*Allahu Akbar!*" he cried.

* * *

Michael Bhardwaj had been teaching ACP Chemistry 1 & 2 at North Central High School for the past twelve years. He had created a fulfilling and engaging life for himself in Indianapolis, marrying a dark-haired beauty he had met while attending Indiana State University. They had two wonderful children: a girl, Elizabeth, now ten; and a boy, Thomas, about to turn nine, although young Thomas already sounded like a seasoned attorney, arguing daily for candy and more video game time.

Despite being a father, a devoted husband, and a consummate professional, Bhardwaj had never lost his own childhood excitement for science, for the study of atomic theory, chemical bonding, kinetics, thermodynamics, and descriptive chemistry. He brought that enthusiasm to his classroom, where his students outperformed all others in the district and won numerous contests. He had been nominated three times as teacher of the year and had won the award twice for his commitment to learning. He was the faculty advisor for the high school's science club and recruited guest speakers from the local rotary to give presentations about their careers to his students. He coached his son's little league baseball team and was vice president of his homeowners' association. His wife, an Italian Catholic raised in New York, had insisted upon the children attending church and receiving their first Holy Communion. Bhardwaj had endorsed that decision, and subsequently they had become avid church goers and volunteered for community projects, especially those that benefited the elderly and/or less fortunate.

In sum, Mr. Michal Bhardwaj was a model American citizen, a gifted teacher, and a pillar of his community. He was thirty-eight years old. He had the rest of his life ahead of him.

But it was all a lie.

Bhardwaj was not his real name. His father was not Indian as he had told his wife, nor had his parents been killed in a car crash. They were both alive and well and living in Pakistan. While he wore no beard and currently did not own a Koran, he had been born and raised a Muslim. As ordered, for the past twelve years, he had kept Allah in his heart, secretly honoring who he truly served.

Now he stood in his bathroom, leaning over the sink, unable to sleep and studying the courier card in his hand, trying to reconcile what they wanted him to do, what Allah needed him to do. Yesterday he had received the note and had met with the courier, who delivered to him the package: a handmade suicide vest whose instructions had been written in Arabic, forcing him to clear the cobwebs from his head and revisit his old language. The vest's operation was as simple as his plan:

Just after homeroom, he would enter the hall as students scrambled off to first period. He would be there at the busiest time of day, when his detonation would cause the greatest loss of life—

Where he would watch, for just a half second, as boys and girls full of promise and ambition glanced back, into his eyes, into his tearing eyes, as all of them were shredded by the explosion.

He trembled and whispered, *"Allahu Akbar."*

* * *

This bomber's name was inconsequential. He had smuggled himself into the country by exploiting the illegal cigarette trade in Ontario to buy passage aboard a high-speed boat that had ferried him to New York. Now he was up in St. Paul, Minnesota, seated in the emergency department waiting room of St. Joseph's Hospital and repeatedly clutching the courier card in his pocket, as though drawing fortitude from the paper and ink. He was hours early, because there was nothing else to do when you were waiting to die.

The vest was well-hidden beneath his parka. The igniter was easily accessible.

"Are you being helped?"

He glanced at a broad-shouldered Hispanic woman whose photo ID clipped to her scrubs read Carmen Guzman. He cleared his throat. "I'm meeting a friend. He couldn't sleep. He's not feeling well."

"All right, you'll check-in right over there."

"Thank you."

She gave him a curious look then returned to her desk at the triage station. He flicked his glance to the old woman seated down the row from him. She was rocking to and fro and whispering something under her breath.

The automatic doors parted and in walked a bearded man in his twenties clutching a small boy. He crossed to the desk, his face stricken.

While this scene unfolded, the bomber—whose name would never be known by the infidels but remembered forever by Allah—rose to stretch his legs. Soon... Soon... *Allahu Akbar.*

* * *

The Long Island Railroad was the busiest commuter rail system in the United States, serving over 335,000 people each day. Travelers from as far off as Montauk Point, New York could board a train and ride all the way to Manhattan. Reaching the city required ticket holders to pass through either the Woodside or Jamaica Stations, depending upon their point of origin.

Woodside was located on 61st Street and Roosevelt Avenue in Queens and had three platforms each extending some twelve cars in length. The northern platform serviced trains bound for Manhattan, while the central island platform was used by eastbound or outbound Port Washington trains, where the line terminated. The southern platform beside track number four of the main line accommodated eastbound main line trains. There were six tracks in all. The ticket office opened at 6:10 a.m. on weekdays.

Jamaica was on Sutphin Boulevard and Archer Avenue and was the LIRR's central hub. Here the Mainline, Montauk Branch, and Atlantic Branch all came together like capillaries feeding into larger arteries. Over 200,000 commuters "changed at Jamaica" each day, making it the busiest station in the country. Five island platforms allowed passengers to board or exit trains from either side. Each morning, westbound trains from three separate lines arrived simultaneously, allowing passengers to cross over the platform, through one train, and into another in a well-choreographed shuffle of ants on the move. The station's main entrance was housed inside a century-old building, along with the LIRR's headquarters, a waiting area, and ticket counters.

Because the Long Island Railroad had become such a vital and dependable link for commuters, a simultaneous and long term disruption of service at Woodside and Jamaica Stations would be a staggering blow to the state's economy. All railway service between Manhattan and Long Island would be cut off. Moreover, a terrorist attack on those stations would deliver a secondary and psychological blow to commuters who would second-guess their modes of transport, the way many had after 9/11. The highways would become further congested. Productivity would drop off, even as fear spread like a super virus.

To this end, the leadership of *Al-Saif* had contacted a very special cell and given them a very special mission.

They were a brother and sister team, each wearing the largest and heaviest vests, or so they had been told. Mirsab, whose name fittingly meant "sword of the prophet," had received a card with coordinates for Jamaica Station. His dry run the day before revealed that he should stand on the platform near track #2, beneath the enormous steel and glass canopy. All around him, hundreds of commuters would dodge between platforms, racing to catch their next train, while his next stop would be Paradise.

In the meantime, Zehna, who had been given coordinates for the Woodside Station, would stand on the northern platform, also crowded with travelers bound for Manhattan. She could cast her deep brown eyes upon the infidels and torch them with the purity of her heart.

While both stations were heavily policed by the Metropolitan Transit Authority, Mirsab felt certain that he and his sister would pass unnoticed through the crowds, with everyone bundled up against the cold. As he sat in his old Camry, parked on the street about five minutes from the station, his cell phone rang.

"I'm scared," she said.

"You can't be."

"I mean I'm frightened of dying."

He raised his voice. "We're here for Allah, for the jihad. Remember, we create the fear. We do not feel it ourselves."

"You have no doubts?"

"Of course not."

"I wanted to get married. I wanted to have a baby."

"You'll have those in the afterlife."

"You're right. I love you, brother."

"And I love you. But don't fail us."

"I won't. *Allahu Akbar.*"

* * *

Nasser El Bayed instructed the cab driver to take him to Orlando International Airport. He was flying out on Southwest Airlines, located in Terminal A. He wore a bulky down jacket and carried a nondescript backpack. He had no luggage to check through.

Judging from his appearance and his current ID, which read "Carlos Ramirez" of 1446 Walden Lane, Casselberry, Florida, most people thought El Bayed was Puerto Rican or Mexican. Cuban, perhaps, since he was clean shaven and wore a crew cut. And while he suspected there was Hispanic blood in his ancestry, he was, in fact, born and raised in the United States, the son of parents who had emigrated from Saudi Arabia. He spent one year at a local community college, where he had failed all of his classes because of a video game addiction. A month later, he had taken a trip overseas to visit his grandparents in Riyadh, where he had met Dr. Ramzi Shammas, a friend of his grandfather. Dr. Shammas had taken El Bayed under his wing and had spent an entire summer teaching him about Allah and about jihad. Time ceased. Food tasted better. He had never slept so peacefully. El Bayed had met other young men like himself, and he had returned to the United States with a feeling of elation, a feeling of purpose.

The driver followed the signs to Terminal A and dropped off El Bayed on Level 2 designated for departing flights. He tipped the man fifty dollars. The driver, who had mentioned that his daughter was just starting college, thought there was some mistake.

"It's yours," El Bayed told him.

Allahu Akbar.

Chapter Forty-Three

"Those boys made a deal with the devil—but they weren't smart enough to realize that you do not trust the devil."

—Johnny Johansen (FBI interview, 23 December)

Nazari's fleet of Intrepids rocketed at full throttle beside the pale yellow glitter of Port O'Connor and the rows of stilt houses wandering northward along the shore. The blue-hulled boat took the lead, with the others completing an arrowhead formation. They passed a cut in Blackberry Island where the still waters of Barroom Bay blurred into view. A few seconds later, they banked hard as they exited the channel, heading south into Matagorda Bay toward a broad swath through the peninsula where ships entered and left the Gulf of Mexico. A small, kidney-shaped island emerged to their left, and beyond it, lights from the peninsula airport stained the bellies of low-lying clouds.

Despite running blacked out, Johnny and the others were detected by Nazari's men. It was impossible to mute their engines or waterjets or conceal their wake. As the lead boat's captain steered for the main shipping channel, Josh said he wanted to close with the enemy. Johnny nodded and signaled to Corey, who left the wheelhouse to man the port side minigun.

Nazari's boat entered the cut, and once his trailing boats did likewise, their sterns lit in strings of short-circuiting lights. In the next instant, rifle fire drummed across *The Marauder's* hull, pinging and ricocheting in a drunken rhythm that had Johnny gritting his teeth and cursing the fact that the boat was nothing more than a bullet magnet, just like any other vehicle. One after another, the jihadis emptied their magazines, then reloaded.

Josh rolled the wheel to starboard, giving Corey a wide open bead on the port side boat, now drifting away from the group.

Johnny squeezed a fist in sympathetic anger as Corey set free a wave of tracer-lit fire, rounds tearing into the boat's engines, drilling holes in the console, and ripping across the hull, with fiberglass splintering and boomeranging away as though it were balsa. One of the jihadis threw himself overboard before being mauled by a deluge of lead.

Even as the Intrepid slowed and drifted mindlessly toward the eastern shoreline, Josh screamed for Corey to get down—

Because a jihadi on the center boat was at the stern and lifting a Rocket Propelled Grenade to his shoulder. About eight or nine of his brothers were hunkered at his knees and returning fire. He hollered at them, and they broke fire and rushed to the starboard side bow, clearing the area behind him.

Gritting his teeth, Johnny watched through *The Marauder's* windshield as the RPG ignited in a flash, and the rocket spat from the launcher.

Josh was one hell of a boat driver, cutting hard to port, trying to protect Corey and the minigun. The rocket struck at an oblique angle... and the impact sent shudders through the entire boat. Fire-lit smoke and showers of aluminum splinters spread across the windshield and vanished as quickly.

"Corey, you okay?" Josh shouted.

"Yeah, yeah, banged my head, but I'm good to go."

Willie left the wheelhouse and slid around the starboard side, crouching low to check for damage. "Not bad," he said over the radio. "Glancing blow. I think they chipped the paint. Bastards." Johnny leaned out for a look himself, and the damage was more extensive than that, with a few pieces of the armored hull missing, a jagged gash along one section, and a huge dent reaching back toward the wheelhouse.

They got another one!" shouted Corey.

A jihadi on the port side boat had taken a cue from his colleague. His launcher was balanced on his shoulder, while a comrade tugged off a plastic cap on the rocket's nose, inserted the rocket, and then stood back.

"Hang on! Emergency stop!" Josh said, reversing engines and bringing *The Marauder* to a sudden halt within one boat-length, the bow plunging, water surging over the hull, the rocket streaking by so fast that if Johnny blinked, he would have missed it.

As soon as the boat leveled off, Corey began lecturing the jihadis with the mini-gun, each of his arguments wrapped neatly in a brass jacket. The gun's reptilian tongue extended from his rotating muzzles all the way to the enemy boat's stern, where it shredded the jihadi with the empty launcher. Wavelets beneath Corey's strobing bead were tattooed crimson and gathered into colonies like strange jellyfish writhing toward the light. Dissonant gunfire and droning engines made it difficult for Johnny to form a thought within the water spout of white noise.

And then... just like that... Corey ceased fire, and it was over.

If any jihadi had survived in that second boat, he was cowering on the deck, because the shattered controls had been abandoned and the craft wheeled in an aim-less arc, one engine belching smoke, the bow rising, the stern beginning to take on water.

Farther out, the other two boats neared the mouth of the channel, having extended their lead because of Josh's emergency stop. Recognizing that, Josh wrenched the throttle again, and Johnny called out to Corey: "Watch your fire. Be sure what's behind your target."

"Roger that, Johnny. Never left my mind."

"Wait a second, what the hell?" Josh asked, pointing at the boats. "Look."

Johnny squinted through the night vision goggles. Instead of turning eastward toward the Port of Houston to rendezvous with that container ship, Nazari and his shadow were heading due south—straight into the gulf.

"Where the hell's he going?" Johnny asked.

"Let's find out." Josh slammed forward the throttle, the boat racing toward fifty knots.

As they sewed up the gap, Corey shouted, "More RPGs!"

Two jihadis had brought their launchers to the stern and were tilting them so that the rockets' exhaust would pass harmlessly to the sides of the boat.

Once more Josh screamed and throttled down, even as he cut the wheel in a vio-lent J-turn that sent *The Marauder* banking so hard that, for just a second, she was lying on her port side.

Corey hollered and, from the corner of his eyes, Johnny saw him get washed over the railing and into the waves.

In the next breath, the rockets whooshed overhead like fragments of lightning that had broken off to burn for a nanosecond then die.

"Corey's over the side!" Johnny reported. He called for Josh to stop and slammed open the wheelhouse door to scan the two-to-three foot swells on the starboard side with his night vision goggles.

After a few seconds that took a year off Johnny's life, he spotted Corey, nearly invisible among the waves and struggling to remain afloat against his heavy plates, boots, and the rest of his gear.

Johnny rushed to slough off his own plates and gear belt. He took a flying leap off the stern. Water temperatures in the Gulf of Mexico during the winter months were generally unpleasant, hovering in the fifties and sixties, Johnny remembered. The shock hit hard, like a thousand needles wielded by a thousand rookie nurses trying to find a vein. He surfaced and spun around, reacquiring Corey about ten meters away.

"Hang on, I'm coming," Johnny said.

"Okay."

"You all right?"

"Yeah," Corey said, spitting salt water. "Wave ripped me right off the boat. Knocked the wind out me, too." He shivered hard and spat again. "Taking everything I got to stay up right now."

Willie tossed out a rescue float with attached nylon line, and Johnny seized it as Corey swam up behind him. After Johnny's signal, Willie began reeling them in toward the stern platform above the waterjets. Willie hoisted Corey from the water, while Johnny got up, onto his elbows and dragged himself from the miserable ice bath. Shuddering, he and Corey stood and jammed themselves into the wheelhouse, where Josh had switched on the heat and wasted no time bringing the boat around, locking them back into the pursuit.

"They have a good lead on us, but again, where are they going? I have nothing on radar besides... wait a second. I do have something. Damn, now its gone." Josh pointed at the radar screen. "You saw that, didn't you?"

"They wouldn't head out to sea—unless they're planning to meet someone," said Willie. He took up Johnny's night vision goggles and began scanning the distance.

Behind him, Corey and Josh seized some blankets from one of the cargo compartments, using them to dry off as the boat bounced more roughly over the swells.

The gulf broadened around them, the horizon reaching toward infinity, with Nazari's darkened boats visible only to Willie and Josh. As the wind picked up, so too did the waves, a few swells rising to four feet.

Johnny shouldered up next to Willie, who shoved the goggles into his hands and said, "Look past the boats. Tell me what you see. Tell me I'm not going crazy."

"You're not," said Josh. "I got it, too."

Frowning, Johnny lifted the goggles and rolled up the magnification.

What he saw convinced him that Nazari was a major player—perhaps *the* player—because his jihadi colleagues had gone to great lengths to ensure his escape.

* * *

The men aboard the sixteen-foot skiffs anchored on the Thames River in New London, Connecticut where led by Mentu Sekani, a member of the Muslim Brotherhood for nearly thirty years and an imam who had helped Dr. Nazari build his organization in the United States. Two to three times a week Sekani and his team fished on the incoming tide, their boats moored to the various substructure footings of the Gold Star Memorial Bridge. The footings kept their skiffs from drifting on the tide, and the submerged growth provided chum that attracted bigger fish. When the fish were biting, the group routinely stayed out until well after dark. They were barely seen among the footings between the bridge's two huge spans.

It was during this reliable obscurity that they had completed their task, working with their dive teams trained in Iowa. The infidels assumed that terrorists would target the Navy base or Electric Boat Shipyard in New London. They gave little to no credit to a collection of lowly fishermen in and around some bridge pilings. They had no idea of just how well *Al-Saif* understood its own limitations and resources—and just how creative and cunning they could be, always exploiting the infidels' security lapses for maximum impact.

The only leak in Sekani's operation had come from the bald-headed black man who had been working as a liaison/courier between them and their supply chain. He had been eliminated, and now all was in place.

Destroying a bridge that spanned the Thames River would result in thousands of deaths and a crippling effect on the state's economy. However, there were other consequences, much larger and more symbolic ones that the infidels would discover in the hours following the attack.

Sekani finished zippering up his jacket, then pulled his cap farther down over his ears. It would be good to get off this cold and windy river. Some warm tea in his belly and a soft pillow were in order. His men would take care of the rest, and Sekani would watch the spectacle from his hotel room in New London.

He rubbed his eyes, started his boat's motor, then signaled to the others. For just a few seconds, he was a boy again, fishing along the Euphrates, watching as his father pilot the boat with a narrowed gaze and the wind tossing his hair. Living among the infidels had drawn the life from Sekani, and his only solace was in knowing they could not steal his memories, not these, not the peace they brought through Allah's will.

His father would visit him again this evening and say how proud he was of the men, of Sekani, of the jihad. The Mujahideen had returned, he would cry. The bridge would fall and the sword would rise toward the heavens.

* * *

Josh and Corey had spent time in Colombia and Honduras interdicting drug smugglers alongside the DEA; thus, they knew exactly what lay out there, half-submerged, with a conning tower like the dorsal fin of a killer whale. To Johnny, it was just a small submarine, but to them, it was a "narcosub" that should not be underestimated. They had witnessed firsthand the level of sophistication, stealth, and maneuverability these craft provided. Many of them had been designed by Russian engineers contracted by the Colombians. They were constructed under the triple canopy of the jungle, smuggled down through rivers barely deep enough to permit their passage, and released into the ocean to do the Cartels' bidding.

More curious was exactly how the submarine had wound up in these waters. Clearly, it had not sailed on its own and run the risk of refueling along the way. It had somehow been here all along or been delivered.

As the two boats raced toward it, a hatch atop the conning tower popped open, and a figure switched on a flashlight and signaled three times.

Corey abandoned his blanket and worked his way back outside and toward the minigun station. Willie jumped on the fifty caliber and told Josh if he wanted to bring the boat around, he would be happy to "lighten their load."

"We need to get in there from the flanks," Josh told him. "Corey's got no shot, and neither do you—without hitting Nazari's boat."

Johnny's breath turned shallow. In his mind's eye, he scowled at each of the jihadis they had lost—LaPorte, Shammas, and Rasul—along with the snipers and that agent in Detroit. They had all died before he could learn the truth. Nazari was the only one left with answers. They could *not* lose him, not after coming this far.

Now Johnny felt Daniel's weight against his arms as he held his brother and listened to his dying words: *"I'm sorry, Johnny. It's my fault. I should have..."*

"You should have what?"

Daniel's lips moved, but his words were drowned out by the incessant and familiar barking of three dogs...

Johnny considered what he had asked of his friends—to leave their families and loved ones behind. To sacrifice everything—even their lives—for the truth. They had tried to let him off the hook, but *he* had dragged them into this. If he let them down now, how could he look them in the eye without suffocating from the guilt?

He thought of Elina and what he had put her through, the tears and the worrying and the burden of comforting their grieving nieces. Moreover, if he had not pried into Daniel's murder, her dogs would still be alive—her precious dogs. And his.

At last Johnny thought about who he was—a United States Marine—and what he stood for—the greatest country on Earth. *Oorah.*

Suddenly, he could breathe again.

There it was. That son of a bitch on the boat would not get away. He would be captured, interrogated, and punished. The Marines had arrived and had the situation well in hand.

Coursing now with adrenaline, Johnny gaped as the men in the rear boat opened fire, rounds striking in thumps and sparks, a few caroming up and across the windshield like insects scuffing the ballistic glass.

Josh tugged on the wheel, cutting forty-five degrees to starboard, trying once more to give Corey the angle he needed on the other boat.

Seeing this, the jihadi driver broke to starboard himself, continuing to shield Nazari's Intrepid with his own.

"He knows what we're doing," shouted Josh.

Willie charged away from the .50 caliber, came into the wheelhouse, and seized his big MCX MR from a rack.

"Don't miss," Johnny told him.

"With all this bouncing around, it'll be a miracle if I even get close," Willie answered. "But I'll give him something to think about."

Johnny watched as Willie came up behind Corey and slipped beside him, exploiting the minigun's blast shield for protection as he stared through his scope.

The MCX MR cracked, and Johnny thought he spotted a spark leap across the other boat's console. He blinked hard and squinted back into the night vision goggles as Willie fired again, this round tearing into the windshield at the boat driver's shoulder.

At the stern, the jihadis broke into automatic fire, waves of it, and Josh veered to port, steering Willie and Corey away from the fray.

Abruptly, Willie shoved his rifle into Corey's hands, then darted back to the stern and took up the .50 caliber, whirling it around and finally getting a clear and open line on that boat. The big gun chugged like a freight train, hurtling lead that chewed hungrily into the fishing boat's hull. Josh would have described the damage as a dozen blows from Mjölnir—"that which smashes," better known as the hammer of Thor. While hot brass spilled across their deck, jihadis on the other boat leaped overboard while a few others crumpled to the deck, missing arms, legs, even a head, as the Intrepid continued in its turn with only the driver's ghost at the wheel.

"Hold fire!" Johnny ordered. "Corey, get inside! We're going in hot!"

Nazari's Intrepid was approximately five hundred meters out from the submarine and closing fast. Johnny counted at least seven men onboard, including Nazari himself, who was crouched near the controls, along with the other two jihadis from the Lexus.

Josh broke into a zigzagging advance, trying to keep the gunmen guessing, but those 7.62 mm rounds kept chipping away at the hull, converting armored plates into gemstones that shimmered in the half-light. The closer they drew, the more intense the fire became, and it was then, during that torrential onslaught, that Johnny recognized the simplicity of their mission and what they must do. He recalled a seminar Corey once gave about narco sub limitations and vulnerabilities. Slow submerged speed, limited battery capacity, and *no watertight compartments.*

"Get us between them and that sub," he told Josh, then turned to Willie. "And when he does, you get on the fifty and put some nice holes anywhere in that sub, you hear me?"

"Roger that, boss!" Willie answered.

Johnny regarded Corey. "You get on the minigun. Keep your fire on Nazari's boat, right on the waterline. We'll scoop them out after it sinks."

"Sounds like a plan." Cory slid to the back of the wheelhouse, ready to dodge to his station.

Hurtling themselves through the incoming fire, they came up behind their prey, just as the Intrepid drew within twenty meters of the submarine.

Without warning, the gunfire tapered into nothingness.

Willie let out a snicker. "Ha! Look at that. They're out of ammo!"

"Are they really?" asked Corey. "I'm not sure. They just stopped firing."

The driver killed the trio of Mercurys, and the Intrepid whispered toward the sub, its wake as quickly swallowed by the gulf.

Josh allowed them to coast forward, and Johnny glanced worriedly in his direction. "What the hell now?"

"I don't know."

Johnny lifted his night vision goggles and squinted. Jihadis were scrambling on the deck, and through the group came Nazari and his two buddies. They leaped over the side and began swimming fiercely around the boat, toward the sub.

Out near the stern, one of the jihadis clutched his AK and waved at Johnny and Josh. His comrades surrounded him, all with their arms raised high in the air.

"I don't believe it," said Johnny."

"Neither do I," Josh said. "These Hajis don't surrender."

The Marauder motored closer to the fishing boat, coming within fifty meters, then Josh turned to come around them, in pursuit of Nazari.

A man on the Intrepid pushed his way to the front of the group and swung a loaded RPG onto his shoulder.

Johnny looked back to Corey, but his friend was gone—having already manned the minigun. Corey was about to open up when the RPG flashed—

And *The Marauder's* bow ignited like a supernova.

Chapter Forty-Four

"They wanted this to be a wakeup call for America, and despite our best efforts, they still got what they wanted."

—Willie Parente (FBI interview, 23 December)

Were it not for the five foot swell that had lifted the fishing boat at the last second, Johnny and his friends would be dead.

The jihadi with the RPG had been targeting the wheelhouse, but his sights had drifted, and the rocket struck across the bow, where armor plating protected the multipurpose compartment below deck.

Johnny yelled for them to get down as a tremendous ball of roiling flames swelled over the windshield. The concussion wave struck in peals of thunder rattling through the boat and sucking air from the wheelhouse.

With his ears ringing and feeling as though he had just been sucker punched with a roll of quarters, Johnny clambered back to his feet, in time to glimpse a mushroom cloud of fire with burning debris shooting through it like bottle rockets, leaving contrails arcing to form petals of smoke.

As the flames clawed higher, tiny crowns bubbled along the fires, turning dark brown like scabs that vanished and reappeared. The stench of melting rubber and hydraulic fluid had Johnny gagging. And then, as fires turned in on themselves, coiling into rings of gray-and-black smoke, Corey yanked open the wheelhouse door. He was coughing and bleeding from minor shrapnel wounds to his neck and forehead. He seized a fire extinguisher from the wall and charged back to his station, blasting the bow with white foam.

Josh was already assessing the damage over the radio. A portion of the boat's superstructure had been torn apart, the bow door assembly was a mangled mess, but the explosion had not breached or compromised the integrity of the hull.

While he continued his report, Johnny burst outside to man the M240 while Willie got on the .50 caliber machine gun. Together, they unleashed hell on that last boat, its hull freckled with so much fire that Johnny gave it five minutes before it sank. A few of the jihadis dove overboard, while the rest never made it that far.

The moment they stopped firing, Josh blurted out that he still had power. With the bow smoldering and a gaping hole appearing in the armor plates just above the water line, he banged the throttle and took them around a widening half-circle of debris, some of it still burning in pale yellow puddles.

Corey had the submarine in sight, with Nazari and his cohorts about ten meters away and swimming with a ferocity that impressed even Johnny. The submariner who had signaled remained in the conning tower and was now armed with an AK-47 instead of a flashlight.

As he caught sight of *The Marauder*, he opened up, and Johnny shouted for Corey to get busy. Salvos of minigun fire not only sheered that man in two, but they chewed through the conning tower then across the bow. A few tracers strayed wide to thump and hiss into the water.

Another man appeared in the battered tower, pushing past the body of his colleague and bailing out with a rifle in hand. He was followed by another crewman who remained there and squeezed off a few rounds. Corey responded with a withering volley of his own. The submariner slumped in the hatch, while the other man who had leaped in the water tugged himself onto the bow. He yanked a pistol from his holster and jammed it into his head. The shot echoed.

Fearing Nazari and his buddies might do likewise, Johnny hollered for Josh to throttle up while he tugged off his boots. He switched on his radio and made sure his headset was tight. "Hey, boys, Johnny here, radio check. Do me a favor. Keep an eye on me."

As soon as they came within ten meters of Nazari and his associates, Johnny hit the waves. Memories of his swim qualifications, especially the one he needed to become a Reconnaissance Marine, drove his arms and legs to work in perfect concert. His breathing grew measured. And his prey drew near.

* * *

The old horse barn in St. Bernard, Louisiana reeked of manure, but there was nothing Achmed could do about that. He had not arranged for this safe house, nor was he responsible for any of its unpleasantness. His job was to impart his wisdom as an old mujahedeen fighter in Afghanistan and coach his cell of young men toward sudden and magnificent jihad.

Parked inside the barn were two Ford F59 food trucks with twenty-foot long Morgan Olson bodies. Trucks like these had become "hip" or "chic" among the infidels during the past decade, each offering homemade sandwiches and tacos and cupcakes, the thought of which turned Achmed's stomach. And so it had seemed fitting, ironic, and clandestine that he and his men would deploy these symbols of American gluttony to communicate Allah's will.

The first truck offered *Blue Bayou Catfish*, and splashed across its sides were blue-and-black logos of bewhiskered fish dressed like rap music stars wearing gold chains and sunglasses. The second truck featured a chorus line of dancing pigs to summon an appetite for gourmet pulled pork created by some infidel named "Bubba." The interiors of both trucks had been gutted and replaced by Baktar-Shikan Missile Systems seated on their tripods and recently delivered to them from out west. Each truck housed two complete systems, along with sixteen missiles. New hatches had been cut into the driver's side of each truck to account for the exhaust. Each truck contained a three man crew: two missile operators and a driver. All six men were now assembled before Achmed as he gave them their final briefing:

The *Blue Bayou Catfish* truck was heading to nearby Chalmette and the ExonMobil Refinery. The truck would approach on West St. Bernard Highway, cross St. Claude, the railway tracks, then enter the unguarded parking lot. There the crew would raise the side panels and destroy the refinery plant processing center, along with as many storage tanks as possible.

Concurrently, the crew of Bubba's Pulled Pork would drive to Bell Chase. They would approach from Levy Road and park across the street from the Phillips66 Alliance Refinery. From that location, they would carry out their attack at nearly pointblank range.

Achmed grinned to himself as he imagined local law enforcement staring slack-jawed at missiles being fired from trucks painted with cartoon characters.

For his part, he would remain behind and in control of two remote detonators. His crews were unaware that their trucks were wired with explosives. Once finished with their tasks, Achmed had been charged with martyring them, after which he, too, would be wrapped in the virgins' arms.

* * *

Johnny had locked his gaze on Nazari, who, along with his two men, continued to swim toward the submarine. Nazari's colleagues continued drifting behind their leader, once again acting as shields.

Josh switched on *The Marauder's* high-powered spotlight. The laser-like beam swept across the waves, found the three escapees, and painted them a garish white.

While Johnny kicked harder to close in, a gunshot split the air, the round striking the swells with a hollow knock not a meter from Nazari's head.

With a gasp, Johnny craned his head toward the boom.

Willie was balanced atop the gunwale, his shoulder resting on the wheelhouse as he leaned into his MCX MR, one eye eclipsed by his scope. The suppressed rifle thumped once more, the round piercing the water an arm's length from Nazari's men. In unison, they ducked under the waves.

"Hold fire," Johnny ordered over the radio. He assumed Willie was only trying to slow them, but even a single misplaced round could hit Nazari.

Just ahead, the high value target himself reached the sub and hauled himself onto the rolling and slippery deck with the aid of a mooring line left trailing in the water. He crawled to the submariner who had shot himself and shoved the corpse over the side to get past him. Once he reached the conning tower, he rushed up the ladder and dragged the other dead man out of his way before disappearing through the hatch.

Desperate now, Nazari's accomplices reached the sub, whirled back, and drew pistols. The jihadi on the right fired two rounds at Johnny, then his slide locked open as a casing got caught there in a stove pipe malfunction. The guy on the left began emptying his magazine, the water alive with splats and plops.

"All right, Willie, give 'em Hell!" Johnny ordered.

Willie engaged the men, his surgically placed rounds beating in time with Johnny's pulse. The jihadis sloughed away from the submarine and floated prone in the water, their heads like buoys rising and falling until they disappeared beneath the waves.

Johnny swam the last five meters to the sub. Using the same line that Nazari had, he scrambled on deck and inched his way carefully across the slick surface toward the ladder. Up near the hatch, his nose crinkled as he struggled to identify a faint odor.

"Hey, guys, I smell something in there—like chlorine."

"Aw, shit, Johnny," Corey began. "We probably hit the batteries and seawater's gotten in there to contaminate them. It's mixing with the lead-acid. How bad is it?"

"Not too bad yet."

"It'll get worse."

"Guess I'm holding my breath."

"Wait. There's hydrogen in there, too. You can't smell it, but it builds up when they charge and discharge the batteries. Ventilation's poor and those vapors are highly combustible."

"So what're you saying?"

"I'm saying don't let him start the engines. One spark and that thing will light up like a Roman candle—"

"—along with the fuel tanks," Johnny said with a groan. "Shit!"

Johnny glanced down into the sub's interior. The rungs of a rusty ladder mounted to the bulkhead led to a makeshift control station fitted with a steering wheel looted from an old Audi. To the right lay a pair of heavy throttle levers—

And in the pilot's chair sat the professor himself. He was studying an array of pipes, gauges, and color-coded shutoff valves mounted to the bulkhead and exposed like a circulatory system. His gaze shifted between the wheel and the pipes until he beat a fist on the console, as though in frustration.

"What's the matter, asshole? You lose your keys?"

Nazari glanced up at Johnny, then bolted from the chair.

With the ticking of straining metal, the sub listed to port and took on more water. Johnny took a deep breath and hurried down the ladder. He moved past the control station, which sat on a ledge above an open hatch leading to the bow compartment where crews ordinarily stored tons of cocaine.

He hopped down from the ladder to the deck, where his bare feet splashed into ankle-high water. *The Marauder's* spotlight shone as a thin shaft from the hatch above, filtering into the narrow confines and producing irregular shadows that could easily hide a man beneath the intestine work of pipes and wires. Seawater arced from the bullet holes along one side and pooled across the narrow main aisle. More pipes, tubes, and wires snaked across the overhead. There were no creature comforts in this metal can; it was strictly a drug transportation platform.

"Johnny, it's Corey. If you can hear me, listen up. There has to be an emergency air intake cutoff valve. I'm thinking it's aft, somewhere near the engines. Find that valve and jam it shut—because the engines can't run without oxygen."

Nazari's anger at the control station suggested he had no idea how to start this boat, which was probably why he had gone aft to find an ignition switch. Still, as an engineer, he had to know something about the smell and volatility of the gas. Maybe his game was not escape but to martyr himself and take Johnny with him. Instead of a suicide vest, he now had a seventy-four-foot long submarine and hundreds of gallons of diesel fuel at his disposal. All he needed was that spark.

After venturing about half way to the stern, with seawater up to his shins and still rising, Johnny stopped. He could leave the sub, go back to *The Marauder*, and light up this bitch with .50 caliber rounds until that aforementioned spark sent Nazari hurtling toward Allah. But then all truths would die with him. Uncovering the rest of his network, along with someone else who might know the truth about Daniel, would be difficult if not impossible without him.

Blinking hard against the fumes, Johnny forged on. The engines came into view—the fading letters of the word YAMAHA seeming to pulsate above the pulleys and belts and braided hoses, along with some NASA-looking conduits wrapped in aluminum. The engines sat abreast, and Johnny leaned forward, probing the elongated shadows behind them.

The urge to steal a breath grew stronger and suddenly overcame him. He allowed a trace of air to enter his nostrils. The chlorine smell had grown much stronger. He was about to cough when Josh's voice buzzed in his earpiece: "Johnny, we have another boat on radar. Big one. He's got a constant bearing, decreasing range, which means an intercept course. Could be Coast Guard. I'm not sure. ETA like ten minutes. We need to get out of here."

"Solid copy," he whispered, wrestling with the itch in his throat. He took a step forward, searching for that valve Corey had mentioned, praying it was not labeled in Spanish.

A shuffling of feet and splashing of water erupted behind him.

Johnny whirled just as Nazari detached himself from the shadows and reared back with a two-foot-long pipe wrench painted neon red.

The wrench arced high in the chlorine-filled air, with faint light flickering off its surfaces before it came down toward Johnny.

Chapter Forty-Five

"Marines never give up, never give in, and never accept second best. So while the rest of us were running out of ideas, Johnny remembered that the one thing that could save us... was us."

—Josh Eriksson (FBI interview, 23 December)

Johnny caught the wrench in one hand as it came within an inch of his forehead. He could not stop Nazari's momentum but managed to divert the blow from his skull to his shoulder. He crashed onto the flooded deck, never losing his grip on the wrench. Corey was barking something over the radio, but the headset slipped from Johnny's ear, his friend's voice tinny for a second then gone.

Meanwhile, Nazari straddled Johnny and maneuvered the heavy wrench down, across Johnny's throat. Using the tool's weight, Nazari forced Johnny's head back, the seawater splashing into his eyes and about to swamp his face. Nazari, while hardly an athlete, had much more leverage, and he drove Johnny's head deeper into the water.

Raging aloud, Johnny squeezed his other hand onto the wrench and drove the jihadi professor up and away like a set of barbells that had pinned him. The second his head was clear, Johnny rolled, forcing Nazari off his chest and throwing him against the bulkhead.

However, the wrench had remained with the professor. As Johnny crawled backward, Nazari pushed forward and swung again, the wrench hammering into the deck, the seawater dousing any spark that might have danced between the metal.

A cluster of pipes off to the right lay within grasp. Johnny seized one and struggled to his feet. Nazari coughed and rose himself, doddering a moment as he two-handed

376

the wrench like a baseball bat. He squinted, as though he had lost sight of Johnny, then leaned forward in a combat stance, leading with his left leg.

Johnny kept his gaze riveted on the wrench, contemplating his next move.

Nazari bared his crowded teeth, his face knotting into a ball of wrinkles spanned by throbbing blue veins. He swung sideways.

Johnny jerked back and dodged the blow—

But the wrench clanged against a pipe fitting.

The professor set up again, wielding the wrench like an axe now, preparing to split open Johnny's head. The weapon came down, and once more, Johnny ducked away, finding himself pinned against one of the engines.

As Nazari drew back for another strike, Johnny lurched forward and seized the wrench in both hands. He tried to pull it away, but his strength was sapped by the lack of air, the chlorine gas, and weeks' worth of stress.

The wrench slipped free from Johnny's hands, and Nazari struck Johnny in the bicep, a glancing blow, but it knocked him off balance. One leg came out of the water, and both hands groped air just as he hit the deck.

Now lying on his side, with the sub's interior beginning to spin, Johnny struggled to sit up. Nazari shambled a few more steps, then fought for balance, his arm extended, the wrench's metal claws scraping against a pipe. That sound, not unlike nails on a chalkboard, startled Johnny into action. He cursed and pushed off the engine to stand. He started for Nazari, but the aisle dilated like a pupil, making it difficult to measure his steps. He sloshed forward, nearly tripped, then banged his head on a copper conduit.

With creaks of buckling metal and a much louder groan, the submarine pitched hard and fast, and suddenly, all the seawater collecting at the stern rose in a powerful wave rushing toward the bow.

Nazari had all of a second to glance back before he was swept off his feet, thrown into the crest, and was riding it toward the open hatch below the control station. He groped for purchase as he spun and rolled.

Barely another second later, Johnny lost his grip and joined the professor, sliding down, across the deck, the submarine pitching even more, perhaps forty degrees now. As he neared the conning tower's hatch, he glanced up at the light and willed himself toward the ladder, but his body would not obey. He rolled and hit the wall beside Nazari, just as another wave crashed across their faces. He gulped seawater and spat reflexively against the salt. The submarine's aft section rasped, along with a strange and somewhat rhythmic thumping that could be his pulse or something else.

Johnny lifted an arm, fingers straining. The bulkheads folded in on themselves as though the boat had already sunk and the ocean's crushing weight would now finish them. Pins and needles sewed across his cheeks. As he began to lose consciousness, a voice echoed from the back of the submarine. *Hey, Johnny? Let's go for a little ride...*

* * *

After Willie and Corey had transferred an unconscious Johnny and Nazari back to *The Marauder*, Willie gave the word, and Josh said he would be on the throttle like a fat kid on a cupcake. Willie glanced at Johnny and smiled painfully over that reply.

As they pulled away, the submarine's screws breached the surface, and something inside—something metallic—must have fallen from a shelf or a toolbox or a locker and produced that fateful spark Corey had warned them about.

The first blast came with a whoosh and violent ejection of flames that extended from the conning tower's hatch just as it hit the water.

A secondary and even more potent explosion caught Willie off guard. The aft section burst apart in a conflagration of flames and wheeling pieces of jagged shrapnel.

Even as the thunderclaps echoed, columns of black smoke appeared and bowed instantly in the breeze. Fires below coalesced into globes of flames orbiting a white-hot mass of burning diesel fuel. Fainter cracks and pops of ammo cooking off punctuated the roar and hiss, while the entire spectacle was reflected across the pale yellow swells, duplicating the catastrophe beneath the waves.

Willie remained there at the gunwale, transfixed by the fires as they traced black cotton balls of smoke in eerie shades of orange.

"Hey, come on," shouted Corey. "I have the first aid kit. Let's see if we can bring him around."

* * *

The Riverine Patrol Boat skipped like a rock over the Euphrates River, exceeding forty knots and accelerating. Daniel was at the wheel, the wind whipping through his wild mane of hair and Charlton Heston beard. Johnny stood beside him, frowning.

"Where we going?" he asked.

"To meet some of my friends up river."

Daniel banked to the right, and the river flowed directly into a mosque with towering minarets and front doors replaced by a waterfall of blood. They passed under the crimson flow, protected by the boat's canopy, then sailed across the *musulla's* Persian carpet with its arch work pattern. They kept on past rows of ornate pillars, heading toward the raised *minbar* where on a dais constructed of live snakes woven together like wicker stood Shammas, Rasul, and Nazari, along with Nicholas Dresden, Edward

Senecal, and Charles Plesner. Each was shirtless and clutching an AK-47 at rest with blood-stained palms.

The boat floated up to these men and slowed to a gentle hover. Daniel regarded Johnny with a snort. "You want the truth?" He gestured to the group. "What else do you need? I mean, look around, Johnny, you have a very vivid if not facile imagination. A blood waterfall? Snakes? Really? Come on, you know what's happening here. For some, it's about jihad. For others, it's about money. It's as simple as that."

"What about you?"

"What do you mean?"

"Did you convert to Islam?"

Daniel closed his eyes and lifted his face toward the ceiling, which peeled off into blinding light. "It was Allah's will."

"Bullshit! What would—"

"What would Dad think? You think I ever gave a shit about the old man?"

"Yeah, I do."

"Forget about me, Johnny. I'm a sheep. A lost cause."

"No, you're my brother!"

Johnny's shout repeated over and over, as though it were trapped forever on the dusty needle of the old man's record player.

Suddenly, he sat up, choking, the burning stench of ammonia filling his nostrils. Familiar voices mingled with the gurgle of waterjets. His eyelids fluttered open, and Corey's grave face came into focus. Between his thumb and forefinger was a tube of smelling salts. "I think he's awake."

Johnny coughed and spat. "No kidding." It hurt to breathe, as though his lungs had been burned. There was pressure on his arms, and somehow he was standing and being ushered through a door. His gaze refocused, and he realized he was inside the wheelhouse.

"What the hell happened?"

"You passed out inside the sub," said Willie. "We got you out. We'll be in Seadrift in about five mikes."

A chill struck Johnny's shoulders. "Where's Nazari?"

"He's okay," said Corey. "We brought him around."

"Where is he?"

"We got him zipped up tight up in the bow compartment. "

Johnny closed his eyes and breathed the sigh of a lifetime.

"Hey, Johnny, we're running out of time," said Willie, tapping his watch. "It's nearly zero five thirty local, meaning we got about ninety minutes."

"Damn." Johnny rubbed the corners of his eyes and regarded Corey. "Athena still helping us with the translation?"

Corey nodded. "They're on it like a tick on a hound dog, but they're still looking for those missing cards. We need to help them."

"Then get on it."

Corey winced. "Johnny, just so you know, our boy down below can't stop them. Each cell has its orders, and they operate independently."

"There has to be something we can do. Maybe Nazari can make a call, maybe he can, I don't know, get in touch with Dresden and Senecal and figure out a way to..."

Willie and Corey shook their heads, rendering Johnny silent.

* * *

They gathered inside the office of Seadrift Dry Storage. Earlier in the evening, Josh had been given a set of keys by old Sooner, who said the place was theirs, whatever they needed, *Semper Fi*, oorah.

Nazari sat in a chair, wrists bound behind his back. His head was lowered, and his beard pressed against a wet silk shirt clinging to his chest. There was something ominous about the way he breathed—a careful rising and falling of his chest, punctuated by a gasp here and there, as though he were sifting through plans in his head and reacting to the devastation.

Corey and Josh had convened on the far end of the office. They teamed up on their computers to help translate the rest of the courier cards into a complete target list.

Johnny sat in a chair facing Nazari, while Willie stood behind the man, close enough to growl in his ear if needed.

"We're not who you think we are," Johnny began. "We don't answer to anyone, so we can do whatever it takes. You're going to sing like a goddamned canary."

Without looking up, Nazari began to chuckle.

Willie throttled him and said, "You think we're joking?"

"*Allahu Akbar.*"

Johnny snickered. "Really. If I were you, I wouldn't think my God was so great right now. You're ready to be martyred—but you'll never get that pleasure out of us."

Willie released him, and the professor nodded.

"We know about your courier cards. We know all about the targets."

Nazari glanced away, his lips tightening in a smile.

"We know about your little dive shop in Iowa, and we know you're in bed with Dresden and Senecal. We also know about Plesner from the FBI."

Nazari faced Johnny, frowned, then raised his voice: "*Allahu Akbar!*"

As Willie began to choke him again, Johnny sighed and lifted his 1911 to Nazari's forehead. "I'll give you a phone, and you'll call your buddies and put an end to these attacks."

Nazari closed his eyes and began muttering something in Arabic, a prayer perhaps.

Willie tightened his grip to the point that Johnny thought their prisoner might pass out—or his throat caved in, whichever came first. He gestured for Willie to release the man and then raised his voice. "Listen to me, asshole. Was my brother working for you?"

Nazari stared through Johnny.

"WAS HE WORKING FOR YOU?"

Nazari closed his eyes.

Johnny bolted from his chair and regarded Willie. "Wait here. Don't do anything." He rushed outside the office and dialed Mark Gatterton. After briefing his friend, he asked, "Once we have the list, can we work around Plesner and get it to the FBI?"

"You said some of those cards have a time. Zero eight Eastern."

"That's correct."

"Then we barely have an hour. We're screwed."

"What do you mean?"

"Johnny, listen to me very carefully. Receipt of a major terrorist threat by the FBI means they have to notify their boss, the Attorney General. They have to call members of the National Security Council, Homeland Security, the CIA, and the TSA. Those groups need to activate their own emergency response teams to sweep through their own operational envelope for corroborating intel to support or refute the credibility of the threat before notifying the president."

"So that's the legalese for everyone having to cover their asses."

"I'm not defending it. I'm telling you what'll happen here."

"I don't believe this..."

"Look, even if you did this anonymously and used the online incident report, there's a three thousand character limit. The target list wouldn't fit in that space, and you'd have to fill out multiple reports and still have to wait for everything to be vetted."

Johnny could barely breathe. "So we're sunk. We can't stop it in time."

"I don't see how. It's impossible."

* * *

Corey sat back and pillowed his head in his hands. "We have two water treatment plants in Phoenix. They're barely seven miles apart. I don't understand why they're targets." He frowned and ran a search on the 91st Avenue plant, which pumped reclaimed water along a thirty-eight mile pipe line to the Palo Verde complex in addition to some place called the Tres Rios wetland project. A map revealed that Palo Verde was the largest nuclear power plant in the country.

"There's your answer," said Josh. "Power plants need coolant water. You shut down the water supply, you shut down the plant. That's why they usually build them near bodies of water. Look at that. There's no water around that plant for miles. They need to pipe it in. Says they get ninety million gallons of treated waste water per day from the combined output of the 91st Avenue plant and the Tolleson plant."

Corey scanned the website and said, "They have a retention pond that holds about a week's worth of water. After that, they're out of commission, and the lights go off."

"And then you got an economic disaster," Josh concluded. "They're playing a game of dominoes, and they know exactly what they're doing."

Johnny came up behind them, out of breath. "Are you finished yet?"

"Almost," answered Corey.

"Get me an electronic copy of that list—A-SAP."

"Roger that."

Johnny started away.

"Hey, one more thing," Josh said. "The Port of Houston hasn't come up yet. What if it doesn't? What did they want with that ship?"

"I don't know. Just add it to the list."

* * *

Johnny returned to questioning Nazari. The professor's face now resembled a grapefruit that had rolled beneath a Mac truck. His shirt was adorned with a necktie of blood, and his slacks bore matching patches on the knees. Johnny scowled at Willie. "I told you not to do anything."

Willie shrugged. "I was just releasing stress and tenderizing him before we put a real fire under ass."

Johnny snickered and regarded Nazari. "If you were a man, you'd stand up for what you believe in, not sit there like a coward. But you're not a man. You're a worthless piece of shit. You hide behind innocent Muslims and pretend to be an American... but you're not. If you want to see how real Americans act, here we are. But not you. *Not you.*"

Slowly, Nazari lifted his head, his eyes igniting with a fanaticism that Johnny had never seen before, despite his years downrange in the Middle East. Indeed, Johnny was right about him. Despite his American citizenship, Nazari had jihad pumping through his heart like radioactive iodine, and there was nothing some jarhead former "action guy" from North Carolina could do to change that. He would not talk. He would not help. He would not do a damned thing.

So Johnny put a bullet in his head.

Or at least he imagined doing so.

Willie cleared his throat. "I know what happens now, Johnny. It's all right. I'll take it from here."

"Roger that. But first, maybe we can talk to Pat. Get Billy involved. Those guys are all that and a bag of chips. They'll have him crying for mama by the time they're done."

"They won't get any farther than you," Nazari rasped.

"Oh, so we're ready to talk?"

"I have a message. *Al-Saif*, the sword, will pierce the heart of America, and she will bleed today like she's never bled before."

Johnny grabbed Nazari by the collar and spoke through his teeth. "I don't think so."

"You have me, you have a list, but there's nothing else you can do. You can't trust your government. You can't trust anyone."

"No, you're wrong. And I'll prove it."

Chapter Forty-Six

"I keep telling myself we did everything we could. I just wish it were more."

—Corey McKay (FBI interview, 23 December)

Nicholas Dresden stared vaguely at the morning newscast beaming from his seventy-inch television. As usual anchors from Fox News were commenting on the latest scandals casting dark clouds over the administration; however, Dresden was only half listening. A school bus's diesel engine thrummed in his ears as he imagined it carrying kindergarteners across the Gold Star Memorial Bridge, on their way to some field trip.

The concrete roadway quaked, great rifts appeared, and then... the road dropped and those children plummeted over the side. Little faces twisted in horror pressed against the bus's rear windows as they vanished into a foaming vortex of concrete and steel.

With a start, Dresden opened his eyes, caught his breath, and took a sip of his coffee, which had already gone cold.

Victoria strode into the living room with a haughty clack of heels. She struggled to secure an earring with French manicured nails. "What are you doing?"

Dresden kicked his bare feet onto the ottoman and pulled his robe more securely around his neck. He glanced perfunctorily in her direction.

"Are you sick?" she asked.

He shook his head. "No one's going to work today."

"You gave them off?"

With a sigh, he rose from the sofa and padded toward her.

"Nicholas, what's the matter with you? If you're in a mood again, I'm not prepared to deal with it this morning. I have a benefit to plan, and I need to be out of here in twenty minutes."

She never saw the kitchen knife jutting from his fist. She was far too busy with her damned earring, her damned benefit, her damned *life* to notice.

He wrapped one hand around her neck, as if to pull her in close for a kiss, then drove the knife up, into her heart. His face grew flush and his hand trembled. She gasped, eyeing him in utter disbelief until her expression twisted in agony, and she crumpled to the floor.

"It's better this way," he told her. "I didn't want you to see what I've done." He began to weep. "We had some good years, didn't we? And you deserved better. I'm sorry. I'm sorry I became one of them. I'm just like Beb Ahmose now. Just like him."

He drifted back to the sofa, where he removed the copy of *Wired* magazine featuring his interview. Beneath it sat an M1911A1 .45 caliber pistol that had belonged to his great grandfather Franz Dresden.

Wiping his bloody hands on his robe, he took a seat beside the pistol. He swallowed and wept again, just as his smartphone vibrated. Senecal's name flashed like a bad fortune on the screen. Dresden ignored it.

* * *

After a quick glance at his watch, Johnny addressed the others gathered around him outside the marina's office. "We have about fifty-six minutes."

Willie looked dejected. "Based on what Gatterton told you, all we can do is sit here because they can't vet our story in time. That's insane."

"Yeah, and we'll live with this for the rest of our lives," said Corey. "We knew this would happen. We have all the targets now, including the missing six. We know they're hitting that bridge up in Connecticut. We know the Hoover Dam's on the list. And now what? We don't even make a call? Is Plesner still running interference for them?"

Johnny raised his palms to calm them. "I have an idea. It might sound crazy, but just listen and keep an open mind. We joke about the Marine Corps Mafia, right? Once a Marine, always a Marine. That's no joke. And that's something we can count on right now."

* * *

In Charleston, South Carolina, textbook buyer and veteran Marine Norm Mack was eating a bowl of Cheerios at his daughter's house, where he was staying for the holidays. His smartphone beeped with a push notification from one of his social media websites. Norm was a member of several private groups for veteran Marines and their families, including one on LinkedIn with over 33,000 members. He thumbed his smartphone and began to read.

A moment later, the spoon slipped from his hand.

* * *

In Orlando, Florida, retired Marine Corps drill instructor Clive Gleeson was roped off in a maze of anxious travelers leading up to the Southwest Airlines ticket counter. Gleeson was a gray-haired black man nearing sixty but still a monster at six feet five, 275 pounds. His wife had passed earlier in the year, and he would have celebrated Christmas alone were it not for the invitation from his son Marcus. Gleeson was flying up to Delaware to spend the holidays with the boy and his family. During a phone call to confirm his travel arrangements, Gleeson received a push notification from the Marine Corps League, Orlando Facebook page.

What he read sent his heart racing, his gaze darting through the crowd.

* * *

In Jamaica, Queens, veteran Marine Richie Zahn, who had served in the First Gulf War when he was just eighteen, was up on the platform and waiting for his train into the city. He worked as a security guard in a Manhattan parking garage on West 25th Street. He was playing a golf game on his smartphone when one of his old Marine Corps buddies sent him a Twitter message. Zahn read the message, then, as instructed by his friend, he visited the 1st Marine Division Facebook page, with its 58,000 likes.

His mouth fell open as he read the latest post, then bounded for the nearest MTA police officer across the platform.

* * *

In Seattle, Washington, Irving Jones was lying in bed, trying to fall back asleep after the tenant upstairs had engaged in a shouting match with his girlfriend at 0300. Not yet thirty, Jones had been an Explosive Ordnance Disposal (EOD) tech who had served two tours in Afghanistan and had been medically discharged eight months prior. His legs were still back in Kabul, shredded across a minefield. His smartphone flashed, and he checked the notification.

"Oh, this is bullshit."

And then he received a Twitter message from a friend. A breath later, a text message came in from an old Marine Corps buddy.

Swearing aloud in disbelief, he switched on his light, grabbed the M9 Beretta from his nightstand, and dragged himself into his wheelchair.

* * *

In St. Paul, Minnesota, triage nurse Carmen Guzman had been staring all morning at the strange man seated in the emergency department waiting area. Admittedly, the overnight shift was a Halloween freak show 365 days a year, but this individual seemed dangerously odd, bundled up in a parka despite the well-heated room and clutching something in his pocket. As he rocked in his seat, he tossed awkward glances at her, and then he frowned at the front doors. Guzman, a veteran Marine who had spent four years as an 0111 administration specialist, had left the corps, gone to nursing school, and had graduated at the top of her class. She stayed in touch with her old friends from the Corps through a Facebook page called "U.S. Marine Corps Females," with over 9,000 likes and some particularly poignant messages from fellow vets. However, she had never come across a post like the one glowing on her phone's screen. She locked gazes with the odd man, and for a few seconds, she could almost see a blood-red aura glowing around his head.

As her breath escaped, she reached into a desk drawer for her purse.

* * *

In Chicago, Illinois firefighter/paramedic Victor Lugano was at the wheel of Ambulance 93 and backing into Engine Company 42's station when his phone beeped. He and his partner had just transferred an elderly patient with Chronic Obstructive Pulmonary Disease (COPD) from a nearby assisted living facility on North Wells Street to Northwestern Memorial Hospital. This was a call they had answered so many times that they could make the run with their eyes closed. Lugano stepped outside the garage and into the imposing shadows of the skyscrapers across the street. He read a text message from a friend who was a firefighter down in Alabama, an old buddy from the 11th Marine Expeditionary Unit. They had fought together in Iraq at the Battle of Najaf.

"Holy shit," Lugano muttered. "Is this for real?"

* * *

In Arlington, Virginia, Mr. Eric Gordon was en route to work at the J. Edgar Hoover Building in Washington, D.C. when he received a phone call from a former FBI colleague who had resigned to help his wife open a Karate school. Like his old friend, Gordon had spent two decades as a Reconnaissance Marine before retiring to accept a job with the Bureau, where he led an Evidence Response Team. After the brief but breath-robbing conversation, Gordon pulled over to the shoulder just as he reached the 14th Street Bridge, which was actually a complex of five bridges spanning the Potomac River to connect Arlington with D.C. He stepped out of his car and turned back toward the oncoming traffic. The broad, stern lines of the Pentagon swept below the rising sun.

Gordon squinted toward the far end of the bridge... and then he saw it.

* * *

In Los Angeles, California, Sergeant LaToya McBride was already pounding away on a treadmill inside the LA Fitness Club on Hollywood Boulevard. She arrived like clockwork each morning at 0430. After her workout, she would shower, change, have breakfast, then drive over to the Marine Corps Recruitment Station in Burbank, where she worked alongside two other recruiters. She had grown up in South Central LA and had enlisted in the Corps over a decade ago. She loved her job and was adept at relating to and recruiting young females unaware of the many occupational specialties available to them in the Corps. The flashing notification on her phone prompted her to slow the machine to a walk.

After reading it, she glanced around the gym, then sprinted for the locker room.

* * *

In Seadrift, Texas, Corey, Willie, and Josh were huddled around one of the computers back inside the marina's office, their wide-eyed expressions aglow as Corey rapped on the keyboard. Meanwhile, Johnny stepped outside to accept a call from Mark Gatterton.

"Johnny, I'm getting notifications and text messages... my phone won't stop ringing."

"I know, it's great, isn't it?"

"Are you insane?"

"Come on, son, we're Marines. We took action."

"But do you realize what you've done?"

"Didn't you read my note?"

"How could I miss it? You posted that message and your target list all over the web, on every social media site there is! It's going up on military forums... it's even trending on Twitter, for God's sake."

"That's right. I hope the damned president starts talking about it!"

"But Johnny, you don't understand—"

"Oh, I understand everything. We didn't have time for the government to vet our story, so I'm letting every Marine who ever served do it. Some of them won't believe me. That's okay. But those who are willing to take a chance on a brother will get down

388

to those locations and remain vigilant. I told them to be our eyes and ears. I told them to call the police, but if some of them put down these bastards before the cops get there, then so be it."

"That's what I'm worried about. This could turn into something—"

"What? Something great? If the Arabs can start a revolution with social media, then maybe we can stop a terrorist attack."

"I just... I can't believe you did this."

"It's pretty bold, I know. But it's not something we decided to do. It's something *we had* to do, despite the system and ourselves."

"I'm at a loss, man."

"No, you're not. We'll make it. Now look here, I'm not sure when we'll talk again, so... thank you. For everything. I mean it."

"I have a feeling you'll still need me when this is over—and I'll be there. Something's in the wind—judging from the call I took a half hour ago. Looks like I'm about to acquire a bigger stick."

"What do you mean? I thought you're too hot for the suits up on the hill."

"Yeah, well apparently today I'm not so controversial—at least according to Cathy Grantham. She's the White House's Counterterrorism advisor. She says I'm an asset. Go figure. And I might be in a position to keep your sorry ass out of the brig. Speaking of jail, what're you doing with Nazari?"

"It's better you don't know."

* * *

Nearly seventeen hundred miles north in Toronto, Edward Senecal tried once more to reach Nicholas Dresden. With a sigh of resignation, he left a voice message: "Nick, it's almost time, and I wanted to take this opportunity to applaud you for your intestinal fortitude, for your visionary leadership, and for—most of all—having the courage to help us lead the United States of America out of some very dark times. No matter what you see or hear, you must focus on the future. We've been friends for most of our lives, and that will *not* change. We'll make it through this together. I'm certain of it. Now, call me when you can. I'm here."

Senecal lowered himself into his home office chair, consulted his watch, then removed a framed photo from his desk. Emile wore his little league uniform and smiled. With a roar, Senecal sprang to his feet and hurled the frame across the room.

"Daddy?"

He faced the doorway. Celine was still in her pajamas and gaping at him. "Are you okay?"

Senecal scooped her into his arms and whispered, "I will be, sweetheart. I will be."

* * *

At precisely 7:56 a.m. Eastern Standard Time, Mirsab stepped onto the platform near track #2. Oddly enough, he felt insignificant among the thousands bustling through Jamaica Station. That feeling would not last long. He was speaking with his sister Zehna, who had moved to the northern platform at Woodside Station and was in position.

Before Mirsab could utter another word into his smartphone, all three westbound trains pulled into Jamaica with a deafening rumble and hiss, the platform reverberating beneath his feet. Zehna spoke again, but Mirsab heard only unintelligible garble.

"What is it?" he asked, raising his voice.

"I said I'm not afraid anymore. And I love you. *Allahu Akbar!*"

"Okay, yes. *Allahu Akbar!* I love you, too."

"Wait. I think someone sees me. It's a policeman. He's running toward me. I'm going to do it now! I'm going to do it—"

"Zehna! Zehna!"

The thundering footfalls of commuters exiting and boarding trains continued— even as the Day of Judgment began...

Mirsab remained there, his mouth falling open, the crowd not missing a beat and schooling around him to pass through cars and make connections.

Before he realized what was happening, people slowed to regard their smartphones. Some gathered in knots to share what they were reading, holding up their screens, gaping, a few covering their mouths, one teenaged girl beginning to cry.

At once, pandemonium struck as though a klaxon had sounded. Commuters stormed like a barbaric horde across the platform, screaming as they shouldered and shoved each other toward the exits, some falling to be trampled, others literally clinging to the travelers in front of them and dragged forward by the wave.

"They bombed Woodside," cried a man from somewhere in the crowd. "We could be next!"

Mirsab trembled. He tightened his grip on the detonator. His thumb drew circles over the firing button. He swallowed, his gaze flicking left and right as more infidels burst from the train cars and swooped by him.

And there he was, standing ramrod straight and immobile.

Scared out of his mind.

He craned his head to the left and saw an MTA officer about two cars ahead. The cop jogged toward him with a middle-aged man in tow. The gray-haired commuter

390

resembled ex-military with his crew cut and square jaw. The officer hollered for Mirsab to freeze and raise his hands. The commuter cursed and referred to him as "Mohammed."

A tremor ripped through Mirsab's torso, and for a moment he thought he had accidentally pushed the button. He wailed inside against the sharp claw of fear tightening around his neck. How could he be such a coward when Zehna had been so brave? How could he shame himself before Allah?

He gritted his teeth and glowered at the MTA officer and barking man beside him. He remembered his profound hatred for these infidels, for their Godless society, for what they had wrought upon the world. He would not be weak. He would fight like Zehna had. He would join her. After a deep breath, he screamed at the top of his lungs: "*Allahu Akbar!*"

"No!" the cop shouted—

But he, along with hundreds of others still on the platform, was too late. Mirsab lifted his head toward Allah and triggered the detonator.

Chapter Forty-Seven

*"Those heroes who stood up and answered the call didn't think
twice. They leaned toward the danger—because they had courage,
commitment, and sacrifice in their blood. Let me ask you something.
Would you answer the call?"*

—Johnny Johansen (FBI interview, 23 December)

Talib Wakim had piloted his houseboat close enough to the Hoover Dam so that he
could spy the four intake towers through a pair of binoculars. A half dozen or more
police cars had just pulled up along the top of the dam, their lights twinkling in the
predawn darkness like a string of crimson beads. Despite these new guests, Wakim
would trigger the detonation at exactly five a.m. Pacific Standard Time.

To fully appreciate the elegance of *Al-Saif's* plan, one must first understand the
Hoover Dam's operation. Water from Lake Mead entered via the four intake towers
and was channeled through four gradually narrowing tunnels or penstocks carrying
a rapid flow controlled by a sluicegate. These penstocks funneled the water down to
the powerhouse located at the bottom of the dam. The intakes provided a maximum
hydraulic head or water pressure of 590 feet, enabling the water to achieve a flow rate
of eighty-five mph. In effect, the entire flow of the Colorado River was channeled
through seventeen main turbines and two additional station-serviced turbines which
provided power for plant operations.

The water's force on the blades of the turbine spun a rotor—a series of magnets—
which was the moving portion of the generator where a magnetic field was created.
The stator was the stationary part of the generator comprised of coils of copper wire.

Electricity was produced as the magnets spun past the stationary wiring of the stator. This concept was discovered by scientist Michael Faraday in 1831 when he found that electricity could be created by rotating magnets within copper coils. The dam generated, on average, four billion kilowatt-hours of hydroelectric power each year for use in Nevada, Arizona, and California—enough to service more than two million people. Anything that inhibited the flow of water into the generators was a dire threat to the dam's electrical output.

And therein lay Wakim's avenue of approach.

As part of his research, he learned that in January 2007, quagga mussels were discovered at a marina in the Nevada area of Lake Meade and two other lakes on the Colorado River: Lake Mohave and Lake Havasu. An inspection funded by the Bureau of Reclamation found quagga mussel infestation in the Hoover Dam, the Davis Dam, and the Parker Dam. The mussels were roughly the size of an adult human's thumbnail and were known as aggressive biofoulers. Juvenile mussels would attach themselves to external and internal dam structures, grow in place, and begin to inhibit water flow. Acute fouling would occur when a large buildup of shells, alive or dead, became detached from upstream locations and flowed into piping systems to clog them.

It was this idea of a tiny mussel threatening a gargantuan structure that intrigued Wakim. If they could not destroy the Hoover Dam, then they would destroy its ability to produce electricity by shutting down the flow of water, which meant attacking the intake towers—towers that were much more vulnerable than the 660-foot-thick wall of the dam itself. At this very moment, each tower was surrounded by one thousand pounds of slurry explosives planted midway between the midlevel water intake gate and the lower water intake gate.

The type, placement, and quantity of these explosives had been confirmed by Nazari's own graduate students back at the University of Northern Iowa because he had provided them with an extra credit test problem:

An abandoned industrial chemical plant is about to be revitalized into a community college campus. Cost cutting includes refurbishing and repurposing the original buildings. The cooling tower adjacent to the main building is an eyesore, has no utilitarian value, and the tower construction materials have significant monetary scrap value.

Task: A) Demolish the tower without damaging any structures in the immediate vicinity.

B) Determine the type, placement, and quantity of explosives necessary to drop the tower within its own footprint.

Tower specifications: 395 feet high; diameter 82 feet at the base, 63 feet, 3 inches at the top; 93,674 cubic yards of concrete; and 1,756,000 pounds of reinforcing steel rods.

While Nazari and Wakim had already formulated solutions themselves, they marveled over the creativity of the answers put forth by the students and felt reassured by the many confirmations they received.

With a nod at the young divers around him, Wakim counted down and triggered four separate remotes.

One after another the towers erupted in a gurgling rumble similar to those produced by depth charges. The water churned and boiled into fountains and amorphous petals as Wakim closed his eyes and imagined what was happening beneath the surface:

Inside each tower was an upper and lower cylindrical water intake gate that was thirty-two feet in diameter and eleven feet high. The upper gate was located about midway down the tower. Each gate weighed 1,473,000 lbs. At this very moment, the upper gate had been blown apart and was descending with tons of concrete rubble. That gate would crash onto the lower gate, destroy it, and plug the mouth of the intake tunnel at the base of the tower.

When he opened his eyes, the concrete walkways that connected the towers in pairs to the dam proper were breaking apart like stale bread, sections tumbling with an unreal slowness that suggested zero gravity. One by one, the towers plunged straight down to remain in their own footprints, as though some unseen giant were pulling blocks in four distinct games of Jenga.

Lights around the dam flickered and died, while the water continued to foam and bubble with swells. Wakim and his men cheered and thanked Allah for granting them the courage to fight in his cause and complete their mission.

They had effectively shut down the Hoover Dam for years, and the loss of power in the region would be catastrophic to the economy.

Wakim smiled, bowed his head toward the young men, then activated another detonator.

Those police officers on the dam would observe a small explosion in the distance, a rather inconsequential camera flash and faint timpani roll when compared to the destruction before them.

By sunrise, the flotsam of fiberglass and flesh would span the lake, while Wakim and his dive crews would rejoice at Allah's shoulders.

* * *

While en route to the Bright Tree Learning Center cited on the target list and located only ten short minutes from his daughter's home in Charleston, South Carolina, Norm Mack called the police and issued a bomb threat. By the time he arrived at the daycare, administrators and teachers were escorting children out of the building and across the parking lot toward a strip mall located on the other side of a tree-lined median.

Norm had "borrowed" his son-in-law's Sig Sauer P227, a .45 caliber pistol with a full magazine of expanding critical defense rounds coined as "manstoppers" in the marketplace of self-defense. He shoved the gun into the deep pocket of his winter coat, then exited his rental car. Several parents were pulling up and hollering toward the groups, their expressions twisting with confusion.

An SUV parked beside Norm's rental car. A dark complexioned man climbed out. He was dressed similarly to Norm in a heavy down jacket. Was this the bomber? Norm tensed, about to confront the man, a capacity for violence never far from his heart, born during the Vietnam war and smoldering for decades.

He turned, opened his mouth, then hesitated. His target opened a rear door and unbuckled a toddler from her car seat. He carried the little girl toward the crowd, crying, "What's happening?"

Norm swore under his breath.

Two police cars with lights flashing rumbled into the parking area, and behind them came a black BMW assumedly driven by another parent en route to drop off a child. As the police split up, one unit heading toward the median, the other parking in a handicap spot near the front doors, the BMW stopped in the middle of the lot.

The car door flung open, and a Middle Eastern woman with a black burka masking all but her eyes bailed out of the BMW and jogged toward the crowd, waving.

But she was only waving one hand.

Norm squinted toward her other hand, where something red flashed near her thumb and a wire snaked up the side of her wrist and into her jacket sleeve.

He tugged the .45 from his pocket, lifted his arms, and took aim at the woman, even as a man from somewhere behind shouted, "He's got a gun!"

From the hollows of Norm's heart came a whisper: *what if you're wrong? What if you're seeing things? Are you prepared to kill an innocent woman?*

But he could not be wrong—because it had all been preordained: his life after the war, his becoming a book buyer, his befriending Daniel Johansen, and, finally, his meeting up with Johnny and informing him of Daniel's suspicious activity. Johnny had gone way up river and returned with a staggering truth and a monumental call to action. His was a call that no Marine could ignore, and this woman must be the bomber because there were no coincidences in this world. God had allowed Norm Mack to survive the Battle of Lost Patrol and live out his life for a reason—so that he could face this woman, knowing what he had to do, acting without hesitation, understanding that the evil in her heart was as cold and hard as the gun in his hands, and that her desire was to murder as many young families as possible, all in the cause of Allah.

Had Norm not made his call, she would have walked into the daycare and blown herself to smithereens, taking countless young lives with her. Now she was exploiting the chaos to pursue her prey and join the crowd, where she could *still* carry out her heinous act—and for just a second Norm imagined a flurry of tiny severed limbs tumbling end over end through the air, pink flesh glowing in an undulating blast wave.

But that would not happen. This bitch was unaware that Norm Mack, 1st Battalion, 9th Marines, 'D' Company, 1st Platoon, along with his brothers and sisters across the United States, had returned to their posts.

"Hey!" Norm shouted.

The woman turned—

And the malevolence in her eyes distorted the air between them, the periphery bleeding away so that Norm saw only her in his weapon's sights. He had never been more sure about taking a shot in his entire life.

He squeezed the trigger, his first round a surprise, as it should be. He caught her in the neck, the wound masked by her burka. His second shot hammered her left cheek, kicking her back, onto the asphalt.

Bending his arm and ducking, Norm winced, expecting her to detonate and take him with her. But her hand had fallen away, the detonator hanging limply from her sleeve. Adrenaline carried him to her, where he dropped to his knees so he could unzip her jacket. The flaps fell back, but not before the police wrenched him up and away.

A hush fell over the parents behind him as they gaped at the suicide vest strapped to the woman's chest.

The dark complexioned man clutching his daughter stared in wonder. "There are bombs going off all over the country right now! She was another one. She was going to kill us all." He glanced more emphatically at Norm. "You saved us—but how did you know?"

* * *

With anchors from CNN reporting explosions at the Woodside and Jamaica Railroad Stations in New York, nearly everyone on line at the Southwest Airlines ticket counter was either glued to a phone or the flat screen televisions—

Everyone except the young man standing a few rows back from Clive Gleeson, the one he had been eyeing for the past minute. As a drill instructor for over two decades, Gleeson had honed his ability to read the unseen, untapped potential—or lack thereof—in young men who desired to become Marines. He could sense from a man's demeanor, his comportment, and even his gait how difficult it would be to transform him into a first class warrior, an instrument of destruction. Was he a loner or a team player? Did he understand the entirety of his training? Did he have a high threshold for pain? Could he lead other men to their deaths?

Sometimes the answers were obvious. Sometimes not. But Gleeson was a master at reading the twitches on faces, the tremors in fingers, the tightly shut lips of men holding their breaths. The slightest quaver in a recruit's tone set off alarms. In that regard, Gleeson was an unusual man jammed into an atypical crowd of holiday shoppers—

And one jihadi.

Since he was a Marine, Gleeson was incapable of being shy, and so he drifted out of line, circled around the ropes, and slipped up behind the young man in question. Why was this kid's left hand tucked up into his sleeve? Where was his phone? Was he trembling?

"*As-salam alaikum*," Gleeson said, recalling his Arabic.

The young man whirled to face him, his eyes bugging out.

Gleeson seized him by the neck with one hand, while patting down the kid's chest with the other. He felt the vest. The explosives.

The kid glanced down at his own hand, which had popped out of his jacket to reveal the detonator.

Gleeson raised his voice. "Let's see if your bomb can get past me—one big, fat motherfucka Marine!"

With that, Gleeson tackled the kid to the floor, smothering him, even as the son of a bitch jammed down the button.

* * *

As Carmen Guzman opened her purse, she blamed the institution for putting her in this position. St. Paul's administrators had recently cut back on the number of off duty cops they had hired and was now providing a local security force whose qualifications, experience, and reliability were sorely lacking. The emergency waiting area's lone guard was currently outside, sneaking another cigarette, while the flat screens mounted from the ceiling flashed with news of bombings in New York, Arizona, and Orlando.

The awkward man she had been studying all morning bolted to his feet and lifted his arms, with something clenched in his right hand. His crazed expression drained the color from his face. He opened his mouth, as if to shout something—

But Guzman was ready. The compact .45 she kept in her purse was tight in her hands, and the 4.4 pounds of single action trigger pull was simple to manage. Her first shot caught him in the chin, and her second struck his head as he was falling backward.

She had given him no time to announce how great his God was. She had claimed that time for herself so that she could make a statement on behalf of the United States Marine Corps, whose officers and enlisted had trained and inspired her.

As her ears rang loudly from the gunshots, the other nurses began screaming, and the useless security guard from outside came stumbling through the doors.

"You shot him?" the guard cried.

Trembling, Guzman lowered her arms and grimaced from the smoke wafting into her face. The guard rushed to the man, spotted the detonator hanging out of his coat, then glanced back. "He's wearing a bomb!"

"I know," Guzman said, her voice barely above a whisper.

One of her colleagues arrived at her shoulder. "You brought a gun to work? They'll fire you now."

Guzman cocked a brow and shivered. "You think I care?"

* * *

Mentu Sekani had ordered his men to anchor their skiffs directly below the northbound span of the Gold Star Memorial Bridge in New London, Connecticut. The men understood the reason behind this order, and not a single diver had borne even the slightest misgiving in his eyes. Above them, the traffic had thickened because the speed limit had dropped from 55 to 25 mph due to icing on the roadway. Sekani estimated that at least six hundred commuters were present when he gave the order to detonate the charges.

The explosions came in a rolling, baritone rumble that ripped up and through their boats, shaking the gunwales. The water heaved, and the footings of the southbound trusses splintered apart, rupturing from beneath the surface. Steel trusses creaked and squealed; rivets popped free and clanged; and great fissures appeared in the concrete beneath the roadway. Sections of bridge between the crumbling footings broke off and plummeted toward the river. Cars, commercial vans, and tractor trailers flew off both ends. Reinforcing beams swung like mangled limbs, slicing through clouds of smoke and jets of salty water. Even as these sections smacked into the river in a chain of echoing booms, chaotic cracks of thunder emanated from the footings of the northbound span. These second charges resounded like the misfiring beats of a diseased heart until the footings shook, cracked, began to disintegrate, then gave way.

At the same time, the waves produced by the collapse of the southbound span, along with the continued plunging of debris, swept over Sekani and his men. It was then that his head lolled back and he raised his arms. He shouted to Allah as the tons of concrete, rebar, and steel trusses above them began breaking free.

His vision narrowed, as though he were staring through a telescope, and in those final few seconds, as the roadway hung by gossamers, he rejoiced. They had taken out both spans of the bridge, yes, but they had accomplished something even greater. They had issued a bold statement to America's military, most notably its Naval forces.

Al-Saif's intel indicated that ten Los Angeles Class and six Virginia Class nuclear submarines called New London, Connecticut home. At any given time half of the assigned submarines were deployed. Several were on call to the U.S. Naval Submarine School for student training.

With Christmas fast approaching there were eight subs in port along with an Ohio Class, *USS Michigan*, SSGN-727 awaiting dry dock space at the nearby Electric Boat Shipyard. *Michigan*, a former Fleet Ballistic Missile submarine had been converted to a cruise missile platform carrying 145 Tomahawk Cruise Missiles, the equivalent of what was typically deployed in a surface battle group.

Also in port was a holiday visitor, the Astute Class, *HMS Ambush*, S-120, a nuclear fleet submarine of the Royal Navy.

What the skippers of those submarines would learn in the hours to come was that the bridge collapse had cut off passage to and from Long Island Sound and the Atlantic Ocean beyond.

Their boats were trapped.

Al-Saif had just proven that even the greatest submarine fleet in the world was not impervious to attack. If someone would have told the President of the United States that jihadis could render immobile a collection of nuclear submarines in one fell swoop, he would have grinned and snorted. He would not be smiling now.

With gooseflesh fanning across his shoulders and his heart swelling over the magnificence and audacity of their attack, Senaki raised his palms toward that gargantuan slab of concrete now floating above him. From the corners of the slab came sedans and SUVs and motorcycles soaring through the air like birds flying south for the winter. Shadows lengthened across the waves, and before Senaki could gasp, the world came down on him.

Chapter Forty-Eight

"Old Mad Dog Mattis said there is no better friend, no worse enemy than a United States Marine. Today, everyone knows that, especially those bastards trying to kill us."

—Willie Parente (FBI interview, 23 December)

The white, nondescript truck's rear axle was practically dragging along the pavement as it started across the 14th Street Bridge in Arlington. Eric Gordon had confronted similar trucks while downrange in Iraq and Afghanistan, and these were, more often than not, jammed with explosives intended to maim and/or kill as many coalition forces as possible.

As the vehicle slowed in heavy traffic, drawing within twenty meters, Gordon locked gazes with the bearded driver, who tugged on the brim of his ball cap to better shield his cherubic face.

Seeing that the man was just getting onto the bridge and probably not in his intended strike zone, Gordon began waving his hands, crossing between cars as he did so. Traffic slowed to a standstill as he motioned for the driver to lower his window. The man drew back his head but complied.

"Hey, there!" Gordon shouted. "Maybe you can help me out. What do you got in the truck?"

The driver's gaze registered alarm. He turned to the passenger's seat.

Gordon thrust himself at the truck, grabbing the side view mirror with one hand to hoist himself up. He launched himself in through the open window while reaching across the driver's lap. On the seat were a remote detonator and a pistol—a 9mm judging from the size of the barrel.

The jihadi reached the pistol before Gordon could, but Gordon locked a hand around the man's wrist as the gun went off, the round blasting through the windshield, the boom stinging Gordon's ears as he wriggled himself across the door and got his other hand on the weapon.

Using the gun for leverage, Gordon reared back with his free hand and punched the jihadi in the right eye. The blow sent his head twisting, his grip loosening, and Gordon wrenched the pistol from his hands.

However, before Gordon could turn the gun around, the jihadi jammed down the accelerator and spun the wheel. He smashed around the sedan in front of them, the car's bumper peeling off as they plowed between lanes. Side mirrors snapped off and car doors crunched as the truck bulldozed toward the center of the bridge.

Gordon dropped the gun and went for the detonator, but again, the jihadi was faster and snatched it into his hand.

Before he could release the detonator's safety toggle, Gordon elbowed the driver in the face then clutched the wheel and rolled it to the right.

Aided by its extreme weight, the truck traversed the sidewalk and crashed into the concrete barrier wall with such force that it broke through.

The cabin grew quiet as wheels spun in midair and the truck's hood tipped down toward the Potomac. Next came the cold rush of air through the open window as the jihadi's detonator flashed red.

Eric Gordon did not care if those commuters on the bridge understood what he was doing. He did not care if they shared his political views or his religion; he was not interested if they supported the troops or if they were completely apathetic about their nation's place in the world. He was giving his life for them without question because he was a Marine and held to the highest standards. His dedication, commitment, and faith in the ideals of the United States of America were all the motivation he needed. He did not expect a thank you, a posthumous hero's parade, or any mention of his name in a news report. Protecting his family and his fellow Americans had always been his mission, and he would do so until his last breath. As the recon creed so boldly stated, he would *maintain the tremendous reputation of those who had come before him.*

The truck never reached the water, and Gordon was thankful for that. He preferred summer over winter, and the extreme heat that engulfed the cab was far more welcome.

Up ahead, shimmering out of the darkness, came a group of men. As he drew closer, he cursed with joy and laughed aloud. Every Marine Corps friend he had lost downrange stood there in full combat gear, waving him on and smiling from ear to ear. As Gordon reached them, he glanced down at his body; he was no longer made of flesh but of something else, something without limitations, something that connected them forever.

* * *

Achmed was behind the wheel of a rental car and had followed the *Blue Bayou Catfish* truck all the way to Chalmette. As planned, the truck's driver had taken them to the unguarded parking lot near the ExonMobil Refinery, where they had matter-of-factly lifted the truck's side panels and set up.

The tripods held fast as they began their attack on the refinery's processing center and storage tanks. Missiles tore away with a hollow roar, trailing exhaust clouds that unspooled across the facility like spider webs.

One after another, the tanks burst apart, hurtling themselves across the yard to trigger secondary explosions that ignited the early morning sky. The flames waltzed with each other, reminding Achmed of Kuwait's burning oil fields during the first Gulf War.

A video texted to him from the other team confirmed they, too, were having great success at the Phillips66 Alliance Refinery. They reported that two police cars had rolled up but were summarily dispatched in dramatic fashion. The team had brought one of their launchers to bear on the units and obliterated them and their occupants.

Because the refineries were infrastructure targets and not time-specific, Achmed had chosen to strike them by eight a.m. EST so that they could be added to the list of locations under attack and further add to the widespread panic and fear across the nation. Both refineries were now suffering catastrophic damage due to secondary explosions and unquenchable fires. More importantly, both were vital in the production of domestic gasoline. The impact on domestic transportation would be immeasurable. Even with oil reserves readily available in the local area, the loss of refining ability would contribute to the country's economic disaster.

After his ExonMobil team launched their last missile and checked in with him, Achmed threw his car in gear and thumbed a remote.

The *Blue Bayou Catfish* detonated in a spectacular fireball that lifted the rear wheels several feet in the air. With a carcass aglow in flames beneath cloaks of smoke, the truck would sit there and continue to burn, its tires melting across the lot.

Whispering his thanks to Allah and tightening his grip on the wheel, Achmed started off for the Phillips66 Alliance Refinery, so he could martyr that team.

In a moment of weakness, he wished he could remain alive so he could watch the birth of this glorious caliphate. All the other stars in the morning sky would switch off in deference to a lone star and a crescent moon. Yes, once America was brought to her knees, the other democracies would follow, and an Islamic state would rule the world.

* * *

Victor Lugano had become a believer in a matter of sixty seconds. He had been standing there outside his Chicago firehouse, reading that text message from his friend in Alabama, when two of his fellow firefighters joined him outside to share the news: explosions had occurred in New York, Orlando, Arizona, and there were reports of oil refinery fires in Louisiana, with more bombings happening around the country. The nation was under attack. Lugano had gone to a Marine Corps Facebook page as his friend had instructed and had read the target list. GPS coordinates in Chicago placed an attack on the corner of West Grand Ave and North State Street—

Which was right around the corner from his firehouse. He and his colleagues had taken off running, while a third remained behind to call law enforcement.

They stood there now, just outside the Rock Bottom Brewery, staring across the intersection at the towering Hilton Garden Inn and the bus stop to their immediate right. Walled in by skyscrapers and with rush hour traffic beginning to mount, the corner buzzed with activity, and a bomber—be he on foot or in a car—would be difficult to spot. Lugano paced up and down the corner, scrutinizing the throngs of pedestrians who came down the block. About ten commuters huddled beneath the glass awning at the bus stop, trying to avoid the wind. Lugano motioned to his buddies that they should cross the street for a better look.

Before they could move, those at the bus stop turned their gazes skyward like extras in a *Superman* movie. Several pointed.

From the gray morning sky came an improbable sight: a parachutist descending toward the street corner.

But this was not just any parachutist. He was dressed in a Santa Claus suit replete with fat belly and long, white beard.

"Must be some radio station publicity stunt," said one of Lugano's buddies.

The floating Santa deftly maneuvered himself toward the road, just as a bus, CTA Route #65, came rolling up West Grand, toward the Redline stop at the northeast corner of State. Santa swooped behind the bus and touched down with practiced ease. He detached his chute and jogged after the bus as it stopped at the corner. As he ran, a curly black beard shone beneath the fake one, while his belly bounced with a suspicious rhythm of its own. He clenched something in his right hand.

This was no radio station publicity stunt. This was a statement being made by jihadis who deemed Santa Claus yet another symbol of American greed and corruption.

Although Victor Lugano was no law enforcement officer and unarmed, he had something else in his possession that, at this moment, could be more powerful than a pistol or a shotgun. He had the training and mindset of a United States Marine.

Without a second's hesitation, he bounded after the man, taking a flying leap and tackling the jihadi from behind just as he reached the back of the bus. Lugano hit the ground, then forced the man onto his back, where he straddled him, ripped off his fake beard, then tore open his jacket, which had been fastened with safety pins.

Haji Claus had enough C4 to take out the bus and most of the street corner.

Lugano's gaze flicked to the man's hand, where he clutched the detonator, his thumb heavy on the trigger.

People at the bus stop screamed as they caught sight of the man's chest. Lugano's colleagues were hollering and rushing up behind him. Diesel exhaust blasted into his face as he glared back at this scumbag jihadi, who began to say something—

But Lugano interrupted him with a curse and battle cry, "Oorah!" He smothered the jihadi to protect those around him.

Something *clicked*. Lugano gritted his teeth and accepted the explosion.

* * *

In Indianapolis, Indiana, Chemistry teacher Michael Bhardwaj stood before his crying and breathless homeroom students at North Central High. "Ladies and gentlemen, you heard the announcement. We're on lockdown."

"Mr. Bhardwaj?"

The young lady with her hand raised had swollen eyes and bright red hair. Her name was Allison Smythe, and she was in Bhardwaj's fifth period class. She was an excellent student, well-read, and polite to a fault.

"What is it?"

"Are we going to die?"

Bhardwaj lowered his head. At that second he realized he could not bear the truth of what he was and what he wore beneath his loose-fitting sweater. He had lied to himself about his inner strength, about his dedication to Allah and the cause. He had fallen in love with his wife, his children. He had fallen in love with America. Those feelings were real. He could not turn his back on freedom—but neither could he turn his back on *Al-Saif.*

He cleared his throat and answered the girl, "We'll all be okay. Now all of you wait here. I'll be right back."

Out in the hallway, he vomited across a row of lockers. A security guard at the far end shouted, "Stay in your classroom!"

Returning an awkward wave, Bhardwaj sprinted in the opposite direction, toward doors at the end of the hall. While locked from the inside, he could still slam past the broad handles and escape.

The cold air seized him as he stole his way around the building, toward the parking lot and 86th Street, where the dates for winter break were glowing on the electronic sign. Five or six police cars were rolling into the lot, and as Bhardwaj turned back, he spotted the security guard bounding after him.

With no where else to run, Bhardwaj started for the school sign, beating a wide path and drawing the attention of officers as they exited their vehicles.

By the time he neared the sign, he was heaving and panting, his nose already running in the cold, his eyes burning.

Mr. Michal Bhardwaj—model American citizen, gifted teacher, and pillar of his community—could hide no more.

He was thirty-eight years old.

The police officers rushed toward him with guns drawn.

"Stay back," he shouted, lifting his sweater to show them his vest.

As if controlled by a switch, the officers broke off their pursuit to remain about fifteen meters away. A few lifted their palms to show they respected his space.

Bhardwaj could not allow himself to be taken into custody. He had failed *Al-Saif,* and if he remained alive, they would kill him and punish his family.

"I don't want to hurt anyone," he shouted, his voice cracking.

He thought of Tommy and Elizabeth and the expressions on their faces when they heard the news. His eyes blurred even more with tears.

Before he could break down any further, he glanced at the sign, the school, then up at the American flag flapping in the cold breeze. He closed his eyes and surrendered to the inevitable.

* * *

At the marina in Seadrift, Texas, Dr. Mohammad Nazari was eavesdropping on the streaming news reports coming in over the Marines' computer. During the last five minutes, he had pieced together an unsettling truth: Johnny Johansen had published the target list on the internet and Marines were rising to the occasion to thwart Nazari's cells. However, in many cases they were failing, as they had at the Hoover Dam and now at the North Anna Nuclear Power Plant northwest of Richmond, Virginia.

According to CNN, a lone surviving Information Center employee told authorities that a semitrailer and three pickup trucks, all advertising an exhibit of the Vietnam Traveling Wall, pulled into the Information Center parking lot at 0750. A half-dozen men stormed the center and attacked the five employees.

During the initial barrage of gunfire, the office manager was able to hit the panic button before being struck down. Four security vehicles were dispatched from the station admin building three miles from the center and, upon arrival at the scene, confronted three ATVs in the wooded area midway between the Information Center and the Spent Nuclear Fuel Storage facility roughly 1,700 feet due east. The security team was taken under gunfire even as two of the ATVs launched Baktar-Shikan missiles at the twenty-seven spent fuel storage casks sitting in the open on a concrete slab. Additional missiles were fired into the casks. The exact number was not yet known.

A long distance inspection with binoculars and rifle scopes already revealed that at least eight of the casks had been breached. Smoke and flames were obscuring a detailed inspection. Highly radioactive materials were now exposed to the atmosphere. The contamination plume was drifting northeast toward Chesapeake Bay to create a fifty mile or more contamination zone affecting over two million people, according to experts chiming in via Skype.

No lowly ex-Marine on his way to a minimum wage job at the auto parts store could have stopped that.

For the attacks on the North Anna casks and the water treatment plants supplying Palo Verde, Nazari had relied heavily on intelligence he had received from Zahir Al-Jabiri, a Muslim-American turned jihadist. Between 2002 and 2008, Al-Jabiri worked at five different nuclear power stations: Limerick, Peach Bottom, and Three Mile Island in Pennsylvania; Salem Hope Creek in New Jersey; and Calvert Cliffs on Maryland's Chesapeake Bay. During his six years of employment he had "unescorted access" to the interior of all five plants.

Ironically, Al-Jabiri was a self-declared al-Qaeda sympathizer who spoke openly of his jihadist beliefs, referring to his fellow non-Muslim workers as "infidels." His extremist views were well known within the plants, yet no one contacted the Nuclear Regulatory Commission or the FBI because they wrote him off as a disgruntled nerd and never took his jihadi claims seriously. Al-Jabiri correctly discerned that the NRC holds the Federal Government responsible for the defense of nuclear power plants, not the plants themselves or the rent-a-cops they hire. Once a member of al-Shabaab, the jihadi group based in Somali, he was captured in Yemen in 2010. While in custody he murdered two police guards and was held in Yemen's Sana'a prison until April, 2014 when he disappeared, or, rather, was rescued by an *Al-Saif* cell.

Nazari's many conversations with Al-Jabiri allowed him to analyze and expose two key vulnerabilities of American nuclear power plants: their on-site spent fuel storage and their coolant water resources. Instead of hitting them head-on (which was far more difficult and required much greater resources), they had found chinks in the infidels' armor through which they had quietly slipped their blade.

Closing his eyes, Nazari pricked up his ears and listened to yet another news report coming in from Memphis, Tennessee.

* * *

There were supposed to be only six targets.

However, as Nicholas Dresden sat before his television, his hands still covered in his wife's blood, the bombings grew in number and size.

His partner Edward Senecal and men like Charles Plesner who had arranged their communications with the terrorists had double-crossed them. Dresden understood they had made a deal with the devil, and he had suspected that the devil would deceive them. He should have withdrawn his support. If it came down to it, he could have had Senecal murdered. But he had been too afraid to act, to take a risk, to bet on himself. He had bowed to Senecal's threats and had lived in denial—until now.

Fox News reported that FedEx's World Hub at the Memphis International Airport had just been attacked. This particular target had been Senecal's brainchild:

An American jihadist flying a Cessna 182T with a full fuel tank had lifted off from Isle-A-Port, a grassy field with virtually no security and located just seven nautical miles northwest of the hub. The plane had a useful load capacity of 1,140 pounds. The pilot weighed approximately 150 pounds. The other 900 pounds were dedicated to explosives provided by UXD.

Flight time to the facility had been three to five minutes. The pilot never flew above 500 feet or 110 mph. There was no time for any countermeasure.

Footage showed pervasive fires spreading throughout the complex. As those images flashed across the screen, the anchor rattled off statistics. She said it took over twenty minutes to drive from one end of the world hub to the other and that the facility had approximately 180 aircraft gates and roughly 15 million square feet of sort space. She reported that over 3,500 day sort associates and 3,000 support personnel had been working inside at the time the plane crashed into the roof of one building.

Inside were over forty miles of conveyor belts and state-of-the-art automated package-sorting systems that processed over 500,000 packages per hour.

The entire hub was being evacuated, some conveyors partially destroyed and shut down, the fires still raging out of control as first responders arrived at the scene. Of course, this was the busiest time of year for the company, and an attack like this struck an enormous blow to their business. More importantly, the attack would remind the American public of 9/11, which was why Senecal had insisted upon at least one act perpetrated by aircraft.

While the idea of collateral damage had always been at the fore of Dresden's mind, he could barely comprehend what was happening now:

A white box truck had just driven straight through the doors of the Family History Library in Salt Lake City, Utah. The truck had exploded, leveling the entire facility and shattering windows over a quarter mile away. Anchors speculated that the jihadis had chosen the library because it was an easy to strike religious target. Mormons took their family history very seriously. They believed that by tracking down and identifying earlier family members, prior to Joseph Smith and the founding of The Church of Jesus Christ of Latter-Day Saints, they could baptize their dead relatives and assure them a place in heaven and a huge family reunion.

More footage taken by pedestrian smartphones came in: a Santa Claus exploding in Chicago; the bridge collapse in New London as captured by the smartphone of a delivery driver snarled in traffic; and a shooting at a daycare facility in Charleston.

A daycare, for God's sake.

Dresden glanced over at his wife, lying there, a mannequin who could no longer nag him to get up and wash his hands. Back on the TV, bloody children were being evacuated from the airport in Orlando. A report came in of an explosion at a high school in Indianapolis. At a Wal-Mart in Atlanta, a veteran Marine had shot and killed a suicide bomber seconds before he detonated at the returns desk.

Lowering his head, Dresden reached for his great grandfather's pistol. At least his suicide would communicate his regret. He had never lived in the gray twilight, and so it was fitting that his life and death would become infamous. In contrast, Senecal would thrust out his chest in defiance and cackle at the authorities.

Beb Ahmose had been right. This war would never end, but at least now, Dresden could withdraw from the battlefield.

If there was a God, an eternity, he was ready to make his case or accept his punishment. Yes, old age had weakened his resolve, but he had dared mighty things... and now... one last feat.

Chapter Forty-Nine

"It started with Marines, but then every branch got involved. We heard about those Army officers who stopped that train bombing in Maryland and that kid from the Air Force Academy who cut off the bomber near the Denver Federal Center. We also saw those two sailors in Honolulu who saved that hotel. Once again, we were all just Americans."

—Josh Eriksson (FBI interview, 23 December)

Johnny and the others huddled around Corey's computer, watching streaming video of a field reporter from KTRK standing somewhere outside the Port of Houston. Behind her, heavy black smoke and tongues of fire rose as though from a battlefield. Her voice cracked as she described the scene. Crew members aboard the container ship *Mawsitsit* had set up "some kind of missile systems" on deck and were firing at the tank farm across the port. Police and fire assets were already on the scene, as well as marine patrol units from the Harris County Sheriff's Office. Local and government agencies were being coordinated through the Houston Area Maritime Operations Center (HAMOC). Coast Guard and Customs and Border Protection personnel were also involved. Automatic weapons fire was being traded between the ship and units at the Bayport Container Piers and sheriff's deputies in the water near berth T5. The situation remained fluid.

"That tank farm wasn't on the list," said Josh.

Willie shrugged. "Target of opportunity?"

Corey lifted an index finger. "Narco subs have a limited range. You know what I'm thinking? Maybe that sub was brought in aboard the container ship. They dropped it off somewhere out in the Gulf. Maybe our boy was going to escape in the sub, and they would rendezvous with another ship while heading down to South America."

Johnny crossed the office and leaned over Nazari. "We're right about that, aren't we? Doesn't matter, though. When this is over, we'll be nothing but stronger."

Nazari smiled through his swollen face.

Cursing, Johnny went back outside to answer a call from Billy Brandt, who was still in Riyadh. "Hey, Johnny. Long time. Pat's told me everything you need, and I got you covered on my end. They want me to text you transit instructions."

"Thanks, man."

"I can't believe we're in the middle of this."

"I know, it's crazy. Say a prayer."

"I will. Let me know if you need anything else."

"Roger that."

Back inside, Johnny cursed and gritted his teeth over more news reports. Multiple explosions were reported at the East Los Angeles Interchange, where four of the city's freeways converged into one of the most heavily trafficked junctions in the world. Johnny had hoped highway patrol and other law enforcement personnel would be alerted in time, and now his heart broke as he listened to a KTLA reporter at the scene. Eyewitness accounts suggested that at least two truck bombs were involved, along with evidence that more explosives were already in place beneath spans crossing the Los Angeles River. Multi-car crashes were mounting, along with the death toll as drivers half asleep and unaware of the dangers ahead drove into oblivion. Nearly half a million commuters would be affected by the attack.

Ironically, the interchange was named after Private First Class Eugene A. Obregon, a U.S. Marine who had received the Medal of Honor for his sacrifice during the Korean War. Disrupting the busy interchange had been the jihadis' main goal, yes, but their deranged leader knew this artery held special significance for America's military veterans.

A text message flashed on Johnny's phone. "Gentlemen? Let's roll." He regarded Nazari. "When the Feds are done with you, they'll send you back to Allah—one piece at a time."

"I don't think so, Johnny. The network is huge. You think capturing me brings it down? I'd keep watching my back. Forget about easy day, no drama. That's all over for you now."

Johnny grabbed Nazari by the throat and dragged him to his feet.

* * *

By 0510 the LA Fitness on Hollywood Boulevard was packed with early morning gym rats who had begun strutting on cardio machines or lifting weights under the grunts and guidance of personal trainers.

But then, as the word spread, people broke off from their workouts to simply watch, in awe, in fear, their gazes held trance-like by giant TVs flashing carnage from multiple cities across the nation.

Sergeant LaToya McBride had fled to the locker room, where she had retrieved her Glock 19 compact pistol from a workout duffel. She carried the weapon at all times, especially after those gang bangers had come into her recruiting center last month and had threatened to kill her if their buddy could not enlist in the Marine Corps.

The target list had the club's address but did not specify a name, so with her holstered weapon tucked into the waistband of her shorts, she jogged toward the main entrance and outside, where she rushed down the staircase and onto the Hollywood Walk of Fame. Terrazzo and brass stars stretched away toward a CVS Pharmacy on the right and a DSW Shoes outlet on the left. A ghostly calm had settled over the boulevard. Palm trees lining the curbs swayed between streetlights. She swore she heard a whisper within the palm fronds, the sound of her father's voice... Across the street lay a parking garage for the Roosevelt Hotel, a sandwich shop, a little Pizza place, and the Hollywood Liquor Store.

Any one of those establishments could be a target. And what if the GPS coordinates were wrong? Perhaps terrorists were planning to blow up the hotel...

A taxi pulled up and out rushed a short, heavyset man wearing a sweatshirt and baggy workout pants. He had a face full of stubble and eyed her suspiciously as he paid the driver.

"Something wrong?" he asked.

"You haven't heard? We're under attack. Bombings all over the country. It's happening right now."

"Really?" He nervously thumbed his smartphone. "Holy shit. On TV inside?"

"Yeah."

He hit the stairs with remarkable speed, as though he were not as heavy as his chest suggested. She rushed up behind him as he slammed past the glass doors.

Inside, the entire club had fallen silent, the TVs switched off.

And there, down below, in the center of the first floor, stood a man at least six feet five, with a curly beard trimmed to the proper fist-length. He had spread his arms, tossed back his head, and was in the middle of a diatribe, his voice echoing up to the second floor balcony of treadmills. His chest, covered in explosives, rose and fell as he spoke of Allah's vengeance and the punishment all infidels must now endure, especially the gays, lesbians, bisexuals, and transgender "abominations" who frequented the club.

"We're all dead!" someone hollered from behind her. "He'll press the button! We're all dead!"

"Shut up!" the bomber cried. "And no one move! No one!"

McBride was a good shot but not a great one. However, she was a Marine, meaning she was incapable of making excuses. She had no time for them anyway. She felt badly for her parents, her father in particular, who was battling pancreatic cancer and who told her every Sunday that she was his pride and joy, his Marine.

The bomber stood approximately thirty meters away. He was still consulting the heavens, as if waiting for some confirmation to set off his C4.

Drawing her weapon, McBride bounded down the staircase, hit the first floor, then ran toward the jihadi.

Her first two rounds missed, ricocheting off equipment and garnering his full attention with a piercing echo. A third shot struck his vest. She thought he might detonate. He lifted his detonator.

She fired again, his shoulder wrenching under the impact. She closed her eyes and launched herself into the air.

What LaToya McBride did not know was that her father had passed away just four hours ago. No one had found him yet. And now he was telling her about that himself.

* * *

Irving Jones sat in his wheelchair, sipping on his venti coffee (black), and feeling restless. The barometer was dropping, and his stumps tingled in confirmation. He despised his chair, which made him feel like half a man, but he had rushed out, saving the time of grappling with his prostheses and worrying that every second counted.

After receiving the alert via his smartphone, he had hauled himself down to the Space Needle, which was only a mile away from his apartment building. By the time he arrived, a half dozen veterans like himself were already there, and police had cordoned off the area. The talking heads on TV believed that some west coast attacks might have been called off by the jihadis because the target list had been posted on social media. Still, attacks in Utah, Arizona, and Hollywood, California had occurred, and the so called "experts" on TV were using words like "asymmetric" and "unprecedented." As always, they had keen eyes for the obvious.

Despite the President's instructions for everyone to remain at home, the Starbuck's at the Pike Place Market in Seattle was packed with those clinging to their daily routine and a few like Jones who remained in the crowd to eavesdrop on conversations and pretend that a semblance of normalcy still existed. Still, the manager, a plump thirty-year-old with a quirky handlebar mustache and dime-sized gauges in his ears, had announced that he would be locking the door now and closing down for the day. Those still inside could exit one at a time. Jones decided he would remain there until he got kicked out, otherwise he would just return to an empty apartment and watch coverage of the attacks. Being around people was preferable to sitting alone, sucking down Bud Lights, and growing more pissed by the minute. The same bastards that had taken his legs had attacked his country. It was as simple and agonizing as that.

A swarthy, college-aged barista, one of the newer kids who had served Jones coffee several times before, left his station and loped toward the restrooms near the back. The manager nervously twirled his handlebar moustache between his thumb and forefinger, then shouted for the barista to hurry up because the place was still swamped. If the kid actually cared, his expression and pace might have revealed that. He ambled on without a care in his young, vacuous mind.

Jones took another long pull on his coffee, savoring the warm, slightly nutty flavor. He was just opening his mouth to exhale when the screaming came from behind.

The barista had returned from the bathroom wearing a suicide vest and holding a detonator in his right fist. He waved a 9mm Glock 17 and ordered everyone to freeze. The front door was locked, and as several people dove for it, the kid hollered once more, threatening to kill them all. He uttered something in rapid-fire Arabic, then eyed the crowd of about twenty-five and shouted, "Infidels, listen to me! Sharia is the law of the land—and soon you will all obey!"

Whether this kid was supposed to blow up the Starbucks—or perhaps the Space Needle—Jones was not sure. He *was* certain that he could get his right hand on the Beretta in his pocket without the barista noticing.

As the kid paraded to the center of the shop, detailing his hatred of America, Irving Jones, veteran Marine who had earned his EOD Badge or "crab" and who had served two tours in Afghanistan, realized that his career was not over, that he had one last bomb to render safe.

Once again, movement came near the front door.

The barista whirled in that direction.

Jones drew his weapon, but an old woman near the counter saw his gun and screamed.

In that instant, Jones and the barista fired in unison, the barista striking Jones twice in the chest, he catching the punk with a grazing shot to the head and a better placed round to the neck.

With cymbals clashing in ears, Jones grimaced while the crowd clawed at each other like animals to get past the door. As the shop fell silent, Jones fought to catch his breath. Blood puddled onto his chest and dripped down into his underwear. Just then, someone knifed out of the restroom, a man in his forties wearing jogging gear. He glanced at Jones and did a flying leap over the barista, who was lying face down. The jogger broke an Olympic record during his exit.

"I'll get you some help," came a muffled voice. Jones strained to look up. The manager stood over him, punching numbers into his smartphone.

Form the corner of his eye, Jones saw the barista's arm flinch. He craned his neck and lifted his pistol, but his vision grew dim, his arm incapable of holding the weapon on target.

"Oh my god," uttered the manager.

The barista suddenly rolled onto his side and exposed his blood-stained teeth.

Mustering all he had left, Jones screamed, "You got nothing!" He fired once more—but the barista had already squeezed his detonator.

They had taken his legs. Now they would get the rest. And the manager, too. But no one else. No one else.

* * *

Sooner, the old cowboy and marina owner, was nice enough to loan Johnny a second and much larger fishing boat, a Wellcraft 340 with large cabin for transporting their prisoner. Johnny had leaned over and whispered in Sooner's ear: "See this guy over here. Don't forget his face. You might see a lot more of him."

Sooner removed his faded Stetson and scratched his head. "Holy shit, Johnny, you're scaring me."

"You? Scared? You're a hero, dude. Thanks for all your help."

"Y'all don't thank me. *Semper Fi.*"

"*Semper Fi*, roger that."

Johnny escorted a silent Nazari down to the fishing boat. They departed with an unceremonious rumble of the outboard and with Josh at the wheel.

Their instructions were simple:

Transit now through Fisherman's Cut and Little Mary's Cut, then exit into the Gulf of Mexico north of Pelican Island. With Pelican Island abeam to starboard take course 150 at twenty-five knots for one hour.

Johnny passed along the route to Josh, who nodded and said. "They're playing it by the book."

"What do you mean?"

"They need to take possession outside the contiguous zone. That's about twenty-four nautical miles beyond the Texas Mean Low Water Mark."

"I get it," Johnny said. "That puts us outside U.S. jurisdiction."

The UN Law of the Sea Treaty (UNLOS) enacted in 1982 had established that boundary and Johnny recognized the importance of making the exchange outside the U.S. because the CIA was involved.

"Yeah, the spooks don't like playing in CONUS because in most cases it's illegal," said Josh. "But those boys have been known to break a rule or two. And, oh, yeah, can you ask him how we'll recognize the contact."

Johnny sent the text, and Brandt replied: *you'll know us when you see us.*

* * *

While they were expecting an official vessel—a submarine or a Coast Guard cutter—what greeted them was nothing short of remarkable.

At 228 feet in length, the *Water Hazard* was one of the world's largest aluminum and composite private yachts and was registered to famed Texas pro golfer Dennis Perry. Johnny and the others were stunned by the vessel's immense size. According to Corey, who found stats for the yacht on his phone, she cost over seventy million dollars, had a top speed of seventeen knots, and could cruise 8,000 nautical miles at fifteen and a half knots. She was like a floating chateau sans the vineyard, with many open dining areas, a sunken cocktail lounge, a lap pool, a home theatre, an aquarium, helipad, and guest quarters that rivaled those of the finest hotels on the planet. She was even equipped to service up to thirty divers at one time, along with decompression chambers and every piece of dive and camera gear imaginable. The bridge, Corey noted, was appointed with rare woods, Italian leather, bright brass, and state-of-the-art electronics that afforded it a kind of retro steampunk vibe.

Corey elbowed Johnny and pointed, "Check it out. All the communication antennas are folded horizontal to receive a chopper as soon as they're out beyond radar range."

"Roger that."

"Where will they take him?"

"Hopefully straight to hell."

They pulled up alongside the aft deck, where a forty-two-foot-long custom built Game Fisher could be launched and returned to its berth inside the yacht.

WaveRunners and other, smaller vessels, were also stored onboard. Crew members in bright white uniforms fastened their mooring lines, and two middle-aged men dressed in dark winter coats and wool caps climbed aboard the Wellcraft and shook hands with Johnny and the others.

"All we get is a hello?" Johnny asked. "Not even your names?"

The older of the two remained stoic. "Does it matter?"

"It does to me."

The agent rolled his eyes. "I'm Louis. My partner's Tim. Are we good?"

"We're good now, you old bastard. Nice little boat."

"It's a loaner from a Company friend. Best we could do on short notice."

"No shit. So Louie, why didn't they say you were coming?"

"I wasn't—till I heard it was you. Johnny, this is a huge score, man, much bigger than anything we ever pulled off in Iraq. How'd you get him?"

"I don't know, really, we just—"

"Don't tell me. Shook some trees?"

Johnny grinned. "Yeah. Easy day."

"You're full of shit. So where is this bastard?"

"Down below."

Willie grabbed Louis's wrist. "He got banged up a little. Don't judge us."

Louis grinned and spoke from the corner of his mouth. "It happens."

"Take good care of him," Johnny said with a wink.

As Louis and his partner went below, Willie asked, "Time to go home?"

Johnny sighed. "We're not finished yet."

Chapter Fifty

"It's ironic that after all we went through, Johnny still doesn't know why Daniel and Reva were murdered. Then again, maybe it's better he doesn't know."

—Corey McKay (FBI interview, 23 December)

"My name is Joe Koos, Special Agent in Charge, Houston Division, Federal Bureau of Investigation. We're here at the La Quinta Hotel, Lake Jackson, Texas. Current time is four forty-five p.m., twenty-three December. Present are Mr. Johnny Johansen of Topsail Beach, North Carolina, along with special agents Kevin Clark, Brad Whidden, and Ryan Seebeck." SAC Koos, a graying redhead of medium build and small blue eyes, switched off his digital recorder and added, "You know what? Let's talk off the record before we proceed."

"That works."

"So, Johnny, Mark filled me in on as much as he could, but obviously we need to hear it all from you."

"No problem. Just a quick question. Where's Plesner?"

"Assistant Director Plesner is missing."

Johnny snorted. "What about Dresden and Senecal?"

"Mr. Senecal, we believe, is up in Toronto. He made several attempts to contact Dresden this morning, prior to the attacks."

"So go up there and get him."

"It's more complicated than that. We can't extradite him if the Canadians know the death penalty will be imposed, and in this case, I'm sure it will be. We'll get assistance from the mounted police and the Canadian Security Intelligence Service, but I'm sure he's already gone into hiding."

"And Dresden?"

"He stabbed his wife then shot himself in the head this morning. A neighbor called it in."

"Guilty conscience."

"Or maybe he realized you guys were on to him."

Johnny frowned. "Doubt it."

"Look, if what you and Mark claim is true, then we have a massive security breach, and there's no way of knowing how long Plesner's reach is inside the Bureau. He might have allies still feeding him intel." Koos frowned at his recorder. "We wouldn't want anything you say to bleed back to him."

"Roger that. So have you launched a manhunt?"

"Absolutely. Intel on him is being passed along a select chain of command, face-to-face, and on a strict need to know basis. We've organized a special task force involving all the alphabet agencies. We'll find him."

"Well, if you don't, give us a call."

"You don't want to go there, Johnny."

"What do you mean? I've been there for the last couple of weeks, while you people were being duped by your own boss. But don't call me bitter. I'm just a dumbass Marine—or so your boss thought."

Koss pursed his lips. He seemed to mull over a reply, changed his mind, then simply asked, "Are you ready to talk?"

Johnny leaned back in his chair, took a deep breath, then measured his words. "First, let me say this. Those boys in the other room? I've known them for years. I want you to understand why they helped me and why everything they did is still my responsibility—no matter what they tell you."

"You're not in trouble, Johnny. Just the opposite."

"I wish I could believe you, but a man in my situation can go from *he*-ro to *ze*-ro in no time. Doesn't matter, though. If somebody has to take the fall, then let it be me."

* * *

By 1900 an exhausted Johnny and the others were prepared to leave the hotel and begin the twenty-hour drive home. However, SAC Koos reminded them that Charles Plesner, along with his jihadi allies, still wanted them dead. Koos insisted they spend the night at the hotel under FBI protection. Meanwhile, he would make arrangements for them to be driven back to North Carolina with FBI escorts. Vehicles and agents would be changed between field offices to maintain security. Once they arrived in North Carolina, Johnny should stay at a location unknown to the jihadis. The FBI would maintain protection and surveillance of the area for no less than a week afterward. Johnny should accept this without argument.

"You putting us under house arrest?" Willie asked Koos.

"Not at all. Like I said, it's for your own protection."

Willie smirked. "Maybe you're the ones who need protection."

The agent shook his head. "Nice."

* * *

At 2105 Corey, Josh, and their "escort" returned from a local grocery store with sandwiches and twelve packs of Michelob Ultra. They sat around Johnny's room and watched the news. CNN was now reporting that some veteran Marine named "Johnny Johansen" had warned of the attacks with a detailed list and that the number of incidents had grown to over 100. Reporters were trying to locate Mr. Johansen and ask how he acquired the list. Computer geeks had traced Johansen's IP address to Seadrift, Texas.

"What are you going to do, Johnny?" Corey asked.

"About what?"

"About becoming famous."

"Look here, we did the Bureau and the Agency a huge favor, so they're doing one for me. They'll help bury this to keep our families safe and allow us to do business. Besides, I ain't Johnny. My name's James Clayton Johansen. That's a common last name. I'm good to go."

"I don't know," said Willie. "I think they'll find you. Pictures will float online."

"We'll see."

The news was interrupted by a press conference in which the POTUS announced that the National Guard was now under federal authority, Martial Law was currently in effect, and all commercial, corporate, and private aircraft were temporarily grounded until at least 0900 Eastern Standard Time tomorrow. U.S. Army troops had been deployed along the Mexican and Canadian borders to augment U.S. Customs and Border Protection assets. Every Islamic enclave and social center in the United States was now under National Guard security for fear of retaliatory attacks. Federal and state investigations had been launched to apprehend and bring to justice all those involved in these cowardly acts. The Central Intelligence Agency had already captured a High Value Target and possible mastermind behind the attacks. That individual, whose identity was being withheld for reasons of national security, was now being questioned by authorities. FEMA representatives were on the ground in all fifty states to support local, State, and Federal authorities in responding to the attacks by using unique consequence management authorities, responsibilities, and capabilities.

The press conference lasted another ten minutes, after which field reporters began an extensive story on the bridge disaster in New London, interviewing several motorists who had barely escaped the collapse. Spokespersons from the U.S. Navy announced that at least one Trident ballistic missile submarine from Kings Bay, Georgia; two Los Angeles class submarines from Norfolk, Virginia; and two Virginia class submarines also from Norfolk were being relocated to the Electric Boat piers, New London to maintain readiness in that area. Rescues and body recoveries were still underway, and vehicle and bridge debris removal from the Thames River channel would commence in the days to come. All I-95 north and southbound traffic needed to bypass New London and join with I-395 to access destinations north and south of New England and beyond. Survey teams would be assembled to investigate possible sites for a new bridge and/or turnpike bypass loop to reconnect I-95 north of the submarine base. This was a long range project because such a bypass would cut through heavily populated areas and legal issues involving eminent domain needed to be resolved.

The coverage continued, moving west to the Hoover Dam. Johnny sighed in disgust over images of the damaged intake towers accompanied by a sidebar of the explosions captured by a phone camera, the towers dropping in the flickering light.

"I saw this earlier," Willie said. "They said two years to rebuild. They opened the bypass spillways to feed the river downstream to the lakes and dams. They need to relocate the power distribution, too. Looks like rolling blackouts in Vegas. What happens in Vegas... well nothing happens right now. Nellis and Creech Air Force Bases have first dibs on the power."

"It's not all bad," said Corey. "They estimate that sixty to seventy of the smaller attacks were either stopped or suppressed by Marines, along with our sister services, who answered the call. We did good, Johnny."

"Right on," Willie grunted.

Johnny shut his eyes and saw Staff Sergeant Paul Oliver answering that same call in Fallujah all those years ago.

By the time he opened his eyes, another report focused on the North Anna Nuclear Power Plant attack. The station would continue operating under special contaminated restrictions during clean up of its adjacent spent nuclear fuel storage site. Experts already predicted that the shellfish fishing industry, seafood processing, and the tourism industry in the mid-Atlantic region was already destroyed, costing thousands of jobs and millions in revenue. Despite frequent government public service announcements to the contrary, the public would be unwilling to ingest seafood harvested from the Chesapeake Bay area or allow their kids to stick so much as a big toe into the Atlantic Ocean within one hundred and fifty miles of the contaminated zone. Images of the Fukushima Daiichi Nuclear Power Plant disaster were still fresh in the public's mind. An environmentalist reporting via phone noted that the bay supported 3,600 species of plant and animal life, including more than 300 fish species and 2,700 plant types. There was no way to contain the spread of contamination via these fish, birds, and plant species or to estimate the impact of possible genetic mutations in subsequent generations.

And worse, the Chesapeake Bay watershed included parts of six states and was home to some seventeen million people, including the cities of Washington, D.C., and Baltimore, Maryland. The watershed's many rivers were the primary source for drinking water. Finding alternate potable water for the region would become a secondary crisis.

Meanwhile, out west, the Palo Verde nuclear power plant was operating only one of its three pressurized water reactors at a time to conserve coolant water until repairs to remote piping and pumping stations could be completed. Best estimate was five to eight weeks. Four million customers serviced by the nation's largest nuclear power plant were already experiencing severe rolling blackouts, and the winter temperatures were exacerbating the situation.

A reporter on scene at Jamaica Station wept on camera as the death toll there climbed to over one hundred, with 476 injured. There were nearly as many causalities at Woodside Station, but these were only preliminary estimates, with numbers sure to climb. The damage was still being assessed, but congestion the likes of which New Yorkers had never seen was sure to paralyze roads and highways as those train commuters resorted to cars.

The two oil refineries attacked in Louisiana and the tank farm in Houston were all but destroyed. The economic impact on the nation was immeasurable at this time. Some economists predicted that gasoline prices could more than double in the weeks and months to come.

In an interview that turned into a shouting match, a congressman from Oklahoma argued that the government should impose a mandatory draft for the National Guard to meet the threat of an enemy inside our homeland. He stressed that these could be the first of many more attacks, and were it not for the brave citizens mobilized by social media, many more lives would have been lost. "We need to make changes to the federal death penalty laws so we can execute all of these jihadis regardless of their level of participation." He was counterattacked by a congressman from Colorado who said we should not overreact and more carefully consider our response because the world was watching our reactions. While they screamed at each other, Willie, Josh, and Corey shouted at the TV.

Johnny drifted away from the group and into the bedroom, where he shut the door and dialed Elina. He trembled like a schoolboy as the phone rang and, after an eternity, she answered.

"Hey, you..."

Her voice cracked. "Thank God you're okay. I guess you've been busy."

"Little bit. How're you doing? How're the girls?"

"We've been watching the TV."

"I figured."

"You put out that list. How did you know?"

"Long story. And for now, let's keep it quiet. So, uh, I need you to pack up. Tell Matt and Jada that an FBI agent will meet you down there. He'll escort you up to Josh's house. We'll stay there for a little while till we sort this out. Now I have to go."

"Okay, see you soon. And Johnny?"

"Yeah?"

"I hope you found what you were looking for."

Suddenly, Johnny was a little boy again, leading Daniel across the plywood bridges, through the swampland, and toward little league practice. He was so overcome with emotion that he could barely speak. "Hey," he whispered. "I love you."

Epilogue

"I have no idea what'll happen to us now, but we'll always be Marines, always be friends, and always be together."

—Johnny Johansen (FBI interview, 23 December)

Johnny rapped on the apartment door, then stood back, placing himself in clear view of the peephole.

"Who is it?" came a voice from the other side.

"FEDEX." Johnny gestured to the patch on his borrowed jacket. "Need you to sign."

"We're not expecting any deliveries."

"I have a letter for Mr. Abdul Azim Mohammad. It's from the University of North Carolina Wilmington. Signature required."

The deadbolt clicked. The second lock thumped open—

And Johnny booted open the door, knocking Abdul onto his rump. The kid's complexion faded as he crawled backward, crying, "Please, don't shoot me!"

"Shut up." Johnny closed the door, keeping his pistol trained on the kid. "Why did you run?"

"What're you talking about?"

"You know *exactly* what I'm talking about."

Abdul hesitated, fighting to catch his breath. "Wait a minute. I know you. You're Dr. Johansen's brother, the Marine. There was a picture in his office. How did you find me?"

"That's my business."

"Only my parents know where I am. Did they tell you?"

His parents had not told Johnny per se, but Ashur Bandar had obtained the kid's whereabouts. It was during the drive up from Texas, while Johnny had been sitting there in the SUV, scrutinizing every loose end regarding his brother, that he remembered Abdul Azim Mohammad had gone missing. He called Detective Paul Lindquist to enquire if the kid had ever been found. Lindquist said he had not, but inevitably the conversation shifted to the attacks and Johnny's involvement, with Lindquist stammering as though Johnny were a celebrity. Johnny politely ended that call and dialed Bandar.

Wilmington's tightly-knit Muslim Community would not volunteer information, especially to outsiders like Lindquist and the Holly Ridge Police Department. Bandar, however, was a Muslim-American whose cousin was a member and benefactor of the Islamic Center of Wilmington. Connections were made, words exchanged, and information finally leaked. Bandar had called Johnny, and, while trying to catch his breath, he had delivered the intel. Johnny drove alone to Atlanta and spent the past day reconnoitering *100 Midtown* at 10th Street, Atlanta, an apartment complex near Piedmont Park, popular with both Georgia Tech and Georgia State University students. Abdul was staying with a GSU buddy in a two bedroom, single bath unit up on the fifth floor. The buddy had left earlier, wearing a Home Depot apron.

"Son, it doesn't matter how I found you. I'm here, holding this gun, and asking you a question. Why did you run?"

"I decided to hang out with a friend."

"My brother was killed. You were his student and lived in the area. Then you were gone, and no one's talking to the police. Do you think I was born yesterday?"

Abdul snorted. "You think I did it?"

"What am I supposed to think? You're not telling me shit."

"And you've come here for revenge?"

"Maybe I have."

"Look, I didn't know what to do."

"So you ran."

"All right, I did. But I didn't kill him."

"Who did?"

"I don't know exactly. But *they* did it."

"They as in..."

"Jihadis."

"Why?"

Abdul hesitated, and his eyes grew distant. "It was all my fault. I met Reva, too. She was a really nice lady. I should've kept my mouth shut."

"What do you mean?"

"I went to him because he was in charge of the whole department. He was the best professor there. He talked me into entering contests and stuff."

"Did you talk him into converting to Islam?"

Abdul frowned. "No. We never discussed religion. Mostly engineering. And sometimes he talked about you and your father."

"What did he say?"

"He said you and your dad were like dogs, and he was the sheep or something. I don't know why he said that."

"He ever tell you about finding stuff? Like a note, maybe?"

"I gave him the note."

Johnny tightened his grip on the pistol. "Really."

"I was working with this visiting professor on an engineering project."

"Shammas?"

"Yeah, you know him?"

"I know they killed him."

"Good."

"You're glad he's dead?"

"He was one of them. I know because I started hearing things, phone calls he was making, conversations he had with students in the MSA who I knew were frustrated. One day this guy came around looking for one of Shammas's students. I talked to the guy in Arabic and pretended I was one of them. I told him the note was for me."

"And you gave it to my brother?"

"I translated it for him."

"Why?"

"Because your brother hired Dr. Shammas. If the guy was a jihadi, I thought he should know. Plus I was scared that jihadis were being recruited at my school."

"What did the note say?"

"Something about going to a place called Reliance Tactical, talk to some guy named LaPorte, and get some keys."

"And what did my brother think?"

"He told me to keep an eye on Shammas. While I was doing that, I think he followed the note. I didn't see him after that. And the next thing I know, they're telling me he was killed."

"Who's they?"

"Friends at school. Somebody saw it on the news."

Johnny tensed. "So Abdul, why the *fuck* didn't you go to the police and tell them what you knew?"

"Because I thought I'd wind up like your brother—and now just being a Muslim could get me killed."

Johnny lifted his voice. "I understand that, but do you have any idea of what you've put us through? I've been wondering if my brother was a jihadi. And it was killing me. And you knew all along."

"Dr. Johansen wouldn't have helped them. He was the best teacher I ever had." Abdul choked up and bowed his head. "He convinced me to become an engineer."

Johnny swore through his breath and lowered his pistol. Yes, Abdul had run. Yes, he should have come forward, but he did have the foresight and courage to intercept that note and bring it to Daniel. He was willing to cross religious and cultural lines to help protect America, his country.

"Hey, kid, listen to me. My brother was trying to tell you something. There are three kinds of people in this world: wolves, sheepdogs, and sheep. The wolves are the bad guys and they want to eat the sheep. So the sheepdogs come in to protect those who are unable or unwilling to protect themselves. It's as simple as that. When you brought that note to my brother, you chose to be a sheepdog, just like him. You shouldn't feel bad about that. My old man used to say that men are like steel: they both need a little temper to be worth a damn."

"But you're right. I shouldn't have run away."

"Well, you can own that now."

"I already do. I've been thinking about your brother every day. I never thought they'd kill him. I just thought Dr. Shammas would get fired or something."

"All right. On your feet. I'm taking you out of here."

"Taking me where?"

"There's a guy downstairs named Lindquist. He's a detective. He's waiting for me. He thought we were coming up here together, but I wanted some alone time with you first. You'll be safe with us."

"I can't go with you. If the jihadis are watching, you know what they'll do, Johnny? They'll kill my family. Is anything I told you worth that?"

"We'll get you out of here discreetly."

"I guess I don't have a choice."

"No, you don't. You're a sheepdog. We don't hide. We hunt."

* * *

Back home in North Carolina, Johnny felt compelled to dig through a box in his attic, a box filled with the artifacts of his youth, namely that old Hardy Boys adventure novel *The Mystery of Cabin Island*. After all these years, he would sit down and read the book, owing this moment to his brother. The spine creaked as he opened the novel, and the right there on the title page was a handwritten inscription from Daniel:

Dear Johnny, even though you are stupid and need a younger kid to help you, I still like you, and you are a good brother. Happy Birthday. Love, Daniel.

Yes, men *were* like steel, but they needed tears as much as temper to remember what was important in this life.

Johnny wiped his cheeks and began to read.

* * *

In the weeks following the attacks, the Muslim-American community put huge pressure on the government to raise the level of protection, since they continued to be targets of blowback and hate crimes. Fights broke out in supermarkets, while vandalism and shootings at Islamic centers across the nation occurred on an almost daily basis. As they had in the weeks following 9/11, American flags flew in great numbers from homes across the country, and the thirst for revenge grew.

With evidence provided by Johnny's group and Mark Gatterton, officials acceded that Dresden and Senecal were aiding and abetting the terrorists. Nazari's name had still not been released, and Plesner's disappearance was being covered up by the FBI. Senecal was apprehended while trying to escape Toronto and was in custody in Canada, fighting extradition. With all of his money, Johnny assumed he could stall authorities for years.

The United States Attorney General, along with the Assistant Attorney General for National Security, had launched an independent investigation into the breaches and failures within the FBI and the Department of Homeland Security. Pundits were already musing that they would produce a document of findings as lengthy and perhaps more convoluted than the 9/11 Commission's original report.

In the meantime, Johnny put his house up for sale. Marines who knew him and realized he was the one who had posted the target list wanted him to get credit for his acts, and photos of Johnny swept across the internet before the Bureau or anyone else could stop them. The media descended upon his neighborhood, and the circus would not let up. Holly Ridge and Topsail Beach Police Departments strained their resources to ward off reporters and spectators. As a consequence, Johnny and Elina decided they would head out west for a while and lay low with friends in rural Colorado until the storm blew over.

Johnny was packing up the garage when his phone rang. "Mark, what's going on?"

"Hey, man, Director of the FBI and this Under Secretary from DHS want to meet with you guys A-SAP."

"Really? Do me a favor—remind them we've already talked to the FBI and those security reps from DoD, State, and that big shot from the National Security Council. We're exhausted. We've told them everything we know. We're done talking."

"Johnny, this is the director of the *entire* FBI. This is big. They won't take no for an answer. And I know your company hopes to get more government work, if you know what I'm saying."

"Look here, if they want to talk, they come down here."

"I'll run it up the flag pole and get back to you."

* * *

The Special Missions Training Center was located in Courthouse Bay, a subdivision within Camp Lejeune and its Joint Maritime Training Center. Over 175 personnel from the military, along with government civilian employees and civilian contractors conducted daily operations in and around the facility. Each year, instructors trained nearly 2,000 operators who had signed up for a variety of Coast Guard and Navy courses, including four classes that focused on riverine combat training and utilized patrol boats not unlike the ones Josh and Corey commanded in Iraq. Some of the courses were designated high risk and required students to complete a Physical Activity Risk Factor Questionnaire (PARFQ) form on the first day of the class. Johnny had joked that their meeting should be considered "high risk" by their government friends, who, if they knew what was good for them, should fill out PARFQs themselves. Since Corey had been employed at the SMTC back in his civilian contractor days, he leaned on his contacts to book them a conference room. The CO had contacted him to say that their VIPs had arrived late at 1710 local time and with an entourage of security in tow.

Dressed business casual, Johnny and the others strode up to the single-story brick building whose entrance was bordered by crepe myrtles and featured an enormous anchor displayed on the front lawn.

Inside, they found FBI Director Matthew Bartone seated at the head of a broad conference table. At nearly three hundred pounds, Bartone was an imposing man who had been born and raised in New Jersey and was a graduate of Seton Hall University. He came from a family of law enforcement personnel and had spent his entire career in the FBI. Known as a straight shooter and often brutally honest with his critics, he had become a source of irritation for the current administration because of his political leanings.

Beside him sat a woman in a navy blue business suit who was pouring over documents and manila folders. She was lean, a runner perhaps, with naturally blond hair graying at one temple. She eyed them over the rim of her glasses as though they were bulldogs pissing on her rose garden. She echoed Bartone's greeting but failed to rise or shake hands.

"Gentlemen, this is Wendelin Voigt, Under Secretary, National Protection and Programs Directorate from the Department of Homeland Security," said Bartone.

"Say that three times fast," quipped Willie.

Voigt gave Willie a look, then cleared her throat. "Now, gentlemen if you'll have a seat, we'll get right down to it." She slapped shut a file and took a long breath, as though bracing herself. "We came here to congratulate you for a job well done—despite the numerous times you took the law into your own hands and committed nothing short of murder, for which you received little more than a slap on the wrist."

"We always drew our licensed and registered weapons in self-defense," Johnny retorted, a phrase he had rehearsed after his many interrogations. "Ma'am, if I may, you're not having a good day, are you."

Bartone intervened before she could answer. "Johnny, the conspiracy, the cover-ups, and the massive security breach you gentlemen uncovered saved us from an even worse attack. We're all grateful for that. But Secretary Voigt and myself? The politics here... well, you know how that goes. This isn't exactly our shining hour."

"I read you loud and clear, sir. And I can see how what we did put your heads on the chopping block. So now you think you're causalities of war, but if you think about it, all you have are jobs to lose. If I asked you who Clive Gleeson, LaToya McBride, and Eric Gordon were, would you even remember? How about Victor Lugano and Irving Jones? Those names ring a bell? They were Marines who gave their lives for us. They're the *real* casualties—not anyone else."

Voigt tapped a finger on her folder. "Mr. Johansen, your evaluations say you have a big problem with your mouth. Just imagine how far you could have gone in the Marine Corps if you weren't so outspoken..."

Johnny snorted. "I have no regrets. Besides, if I were still active duty, all of this might've turned out differently."

Voight sighed, removed her glasses, then continued: "Mr. Johansen, despite what you might think of us, we'd like you and your partners to continue working with the government, drawing upon your own sources of human intelligence that helped thwart many of these attacks."

"She's trying to say you're a valuable asset," said Bartone. "The NSA can continue its data mining operations until the end of time, and we can fly all the drones we want, but the jihadis have gone old school, and they'll keep slipping under the wire if we don't stay on them—any way we can."

"Sir, like you just said, you have all the assets in the world, and you want to lean on some good ole boys from North Carolina? Or is hiring us another political game?"

"We appreciate your modesty, Johnny. This isn't a game. We've seen what you can do. You bring to the table some real battlefield ingenuity that these jihadis will never see coming. I'd like you to join us right now."

Johnny glanced over at the guys. Josh frowned and chuckled under his breath. Willie shook his head. Corey pursed his lips and shrugged.

Bartone continued, "Look, gentlemen, the country has lost even more faith in its government, and I know you boys would like to help restore that, wouldn't you..."

"Sir, with all due respect, our last job with the government didn't work out so well. Our boss tried to kill us."

Bartone's tone grew more emphatic. "We're in the same fight here."

"Really? Do you have Plesner?"

"That's classified," snapped Voigt.

Bartone raised his palms. "There's no reason for paranoia."

"Oh, really? So he's still out there—because if you had him, you'd be telling the whole world."

"Johnny, you can't—"

"Sir, look here, we love our country more than anything, and we'd be happy to sell our consulting services to the government, but you need to get your house in order."

"Exactly. And we can do that with your help. It's a very lucrative deal. You'd lose a lot if you turned it down. You know how government contracts work. It'd be tough for your company to compete if the jobs get awarded to inside bidders before you even knew about them. That's already a problem, and now it'll only get worse."

"So if we don't work for you, you'll find another way to shut us down," said Josh. "That's bullshit, man."

Johnny raised a hand to calm his friend, then he narrowed his gaze on Bartone. "You're saying you want to hire us, but this has to be killing you. We made your agencies look really bad. So let me guess: you got orders to come down and offer us the job. You wouldn't have come willingly."

"It was strongly suggested to us," said Voigt.

"By who?" asked Willie.

"Who do you think?" Bartone countered. "This comes from the top."

Johnny stood. "Well, Director Bartone? Secretary Voigt? Thanks but no thanks." He regarded the others. "We're out of here."

Bartone rose. "Johnny, wait. Let's talk numbers. Don't do something you'll regret."

Johnny turned his back on the director and moved toward the door. With a sarcastic wave good-bye, he said, "Easy day. No drama."

As they left, Johnny overheard Bartone confide in his colleague, "They'll come around. They always do."

* * *

Moments later, Johnny led the others toward his truck at the far end of the parking lot. He felt vindicated for sticking it to those Feds who wanted to use and exploit them. They had wrapped the package in patriotism, but Johnny could smell the manure a mile away. Bartone was right about one thing: Johnny, Corey, Willie, and Josh did love their country and never forgot their fellow Marines who had sacrificed everything. One day Johnny and the others might help, but on their terms.

Corey cursed and said, "Did we just do that?"

Johnny snickered. "If you don't believe you're all that and a bag of chips, who will? They want janitors? Let 'em hire janitors."

"That's right," said Josh.

"Yeah, but we just turned down a whole lot of money," Willie said. "We could've just *listened* to the numbers..."

Johnny cocked a brow.

"You're not curious?" asked Willie.

"No," Johnny snapped.

"So what now?" Corey asked.

Johnny threw an arm around his friend. "Now we put on our man pants and get busy. Those fools can't screw us out of every contract, especially the local and state jobs. I'll see what I can pick up out in Colorado. Gentlemen, we're back to work like a fat kid on a cupcake. Imagine that."

As they walked on, the sun finally set over Courthouse Bay and the Special Missions Training Center. Anyone watching from a distance would have seen four men with shoulders held high against the looming darkness.

Acknowledgments

This novel is the collective work of many talented researchers and warriors who graciously volunteered their time. They are, in fact, the "secret corps" behind the conception and completion of a very challenging and rewarding project.

Mr. James Ide, Chief Warrant Officer, U.S. Navy (Ret.) is my long-time collaborator who helped me develop the story from the initial sixty-seven page outline to the final polished manuscript. His technical prowess and military experience are most evident in the clues presented in this murder/mystery and in the epic attacks described herein. Jim challenged me at every turn to make this story more credible and exciting. His contributions are significant, and I'm deeply indebted to him for the many hours he dedicated to this project.

My agent, Mr. John Talbot, encouraged me to develop this story and offered some valuable suggestions during the early stages of brainstorming. His note to "keep the action in and around the United States" served as a strong framework for the entire plot.

The men I'll refer to as "the Marines from North Carolina"—James "Johnny" Johnson, Joseph "Willie" Parent, Josh Iversen, and Corey Peters—spent countless hours answering my questions and submitting to interviews regarding themselves and their families. I was even fortunate enough to speak with their wives. These discussions were personal, even painful, but they forged on, reminding me how incredibly fortunate and honored I am to know them.

Veteran Marine Corps Corporal Paul R. Bagby and veteran Army Specialist Fourth Class Chris Lipp served as "beta readers" and provided their reactions and criticism while the novel was being written. Their hard work and encouragement are deeply appreciated.

Mr. John Guandolo, author of *Raising a Jihadi Generation*, addressed my pointed questions and provided remarkable insight into the minds of Islamic radicals. John is not only an excellent author but a veteran Reconnaissance Marine, a former FBI special agent, and a counterterrorism expert with a keen understanding of Sharia Law and the Muslim Brotherhood. His work can be found at www.understandingthethreat.com.

Mr. Adam Painchaud, senior director of the Sig Sauer Academy, described in detail information I needed about weapons, ballistics, and tactics. His generosity and great sense of humor contributed much to this manuscript.

Troy L. Wagner, TMC (SS), EOD, U.S. Navy, is a retired chief torpedoman, a submariner, and a specialist in explosive ordnance disposal who provided considerable knowledge and insight into our attack scenes.

The talented and gracious Mr. Matt Bowlin gave me permission to write about him in this novel. If you would like to hear and/or purchase some of his remarkable and patriotic music, visit:

www.mattbowlin.com or www.facebook.com/MattBowlinOfficial

My former student Mr. Will Wight provided me with guidance regarding e-book and trade paperback conversion. His own excellent and engaging work can be found on Amazon.com and at www.willwight.com.

Many other friends and military experts answered questions, provided me with research, or indirectly influenced this book, including:

Gunnery Sergeant Eric N. Gordon, USMC (Ret)

Colonel Mark John Aitken, U.S. Army

Command Master Chief (SEAL) Steve Rose, U.S. Navy (Ret)

Dee Rybiski, FBI Richmond Division Community Outreach Specialist

Mr. Tom O'Sullivan, Senior Director, North American Rescue

Mr. Derwin Bradley, Master Police Officer, Orlando Police Department

Mrs. Carol Ide (my keen-eyed proofreader)

Mr. Steve Berger, Mr. Chris Fallen, Mr. Pat Rugg, Mr. Gary Mulchan, Mr. Michael Janich, Mr. Kurt Telep, and Dr. Rudy McDaniel.

I could not complete this book without the support of my wife Nancy and my two beautiful daughters, Lauren and Kendall.